PENGUIN BOOKS

This Child of Mine

Bestselling author Sinéad Moriarty lives in Dublin with her husband and their three children. *This Child of Mine* is her eighth novel.

This Child of Mine

SINÉAD MORIARTY

PENGUIN BOOKS

For you, the reader, with grateful thanks

PENGUIN BOOKS

UK | USA | Canada | Ireland | Australia
India | New Zealand | South Africa

Penguin Books is part of the Penguin Random House group of companies
whose addresses can be found at global.penguinrandomhouse.com

Penguin
Random House
UK

First published by Penguin Ireland 2012
Published in Penguin Books 2013

001

Copyright © Sinéad Moriarty, 2012
All rights reserved

Typeset by Palimpsest Book Production Limited, Falkirk, Stirlingshire
Printed in England by Clays Ltd, St Ives plc

ISBN: 978-0-241-98085-9

www.greenpenguin.co.uk

London, June 2011

Sophie sank back in the couch and put her bare feet up on the cof-fee-table. It was one of those hot, sticky London summer evenings. Holly came in with two glasses of wine and plonked down beside her. 'Anything good on?' she asked, as Sophie channel-surfed.

'Nothing. Oh, hang on,' Sophie stopped on BBC1. They were interviewing some artist. The camera was showing an enormous orange canvas.

'Oh, God, no!' Holly groaned. 'Not another artist. You're obsessed. I know I'm never going to see you next year when you're at art college. You'll be too busy with all your arty-farty friends for me.'

Sophie smiled. 'Holly, you've been my best friend for as long as I can remember. You'll never get rid of me. I love coming to your house.'

'I should think so, too.' Holly grinned, as she sipped her drink.

Sophie turned back to the TV. The artist's name was Laura something, and she was Irish – Sophie could tell by her accent: she sounded a bit like her mum. The interviewer asked Laura about the orange painting.

Laura explained that she had painted the picture the previous year, on the day of her daughter's birthday, and that orange was the colour she saw when she felt pain.

Holly stared at Sophie. 'That's just like you.'

Sophie sat forward to listen closely.

'Your synaesthesia has influenced a lot of your painting, hasn't it?' the interviewer said. 'Could you explain how the condition affects your life?'

'Having synaesthesia has made me see the world differently from most people. As an artist, it's a blessing. I don't see emotions,

I see colours. I visualize numbers and letters as colours. Music translates to colour. Everything is illuminated. And the real beauty of it is that everyone with synaesthesia has their own palette of colours. So we all see things in a unique way.'

Sophie was riveted.

'What colours do you find come up most regularly?' the interviewer asked.

'Well, blue is my happy colour, orange is pain and green is fear.'

Holly turned to Sophie. 'You see? You're not the only freak in the world.'

The camera panned from the orange canvas to another painting, a purple and green one. The interviewer asked Laura about it – she had just sold it to the rock star Hank Gold for two hundred thousand euros.

'It's nice to have finally found a level of success after years of struggling, but money is not what drives me.'

'What does?' the interviewer asked.

'Regret,' she said softly.

'Does that have to do with your baby daughter drowning all those years ago?' he probed.

There was silence. All you could see was the purple and green canvas, and all you could hear was Laura's laboured breathing.

'It must have been a terrible time for you,' the interviewer suggested.

'It still is,' she whispered.

'And they never found your little girl's body,' he noted.

'No, and I believe she's still out there.'

'Do you?' He sounded surprised.

'Yes.' Laura's voice grew stronger. 'I never believed she drowned. I always hoped I'd find her or that someone would discover her and bring her home to me.'

The camera moved from the painting to Laura's face.

Holly gasped. 'Oh, my God!'

Sophie's glass hit the floor and shattered into a thousand pieces.

PART I

Then

I.

Anna

December 1992

Anna beamed at herself in the bathroom mirror. Carefully, she applied makeup to hide her green complexion. Never had she been so thrilled to feel sick. The worse she felt, the happier she was. She hummed as she put on her mascara.

Barry came in and kissed her cheek. 'I'm off, early meeting. See you about seven.'

'OK. I'm going to yoga at six thirty so I'll be home after that.'

'Yoga?' Barry said. 'Are you sure that's a good idea?'

Anna smiled. 'It's fine. Honestly, this time is going to be different. I'm not scared or worried. I know that my mum sent me this one. I know this one's a keeper. Besides, yoga is one of the few things I can do with this big bump.'

'OK, but please don't overdo it. Take it easy.'

Anna turned away from the mirror and placed her hand gently on her husband's arm. 'Before Mum died, she promised me she'd send me a baby. This is her gift to me. Nothing is going to go wrong this time. I promise.'

Barry attempted a smile. 'I hope you're right.'

He left for work and Anna continued layering on her makeup. She hated anything tight around her bump, so she opted for a black shift dress and her flat black boots. She had promised the kids she'd make Santa Clauses with them today so she had bought a big bag of cotton-wool balls, glitter, glue, twenty paper plates and twenty red markers.

She packed the materials into her backpack and headed off to school. If it wasn't raining, Anna liked to walk. It took half an hour and it cleared her head so that when she reached the school gates, she had left her worries behind and could focus on teaching.

Of course, there had been many days over the last few years when she hadn't been able to leave her troubles behind. There had been some days when getting up at all had been a struggle. Days when she had literally had to drag herself out of bed and ask Barry to help her get dressed because she was crying so much she couldn't see the buttons on her shirt. Days when she had been catatonic with grief and wanted nothing more than to pull the duvet over her head, curl up in the foetal position – which was ironic when you thought of it – and grieve for the children she'd never have.

Seven miscarriages in five years. The longest she'd managed to hold on to a baby was fourteen weeks. That had been the hardest one. She'd finally made it past the three-month mark, had allowed herself to hope, to get excited . . . and then it was gone. Snatched away from her. That had been number five. The last two she had lost at seven and nine weeks. And then her mum had got sick and she'd put everything on hold to look after her. She was an only child and her dad had died when she was twenty-three, so there was no one else. She was all her mum had. Ovarian cancer, the silent killer, the doctor called it. And it had been – silent and deadly. Within four months her mother was gone.

But even then she'd only taken four full days off work. She didn't like letting the kids down. She was their only stability. Their little lives were filled with drugs, alcohol, abuse, poverty, neglect and violence. How could she, the one constant in all that, disappoint them? She couldn't. So even on those days when she had woken up feeling as though she was drowning, as if the water was coming up and engulfing her, dragging her down into the depths of depression, even on those days she had got out of bed and gone to work.

She had always been glad she had, because when she saw their little faces, her heart lifted. She had recognized in their eyes some of the grief she felt. They had no choice, no way out. They were stuck with deadbeat dads and alcoholic mums. They were trapped in homes where love was a distant memory. Where cruel words and violence were a daily occurrence, hugs and clean clothes an anomaly. Where help was not at hand because overworked social workers were crumbling under the weight of their caseloads.

Anna had received the precious gift of a happy childhood. She had been loved, cherished, encouraged and nurtured in every way. It was something most of her pupils would never experience, so she felt it was her duty to show them that there was another way. She wanted to show them that their dysfunctional lives were not 'normal'. She wanted to give them love, kindness, affection, warmth and, most of all, hope.

Anna knew that school for most of those children was a sanctuary, the one place where they could be at peace for a few hours. Barry told her she put far too much energy into teaching a bunch of kids who were just going to end up being junkies, like their parents. In the seventeen years that Anna had been teaching at the school, the majority of her students had not grown into upstanding citizens, but a handful had got jobs that didn't involve criminal activity and two had even gone on to college. It was a meagre statistic, but it still made her proud to know that, in some small way, she had helped those children. That when they had come to her at five years of age, she, their first ever teacher, had paved the way for something better. She clung to those success stories and tried every day to do her very best for the children.

She got to school early and set up for the day. She liked to have everything ready for the children when they arrived. They found the familiarity of the classroom and the structure in their day reassuring. At nine o'clock they came streaming in. She had twenty in her class this year: eleven boys and nine girls. Of those twenty, she had six very bad cases. Three single mums who were alcoholics, one single mum who was a junkie and had moved in with a well-known drug dealer, another single mum whose husband was in prison for armed robbery, and one mother who was routinely physically abused by her boyfriend.

Each year, when the children arrived on their first day, she could tell immediately which ones were neglected. There were the obvious signs, like dirty clothes, head lice, no coats or warm jumpers, but then there were the other things – language delay, stuttering, low self-confidence, inability to engage in any class-work. There were also the children who reacted outwardly instead of inwardly to their unhappy situations: they were hyper-active, destructive, disruptive, couldn't sit still or concentrate for more than a minute on anything.

This year she had one very difficult boy, Ryan. His mother was addicted to crystal meth and his dad was serving fifteen years for armed robbery. Ryan was very physical and difficult to manage, but Anna loved him. She could see through his aggression. Behind it, he was just a scared, scarred five-year-old, who was completely neglected. She was determined to try to show him another way.

The children ran into the classroom and those who had coats took them off. Ryan, Kylie, Francie and Jason never had coats. Anna sat the children down in a circle on the floor and asked them to talk about their weekend and to tell her about the good things or the bad things that had happened.

Sally went first. 'My mammy took me to the cinema.'

'Wow, that's great! How about you, Ronan?'

'I fell off me bike and hurted me leg.'

'Oh, you poor thing – is it OK now?' Anna asked.

'Yes, Mrs Roberts, it is. My mammy put a big plaster on it.'

'Good. Derek, how was your weekend?'

'Shite. Me da was pissed drunk and stood on my Lego what I'd just spented an hour making.'

'Derek, you know we don't curse in class, it's not nice. I'm sorry your Lego was broken. Were you able to fix it?'

'Me ma told me da he was a useless fucker – oops, sorry, Mrs Roberts – but that's what she said. And she maded him fix it, so it's OK now.'

Anna moved on to Kylie. 'How about you?'

Kylie shrugged. 'Nothing.'

'Did anything happen?'

'I dunno.'

'Were you inside all weekend or did you go out anywhere?' Anna prodded. 'Did anything bad happen? Anything that made you sad?'

Kylie stared at the floor. 'Me ma fell down the stairs and me granny haded to call an ambooance and she haded to get ten of them stitches here.' She pointed to her eyebrow.

'I'm sorry to hear that, Kylie. Your poor mum and poor you. You must have got a terrible fright.'

'There was lots of blood.'

'Oooooooh!' The other children were impressed.

'Millions of blood.' Kylie warmed to her theme, enjoying the rare attention. 'Blood everywhere. On the walls and the carpet and it was all squirting out of her head.'

'OOOOOOOOH!' Her classmates liked this detail.

'M-m-m-my da p-p-p-punched my m-m-m-ma one time and her nose squirted b-b-b-blood like an alien,' Francie piped up. Then he went bright red and looked at Anna wide-eyed. 'But it was ages ago. Like a m-m-m-million years ago.'

Anna knew that Francie's dad spent most of his spare time beating his mother and once, about six weeks ago, Francie had come into school with bruises on his arm. Anna had notified the principal, who had called Social Services. A social worker had gone to speak to the parents, but they had denied it. Francie hadn't had any bruises since, but Anna had seen his mother trying to hide bruises on her neck with a scarf. So, yet again, a child had fallen through the cracks.

'Now, everyone,' Anna said brightly, to distract them from their gory tales, 'today we're going to make Santa Claus faces.'

'Boring!' said Ryan, jumping from one chair to the next.

'It'll be fun – come on, Ryan, I'll let you hand out the cotton balls for Santa's beard.'

'Santa never came to my house last year. My ma said he losted our address,' Ryan said, almost absentmindedly.

9

Anna put her arm around him. 'Well, I bet he'll find it this year.' She made a mental note to make sure that Ryan's family received one of the twenty hampers the school delivered to the neediest families every Christmas.

She was on her way to get the materials for the Santas when she heard Jordan say, 'Maybe Santa didn't lose your address, Ryan. Maybe he didn't come because you're so bold.'

'Shut up, you,' Ryan shouted.

'Don't say that, it's bad words.'

'Fuck off, then, you ugly minger.'

'My ma said your ma's a dirty junkie.'

'That's enough!' Anna stood between them. 'I want you both to say sorry for being mean.'

They muttered, 'Sorry,' to each other and Anna managed to get all the children sitting down to make Santa Claus faces. A few minutes later Ryan was up again using his paper plate as a Frisbee.

They stopped for a break at ten twenty. A healthy mid-morning snack and lunch was provided for all the children daily, because the school knew that some of them didn't get fed at home.

'What's this?' Molly asked, holding up a kiwi.

'It's a fruit. It's yummy, very sweet and soft.' Anna cut the kiwis and divided them up between the children.

'It's hairy, Mrs Roberts.' Timmy sniffed it. 'And it smells disgusting.'

'It looks like a monkey's arse.' Jenny giggled.

Anna finished scooping the kiwis on to plates.

'There's no way I'm eating that,' Molly said. 'It's all green and mushy. It looks like snot.'

'Yuuuuuuuuck!' the children squealed.

Anna took a deep breath. 'Molly, I want you to taste it and then decide if you like it or not.'

Molly clamped her mouth shut.

'I'll have it,' Jason said, slurping up Molly's portion.

'You ate snot!' Molly shrieked. 'You're disgusting and you smell.'

'That's enough, Molly,' Anna scolded. She knew that Jason

rarely, if ever, had breakfast or a bath. His mother spent most of her time out of her mind on heroin.

'You're a cunt,' Jason roared, and bit Molly's arm – her yells could have been heard in Timbuktu.

Anna took Jason by the shoulder and marched him to the other side of the room. She crouched down. 'Jason, I know Molly was taunting you but –'

'What's taunting?'

'Teasing. But you had no right to call her that really terrible word and to bite her. You know biting is naughty.'

'Don't tell. Me da'll kill me.'

'I'm sorry, Jason, but I have to report bites. Molly's mum is going to see the tooth marks tonight anyway.'

'I'm dead.' Jason sighed.

Later that day, Anna stood with Molly's mum and Jason's dad, explaining what had happened. 'So, unfortunately, they had an argument about the kiwi. Molly was teasing Jason and then Jason got a bit angry and bit Molly.'

Molly's mother stared at the marks in her daughter's arm. To Jason, she hissed, 'Listen here, Jaws, you'd better apologize to my Molly for taking half her arm off. I might have to get a tetanus injection for that.'

'Sorry,' Jason muttered.

'He called me a cunt,' Molly said, loving the attention.

'What?' Her mother was shocked.

Jason's dad swivelled to his son. 'You little prick. What the fuck is wrong with you, cursing and biting at school?'

Jason looked at his feet. 'Sorry.'

Anna patted him on the back. 'Good boy, Jason. Now, Molly, you need to apologize for teasing Jason.'

Molly's mother wagged a finger at Anna. 'Excuse me, she'll be apologizing for nothing. Jaws here needs a muzzle to stop him ripping the arms off innocent bystanders and from using bad words in the class. I've a good mind to call Social Services about this.'

'What the fuck are you on about?' Jason's dad asked. 'He's said sorry to your precious daughter. It's over now.'

Molly's mother folded her arms defiantly. 'What if he decides to go for her again because he can't handle a bit of teasing? What if next time he bites her ear off, like that Mike Tyson?'

'He's not a fucking heavyweight boxer, he's a little kid.'

'It's hardly surprising he's got problems, with a junkie for a mother.'

Jason's dad narrowed his eyes. 'Leave my wife out of it.'

'She's out of it, all right,' Molly's mother proclaimed. 'She's out of her tree morning, noon and night.'

Anna stepped in. 'OK, folks, we need to keep this civil. Jason has apologized and –'

Jason's father shook a fist at Molly's mother. 'Don't you slander my wife, you stupid cu–'

'STOP!' Anna jumped in before a fight broke out. 'The incident is over now and tomorrow we'll start afresh. Molly and Jason, I want you both on your best behaviour in the morning. Now we can all go home and cool down.'

Molly and her mother stormed off. Jason's dad turned on the little boy. 'If you ever embarrass me like that again I'll fuckin' kill you. I've enough on me plate trying to get your mother off the gear. I don't need you causing me hassle.'

Jason's eyes watered. 'I'm sorry, Da.'

'Mr Cooney,' Anna said, 'Jason is trying very hard in class and his behaviour is generally good. I'm very pleased with his progress.'

Jason's dad looked surprised. 'Oh, right. Well, that's good to hear. If he keeps his fangs to himself he should be all right so. Come on, Jaws, let's get a burger – I'm fuckin' starving.'

Jason looked over his shoulder at Anna, and smiled gratefully.

2.

Laura

Christmas Eve 1992

Laura groaned. Her head was thumping. She had the worst hangover ever. She lay back on the couch and closed her eyes.

Joan came in and glared at her. 'Where were you until three this morning? Have you no shame?'

Laura sat up, the last thing she needed was her mother knowing she'd been drinking last night. If Joan even suspected it, there would be World War Three.

'Relax, Mum. I was just out with the girls, we stayed in Chloë's house chatting, it's no big deal.'

Joan clicked her tongue. 'It *is* a big deal. Pregnant women need rest. You're always out – you need to stay at home and put your feet up so the baby has time to grow. The doctor said it was on the small side and that you were to stop gallivanting about and take it easy.'

Laura rolled her eyes. 'Leave me alone. You're such a nag.' She switched on the TV and turned up the volume.

Joan stood watching her daughter and prayed silently for patience. When Laura had told her she was pregnant and wanted to have an abortion, Joan had been shocked. To find out, in the space of thirty seconds, that your nineteen-year-old daughter is pregnant by a stranger and wants to have an abortion is too much for any mother. She had begged Laura not to terminate the pregnancy. No matter what people said, abortion was wrong in Joan's eyes, and she could not – would not – let that happen.

She had promised Laura that she'd help her raise the baby, and eventually Laura had relented.

For the millionth time Joan wondered how her sweet daughter had turned into this angry, selfish stranger. If she was being honest she had to blame Harry for some of it. He had spoilt Laura far too much. And after he was diagnosed with lung cancer, he had gone into overdrive. He had said that whatever time he had left in this world was going to be happy, and he was determined to enjoy the money he had made. He never said no again. He gave Laura and her elder brother Frank everything they wanted. In those last two years of his life, before the cancer had beaten him, they had gone all over the world, dined in the finest restaurants, shopped in the swankiest stores and had the most elaborate birthday parties imaginable.

But he had died when Frank was eighteen and Laura was sixteen and had left a huge hole in their lives. Joan was glad Harry wasn't here to see this. Laura had become uncontrollable since he had died. He would have been heartbroken to see his beautiful daughter pregnant at nineteen. He had called Laura his little princess, and it would have devastated him to think she had had unprotected drunken sex with a stranger, whose name she couldn't even remember.

'He was just some American musician over in Dublin for a few days with his band,' she had said, when Joan had demanded to know who the father was. 'I met him one night at a party. He's long gone.'

'But you have to find him and tell him,' Joan insisted.

Laura had laughed. 'Find him? Mum, I don't even know his name. I was drunk, it's over. I'll get rid of it.'

That was when Joan had started to plead with her to keep the baby and now here she was, a forty-two-year-old woman, soon to become a grandmother.

Joan left the room before she told Laura what she thought of her. She couldn't face another argument – and it was bad for the baby to have Laura shouting and screaming. She passed Frank on the way out.

'Talk to your sister, will you, Frank?' she asked her eldest and finest. 'She was out until three a.m. It's not good for the baby.'

Frank grimaced. 'Sure, Mum, I'll have a word.'

He went into the lounge, picked up the remote and switched off the TV. He sat down opposite his younger sister.

'Hey, I was watching that,' Laura grumbled.

'How's your head?' he asked.

'Bloody awful.' Laura groaned.

'Hardly surprising – you really went for it last night.'

'Yeah, it was a fun party. I needed a blow-out.'

'You were very messy. It looked pretty bad, Laura.'

'I was not messy,' Laura said indignantly. 'The drink went straight to my head, that's all. It must be the bloody hormones or something.'

'You were out of your head. You were all over Danny like a cheap perfume.'

Laura blushed. 'Sod off.'

'He had to peel himself away.'

'That's bullshit. He was all over me.'

'Laura, you were completely pissed. A pregnant girl falling around is really embarrassing. Seriously, sis, go easy on the drink.'

'I wasn't that bad.'

Frank raised his eyebrows. 'You set Tara's hair on fire when you were trying to light a cigarette. Seriously, smoking when you're pregnant is not cool.'

Laura giggled. 'Did I really burn her hair?'

'It's not funny – she freaked.'

'It only caught fire because she had so much hair spray in it.'

'Luckily for you, Nick threw his scarf over it so she only lost a few hairs.'

'Tara could do with a trim.'

'No one thought it was funny except you.'

'Did Danny say anything?'

'About the hair fire?'

'No, the other thing, me being a bit keen.'

'No, but he was stone-cold sober. None of the guys on the team are drinking because we've got a big game next week.'

'Sober? Oh, God, I thought he was drunk too.' Laura put a cushion over her face.

'He had to help me carry you out to my car.'

'Stop! Don't tell me any more.'

'You also called Vanessa an air-head.'

Laura rolled her eyes. 'Well, she is. She thought Marc Chagall was a French rugby player.'

'She's not thick. I know he isn't a rugby player because I can name that French team in my sleep, but who the hell is he? A singer? Chef?'

'Duh! He's, like, a really famous amazing French painter.'

Frank yawned. 'We're not all studying history of art, Laura. Some of us are studying real subjects.'

'Give me a break. Social science is a sad excuse for a course. The only reason you're in college is so you can play more rugby.'

Frank smirked at his sister. 'Social science was a stroke of genius. There are only three guys in the class and one of them is gay. All the rest are babes.'

'Most of whom you've shagged.'

'Not most, but I'm working on it.' Frank flexed his muscles. 'This body was made for lovin'.'

'It's not fair. You can go around sleeping with tons of people and no one thinks you're a slut, and I get pregnant on my third bloody shag and I'm labelled a whore.'

'The key is not to get pregnant.'

'I'm paying for my mistake every day.'

'I know,' Frank said, with a sigh, 'but you have to deal with it and stop pretending it's not happening. You're huge now and you can't hide it any more. You need to cut out the drinking and smoking.'

'That's easy for you to say. You're not trapped with a baby for the rest of your life.' Laura's eyes welled.

Frank patted her arm. 'Come on, you know Mum will help and I'll do my bit. You'll be OK.'

'I'm scared, Frank. What the hell am I going to do with a baby?'

'You'll just take it one day at a time. Now get some rest. You'll feel better when the hangover wears off.' He stood up. 'I've got to go. I've got training.'

Laura watched Frank leave and began to feel panic rising inside her. She was getting these waves of terror every other day now, as her due date drew closer. She felt bile rising in her throat and ran upstairs to the bathroom where she threw up.

Wearily, she dragged herself into the shower to try to wash away the night before and the smell of vomit. While the water could wash away the smell, it couldn't do anything about her feeling of claustrophobia. She felt as if she was drowning under the weight of this unwanted pregnancy. She hated it. She hated being trapped. She didn't want to be a mother. She didn't want a kid. She could barely look after herself. She wanted to have fun. But she knew that once this baby was born, she'd never be free again.

Laura dried herself slowly and then, afraid to spend any more time on her own with her dark thoughts, she decided to call her best friend Chloë. She needed to get out of the house.

'Come on over,' Chloë said. 'A few of the girls are calling in for wine and mince pies tonight, except I forgot to buy the mince pies.' She giggled.

'Great. I'll see you later.'

A few hours later, Laura went downstairs. Joan was sitting on the couch watching a cookery programme.

Laura took a deep breath. 'Mum, I'm just popping over to Chloë's. She has a Christmas present for me,' she lied. 'I won't be long.'

Joan looked up. 'I want you home at eleven, do you hear me? You need an early night and I want some help with the Christmas dinner tomorrow. There's a lot to do.'

'Yeah, sure.' Laura rushed out of the door before her mother interrogated her.

When she got to Chloë's, Hayley and Amber were already there, tucking into white wine. Chloë's parents had a big wine cellar in their house, and whenever her mum and dad went out, Chloë would go down, pull out some bottles from the back where they wouldn't notice and share them with her friends. Tonight, she had selected three very dusty bottles of white wine.

'Oh, my God, Chloë, this one says 1938 on it. I hope it isn't mouldy or anything,' Hayley said, waving the bottle in the air.

'It tastes a bit funny.' Amber scrunched up her face.

'It's not great.' Chloë stood up and went to get a large bottle of Sprite. She mixed the lemonade with the wine in her glass. 'That's better.' She knocked it back.

The other girls did the same. After two drinks, Laura felt much better.

'Wow, Laura, you really are getting big. You look like you've got a bowling ball in there.' Amber smirked.

Laura shuddered. 'I really don't want to talk about it tonight. Honestly, guys, I can't take much more of this. I am way too young to have a kid. It's like having a noose around your neck.'

'I can't even begin to imagine it. I mean, my little brother is five and he wrecks my mum's head and she has a full-time nanny for him,' Hayley said.

'Maybe that's what you need, like, proper help. Why don't you hire a nanny?' Chloë suggested.

Laura lit a cigarette and inhaled deeply. 'I wanted to, but my mum said no way. She keeps going on and on about taking responsibility and raising my own child, blah-blah-blah. I'm sick of it.'

'It's such a bummer you didn't get that musician guy to wear a condom,' Hayley said.

'Such bad luck,' Chloë agreed.

'I think about it every day.' Laura sighed. 'Why was I so stupid?'

'Probably because you'd just done five tequila shots,' Hayley reminded her.

'I'll never drink tequila again,' Laura said, shaking her head.

'Didn't Danny look amazing last night?' Amber gushed, changing the subject.

They all nodded in agreement. Laura tensed. Danny was her guy. Well, he wasn't actually *her* guy, but he was Frank's friend and she had fancied him for years. They had kissed a few times but then she'd met the American musician, got plastered and pregnant and blown her chances. Her friends knew she still really liked Danny so they didn't flirt with him out of loyalty.

'I saw you talking to him for ages, Laura,' Hayley said.

'It was less like talking and more like swaying and spilling your drink all over him,' Amber said drily, running her fingers through her auburn hair.

'Frank said I was a disgrace,' Laura admitted.

'You were not.' Chloë was loyal to the end. 'You were just chatting.'

'I'm sorry, but I think friends should be honest with each other and you were all over him,' Amber said. 'You followed him around all night.'

'It wasn't that bad,' Chloë said.

'You were just a bit pissed,' Hayley added.

'Paralytic.' Amber stubbed out her cigarette. 'He had to help Frank carry you out to the car. I met him on the way back in. We had a really good chat, actually. He said he's worried about you. That you seemed to be drinking too much and kind of a mess, and he's worried for the baby. I mean, it is pretty dangerous, you know.'

Laura jutted out her chin. 'And what did you say?'

'I just said that being pregnant was hard for you and that you weren't going out much any more because you were so ginormous. So when you do get out, you get overexcited and drink goes to your head. He was really sweet about it. He said he felt really sorry for you and that it was such a pity you'd wrecked your life.'

Laura thought she might be sick.

'It's not wrecked!' Chloë said.

'It's just complicated,' Hayley added.

'I'm just telling you what he said.' Amber reapplied her lip-gloss. 'Anyway, I have to go. I'm meeting my parents at Midnight Mass.'

'I'll come with you.' Hayley got up and put on her coat. 'Happy Christmas, everyone!' She kissed Chloë and Laura, and the two girls headed out into the night.

Laura took a long drink of wine and sighed. Chloë put her hand on her friend's arm. 'Ignore Amber. She's a bitch. You know she fancies the pants off Danny.'

'Well, she can have him. He clearly has no interest in me now. God, Chloë, I wish it hadn't happened. What am I going to do? I can't be a mum, I just can't. I'll never be able to do anything spontaneous again. I'm never going to be able to go away with you on your college summers. Everything has to be planned and checked with Mum first. I'll never be able to travel and go and live in Paris, like I always wanted to, and study art. I'll be stuck in Dublin for ever. This is it – this is my life. And no one is ever going to want to marry me. Who the hell wants someone else's kid? And, besides, they all think I'm a slut and it was only my third time having sex. It's just not fair.' Laura laid her head on the table and bawled.

Chloë rubbed her back. 'No one thinks you're a slut. You're stunning-looking so guys are always going to fancy you. You've got the most amazing blue eyes and your hair is, like, to die for, so thick and curly. Come on, Laura, it'll be OK. You'll get through this.'

'But the thing is, Chloë, it's never going to end. I'll never be free again. This baby is always going to be there, needing to be looked after.'

'I know it's scary but you'll be a great mum, a cool young mum. You can be friends with your kid and have fun together.'

'I wish I'd never told Mum I was pregnant, just gone to London and had the abortion.'

'Come on, Laura. I know it's hard on you but you'll love the baby when it's here, and I'll help babysit.'

'I just want to run away from it all. I wish –'

The kitchen door swung open and Chloë's father walked in. 'Ho ho ho, and a very merry Christmas,' he said, swaying slightly. 'I see you've been having your own little party.' He nodded at the empty bottles on the table.

Chloë jumped up and tried to hide the evidence, but it was too late. Mr Jackson-Black picked up an empty bottle and peered at the label.

His face went pale. He turned to his daughter and, in a controlled but quivering voice, asked, 'Chloë, are you aware that this is a Château d'Yquem 1938 Sauternes?'

Chloë looked sheepishly at him. 'I thought the ones at the front of the cellar were your favourite so I took the oldest-looking ones.'

Mr Jackson-Black was hyperventilating. 'Do you have any idea how rare this is?'

'It was at the back and it was all dusty so I thought you'd forgotten about it.'

'FORGOTTEN ABOUT IT? I was saving it for a very, *very* special occasion.'

'Well, it is kind of a special occasion – it's Christmas Eve. And, anyway, it tasted rotten so we had to mix it with Sprite.'

'SPRITE!' her father exploded.

'Jeez, Dad, chill. You've got ten zillion more bottles down there.'

'Not of the Château d'Yquem 1938 I don't.'

Laura stood up. 'I'm very sorry. We'll replace it for you.'

'*It costs a bloody fortune!*' he roared.

'What?' Chloë and Laura were horrified.

'But it tasted awful, Dad, honestly. It must have gone off or something.'

Chloë's dad leaned in so that his face was close to his daughter's. 'It had not "gone off". You and your brainless friends have just drunk one of the finest wines in my cellar and you destroyed it by mixing it with LEMONADE. If I ever see you near my wine again you'll be grounded for life. I'm going to bed now before I say something I regret. Tidy up and remove the bottles from my sight.' To Laura, he added, 'It's time you went home, young lady. You shouldn't be out this late and you certainly shouldn't be drinking. Have you no consideration for that child? Go home.'

'Dad!' Chloë glared at her father and walked Laura to the door. 'Don't mind Dad. He's just obsessed with his stupid wines.'

'It's cool, don't worry. Merry Christmas.' Laura hugged her friend and walked down the driveway, pulling her coat round her. She shivered, but it wasn't because she was cold. She saw white, but it wasn't because it had snowed: it was because of the way Mr Jackson-Black had looked at her – as if she was trash, a loser, a nobody, a has-been.

3.

Anna

Christmas Eve 1992

Anna reached up to hang the fat Santa they had got in Las Vegas on the tree. Barry had thought she was mad buying a Christmas decoration in the scorching heat but she liked to collect them from all her travels. That Vegas holiday had been a good one. It was before they had started trying for a baby, before everything had got complicated and stressful and tense between them.

Vegas had been fun and carefree. They had gone to shows, eaten in fantastic restaurants, gambled at the blackjack tables until the sun came up and then slept all day in their oversized room. Everything in Vegas had been super-size. They had gambled too much, eaten too much, drunk too much, and had lots of passionate sex. It had been wonderful.

But then they had decided to try for a baby and everything had changed. As the months had turned into years, Anna had become more and more obsessed with being a mother. She'd read every book she could find. She'd stopped drinking alcohol and caffeine; she'd cut down on her sugar intake; she'd taken awful Chinese herbs that made her feel sick. Sex had become robotic, functional and, finally, loveless. She knew Barry was at the end of his tether. He was sick of the whole baby trail. After the last miscarriage he had begged her to stop. He'd said they could just have a life without children: her obsession with getting pregnant had turned her into a person he no longer recognized. They never had fun any more. Everything was so serious and sad and depressing. He wanted to live a little, to stop being ruled by her monthly cycle. He'd said he was feeling worn out and ground down. He wanted to turn back the clock to before they had started trying to have a baby.

But she couldn't do that. She wanted to be a mother. She yearned for a baby. She ached to have her own child. It was all she could think about. Every second of every day was taken up with how, why, when . . . She hardly went out because she couldn't bear to listen to their friends chattering about their babies and moaning about their sleepless nights. She'd wanted to scream, 'I have sleepless nights, crying for the baby I don't have and for the babies I've lost. You're lucky to be up with your babies. You should be thanking God, not complaining.' She'd known it was irrational, they meant no harm, that they were exhausted, struggling with newborns and toddlers, but she still couldn't stand listening to it. She had preferred to stay in and read books or watch movies. It took her away from herself for a few blissful hours. It briefly silenced the noise in her head and gave her a little relief.

But Barry had wanted to go out. He'd wanted to get drunk and talk about football, cars and politics with his mates. He'd wanted to get away from their house, from their situation and, she feared, from her. When they were out together and someone mentioned babies, Barry would check to see if she was OK. But when he was alone she'd known he could forget about infertility and immerse himself in the lively banter he so enjoyed with his friends. In the last year they had barely gone out together at all. When they did go out, they usually went to the cinema. They didn't need to talk there. They didn't need to fill the silence. In the dark cinema they could pretend everything was normal, ignore the cracks and the rot that had seeped into their marriage.

When Anna's mother had got sick and died, Barry had thought it would push her over the edge, finish her off. But it hadn't. In a really strange and surprising way it had helped. For four months she had stopped thinking about babies all the time and focused on her mother. She had gone to see her straight after school every day, and when she was too sick to manage, Anna had moved in with her. She had loved those few weeks she had spent in her old home. She and her mother had always been close and the time they had had together in those last months was precious. Her mum had told her not to worry so much, that a baby would come to her. She had told her that she knew Anna was destined to have a child of her own. She had to put her trust in God. She also warned her not to neglect Barry because she could see that he was suffering too, that he was heartbroken about the miscarriages, but men reacted to grief differently.

Anna and her mum had talked about everything. They had looked over old photo albums, laughed a lot and cried a lot. It had been very cleansing and cathartic. Anna had got out a lot of her sadness and pent-up emotion. Instead of pretending she was strong, she had allowed herself to fall apart, and her mother had encouraged it. When she had died, although part of Anna was devastated, another part was glad. The last few weeks had been awful for her mother and she was happy that her suffering was over. She also knew how lucky she was to have had such an incredible mother in her life for thirty-eight years. They had said all the things they wanted to say to each other; they had loved and been loved. She believed with all her heart that her mother would send her a baby. God had taken her mum so now He owed her a baby. She knew her mother wouldn't let her down. She'd make it happen.

Three months after she had died, just when Anna was beginning to panic, she had found out she was pregnant. And she had known that this baby was a keeper. All her nerves were gone. This baby made her feel close to her mother, as if she was still with her. This child kept her warm inside. This life would replace the one that was lost.

Anna put on some Christmas music and looked out of the window. She couldn't wait for Barry to come home so she could tell him about the Christmas play. She wanted to make him laugh again, like she used to. They had never been able to return to their Vegas days, but since she'd got pregnant this time, things had been better between them. This was going to be a great Christmas.

She giggled to herself as she thought about the children's play and the mayhem in Bethlehem . . .

The nativity play was one of Anna's favourite tasks with the class. She knew that, with schools becoming multicultural, it would soon be a thing of the past so she was cherishing the few years she had left with her mini Marys and Josephs.

As usual, all the girls wanted to be Mary and all the boys wanted to be Joseph. Anna reminded them that there were lots of other important roles – like the narrator and the innkeeper and the donkey and the three wise men and the shepherds and the angels. Then all the girls decided they wanted to be angels and the boys wanted to be the donkey. Everybody had a part. Kylie was Mary, and Francie a shepherd – he didn't want a speaking part because of his stutter. Jason was the angel Gabriel, and Ryan had begged to be the donkey. Anna had thought this was a good idea as it was a physical role that should keep him out of trouble.

On the night of the concert, after weeks of preparation, Kylie refused to get up on the donkey.

'Why not?' Anna asked.

'I don't want to say.'

'Come on, Kylie, you can say it.'

'I'm just not riding him.'

'Are you afraid of falling off?' Anna asked.

'No. It's because Mary is the Mother of God and there's no way she'd be riding around on a donkey that smells dirty.'

'OK, that's enough,' Anna said. 'Just get up now.'

Ryan stood up, hands on hips. 'Well, I'm not letting you get up on me anyway, Kylie, because I don't want your smelly knickers on my back.'

'Stop it, both of you,' Anna said firmly. 'We're going to use this blanket as a saddle. Now, I want you all to be nice to each other and no more cross words.' She placed the blanket on Ryan's back.

She peeped out from behind the makeshift curtain to see if the parents were all settled in their seats. She was relieved to see that each child had a family representative in the audience, whether it was a parent, grandmother, older sister or brother. Even Ryan had someone: his sixteen-year-old sister had come to support him. Anna was thrilled. Kylie's mum looked a bit unsteady, but the granny was there too, so hopefully she'd keep her in check. Jason's dad was in the back row beside Francie's mother, who was wearing dark glasses that didn't hide her black eye.

'OK, everyone, are you ready? We're going to start now.' Anna smiled down at her little class. She had made the costumes with the children. The angels were wearing white shirts and had halos made of tinsel. The shepherds wore the traditional tea-towels on their heads. Mary had a blue dress and a matching tea-towel, and the kings had crowns made of cardboard and gold paper.

'Right, narrator, off you go.' Anna gently nudged Karen on to the stage.

The little girl went bright red. 'A very long time ago, like ages and ages ago, in a place called Naz– Naz– . . .'

'Nazareth,' Anna prompted.

'Oh, yeah, Nazareth, there was a girl called Mary and she was gorgeous-looking and everyone fancied her. And she was a lovely girl, not a slut at all, and she never took drugs or anything like that. No way. Anyways, one day she was having a cup of tea and the angel Gabriel came to see her.'

Jason strutted on to the stage and stood in front of Kylie, who was pretending to drink a cup of tea. 'Howrya, Mary?'

'Grand, thanks. Howzit going?' Mary said.

'Are you not surprised to see me?'

'Oh, Jesus, yeah, sorry, I forgot.' Kylie's hand flew up to her mouth. 'Sorry, Mrs Roberts, I didn't mean to curse.'

The parents roared laughing.

'It's OK,' Anna said, from the side of the stage. 'Go on.'

'You're all right, Mary,' the angel Gabriel said. 'So, anyways, I came to tell you brilliant news. You're going to have a baby and his name is Jesus.'

'But I'm not married!' Kylie said.

'Neither was your mother,' one of the women shouted up at Kylie.

'Shut up, you witch,' Kylie's granny hissed. 'Leave the poor child alone. Go on, Kylie, you're doing great.'

The angel Gabriel reassured her: 'Don't worry about it because this is God's child and you're going to get married to a different fella called Joseph. He won't mind that the baby's daddy is actually God.'

'He's a bigger man than me.' Jason's dad laughed.

'Shut up, Da,' Jason scolded. 'I'll forget me lines.'

'Is this Joseph fella good-looking? Does he have money?'

Jason looked confused: this was not part of the script. 'Eh, yeah, he's OK, like, and I think his da owns a chipper so you'd get free chips and nuggets.'

'OK, then. I'll do what God says.' Mary and Gabriel walked offstage.

The narrator then said, 'Loads of soldiers came and turfed Mary and Joseph out of their house and they had to go on a donkey for, like, ages, and Mary was huge and fat and knackered.'

Joseph and Mary appeared on stage. Mary was on the donkey, and was looking a bit unsteady. The donkey was busy trying to find his sister in the crowd.

'Howrya, Siobhan,' Ryan shouted, when he saw her. She waved at him. He waved back and Mary fell off.

'For God's sake, Ryan, will you stay still?' Mary shouted at her donkey. Then, to Joseph, she said, 'I'm very tired, Joseph. I think we need to stay in a hotel. This donkey is crap – you should get rid of it.'

'Piss off,' the donkey snapped.

'Stop that,' Anna scolded from the side.

'OK. I'll go and see if there's any room.' Joseph knocked on a cardboard door. 'Hello – any chance of a room with a flat-screen TV and some cheese and onion crisps?'

The innkeeper snorted. 'You must be joking. There's no room here for the likes of you. Look at the state of you, all dirty and smelly. No way.'

'Come on, please! Me wife is about to have a baby,' Joseph begged.

'OK, you can stay in me shed.'

As Mary was shuffling towards the lump of straw that was the manger, she looked into the audience to see her mother fast asleep.

'WAKE UP, MA! I HAVEN'T HAD THE BABY YET!' she shouted.

'She's pissed, love,' the woman behind her mother said.

Kylie looked crestfallen.

'It's all right, Kylie, I'm recording it. She can watch it tomorrow.' Her granny waved her camera in the air.

The Virgin Mary stormed over to the hay and plonked herself down. The cushion that was her pregnant stomach fell out of her skirt.

'You just went into early labour,' a man shouted. Everyone laughed.

Kylie stuffed the cushion back up.

The narrator came back on. 'So, anyways, some shepherds and some kings then followed the shining star and came to see Mary and the baby and give them loads of presents, a bit like Santa. I'm getting a bike from Santa for Christmas, amn't I, Mam?'

'Yes, love,' her mother answered.

'Deadly. And I'm getting a Barbie.'

'Get on with the play, Karen. I'm startin' me shift in Tesco's in fifteen minutes,' her mother urged.

'So then the baby was born.' The narrator summed it all up.

The Virgin Mary, who was lying on her back, legs akimbo, began to scream. 'Oh, Jaysus, get the baby out! I'm in agony! Give me some drugs for the pain. Pull it out, Joseph – come on, will you?'

'Push, Mary, push,' Joseph said, getting into it.

'It's coming. Oh, God, here it comes, oh, the pain of it.' Mary let out an ear-shattering scream, and Joseph pulled the plastic doll from under the hay and waved it about proudly by one leg.

The audience clapped, cheered and whooped.

In the excitement, Joseph threw the baby up in the air and then dropped it.

'You've killed him!' Mary roared. 'You've dropped me baby on his head, you gobshite!'

Joseph picked the doll up and shook it. 'No, it's OK. He's grand. Just a bump.'

'Well, I'm not leaving him on his own with you again. You're a crap dad.'

Joseph shook the doll in Mary's face. 'Fine, it's not even my kid. God's the dad, so why don't you get him to look after the baby?' With that, he stormed off the stage.

Anna stopped him. 'You have to go back, it's the last bit of the play.'

'I'm not going. Kylie's a pain. She said I tried to kill Jesus and I didn't. It was an accident.'

'I know, pet, and you're very good with the baby. Now go on back and finish the play, there's a good boy.'

Joseph stomped back on to the stage, followed by the shepherds, angels and wise men. They all sang a tuneless but very enthusiastic rendition of 'Away In A Manger' and there wasn't a dry eye in the house . . . except for Kylie's mother's: she was still snoring.

Anna saw Barry's car pull into the driveway. She waved at him and hurried out to open the door. She was so full of joy she thought she might burst. This year, Santa Claus had given her the best present ever. She was finally getting the gift of motherhood.

4.
Laura
January 1993

'Give me drugs, you stupid cow!'

The midwife gritted her teeth. 'You need to push. The baby's crowning. The sooner you push, the quicker this will all be over.'

'I hate you and I *hate* this baby,' Laura screamed.

'Stop making a show of yourself,' Joan hissed in her ear.

'I'm in agony, Mum. Everything is orange – bright orange. Give me something – painkillers, vodka, anything.'

'It was too much vodka that got you into this mess,' Joan snapped.

'Come on now, Laura, a big push,' the midwife encouraged her.

Laura closed her eyes, let out an almighty roar and pushed the baby into the world. 'Is it out? Please, God, tell me it's out,' she wailed.

'It's all over now,' the midwife assured her. 'You have a beautiful . . . little girl.'

Laura looked up and saw a wriggly, bloody thing coming towards her. She could see green, dark, murky green, as panic enveloped her.

'Would you like to hold your daughter?' the midwife asked.

'Get her away from me.' Laura shut her eyes. 'She's ruined my bloody life.' She began to sob into the pillow.

Joan leaned over and took her tiny granddaughter into her arms. The baby opened her eyes and sighed. Joan kissed her and began to cry softly as she held her close.

An hour later, Laura was sitting up in bed feeling much better. They had given her tea and toast, and when no one was looking she had laced the tea with vodka. She desperately wanted a cigarette, but knew her mother would freak if she smoked in front of the baby. Joan was into aerobics and healthy living, which was so boring.

The baby had been washed and wrapped in a nice clean pink blanket and was tucked up in a cot beside Laura, sleeping peacefully. Laura leaned back into her pillows and took another slug of her tea. Maybe it wouldn't be so bad, after all.

The door swung open and Joan came in. She ignored Laura and went straight to the baby.

'Jesus, Mum, don't wake her up.' Laura was terrified she was going to start screaming again.

'She's the image of you,' Joan said, gazing down at her sleeping granddaughter. 'You were such a sweet baby and then –'

'And then I turned into a nightmare. Yeah, yeah, I know the story, Mum – the perfect child who turned into the horrible teenager.'

'Well, your wild days are behind you now. You've a baby to look after. Responsibilities. Duties.'

Laura's head snapped up. 'Hold on a minute. I didn't want to keep this baby. The only reason she's here is because you said you'd help bring her up. Don't start backing out now or I swear I'll give her up for adoption.'

Joan prayed silently for patience. She faced her daughter in the small hospital room. 'I said I'd help you and I will, but you are the baby's mother and you have to take responsibility for her.'

Laura flicked back her blonde curls. 'I'll look after her on the mornings I don't have lectures, but don't expect me to stay in on the weekends and mind her because I won't. No way. Besides, you hardly ever go out at the weekends any more, so it's no big deal for you to babysit.'

The baby started crying. Joan picked her up to soothe her. 'I think she needs her nappy changed,' she said, handing her to Laura.

Laura folded her arms. 'No, Mum. I don't know how to do it. I can't.'

Joan set about changing the baby's nappy. 'Have you decided on a name? I was thinking Amanda, like your father's mother.'

Laura shook her head. 'No. Amanda is a brown name. I'm calling her Jody because it's a pink name and she's a girl.'

Joan bit her tongue. She'd never understood the way Laura and her father saw names, numbers and emotions as colours. It had been a very strong bond between father and daughter. When Laura was six, she had announced at dinner one night that her name was purple, just like the colour for funny. Harry had dropped his fork. He couldn't believe that she saw the world in the same way he did. Their colours were different. The only colour they matched on was orange for pain. Harry saw yellow for fear, red for happy and brown for funny. But he was thrilled to have a child who understood his world. Frank, Laura's brother, didn't see colour, and Joan was glad. Otherwise she would have felt like the odd one out.

She clicked the Babygro back on and hugged the baby. 'Hello, Jody, I'm Joan. I'm actually your granny and this young girl here is your mummy.' With that, Joan handed Jody firmly to Laura and went to wash her hands.

Laura looked down. The baby stared up at her, unblinking. 'Sorry, kid, you pulled the short straw with me as your mother. I haven't got a clue and I'm only nineteen so you're going to be hanging out with your granny a lot. She's been really lonely since Dad died, so this could actually work out quite well. She can focus her attention on you and get off my back.'

Joan came back in, drying her hands. The door opened. It was Frank, holding a half-dead bunch of carnations.

'Nice flowers. Are they for me?' Laura smiled at her brother.

'At least I tried.' He dumped the flowers on the windowsill. 'Well, there's a sight I never thought I'd see.' He grinned at Laura holding Jody.

'Isn't she beautiful?' Joan gushed.

Frank gave the baby a cursory glance. 'Not really.' He sat on the edge of the bed. 'She looks weird. Is that normal or is she ugly?'

'Frank!' Joan was annoyed.

'What? She's all red and scrunched-up.'

'Your niece is perfect.' Joan kissed Jody's head. 'Don't listen to that nitwit. You're gorgeous.'

'I'm calling her Jody, by the way,' Laura said, trying not to drop the baby. 'It's a pink name.'

Frank nodded. 'Cool. The only Jody I know is a fox.'

'Jody Kerrigan?' Laura asked.

'Yes.'

'She's so dense. She thought the chorus of "Bohemian Rhapsody" was – "I see a little silly wet man, scare him much scare him much, will you do the fand and go."' Laura threw her head back and laughed.

Frank shrugged. 'Who cares about her singing when she's got a body for sin?'

'You're so shallow.'

'Have you not just had a baby by a nameless, faceless man?'

Joan thumped the side table loudly. 'Stop it, you two. You're behaving like –'

'Teenagers?' Laura smirked.

'Immature teenagers,' Joan retorted.

'Sorry, Mum,' Frank said. Then, to Laura, he added, 'So, Danny was asking if you'd had the kid yet.'

'He's a lovely boy,' Joan said.

Laura looked down. 'Did you tell him?'

'I called him before I drove over.'

Laura almost dropped the baby. Joan leaned over and grabbed Jody.

'What did he say?' Laura asked.

Frank took his chewing gum out of his mouth and stuck it on Laura's saucer. 'Nothing.'

'Nothing at all?'

'He just said he couldn't believe you were, like, a mother now. That it was weird.'

Laura fought back tears. 'He'll never go near me now.'

'You've only yourself to blame,' Joan reminded her. 'Now, hold your daughter while I go home and sort out some more clothes and vests for this gorgeous girl. It's been a long day. I need to get something to eat. I'll be back first thing in the morning to help you out.'

'*You*'ve had a long day?' Laura exclaimed. 'What about me? What about my pain and suffering?'

'Hopefully the baby will sleep now and you can get some rest.'

'Don't go, Mum,' Laura begged. 'I don't know what to do. Don't leave me on my own with her.'

Joan buttoned her coat. She went over and patted Laura's hand. 'You'll be fine. Every new mother panics on the first day. But the only way to learn how to look after a baby is to get lots of practice. If you need anything, call the nurse or you can phone me at home. Don't worry, it'll be fine. She's a little dote.'

She gave Jody a final cuddle and settled her in her cot. She turned to Frank. 'I'll see you at home. I made some lentil soup yesterday and some pumpkin bread.'

'Mum! I'll be starving after rugby practice.'

Joan smiled. 'OK, I'll grill a steak for you.'

'Brilliant, thanks.'

'I thought you were too tired to do anything,' Laura huffed.

'Frank needs to keep his strength up,' Joan replied, closing the door behind her.

'Poor little Frank needs his steak,' Laura teased.

'She likes doing stuff for me.'

Laura sighed. 'You can do no wrong and I can do no right. I'm sick of her giving out to me.'

'Try being nicer to her and not getting pregnant.'

Laura rubbed her eyes. 'What the hell am I going to do, Frank? I can't be a mother. I'm too young.'

'Don't sweat it. Mum will look after the baby most of the time, and you can use some of the money Dad left you to pay for babysitters when she's not around.'

Laura looked at her daughter. 'Does everyone think I'm a total loser?'

'Not a loser, more a slut.'

'Thanks a bloody lot. I feel so much better now.'

'Laura, if you don't want to know, don't ask. You having this baby will be the talk of the town for a few weeks and then it'll be old news. Just put your head down and keep your legs closed.'

'Do you think anyone will ever fancy me again?'

'Did anyone fancy you before?'

'Come on, Frank, be serious for a minute. Would you go for a girl who had a kid?'

Frank got up and stretched his arms over his head. 'If I liked her enough it wouldn't matter,' he lied.

Laura sat up straight. 'Really? Seriously? No kidding?'

'Sure – why not?'

'So you don't think I'm a social pariah?'

'No, but make sure it doesn't happen again. Having a slapper for a sister is ruining my image.'

'Cheers!'

Frank peered into Jody's cot. 'Did Jody Kerrigan really think the lyrics of "Bohemian Rhapsody" were "I see a little silly wet man"?'

Laura nodded and they both roared laughing. 'But the best one was that idiot you went out with last year, Nikkie Holmes. Remember, she thought Robert Palmer's "Addicted to Love" was "Might as well face it, you're a dick with a glove".'

'And Dad thought Michael Jackson's "Billie Jean" was "Billy Jim is not my plumber".' Frank cackled.

They laughed until they cried.

'I miss Dad,' Laura said, her tears turning from happy to sad.

'Me too.' Frank squeezed her hand.

5.

Anna

January 1993

Anna was reading *The Very Hungry Caterpillar*. It was Ryan's favourite book and she knew he'd sit still for a few minutes to listen to it. She was twenty-five weeks pregnant now and she felt tired today. She needed to sit down for a while.

Anna read: '. . . pop, out of the egg came a tiny and very hungry caterpillar.'

'Is an egg going to pop out of your tummy?' Timmy asked.

'No, I have a baby in my tummy.' Anna ran a protective hand over her swollen belly.

'Do you have any other children at home?' Penny wanted to know.

'No, this is my first.'

'But you're really old. I thought you'd have millions of them,' Kylie said.

'Are you happy to have a baby?' Molly asked. 'My mammy was crying when she found out she had another baby in her tummy. She said eight is too many.'

'I'm sure she'll be happy when it arrives,' Anna soothed her.

Molly shook her head. 'She wasn't a bit happy when Fintan arrived. She said she wishted she got a new washing-machine, not a baby.'

'My da got his willy snipped for my ma's birthday,' Penny announced.

'*What?*' The other children were shocked.

'Yeah, she said it was the only present she wanted so he did it. He chopped his willy.'

'Chopped it off?' Ryan covered his own protectively.

'Snipped it off,' Penny said.

'Oh, my God, your ma is a wagon. There's no way I'd cut my willy off for any girl.' Jason was outraged.

After years of teaching, Anna had decided that her young children needed to be allowed to chat among themselves for a few minutes every couple of hours. It allowed them to switch off for a bit, relax and speak freely, which she knew was important as many of them had such difficult home lives. But it was time to step in.

'What Penny means is that her daddy went to the doctor to have a little procedure called "the snip". But he didn't cut his willy off. It's just a little thing that some daddies have done when they're finished having children.'

'My granny told my ma to have her tubes tied,' Molly told them.

'What's that?' Penny asked.

'It's where you go in and you get these tubes inside you where the babies are made and you tie them in a big knot and then no more babies can come out.'

'Are the babies stuck in the tubes?'

Molly frowned. 'I don't think so.'

'Imagine if you tied a big knot and a baby was stuck in the knot and he was all crying and shouting, "Let me out! Let me out!"' Ryan giggled.

'Babies can't talk,' Penny reminded him.

'You'd hear him crying so you'd just untie the knot and let that one out and then tie another one.' Molly had figured it out.

Anna clapped her hands. 'Come on, children, enough talking. I want you to settle down and listen.'

'I saw your ma throwing your da's clothes out the window yesterday,' Jason said to Timmy.

Timmy went bright red.

'That's enough, Jason,' Anna said.

'She was shouting, "Get out of here, you cheater, and don't come back,"' Jason said breathlessly.

'Did he cheat at cards?' Jack wanted to know. 'My ma goes mental when my da cheats at cards.'

'No, you thick, he cheated with another girl,' Kylie explained.

'Oh. My da did that and my ma was mad with him, but he said, "If I'm not gettin' any at home I have to look somewhere else,"' Jack told the class.

'What wasn't he getting at home?' Jason asked.

Anna raised her voice over them. 'I'm going to get cross now. I want you all to stop talking and listen.'

'I think he meant nice food,' Jack said. 'My ma is a vegenarian and she's always cooking yucky vegetables and brown rice. My da wants chips and sausages, like me. I bet the other girl what he went off with cooked chips or maybe they went to the chipper on the corner. My ma says that chipper should be shut down.'

'Why?' Ryan looked horrified.

''Cos she said the meat what they put in the burgers is like cow's arse and nose and eyeballs and stuff.'

'Eeeeeeeew,' the kids said.

'It tastes lovely, though,' Ryan noted.

'I love chipper chips,' Kylie said. 'When my ma has a sore head from drinking too much orange juice she gives me money to go down for a snack box.'

'My da said if you eat too much chipper stuff you'll get big and fat and no one will want to marry you,' Penny said. 'He said that's why my aunty Rosie has no husband because her arse is huge.'

Anna tried not to laugh. 'OK, class, come on now, that's enough. Listen to the story.' She continued to read. Halfway through, she jumped up to get Ryan down from a table.

'Oh, Mrs Roberts, your skirt's all dirty,' Molly said.

'It's red,' Kylie said.

'It's b-b-b-blood!' Francie shouted.

Anna spun around. She looked down. There was a big red stain on her skirt.

'BLOOOOOOD!' Ryan roared. 'Teacher's dying, teacher's dying.'

All the children started to scream. But Anna couldn't move. She was having trouble breathing. She tried to speak but no words came out. The room began to spin . . .

She came to in hospital. Barry was beside her, white-faced, gripping her hand. Her obstetrician was standing on her other side.

'Anna, can you hear me?'

She nodded.

'The baby has decided to come early, but we're going to try to keep it inside the womb as long as possible. Even if we can delay the birth for forty-eight hours, it'll be a big help. Now, I'm giving you an injection of corticosteroids to help the baby's lungs mature before delivery. In the meantime, I need you to lie very still. If you need to go to the toilet, the nurse will get you a bed-pan. You are not to move.'

'Is the baby OK?' Anna was desperate to know.

Mr Walsh nodded. 'So far, so good. I'll be back to check on you in a little while.'

Anna lay back and tried not to cry. She had to be calm. She had to be still. She had to let the baby grow.

'I asked him what the stats were for babies born at twenty-five weeks to make it,' Barry said, stifling a sob. 'He said fifty per cent, so we've got a good shot.'

Anna squeezed his hand. She had to stay positive. She prayed silently to her mother: Help me, Mum. Don't let my baby die . . . please don't let it die.

As Anna lay in her bed, praying, she could hear a young girl screaming in the room next door. 'Puke! She's puked on me again!'

A nurse came into her room to look at her chart. 'Is she all right?' Anna asked her.

The nurse rolled her eyes. 'She's fine – but every time the baby needs to be changed or fed or has a little vomit she starts screaming for help. She has us all driven mad.'

'Maybe she's nervous,' Anna suggested.

The nurse shook her head. 'No. She's just a nineteen-year-old girl who got herself pregnant and now doesn't want to look after her own baby. Thank God she has a sensible mother who can help her out.' She sighed and went to the door. 'I'd better go and check on her.'

Anna heard her snap, 'Laura, calm down – it's only a bit of milk.'

Barry sighed. 'I hope if we have a girl she doesn't turn out like that!'

Anna smiled. 'She won't. She or he will be just wonderful. They'll have your kindness and mathematical brain –'

'And your patience and compassion and hopefully your amazing hair.'

Before Anna could reply she felt a searing pain in her abdomen. She gasped and hunched over. 'Barry!'

He jumped up and wrenched open the door. 'HELP!' he shouted. 'HELP!'

Within seconds a midwife was at their side. She saw the blood and called for Mr Walsh.

'I'm afraid this baby is determined to be born,' he said, as soon as he had examined her. 'OK, Anna, here we go.'

Anna's mind and spirit floated above the scene. She saw her baby being born. She was tiny and red. People were rushing about, Mr Walsh was barking orders, and there was blood, lots of it. Anna felt her head getting lighter. She was beginning to drift away, but she forced herself to stay present. I will not miss this, she told herself. I will not leave this moment.

'It's a girl,' Mr Walsh said.

She heard a cry, a tiny kitten-like mew. She felt salty tears on her lips – she must be crying too. Tears of joy. She wanted to hold her baby but the room was getting darker . . .

*

Anna opened her eyes. Mr Walsh was standing next to her bed. She could tell by his face. He didn't need to say it. She knew.

'I'm terribly sorry, Anna. We did everything we could. I'm afraid the baby was just not ready for this world. She suffered a bleed in her lungs and brain. And I'm afraid there were complications with you too. We had to perform a hysterectomy. I'm so very sorry. I know how much this meant to you.'

Anna looked at the ceiling. 'Where is she?'

'Here,' Barry croaked.

Anna turned her head. He was sitting in the corner of the room rocking back and forth, tears streaming down his face, holding their baby girl.

Anna reached out her arms. Barry stood up, walked over and gently placed the almost weightless bundle on her chest. Her daughter's tiny face peered out. Eyes closed. Lips blue.

Barry sat on the side of the bed, his head in his hands, sobbing.

She looked down at her baby girl. Her mother's sign. Her mother's gift. Dead. Not breathing. Born too soon. Too fragile. Too weak. Too helpless. Not for this world.

A nurse offered to take some pictures. 'You'll find them a comfort,' she said softly. She took one of Anna holding the baby and one of the baby's face.

Anna thanked her and asked her to leave them alone with the baby for a while.

Barry didn't speak. He just continued to cry, as if a river of grief had opened up inside him.

'Hope Sophie Roberts,' Anna said, staring at her child. 'Her name is Hope. Because that's what she was to me. Hope. My last and final hope. And Sophie for my mother, who will have to look after her now.' Anna squeezed her eyes tightly shut and let out a primal wail – she keened for her lost love, her broken heart and her shattered life.

Anna held her baby girl close, inhaling her scent. She kissed her, she held her, she cuddled her, she poured all of the love in her heart into her. She sang to her, she whispered to her, she prayed for her, she breathed in her smell, she clung to her . . . until eventually the doctors took her Hope away.

As she watched her baby girl disappear from her life for ever, Anna didn't cry. There were no tears left and there were no words to describe her pain. Barry sat silently by her side, unable to speak, unable to offer words of comfort because there were none. He was a broken man.

During the time she was in hospital, the only person she agreed to see was Joe: her oldest friend, the only person left in the world who had known her from the age of three when his family had lived next door to hers. Joe was a GP and had been so kind to her mother when she was sick. Her mother had called him her surrogate son. It was Joe who had arranged for Anna and Barry to see every fertility specialist in Ireland and two in London. He had shared their disappointments. He had held her hand in his surgery while she cried for her unborn babies. He had given her sleeping tablets when her desperation for a baby became too much. It was Joe who had listened to her, time and time again . . . and now.

He stuck his head around the door. His hair was rumpled and his jacket was creased. He always looked as if he had just got out of bed. 'Congratulations on becoming a mother.' He came over and enveloped her in a bear hug.

Anna half smiled. Only Joe would say something like that. She was a mother. She hadn't thought about it like that. She had given birth to a child. She was someone's mother. Hope's mum.

Joe held her hand. 'Barry said you called her Hope Sophie.'

Anna nodded.

'It's beautiful, Anna. Your mother would be so proud of you.'

Anna turned away. 'My mother would be broken-hearted. I'm glad she's dead. I'd hate her to have seen this.'

'Do you have a photo?'

Anna handed him the two pictures she had of Hope.

43

'She's perfect,' he said.

'She's dead,' Anna said.

'Yes, she is.'

'After five and a half years and eight pregnancies, I have nothing. I don't even own a uterus any more. I think I'm what they call washed up. Used goods. Fit only for the scrapyard.'

Joe fiddled with his glasses. 'Come on, Anna.'

'Come-on-Anna what? Buck up? Chin up? Stiff upper lip? There's nothing left, Joe. I will never have a child of my own. All I ever wanted was to be a mum. That's never going to happen now. It's over. The waiting, hoping, praying . . . it's all over. I will never see a first smile, first tooth, first day at school. I'll never hear the word "Mummy" said to me. I'll never buy a Hallowe'en costume or a Christmas stocking for my mantelpiece. Santa Claus will never come to my house. No Tooth Fairy will leave money under my child's pillow. I'll never dress my daughter in pretty clothes and tell her she's the most beautiful girl in the world. I'll never tuck her in at night and tell her I love her, to have sweet dreams. I'll never know the unconditional love that I ache to give her. I'll never be a mother and I don't know if I can handle it.'

Joe didn't say anything. He just held Anna while the tears that had been buried deep beneath her broken, shattered heart finally surfaced.

After five days she was discharged. She left with a prescription for antibiotics and painkillers. Two days later, on a crisp January morning, Barry and Anna buried their baby girl and all their hope with her. They stood at the tiny grave, united in grief, torn apart by sorrow.

As the coffin was lowered into the ground, Anna felt the light go out inside her. She knew that her life from now on would be half a life. She'd go on living but inside she was dead.

Later that day when she was about to take some sleeping tablets to try to obliterate the pain in her chest, Barry came in, still wearing his black suit, and sat down on their bed. With his back turned to her, shoulders hunched, he asked, 'What did we do that was so bad? Why are we being punished?'

'I don't know,' Anna said.

'You see these losers – drug addicts, abusers, rapists – having kids and here we are, two nice normal people who could give a child a happy home, and we get nothing.' Barry pulled at his tie as if it was choking him. 'I tried not to get my hopes up, I knew we could lose it again, but four months passed, then five and then six, and I thought, OK, this is it. This is the one. Anna was right, this is a keeper. I'm going to be a dad. I'm finally going to be a dad. And now she's gone. Buried under the ground. Our little Hope. My daughter, my little girl.' Barry's face was full of rage. 'WHY, ANNA? WHY US? WHY?'

Anna reached over to him, wincing as her scar throbbed. She held her husband in her arms and they wept for their lost child. Their stolen baby.

6.

Laura

May 1994

Jody was toddling around Laura's bedroom in a pair of high-heeled shoes, squealing with delight. But at only sixteen months she was still unsteady on her feet. She toppled over and began to cry.

'For God's sake, Jody,' Laura snapped. 'Stop trying on my shoes. You're always falling over.'

Jody looked up at her mother, her big blue eyes spilling tears. But Laura ignored her daughter: she was in a really bad mood. Yellow was the colour she could see, mustardy yellow. She was furious that her mother couldn't look after Jody: she wanted to go to Frank's rugby match at the university – not that she was remotely interested in rugby, but Danny was playing and she had been planning her outfit all week.

She'd gone for skinny black jeans, flat black boots and a black Che Guevara T-shirt that he had admired a few months ago. But now Joan had told her she was going out to lunch with six of her friends and wouldn't be back until much later.

Laura knew she didn't really stand a chance with Danny now that she had a kid, but he was always nice to her and chatted to her whenever they bumped into each other, and he wasn't going out with anyone so she held out a tiny sliver of hope that maybe one day they would get together.

She plonked Jody down to watch cartoons while she went to get ready. When she'd done her makeup, smoky eyes and neutral lips, she examined herself in the mirror. Her eyes were the best thing about her face. They were big and deep blue. She liked that because blue was her happy colour. She wondered if Jody would see numbers, letters and emotions as colours too. She had loved that special connection with her dad. She remembered the first time she'd said that her name was a purple name and her dad had been so excited. He had kept hugging her and saying, 'You're a very special girl.' They had laughed about it all the time. It was wonderful to have someone close to you who had the same quirks and characteristics as you.

It was also nice to know that she wasn't alone: when she had said in school that she saw colours for numbers and names, some of the other kids had called her a weirdo. She'd come home crying and Joan had told her just to keep her colours to herself and not tell the other kids so she wouldn't be considered different. But then her dad had come home and told her to hold her head up high and never be ashamed of the gift God had given her. He always called it a gift because it had made him a genius with numbers and had led to his huge success in computer programming.

'Don't hide what you are. Be proud of it,' her dad had urged. 'You're lucky to have this unique view of the world because it'll make you see things differently and that's a good thing. Who wants to be the same as everyone else? Being unique is wonderful. What we have is called synaesthesia and it makes us special. My grandmother had it and my mother too, so hopefully your children will be lucky as well.'

He had made her feel so good about being different. But he was wrong about school: it was better for her not to mention it because she didn't want to be different. She didn't want to stick out or be thought odd. She wanted to fit in. She wanted to be like the other kids. So she had hidden it and used it to her advantage in getting good results. She had found it easy to remember names and numbers and had done well in her exams. But her heart had always been in art.

From as far back as she could remember she had loved painting. She saw everything through colour – when she listened to music she saw colours. Painting was second nature to her, the best way to express what she saw in her head. Her art teacher had told her she was very talented. She had decided to study history of art because she wanted to go to college with her friends and have fun for a few years, then go to Paris to continue with her art. But Jody had come along and ruined that dream, destroyed that hope. She'd never get to Paris now.

Jody came wobbling in. 'Mama.' She grinned up at her mother, her little pearly teeth showing.

'It's Laura. Call me Laura.' Laura was furious with Joan for teaching Jody to call her 'Mama'. She didn't want to be called that. It made her feel worse than she already did. She wasn't a mother – at least, she didn't feel like one. She hated being burdened with a kid and didn't need to be reminded of it every five minutes by being called 'Mama'.

Jody frowned. 'Lala,' she said.

'Yes, good girl, that's it – Laura. Now, come on, let's get you dressed. We're going to a rugby match and I want you to be good, no shouting or whingeing.'

Laura took her daughter into her bedroom, changed her nappy and put her into one of the many flouncy dresses Joan had bought her. She strapped her into her buggy, gave her a bottle and closed the door behind her.

When they got to the match, Laura turned the buggy to face her and whispered to Jody, 'Listen, there's a guy here that I really like called Danny. If he comes over to talk to me, you must smile and look really pretty and sweet. If I have any chance with him, he has to think kids are easy. So, none of your hissy fits today. OK?'

Jody sucked her bottle and blinked.

Laura kissed her forehead. 'I'll take that as a yes.' She took a deep breath and pushed the buggy into the rugby stadium where four thousand students were shouting for their teams. She heard her name called.

'Laura, over here.' Chloë was waving her arms to catch her attention.

Laura manoeuvred the buggy towards her friend, who was sitting with Amber and Hayley.

'Oh, my God, how cute is Jody,' Chloë cooed.

'Do you think it's a good idea to bring her to a rugby game? It's very loud. Won't she be frightened?' Hayley wondered.

'I had no choice – my mum's out.'

'It's not great for your image. I mean, I thought you were trying to get people to forget you had a kid and now the whole university can see her,' Amber said.

'Like I said, I had no choice.'

'You could have stayed at home,' Amber suggested.

'God, Amber, give her a break,' Chloë snapped.

'I'm only trying to help.' Amber flicked back her hair and pouted. She was wearing the same skinny jeans as Laura, but she had really high spike-heeled black boots on and a sparkly top.

'Aren't you a bit overdressed for a rugby match?' Laura said.

'No.' Amber scowled.

'Her thighs look bigger than Frank's,' Chloë whispered, and Laura giggled.

'How hot does Danny look?' Amber said.

'Very,' they all agreed.

Jody began to wriggle and squeal.

'Oh, for God's sake, be quiet,' Laura muttered.

'Here, let me hold her.' Chloë reached over and lifted Jody out of the buggy. Jody went to her happily. She was used to being handed around between Laura's friends when they called to the house. She never made strange. 'She's such a cutie.' Chloë kissed her chubby cheeks.

'I'd kill for hair like that,' Hayley said, looking admiringly at Jody's blonde curls.

'She's the image of you,' Chloë said. 'Like a mini-me.'

Laura shrugged and looked back to the pitch, where Danny was about to kick a penalty. The ball sailed over the goal posts.

Laura jumped up to cheer. 'Did you see that?' she squealed. 'He's amazing.'

'I think someone's still got a crush.' Amber placed her arm on Laura's. 'You really need to focus on someone else. He's a lost cause.'

'Why?' Chloë challenged her.

'Do I have to spell it out?' Amber pointed to Jody. 'He's not into other people's kids.'

Laura willed herself not to smack Amber's bitchy face.

'Well, I think he still fancies Laura.' Chloë smiled at her best friend.

'Frank looks amazing.' Hayley sighed. She had been obsessed with Frank since she had first set eyes on him in college. She had spent the last eight months blushing every time she saw him and becoming either mute or talking incessantly whenever he said hello to her.

Laura shook her head. 'Honestly, Hayley, you're better off without him. He's a slut, determined to shag his way through college.'

'I know, but I can't help myself.'

The match ended and the girls headed to the campus bar where everyone was meeting up. Thankfully, Jody fell asleep in her buggy. Laura pushed her into a corner and went to get a drink. When the team arrived in, everyone cheered their victory.

Frank came straight over to Laura. 'What the hell is Jody doing in here?' he barked.

'Mum went out so I got lumped with her.'

'You need to take her home. This is no place for a baby.'

'She's fine – she's asleep. I'm only staying for a bit.'

Before they could argue any further, Hayley came over. 'Hi, Frank, you were brilliant today,' she gushed.

'Thanks.'

Hayley went a deep shade of red. 'So, how are you?'

'Great.' Frank started to walk away.

Hayley, emboldened by beer, blocked his way. 'How are you

feeling? I mean, you must have a sore arm – I saw you getting stood on in the match. Is it sore? Does it hurt? Are you in pain?'

'No, it's fine.'

'You look really fit. Have you been working out?'

Frank sighed. 'Yes, I have. The team trains three times a week.'

'Oh, right, yeah, I knew that. Of course. So, what are you doing? What are your plans for, like, the rest of the day and stuff?'

'Well, I'm going up to the bar – if I can get past you that is – to get another pint and then I intend to chat up the fox in the red mini-skirt and, hopefully, all going well, shag her senseless.'

Hayley froze.

Laura grabbed Frank's arm and pulled him to one side. 'There was no need for that.'

He shrugged. 'She asked me what my plans were. I was just being honest.'

'A bit too honest,' Laura retorted. 'Come on, you know she fancies you, God only knows why.'

'She's certifiable,' Frank said. 'She follows me around every day asking me how I am, how training's going, how I'm feeling. She needs to be sectioned.'

'She's a really sweet person.'

'She's a stalker.'

'She's my friend.'

'As her friend, you should tell her it ain't gonna happen. I'm not interested in having sex with someone whose arse is twice as big as mine.'

'That's really mean and, anyway, she's not like that. She's quite a prude.'

'You mean she's a virgin.'

'She's saving herself for the right guy.'

'With an arse that size she might be waiting a while.'

Danny came over and handed Frank a pint.

'I need this badly.' Frank knocked it back. 'My stalker's here.'

Danny grinned. 'She just told me how lucky I was to play on the same team as the one and only Frank Fletcher.'

They all laughed.

'Hey, Danny, well played today,' Laura said, still giggling.

'Thanks. Nice T-shirt.'

Laura was thrilled he'd noticed. 'Thanks, so are you –'

A wail cut through the noisy bar. Laura cursed under her breath.

'What's that?' Danny asked.

'It's Jody.' Frank rushed over to her and lifted her out of the buggy.

'Ank, Ank,' she said, giving him a toothy smile.

'How's my girl?' He kissed her and threw her into the air. She squeaked with delight.

Hayley appeared at his side. 'You're so amazing with babies. You're going to be an incredible dad some day. She loves you.'

Frank winked. 'She's only human.'

Hayley blushed again. 'Would you like to have children?'

'I'm not into procreation, I'm into sex. Dirty, raunchy, any-way-I-can-get-it sex. So, unless you fancy coming into the jacks for a quick shag, move aside.'

Hayley gripped his arm. 'Don't you think sex should be about two people who love each other connecting physically?'

'I'm a straight man. Sex is about getting my rocks off.'

'But it's a loving act between –'

Jody wriggled in Frank's arms. 'Look, Hannah –'

'It's Hayley.'

'Right, yeah, Hayley. I just want to have some fun and get laid. You seem like a nice if slightly unhinged person, so why don't you go and find yourself a guy who wants to hold hands and look at sunsets? You're barking up the wrong tree here.'

'Ank, Ank.' Jody slapped Frank's head.

Hayley was not to be deterred. 'Loveless sex is meaningless, but if you –'

Frank cut across her: 'I like meaningless sex. I like getting laid with no strings attached. I like loose women. I want to shag and go. I'm not interested in what their favourite song or movie is – I couldn't care less. I'm in it for the sex, not the conversation. Yes, I really am that shallow.'

While Hayley struggled to come up with a response, Frank took Jody to Laura and Danny. He had Jody on his shoulders. She was gurgling happily.

Danny stared at the baby. 'You brought her here?' he asked Laura.

Laura took a slug of vodka. 'Yeah, well, I couldn't get anyone to look after her and I didn't want to miss the match. Where are you guys going later?' she asked, attempting to get off the subject of her bloody kid, but before Danny could answer, Frank let out a loud groan.

'Jesus, Jody, that's bad.' He thrust his niece into Laura's arms. 'She's got a smelly arse and Uncle Frank doesn't do nappies.'

Laura glared at him.

'Oh, my God, what is that stink?' Amber had arrived, pinching her nose with her fingers.

'Jody's dropped a bomb.' Frank grinned.

'It's horrendous,' Amber said. 'Seriously, Laura, you need to take her out.'

'I'm going,' Laura barked.

'Calm down. I just think you should look after your child.' Amber batted her eyelids at Danny. 'There's a big crowd heading into town to the Dirty Duck. Are you coming?'

'You can't bring a kid in there,' Danny said.

'Laura's heading home now, aren't you?' Amber turned to her. 'It must be Jody's bedtime.'

'Yes, Amber, it is. Thanks for reminding me. Have fun without me.' Laura almost choked on the words.

'Sorry you can't make it. I guess babies kind of complicate things,' Danny said.

'You can say that again.' Amber laughed. 'Come on, let's go before it gets too packed.'

They all put on their coats. 'See you, kiddo.' Frank kissed Jody's head.

''Bye, Laura, have a good night.' Danny walked out of the door, with Amber hot on his heels.

Laura tried not to cry. She looked around for Chloë but her best friend was kissing a cute blond guy in the corner of the bar.

Laura knocked back the rest of her vodka, put Jody in her buggy, and cried, 'I hate my life.'

As she walked home, all she could see was a wall of orange mixed with yellow and white – pain, anger and shame.

Laura felt nothing so she did another line. Her throat was numb. Yes! Now she was feeling it. Brilliant. She was ready to go out and face the world. She wiped her nose, reapplied her lipstick and headed downstairs.

'I'm off now, Mum,' she said to Joan, who was watching *Tom and Jerry* with Jody on her knee.

'Don't be late. I heard you coming in at five o'clock on Thursday. I want you home at a decent hour tonight. You've to look after Jody tomorrow morning. I've got my aerobics class at nine.'

'Fine, yeah, 'bye.'

'Are you not going to kiss your daughter goodnight?'

Laura sighed, and walked over to Jody. She pecked her on the cheek and hurried out of the door.

She swaggered down the road. She felt fantastic. On top of the world. She just wished she'd discovered cocaine before. She'd taken it for the first time a few days after Amber and Danny had got together. It had happened the night after the rugby match when she'd had to go home because she'd had bloody Jody with her. Amber had finally got her claws into Danny.

Laura hadn't felt pain like it since her dad had died. When Chloë had told her about Danny and Amber, she'd run into the bathroom and thrown up. For days all she could see was orange – so bright and searing it made her feel constantly nauseous.

Frank had been his usual blunt self. 'What do you expect? She's available, he's a guy.'

'I'm available!' Laura said.

54

'No, you're not. You have a kid. Danny couldn't handle that.'

'You said to me in hospital that it wouldn't matter, that if a guy liked me, having Jody wouldn't stop him.'

'I lied.'

'What?'

'Come on, Laura, you can't be that stupid. A lot of guys will run a mile when they find out you have a kid.'

'You bastard, I believed you.'

'You were in hospital. I didn't want to make you feel worse. Besides, there are some guys who would take on someone else's kid, but Danny isn't one of them. He's way too conservative. Forget him, it's never going to happen.'

Laura had to leave the room to throw up again.

After four days of being sick and miserable, she'd had to get out of the house. She'd arranged to meet Chloë in the Leopard bar and they had drunk vodka after vodka. But it hadn't made Laura feel better. If anything, she'd felt worse . . . until they'd bumped into Hilary, a friend from school, who had promised Laura she had the perfect solution to her problems.

'I have something that's going to make you feel so good you won't give a damn about Amber, or whatever her stupid name is. Come on, follow me.'

Chloë had only tasted the cocaine, she was too scared, but Laura had hoovered up two lines and Hilary had been right. She'd felt brilliant, full of energy and confidence. Who the hell cared about stupid Danny and Amber? Laura was on top of the world.

The next day she'd called Hilary and asked her where she could get more. Hilary had put her in touch with her dealer, and now Laura was buying it direct from a guy called Rozer. She had met him in town, behind the Brendan Behan statue in Granville Park on a Tuesday at three o'clock, and bought two grams. She didn't have a clue how much cocaine that was but it was the amount Hilary had suggested. She'd said it would do her for a few weeks.

Laura loved it. The coke numbed her pain and now she could see Amber and Danny together without feeling sick. It also helped her to study. She felt really alert all the time. At first she had told Chloë she was doing it, but her friend started to worry about her and begged her to stop. So Laura had to be careful that Chloë didn't find out. She also knew that if Frank discovered what she was up to he'd kill her, so she did it alone and was careful to cover her tracks.

Laura met up with Hayley before the party.

'Wow, you look amazing!' Hayley gushed. 'That dress really shows off your figure. They'll be queuing up tonight.'

Laura beamed. 'I love this dress. I feel really good in it.'

'Is Frank coming?' Hayley asked.

'No, he has to study for his last exam.'

'Oh.' Hayley looked crestfallen.

Laura put her arm around her friend. 'Come on – there are loads more guys out there. Let's go and find some cute ones to chat up.'

They headed off to the house party, where Laura drank vodka after vodka. When Amber and Danny walked in, she went to the toilet and did another line of coke. When she came out she marched straight over to them. 'Hi, guys, how are you?'

'Amazing, thanks.' Amber put her arm around Danny's waist.

'How about you, Danny?' Laura stared at him.

'Um, yeah, fine, thanks.' He looked uncomfortable.

'Cool, so we're all good.' Laura smiled. 'Oh, God, I love this song – come on, Danny, let's dance.' Before Amber could react, Laura had pulled him close and begun to dance with him. Laura knew she was hot, she knew she was sexy. Danny looked embarrassed but Laura also knew that, deep down, he wanted her. She threw her arms around his neck and whispered in his ear, 'I know you fancy me. I can see it in your eyes.'

Amber came over and yanked Danny away. 'You slut. What are you trying to do? Steal my boyfriend? Don't you get it? No guy here would go near you. You're used goods. You had a kid and you don't even know the father's name.'

'You're just jealous because you know your boyfriend wants me,' Laura sneered.

Amber threw her head back and laughed. 'Everyone wants to sleep with you, Laura, but no one wants to call you the next day.'

'Come on, let's go.' Danny pulled Amber away.

As she watched them leave, Laura began to feel her buzz waning. She didn't want to feel the hurt she knew was inside so she went into the toilet and did two more lines. When she came out, she felt fantastic again and ended up snogging Gerry, one of the guys on Frank's rugby team. He was a friend of Danny's and she knew it would get back to him.

'Come on, let's go upstairs and have some fun.' Gerry led Laura up the stairs and found an empty bedroom. He pulled her down beside him on the bed and shoved his hand up her dress.

'Hold on, relax. What are you doing?'

'Getting your pants off.'

'Stop, no!' Laura pushed him aside and sat up.

'What do you mean, "no"?'

'I mean no. It's not going to happen.'

'But everyone knows you're easy.'

'I am not,' Laura spat.

'You have a kid – it's a bit late to be tight now. Come on, Laura, I know you want it.' He put his hand up her dress again.

A kind of rage she'd never known before came over her. She grabbed his wrist and twisted it. 'How dare you?' she screamed. 'You pig! I wouldn't sleep with you if you were the last man on earth!'

He pulled his wrist free. 'A slut like you can't be choosy.'

She jumped off the bed and raced out of the room. 'FUCK YOU!' she yelled, running down the stairs, not caring who heard. 'I HATE YOU ALL!' She tore out of the party and all the way home, spurred on by fury and cocaine.

By the time she got back, the cocaine and vodka had worn off and she was feeling really low. She took her shoes off and massaged her feet, which were covered with blisters. She went into the kitchen to get some plasters and found Joan and Frank sitting up waiting for her.

Joan was gripping something in her hand. Frank pulled his finger silently across his throat. Laura knew she was in big trouble.

'Sit down, please,' Joan said, her voice shaking.

'Not now, Mum. Whatever it is, please don't start now. I've had a really bad night and I just want to go to bed.'

'I said sit down,' Joan barked.

Laura sat at the table, facing her mother. Joan opened her hand, held out a little bag and shook it in her daughter's face. 'Explain this.'

Laura thought she might vomit. It was her stash of cocaine. How the hell had Joan found it? She had hidden it in the toe of her boot at the very back of her wardrobe.

'Is it coke?' Frank asked.

'No, it's just powder, it's just . . . it's nothing . . .'

'Oh, well, that's a relief because Jody found it,' Joan said, her cheeks flushing bright red. 'She was trying on your shoes and she felt something in your boot and pulled it out. When I found her, she'd opened the bag and was tasting it.'

Laura's hand flew to her mouth.

Frank thumped the table. 'Is it cocaine?'

Laura nodded. 'Is Jody OK?'

'I arrived home as Mum was calling the doctor. We didn't know how much she'd taken.'

'I knew it couldn't be much because I'd only left her for a minute.' There were tears in Joan's eyes.

'The doctor said she seemed OK but we had to keep her awake and watch her for two hours. She's asleep now.'

'He said that if she'd ingested all of it she could have died.' Joan began to cry.

Frank crossed his arms. 'He wanted to call the authorities but we managed to persuade him not to.'

'What's wrong with you?' Joan whispered. 'How could you do this? You could have killed our little Jody.'

Laura's whole body was shaking. She was sweating and she felt cold. She could see dark green. She was terrified. She put her head into her hands and sobbed. 'I'm sorry, I'm so sorry. I never meant . . .'

'NEVER MEANT WHAT? FOR YOUR BABY GIRL TO FIND IT AND DIE OF A DRUG OVERDOSE?' Joan stood up and began to hit Laura, slapping her about the head, face and shoulders.

Frank jumped up and pulled his mother back. He sat her down in her chair. 'We all need to calm down. The important thing is that Jody's OK.'

'I'm sorry, Mum.' Laura willed her mother to forgive her. 'I'm an idiot, I know I am. I messed up. I just wanted to forget for a while. I've been really stressed and unhappy. I'll never do anything so stupid again. I swear. Look.' She went to the sink and flushed away the cocaine.

Joan stood up. 'I don't know who you are. The girl I raised, the girl your dad was so proud of, would never have done this. Some kind of monster has taken over my Laura. You're not fit to be a mother. You don't deserve a beautiful child like Jody. You put her life in danger. What kind of a person are you? How could you do that to an innocent child? A child who loves you and craves your attention, and who you ignore most of the time. You're her *mother*!' Joan walked to the door. 'I can't look at you any more.' She slammed it behind her.

Laura looked at Frank. 'Do you hate me too?'

He sighed. 'What the hell are you doing messing with cocaine? How stupid are you? You've got a kid.'

Laura pummelled the table with her fists. 'Don't you get it? That's why I took the cocaine – *because* of Jody. Because I can't be the person I want to be. I can't be a student. I can't be a normal twenty-year-old girl. I'm a mother. I can't be carefree. I can't go to pubs because I have to babysit. I can't flirt with guys because they think I'm a slut. Scrap material. I *hate* my life. I used cocaine to escape from myself. To escape from Jody. To escape –'

Frank grabbed her arm. 'Stop trying to run away. Jody's not going anywhere, and Mum can't look after her for ever. You . . . have . . . a . . . child. Deal with it.'

'It was one night, one stupid mistake, and I have to live with it for ever. Don't you see? It's like having a noose around my neck. I feel as if I'm being strangled. I can't do this, Frank. I can't be a mother, I just can't.' Laura laid her head on her arms and bawled.

'Laura, listen to me. This isn't a choice. You *are* a mother, you *have* a daughter. You've got to get that into your thick head.'

'It's not fair. You screw around all the time and never have to deal with consequences. No one thinks you're damaged goods. People don't look at you like you're dirt. You're not trapped having to look after a kid for the rest of your life. Why me? Why did I get so unlucky?'

'I can't answer that. All I know is that Jody's here and she needs a mother. And so far you're doing a shitty job. And, FYI, no guy wants to go out with a coke-head. Stop drinking so much as well – you're always pissed when you're out. Seriously, Laura, you've got to get your shit together and start looking after Jody properly. She's a great kid. If you stopped feeling so sorry for yourself all the time you might actually enjoy her.'

Laura cried harder.

'Come on, Laura. Look at the positives. You have a gorgeous little girl. Find your happy colour – purple or green or whatever the hell it is. Find it and look at it and focus on it. Come on!' Frank grabbed an apple. 'OK, look at this apple, focus your mind on the colour – greeeeeeeen . . . happyyyyyy . . . greeeeeeeeeen . . . I love greeeeeeen . . . I feeeeel happyyyyyyy now . . . greeeeeeeeeeen.' He waved the apple in front of her eyes.

Frank was right about the colour but wrong about the emotion. All Laura could feel was panic.

7.

Anna

June 1994

Anna stood in the shower, letting the water wash away her tears. She still woke up crying every day. A year and a half later and her pain was the same. Time had not healed her wound. There was still a gaping hole in her heart.

She had gone back to school six weeks after Hope's death. She tried really hard every day to behave the way a 'normal' person would, but inside she was dead. She felt as if her whole body had been anaesthetized. The worst thing that could possibly have happened had happened. Now there was nothing to fear but life itself.

In those first few weeks after Hope had died, she had contemplated suicide. She'd known she had to go back to work or else she would put her head in the oven, turn on the gas and breathe in deeply. Barry had thought she was going back too soon, but Anna had needed to do it. She craved children. She had to be around innocent little people who didn't ask her how she felt all the time. Joe had agreed with her that it was a good idea. He'd thought it important for her to get out of the house and have some structure to her day. He'd helped her persuade Barry that it was a good idea.

Anna had spent most of those awful weeks asleep. She'd been taking sleeping tablets and welcomed the relief of switching off her brain and drifting into dreamless oblivion. But eventually she'd wake up and the pain would take her breath away.

She remembered that first day back at school as if it were yesterday. When the children had come into class and seen her, their faces had lit up. They had run over to hug her . . .

'I missed you. The other teacher they gave us was really narky,' Kylie said, holding on tightly to Anna's legs.

'Here, get out of the way! I want a hug.' Ryan pushed Kylie aside and Anna crouched down. He threw his arms around her. 'Jaysus, Mrs Roberts, I'm made up you're back. The other teacher shouted at me all the time and you never do. You never make me feel bold or thick.'

'I'm glad to see you too,' Anna said, fighting back tears.

'Are you really?' Ryan looked delighted. 'Most people aren't. Me gran always says, "Here's trouble," when she sees me.'

Anna hugged him again.

'Where d-d-did you g-g-go?' Francie asked.

'I know!' Molly said. 'My mammy told me that you lost your baby.'

'What?' Jason was surprised. 'I thought you was sick. Where did you lose the baby? Was it in the shopping centre? My ma lost my brother there one time but we found him. He was hiding in a tent in the sports shop. You should check the sports shop – I bet your baby's there.'

'Thanks, Jason, but the baby is gone,' Anna said.

'Did you not find it?' Penny asked.

Anna shook her head. She was welling up again.

Ryan was upset for her. 'Did you look everywhere? I can help you. I'm a good finder.'

'What you need to do is pray to St Anthony – he's a brilliant finder,' Molly said. 'When my da went missing one time for ages my ma prayed to St Anthony to find him and he did.'

'Where was he?' Penny asked.

'In the pub. He fell asleep in the toilet.'

'I lost my da when I was just a baby and we never found him,' Timmy said. 'My ma says he went to plug Tina's hole and never came back.'

'It must have been a massive hole,' Jason said. 'Did he have a digger?'

Despite herself, Anna laughed. 'Come on, let's get to work.'

'Mrs Roberts, didn't you lose your mammy too?' Molly asked.

'Yes, Molly, I did.'

Molly wagged her finger. 'You have to be more carefuller. That's two people you've lost now.'

'Why don't we all have a look? I bet we'll find them.' Ryan was desperate to help his favourite teacher.

'It's OK, Ryan. The baby and my mummy have gone to Heaven. They're angels now.'

'Oh. Are you sad?' he asked.

'Yes, I am.'

'Can I be your kid instead? I'd love to come and live in your house,' he offered.

Anna smiled. 'You're all like my children and I'm so happy to see you again. I'm really going to miss you guys next year. Now, listen, I want you to remember something. You can be anything you want, if you work hard. You can have your own house and your own car and a good job. But you must concentrate and be good in school. I know that some of you have things going on at home that make you sad and scared. But if you work in school and try hard you can make your own life and be the best person you can be.'

'Like you are,' Kylie said.

'I want to be a teacher like you,' Ryan said, standing close to Anna.

'That would be wonderful, Ryan.' Anna patted his head.

'And me,' Jason said.

'And me . . . and me . . . and me . . .' they all joined in.

For Hope's first anniversary Anna, Barry and Joe had gone to the grave and released twenty white balloons. She'd watched them floating up into the cold January sky. So white and pure and innocent. Sailing up to Heaven, to her mother and Hope.

Joe had insisted on taking them out to lunch, but it had been awful – stilted conversation, pushing their food around their plates, each wishing they were somewhere else.

Barry had slowly but surely pulled away from Anna. At first they had been united in their grief, but it hadn't lasted long. She knew that he dreaded coming home to her, to their house, that he could never move on with these memories dragging him back. She had watched him struggle to be a loyal husband, to be supportive and kind, but it was slowly eating away at him. Now she knew what she had to do.

On the last day of term, Anna packed up her things, emptied her desk drawer and walked out of the school gate without a backward glance. It was over. This part of her life had to end. She couldn't live in the same house and work in the same school and act as if nothing had changed. She had tried it, she had given it eighteen months, but she couldn't do it any more. The pretence was over. She knew if she didn't get away, she'd sink. The grief was still overwhelming.

When Barry came home that night, Anna surprised him with his favourite meal – steak with pepper sauce and dauphinoise potatoes. She had put on some makeup and used their best china. She even opened a bottle of wine. She had been avoiding alcohol because she was worried about its effect on her. Worried that she would get maudlin and also that once she started drinking she might never stop. She would gladly live in a haze of alcohol, avoiding reality and numbing the hurt. She poured a glass for Barry and put it next to his plate.

She heard him come in and went out to greet him. He looked shocked to see her dressed up. Normally by the time he got home she was in bed, watching TV or pretending to be asleep so they wouldn't have to talk.

'Wow, this looks nice.' Barry loosened his tie and sat down opposite her.

'I decided you'd had enough TV meals over the last few weeks.' Anna forced a smile.

'Right, yes, but it's OK – I mean, I don't mind.'

'Oh, I know, I just thought it would be nice.'

'It is – no, absolutely. It's great.'

'So how was work?' Anna asked, as she dished potatoes on to her husband's plate.

'Oh, you know, the same. How about you? Glad to be finished for another year?'

Anna said nothing. She was trying to find the right words, the right moment to tell him.

'Peter and Susan were wondering if we'd like to have dinner with them. Something casual. Just to get out of the house.'

Anna shook her head. 'I don't think so.'

'Yeah, well, I knew you'd say that, so I told them it was unlikely. No worries, it was just a thought.' Barry concentrated on cutting his steak.

'Barry?'

'Yeah?'

'Are you happy?'

He dropped his knife. 'What kind of a question is that?'

'I mean, are you happy with this life?'

'We buried our daughter. What the hell do you think?'

Anna took a deep breath. 'I didn't mean it like that. I suppose what I meant is that I feel as though you've been unhappy for a long time.'

Barry waved his fork at her. 'Don't you put this on me. Don't you start telling me I've been a bad husband. I've stood by through all your obsessive pregnancy stuff. I didn't want to try any more. I begged you to stop after the last miscarriage. I *told* you it wouldn't work but you kept on and on about your mother sending us a baby and all that *crap*. And then it happened and I started to believe it and now look – I buried my baby girl and you ask me if I'm happy. What do you want from me?'

Anna smiled. 'I want you to be happy.'

He glared at her. 'Well, I'm miserable.'

'I can see that, and that's why I'm setting you free.'

'What?' Barry stared at her. 'Is this some kind of joke? Have you taken something? Did Joe give you some new tablets?'

'No, Barry, he didn't. Listen to me. I know I can't make you happy. Our time is over. I'm telling you that you can go. You can go and never look back. I'm telling you that I know our marriage is over. I know that I pushed too hard, too far. I know that Hope living was the only way our marriage could have survived, and even if she had made it, I'm not sure it would have been enough. I love you, Barry. I love you for staying with me through the miscarriages and for holding my hand through the disappointments. I love you for not walking out on me when I know you wanted to, when my obsession with having a baby took over my life. But I know that our relationship has run its course. We'll only make each other unhappy by staying together so I want us to be sensible and end it before we get bitter. I want you to be happy and I can't help you with that any more. Part of me died with Hope. It's time for both of us to move on, in different directions.'

Barry's face was bathed in relief. Anna knew she had made the right decision.

'Are you sure?' was all he said.

'Absolutely positive.' She was firm.

He came over and hugged her. A proper hug full of warmth and emotion and most of all, she sensed, gratitude – for allowing him to move on with his life, for not making him live the rest of his life with her broken heart.

'I love you, Anna.' He kissed her. He sat back down and began to eat with gusto.

Anna played with her food. 'Actually, there's something else. I've decided to move away.'

Barry's shock was written on his face. 'What?'

'I've handed in my notice. I'm going to apply for jobs in London. I want to get away from here. Too many memories of Mum and Hope and all the babies we lost. I need a fresh start.'

'It's all very quick. Don't you think you should give yourself more time?'

'No. I don't need time. I need distance. It feels right.'

He looked at her for a moment. 'You've really thought about this, haven't you? Will you be OK?'

Anna sighed. 'I've thought of nothing else since Hope. It's better this way for both of us. I'll get a new life, away from my memories, and you won't have to worry about bumping into me when you meet some twenty-five-year-old hottie.'

'Anna!'

'It's OK. I want you to meet someone. You're a great husband. You should get married again and I really hope you have children. You'll be a great dad.'

Barry fought back tears. He came around and held her tightly. 'You would have been an incredible mother. I'm sorry, sweetheart, I really, really am.'

'Me too.'

They held each other and cried together for the last time.

8.

Laura

August 1994

While all of Laura's friends went off to spend their college summer in London, she worked in a local restaurant, Dino's, and stayed in at night with her mother, who had grounded her after the cocaine incident. The summer dragged on interminably and Laura felt increasingly suffocated.

She couldn't believe she was stuck in Dublin, working and babysitting. Frank had gone to New York with some of his friends to work on a building site, and Danny was in London with some of his rugby friends. They were renting an apartment in Fulham near Chloë, Hayley and Amber's flat.

Laura kept getting phone calls from Chloë telling her what a wild time they were all having. They were working all day and partying all night. While Laura wanted Chloë to call and keep her up to date, she always felt wretched after talking to her best friend. She felt left out, abandoned and dumped.

She was stuck in a house with her mother, who thought she was a worthless piece of crap, and a child she didn't want. She loved and hated Jody in equal measures. All she saw when she looked at her daughter was a prison cell. It was Jody who was preventing her from living her life, from being in London with her friends, from being a normal student, from having Danny.

Most nights when Joan was asleep, Laura stayed up late watching TV and drinking vodka. It was her pathetic attempt at rebellion. She was very careful to hide the vodka bottles high at the back of her wardrobe so Jody couldn't get her hands on them.

She often went to bed drunk. It helped her get through the summer. It helped her forget about her situation and her status as a loser.

There was a chef at Dino's who was keen on her. He was older, about thirty, and very full of himself. She wasn't interested in him, but she kissed him a few times out of boredom. When he started pulling her clothes off in the storeroom, though, she drew back. She was terrified of getting pregnant again. He said he had condoms, but she was afraid they'd burst or be faulty. He was furious. He called her a prick-tease and proceeded to ignore her, always cooking the meals for her customers last. Not only had Jody ruined her life in college, but she had also made her completely paranoid about sex. Laura felt doomed.

She was feeling particularly sorry for herself one night when Chloë called.

'You sound really down,' her friend noted.

'I'm just so sick of my shitty life.'

'Come over and visit next weekend,' Chloë begged.

'I can't. I've got a kid, remember.'

'I'm sure your mum would look after her for a few nights,' Chloë said.

Laura hadn't told Chloë about the cocaine: she'd been too ashamed. Chloë didn't know that she was grounded because she had endangered the life of her own child. 'I'm not sure she would, Chloë.'

'OK. Well, you need to get down on your knees and beg her because I have some good news for you. News that is definitely going to cheer you up.'

'You bought those leopard-print shoes you were on about.'

'No, much more exciting than that.'

'You bought me the leopard-print shoes?'

'No, forget shoes.'

'You had sex with Tom Cruise?'

'No, but you're getting warmer.'

'Really? You had sex with Brad Pitt?'

'Nope.'

'Johnny Depp?'

'I wish. No. It's not about me, it's about you and someone you like.'

'Danny?'

'Yes! Danny and Amber have split up.'

Laura's heart soared. This was the best news ever.

'He dumped her three nights ago. She's devastated.'

'How devastated?'

'Can't-sleep-or-eat devastated.'

'Amber not able to eat?'

'I know! She has it bad.'

'Poor her.'

'I can hear the concern in your voice.'

'Is she utterly miserable?'

'Utterly.'

'Fantastic.' Laura grinned at the ceiling. 'So what happened?' She wanted to hear all the juicy details.

'According to Amber, he said he wanted a little break. But James said – you know Danny's friend James?'

'Yeah, he's a friend of Frank's too.'

'Right. Well, he told me that Danny couldn't handle Amber any more because she's so clingy and controlling, and every time he even looked at another girl she freaked.'

'I love it! Tell me more.'

'That's it, really, but the other good news is that Amber is leaving tomorrow to meet her parents in the South of France for two weeks' holiday so she'll be out of the picture for a while. And it just so happens that we've arranged to go and see Paul Oakenfold playing in Green Park this Saturday night.'

'I love him! He's the best DJ ever.'

'I've got you a ticket and Danny's going to be there so you *have* to come. You have to find a way to get over here.'

'Leave it with me – I'll work on it.'

★

Laura waited to catch Joan in a good mood, which was extremely difficult as every time Joan looked at her, she remembered the cocaine incident and felt angry all over again. The next night, Laura offered to put Jody to bed, but Joan said no. She liked giving her granddaughter a bath and reading her stories.

She could hear Joan singing 'Twinkle Twinkle Little Star' to Jody. She sounded like she was in a good mood. This was Laura's opportunity. She hovered in the kitchen until Joan came down. 'Is she asleep?' she asked.

'Yes, the poor little thing is worn out. We went to the park today with Lilly and her little boy Tom. Isn't it funny that my friend has a son the same age as my granddaughter?' Joan shook her head. 'Your dad and I got married young. He was mad keen to have kids straight away. He always said he wanted to be a young dad. It was as if he knew somehow his time was limited. He would have loved Jody – she's such a sweet child. And she's very clever. She has lots of new words. Her vocabulary is amazing for a nineteen-month-old.'

'Great, yeah. So, um, Mum, can I –'

'No.'

'What?'

'Whatever it is you want to do, the answer is no.'

'But I haven't even asked you yet! How can you say no when you don't even know what I want?'

'Because I know it's something to do with going out and I told you that, until you can prove yourself to be responsible, you can't go out.'

'Jesus Christ! I've been locked up for weeks – I'm going crazy here. I feel like a prisoner in my own home.'

'It's my house and you put Jody's life in danger.'

Laura threw her arms up into the air. 'I've apologized a zillion times and I've worked all summer and stayed in while all my friends are living it up in London. They're having what students are supposed to have – FUN!'

Joan folded her arms. 'Well, Laura, you don't seem to know

how to have fun in a normal way. You either come home pregnant or on drugs.'

'I made a mistake.'

'No. You made two huge mistakes.'

'OK! I made mistakes but I'm human. People make mistakes. No one's perfect.'

'When you make mistakes, you have to live with the consequences.'

'I live with them every day!'

'No, you don't.' Joan said, sitting down at the kitchen table. 'I'm the one raising Jody. You barely interact with her. That needs to change. I'm not going to spend the next thirty years babysitting your daughter. You have to be a mother to her, Laura, not someone who feeds her and changes her nappy. You need to really engage with her and get to know the beautiful person she is. She needs her mother's love.'

'But you like doing everything for her. I see how happy she makes you.'

Joan nodded. 'She's been a joy. After your dad died I was destroyed. Just getting out of bed in the mornings was a struggle. But then Jody came along and she was so sweet and innocent. I threw myself into looking after her because it helped me get over my grief. In a way she saved me. But I realize now that I've done too much. I have to start taking a back seat. I'm not her mother. *You* are. So, from now on, I'm going to let you put her to bed and bathe her and read her stories and spend time with her. She needs to get to know her mother and you need to get to know your child. And I need to get on with my life. Don't miss out on Jody's precious baby years, Laura. You'll regret it if you do.'

Laura frowned. She didn't like the sound of this. She didn't want to look after Jody more. She wanted to look after her less, if possible. 'But Jody adores you, she doesn't want me.'

Joan sighed. 'That's the whole point. She needs to get to know you properly. You need to bond with each other.'

Laura didn't want to get into this now. She'd deal with it later when she had time to work out a plan. For now she'd tell Joan she had to do more shifts in the restaurant, and in September she'd tell her she had lectures all day and study groups at night or something. She'd worry about it when she got back from London. But right now all she cared about was going to the concert and seeing Danny. She needed Joan on her side.

'You're right, Mum. I do need to take more responsibility and I promise I will. I'll be more mature and level-headed and all that. But Chloë just called and invited me over to London for the weekend. It's no big deal, just two days, and when I come back I'll look after Jody more and be a better person.'

'The answer is no.'

Laura saw a wall of yellow. 'I HATE YOU!' She stormed off to bed, drank half a bottle of vodka and cried herself to sleep.

When she got home from the restaurant the next night, Joan was standing in the hall with her coat on. 'I have to go to Galway. Angela's broken her leg, and Tony's away on business until Tuesday, so she needs my help. I'm sorry, but you'll have to tell the restaurant you can't work for the next few days. You have to look after Jody.'

'Why can't you take her with you?'

'Because I'm going to be flat out, looking after Angela and her four kids. Anyway, it'll be good for you both. You can spend some quality time together. Now, make sure you look after Jody properly. Give her balanced meals, lots of fresh air and not too much TV. You'll have fun with her – she's great company. Look, I have to dash. I'll call you later.'

'But, Mum, I –'

Joan rushed out of the door before Laura could object any further. She stomped upstairs to get some vodka. She was furious. Now she'd be stuck with a kid all weekend. How the hell was she going to fill her days? Her manager at Dino's would go mad when she told him she couldn't work the busy weekend shifts.

The phone rang and she grabbed it before it woke Jody. It was Chloë. 'Any luck? Did you persuade your mum?'

'No – and now she's gone to Galway for the weekend because her sister broke her leg and she's left me on my own with Jody.'

'Oh, God!'

'Look, you might as well give my ticket to someone else.'

'Hang on! If your mum is definitely going to be in Galway all weekend, why don't you come over?'

'Because I've got Jody.'

'Yeah, but we can find a babysitter. I'll ask around in the other flats and see if I can find someone. I'm sure it won't be hard.'

Laura felt the adrenalin pumping through her veins. 'And I've saved up loads of money from the restaurant and not going out, so I can easily pay for flights.'

'Oh, my God, this is great!' Chloë squealed. 'Call Aer Lingus first thing in the morning and book your flights.'

'I'M COMING!' Laura shouted, and everything suddenly looked blue, a lovely aqua blue.

9.

Anna

August 1994

Barry squashed the last box into the boot of his car and closed it. He turned to face Anna. 'So.'

'So.' She smiled.

'Onwards and upwards.'

'Exactly.'

He looked at the house. 'We had some good times here.'

'Yes, we did, very good times.'

He put his arm around her. 'I'm sorry things didn't work out.'

She rested her head on his shoulder. 'Me too.'

'I never thought we'd be the ones to split up.'

'We gave it our best shot. Life threw us too many curve balls.'

'You can say that again.' He sighed. 'I wish we'd been luckier.'

Anna fought back tears. 'We really never got a break. Hope was the last straw. Too much pain . . .'

Barry cleared his throat. 'She was so beautiful . . . It's not fair . . .' His voice broke.

Anna hugged him. They clung to each other over the memory of their lost daughter, their joint heartache.

Anna pulled back first. She dried her eyes. 'God, this is hard.'

He gave her a shaky smile. 'It's been a great ten years, even with all the crap.'

'Yes, it has.'

'I just wish –'

'Don't. We can't change the past.'

He exhaled deeply. 'So, what time is your ferry?'

'Tomorrow at eleven.'

'I'll miss you, Anna.'

'Me too.'

'Will you write and let me know you're OK?'

'I think it's best if we make a clean break. I'll be fine and I know you will too. It'll be easier for me not to keep in touch. Too many memories.'

'OK. Look after yourself. I hope you find peace of mind and happiness in London.'

'Thanks.' She kissed her husband's cheek.

'I transferred the money for the sale of the house into your account yesterday.'

'Great.'

'Good luck with those posh English girls. It'll make a change from the inner-city kids here.'

She smiled. 'Change is good.'

Barry jingled his car keys in his pocket. 'Right . . . well . . .'

Anna hugged him once more, then walked away. 'I'm going back into the house while you drive off. I can't do the big good-bye.'

Barry called after her, 'I wish it had turned out differently.'

'Me too.'

Anna finished packing and closed her suitcase. She went to the drawer in her bedside locker to get her passport. Lying underneath it was Hope's birth certificate. Anna's hands shook as she held it. She sat down on the bed and stared at the document – Hope Sophie Roberts, date of birth 24 January 1993. Anna pressed the piece of paper to her chest. She was glad that she had this to remind her that she had been a mother once, if only for the briefest moment. She was glad that her daughter had been acknowledged in this world, as a person, a human being who mattered.

There was no death certificate. Anna had meant to register Hope's death, but when she'd got to the Register Office she couldn't do it. She couldn't face erasing her baby's existence.

How could a mother go in and tell a stranger to destroy all evidence of her child's life? How could she wipe out her baby's birth? Hope had lived, she had been on this earth. She was Anna's most treasured possession. Anna couldn't destroy that. Not ever.

Anna packed her passport and Hope's birth certificate into her travel wallet and went to her hair appointment.

'What would you like done today?'

'I want you to cut it all off.'

The hairdresser was clearly shocked. 'But you've got beautiful hair.'

'I need a change. I need to walk out of here looking like a different person because then maybe I'll feel like a different person.'

'You're absolutely sure?'

'I've never been more sure of anything.'

The hairdresser began to cut. Anna felt numb as she watched her thick hair fall to the ground around her. Good riddance, she thought.

Joe looked around the coffee shop. Anna waved. He looked behind him. She called his name. He peered at her. 'Jesus, Anna, is that you?'

She held her hand up to her cropped hair. 'Yes.'

'You look –'

'Completely different?' she suggested.

'I'd never have recognized you.'

'Good. I want to create a new me. I'm shedding my old life.'

'But your hair,' he said.

'My crowning glory. It had to go. It was tying me to my past life. I feel lighter, freer now. I also feel less visible. I like that. I want to blend into the background. I need to be invisible for a while until I figure out who I am again.'

'And you've got so thin.'

'That would be the misery diet,' she said, with a wry smile.

'When do you leave?'

'Tomorrow.'

'Are you sure about this?'

She shrugged. 'It's the only decision I can make. I can't stand being here with the memories and the grief, the failed pregnancies and the failed marriage. I have to get away. There's nothing for me here. I know that if I stay I'll sink into a terrible depression that I'll never get out of. I'm terrified of it. I'm afraid to let myself think too much. I need to be distracted. New country, new job, new home, new me.' Her voice cracked.

Joe leaned over and held her hand. 'You know I'll always be here for you, and if the depression does catch up with you, call me. You've been to Hell and back, and I'm worried about you.'

Anna took an unsteady sip of her coffee. 'I don't know what else to do. How did I end up here, Joe? I should be at home surrounded by babies, not starting a new life at forty.'

'You were unlucky. Incredibly unlucky. But, look, at forty you're young. You still have a full life to live. You're a fantastic person and I know you'll meet some great guy and hopefully you'll find happiness again.'

'I don't think you can meet someone if you're dead inside.'

Joe put his arm around her. 'It'll get better over time.'

'Will it? Are you sure? Because right now I feel like a corpse. My heart is shattered, my soul is black. I wake up every day and the pain of Hope's death leaves me gasping for breath. And as the day goes on I feel angry, resentful and bitter.'

'Of course you feel all those things – you're still grieving. The loss of a child is the worst thing that can happen to anyone.'

'I don't want to end up a bitter old woman. I'm fighting it. I'm trying really hard not to fall into the why-me-why-not-them pity party. But it's hard, Joe. When I think of some of the parents of the kids I taught, out of their minds on drink and drugs, completely incapable of looking after their children, I do get angry. Why should they get to be parents and not me? I'm a good person. I could give a child a great home. I've been teaching for many years. I've seen how damaged those little children are by living with neglectful alcoholics and drug addicts.'

Joe stirred his coffee. 'I agree with you. Some people just should not be allowed to raise children, but that doesn't change your situation. You have to focus on yourself, not others. You need to heal your soul and your heart and you won't do that if you let anger eat away at you.'

Anna sank back into her chair. 'I know, but it's hard.'

'Hey, I'm here for you any time you want to rant or rage or cry. I've seen what you went through. I know how much pain you're in. Besides, as well as being your friend I'm your doctor, so if you feel yourself going under, call me.'

Anna hugged him. 'Thanks, Joe. Now that Barry's gone you're the only "family" I've got.'

'You're the sister I never wanted.' Joe laughed. 'I'll miss you.'

Anna stood up. 'I'll miss you too. Now, go home to your wife and son. Cherish him, Joe. Kids really are miracles. Mark's a lucky little boy to have you as a dad.'

Joe kissed her cheek. 'Mind yourself – and remember, call me anytime.'

Anna watched her old friend walk away. Back to his wife and son. Back to his warm home and welcoming family. She suddenly felt desperately lonely. Hope's face flashed in front of her and she had to grab the wall to stop herself buckling under the weight of the pain. She forced herself to breathe, in and out, in and out. After a while she was able to walk on.

For the millionth time she questioned her actions. Was she mad moving away and taking a job at a well-to-do private girls' school in Putney? But what choice did she have – stay here and watch Barry move on with his life while hers stood still?

She was broken. And the only thing she could do to save herself was to run away. She caught sight of her reflection in a shop window. She wasn't Anna any more. She was a thin, cropped-haired, exhausted woman in nondescript clothes. She looked invisible, which was exactly how she felt.

10.

Laura

The next day . . .

Laura slammed down the phone. All flights to London were booked up.

'It's high season,' the woman had said. 'You have to plan in advance. Everyone goes on holidays in August.'

'But you don't understand. I have to get to London. It's an emergency,' Laura cried.

'Is someone sick?'

'No, but there's this guy –'

'Isn't there always?' The woman sighed.

'This one is special. I've fancied him for years and he's just broken up with his girlfriend, who is one of my friends, except she's a bitch. I have to get over there. I know we'll get together now. I feel it in my bones.'

'I'm sorry, love, there's nothing I can do for you here. Why don't you try the boat? It'll probably be booked up but you might get on as a foot passenger.'

Laura exhaled. 'That's a great idea. I'll do it now. Thanks.'

'Good luck.'

Laura got a ticket for the boat. She cried when the man said yes. But now she had exactly one hour to pack and get to the dock before it sailed. She grabbed a pile of clothes for Jody and stuffed them into her knapsack with some nappies, Jody's blanky and a soother. Then she ran into her bedroom and pulled everything she had out of her wardrobe. She needed the perfect outfit for the concert. Chloë had said it was roasting in London. She decided on a tight blue sundress that showed off her eyes. She knew tomorrow would be a blue day so she wanted to be dressed to match.

Laura looked at her watch. Damn! She had to hurry. She called her mother. Joan picked up after three rings.

'How did Jody sleep last night?' her mother asked.

'Not well. She woke up five times looking for her soother. I'm absolutely exhausted.'

'I always put four soothers in so she's never stuck for one.'

'Oh, OK, I'll do that tonight.'

'Did you give her porridge for her breakfast?'

Laura had given Jody just a bottle of milk: she'd been too busy trying to organize transport to London. 'Yes,' she lied. 'How's Angela?'

'She's in a lot of pain, the poor thing. It was a bad break. She really needs my help – she can't do anything. I'll have to stay until Tony gets back from his business trip.'

'That's fine. Stay as long as you need to.'

'I should be back on Tuesday but it might be Wednesday, if Tony's on a late flight.'

Laura punched the air with her fist. Perfect. Joan would never know about London. Laura would be back on Monday with Jody. She'd got a lunchtime flight back to Dublin that day – flights back were no problem to book. She'd ring her mother from London in the morning to reassure her that everything was OK and let Jody say hi to her so Joan wouldn't suspect anything. This was all working out perfectly. Laura hadn't felt so happy in ages.

'It's fine, Mum. Take your time.'

'Are you sure you'll be able to manage with Jody? I'm worried about her.'

'You said I need to look after her more so that's what I'm doing and she's great.'

'Good. Well, there are some homemade soups in the freezer. Defrost them and give them to her. It's very warm, so don't put a vest on her at night. Put the Minnie Mouse pyjamas on her and the light pink blanket. And only half an hour's television a day. It's bad for her.'

Laura decided to jump in. If her mother kept going on, she'd miss the boat. 'OK, Mum. Don't worry, it's all under control.'

'You have to watch her like a hawk. You can't take your eyes off her – she's at the age where she wants to put everything into her mouth. She could choke or fall down the stairs or fall off the roundabout in the park and get concussion or –'

Laura bit her tongue. 'I know, Mum. I'll keep a close eye on her, I promise.'

'Please do. Because if anything happens to that child while you're in charge, I will never forgive you. Now put me on to Jody.'

Laura groaned silently. It was all taking too long. She grabbed Jody away from the TV and put the phone to her ear.

'Hello, my little pet,' Joan said.

'Gany, Gany.' Jody's face lit up.

'Yes, you clever thing, it's Granny. How are you?'

Jody stared into the phone.

'Are you being a good girl?'

Jody nodded silently.

'She's nodding, Mum,' Laura told Joan.

'I miss you, pet,' Joan said.

Jody nodded again.

'She's still nodding. She misses you too.' Laura was desperate to get away.

'What are you going to do today?' Joan asked her grandchild.

Laura rolled her eyes. For God's sake, the kid couldn't speak! She lifted the phone from Jody. 'We're going to the park. Actually, we'd better head off now, before it gets too hot.'

'Good idea. Don't forget her sun cream and her hat,' Joan said.

'It's all done,' Laura lied. 'OK, 'bye, Mum.'

'Bye-bye, Jody,' Joan shouted.

'Bye-bye, Gany,' Jody shouted back.

Laura hung up and Jody began to cry. 'Gany . . . Gany . . .'

'She's gone now but she'll be back soon,' Laura told her.

Jody threw herself on to the floor and howled, 'Gany . . . uh . . . uh . . . Gany!'

'Jesus, Jody, I don't have time for this. You'll see Granny in a few days. Stop whining. I got no bloody sleep because of you last night. Now, come on.'

Jody cried even louder. Laura grabbed her by the waist and pinned her into the buggy while she clicked her straps on. Jody screamed and wriggled, but Laura was stronger and more determined. She strapped her in, then snarled, 'You're not going to ruin this weekend for me. I swear, Jody, you'd better be good or I'll leave you on the bloody boat.'

Jody screamed all the way up the road to the train. Laura shoved her soother into her mouth to plug the noise and gave her the blanky.

On the train Jody, worn out by the crying and soothed by the motion, fell asleep. Laura leaned her head against the window and closed her eyes. She was knackered. It was going to be a long trip. Three hours on the boat to Holyhead in Wales, then a four-hour train journey to London. But she knew it'd be worth it. She hoped Jody wouldn't be a pain the whole time. She didn't want her screeching or whining on the boat and train. She wanted to chill out, not deal with a screaming child.

She wanted to have the best weekend ever. She had butterflies in her tummy. This was it. This was her moment with Danny. She knew they'd get together this weekend. She just had to get Jody out of the way so she could concentrate on Danny. Chloë had better have found a babysitter.

Laura pushed the buggy up the ramp on to the boat. It was packed with families heading off on their summer holidays. Kids were running wild everywhere, shouting their heads off. Laura wanted to get away from them. She didn't want Jody to wake up.

She was enjoying the time out. She looked around and saw a bar to her left. She peered through the glass doors. That's exactly where I want to be, she thought. I need a vodka to calm my nerves and kick off the weekend. She went in, parked the buggy with the still sleeping Jody in the corner, and sat up on a bar stool.

'What can I get you?' the barman asked.

Laura looked at her watch. It was five past eleven and they had just set sail. A bit early, but what the hell? She wanted a drink to celebrate her freedom. 'Vodka and Coke,' she said.

'You're starting early.' The barman grinned.

'I need it to wake me up. I've been up all night with her.' Laura waved over to the sleeping Jody.

'I'll make it a large one so.' He handed her the drink. 'Get that into you.'

She knocked it back. Because she hadn't had time to eat any breakfast, the vodka had an immediate effect. It felt fantastic. The tension in her shoulders and back eased; she felt lighter, less burdened. 'I think I'll have to have another of those large ones.'

'How old is your daughter?' the barman asked.

'Nineteen months.'

'Is there a dad in the picture?'

'Nope.'

'He left you?'

'You could say that.' Laura took a large sip of her second vodka.

'Must have been blind to leave a gorgeous girl like you.'

'Do you really think I'm gorgeous?'

The barman leaned over the bar and whispered, 'You're a knock-out. You'd never think you had a kid. You look too young.'

'Thanks.' Laura lapped up the attention. This was definitely a blue day.

'You're welcome. Credit where credit's due. What do you do?'

'I'm in college.'

'Smart and beautiful, the whole package.' He winked.

Laura giggled and finished her drink. 'God, these are going down so well. I'll have one more.'

'Coming right up.'

As the barman was pouring Laura's third drink, Jody woke up and began to thrash about in her buggy. Laura climbed down from her stool and went over to unstrap her.

'Baba . . . baba . . .' Jody said.

Shit. Laura had forgotten to bring her bloody bottle. 'I don't have your baba. Here, have some Coke.' She handed Jody the bottle of Coke she was using as a mixer. There was about a third left.

Jody sniffed it cautiously, the way children always do when faced with something new. She took a sip, crinkled her nose, then smiled.

'Yummy Coke,' Laura said.

Jody drank the rest. 'Mo baba?' she asked, waving the empty bottle.

'Oh, for God's sake. Hold on.' Laura asked the barman for a bottle of Coke, a straw and a packet of crisps.

Laura sat Jody up at a table in the corner of the bar, handed her the Coke and opened the crisps for her. 'There now, eat up and be quiet,' she said. She turned back to her stool, climbed on and began to drink her vodka.

As she did so, a small woman in a brown dress entered the bar and sat in the opposite corner with a book. The barman went over to ask her if she'd like a drink. She ordered some sparkling water.

What a bore, Laura thought, as she gulped her vodka.

II.

Anna

The ferry . . .

Anna sipped her sparkling water and tried to concentrate on her book, but it was hopeless. The girl at the bar was talking at the top of her voice. She glanced back to the lobby, but it was mayhem out there. Children were running wild, couples were arguing and the place was packed to the brim with bags and picnic lunches and people rushing outside to be sick.

The bar was the only quiet place on the boat. It was too early for most people to drink. A small group of men were sitting in one corner, staring at a replay of some football game and then there was the girl with the loud voice.

'I'm going to London to see Paul Oakenfold play,' she announced.

'He's amazing.' The barman seemed impressed.

'I can't wait.' Although she was clearly already drunk, she ordered another vodka.

As the girl continued to flirt with the barman, a tiny child with blonde curls waddled over and tugged at her dress. Anna hadn't noticed her until she'd stood up.

'What?' the loud girl snapped.

'Baba,' the child said.

'I told you I don't have it. I gave you a bottle of Coke instead and some crisps. Look, you haven't even finished them. Go back and sit down and be quiet.'

The little girl's head drooped. She shuffled back to her corner where she scrambled back up on to the couch and continued eating her crisps. She looked so small and forlorn, about eighteen months old, the same age as Hope would have been if . . . Anna could feel the blood rushing to her head. She forced herself to look away. It's not your problem. Ignore it, she scolded herself, and stuck her nose firmly back into her book.

'I'm pissed,' the girl announced, slamming the empty glass down on the bar counter. 'How many have I had?'

'Five,' the barman told her.

'How long more to go?'

He looked at his watch. 'Well over an hour.'

'So I definitely have time for another,' she slurred.

The barman poured her another drink. 'There you go. Will you be all right while I nip down and change a keg?'

She waved her glass and gave him a lopsided smile. 'I'll manage on this until you get back.'

The child came over again. 'Baba . . . baba.'

'God, Jody, give it a rest. I don't have a bottle.'

The child blinked. 'Baba, peese.'

Her mother swivelled around in her chair and put her face close to the child's. 'Look at me. I . . . do . . . not . . . have . . . a . . . bottle. OK? I'm sorry, I forgot it, probably because I got no sleep last night. Now, go and play with these.' She handed her a pile of coasters. The child went back to the table and began to play with them.

'Jesus, I hope she's not like this all bloody weekend,' muttered the drunk. 'If it wasn't for her, my life would be great.'

Anna could feel her chest tightening. How could this woman be allowed have a child? She was clearly a terrible mother – drunk, neglectful and horrible to her daughter. Anna had seen so many drunks like this over the years in her school and their children were scarred for life.

The little girl was quickly bored with the coasters and waddled back to her mother, who was polishing off her drink. 'Baba, peese.'

'Jesus Christ, child, for the millionth time I don't have it!'

The little girl's lip wobbled and then she began to bawl.

The mother shook her finger at her. 'I'm too tired for this. Don't start whining. If you do, I'll take blanky away.'

The child clutched her blanket.

'Go on over there and be good.'

'Baba,' the little girl whimpered.

Anna tried to read her book. She tried looking away. She tried distracting herself . . . But she couldn't. She had to do something. She just couldn't let it go. She got to her feet and walked over to the drunk mother. 'Hi, sorry to interrupt you. I was just sitting over there and I heard your little girl crying for a bottle. I was just going to pop into the café to get a sandwich, so why don't I see if I can find a bottle or a beaker of some sort for her? She seems thirsty.'

'She's just had a full bottle of Coke,' the mother slurred.

'Baba . . . BABA!' the child screeched.

'Maybe some milk would calm her down,' Anna suggested.

The mother shrugged her tanned shoulders. 'Fine, take her with you. You're welcome to her.' Turning to the child, she said, 'Jody, go and get some milk with this nice lady and be good, no moaning.'

Anna held out her hand and Jody took it. 'Come on, sweetheart, let's go and find you some milk.'

Jody smiled. 'Ye . . . ye . . . baba.'

Anna left her book on the table and picked up her handbag. She took Jody into the café and asked if they had any bottles or beakers. They didn't, but they gave her a little carton of milk with a straw.

The two sat up at a table in the corner of the busy café. 'There you go, pet.' Anna handed the milk to Jody. 'Drink that up. It'll make you feel better.'

'Ank oo.'

'You're very welcome.' Anna smiled at the little girl. She looked like one of those cherubic angels you saw on Christmas cards, all blonde curls, big blue eyes and chubby cheeks.

Jody beamed and drank the milk quickly.

'Slowly, pet, or you'll get a sore tummy,' Anna warned her.

Jody put the carton down, frowned – and was sick everywhere. The lady at the next table jumped up. Anna apologized.

'Don't worry, these things happen,' the lady said. 'I raised five children myself and I've ten grandchildren, I'm well used to it.'

'Thanks,' Anna said, as she wiped Jody's dress.

'She's a beautiful little girl.'

'Yes, she is,' Anna agreed.

'They're a blessing,' the woman said.

'Yes, they are.'

'You must be delighted with her,' the woman added.

'Oh, she's not –' Before Anna could finish, Jody threw up again. 'I'd better take her out and change her.' Anna hurried out of the café and carried Jody back into the bar, where her mother was still drinking.

'I'm afraid she's been sick,' Anna informed her.

The mother could barely focus, she was so drunk. 'Bloody brilliant. Well done, Jody, that's all I need.'

'It's all right. Give me a change of clothes and I'll sort her out.' Anna willed herself not to be rude. She was furious with this pathetic excuse for a mother. How dare she treat her child so badly? She had no right to be so neglectful. It didn't matter that she was young: if you had a child you had a duty to take care of it, not ignore it and treat it like some kind of nuisance in your life.

The mother pointed to a bag in the corner. 'Her stuff's in there.'

Anna picked up the knapsack and took Jody into the Ladies to change her. She took off her red dress and replaced it with a green T-shirt and denim shorts. Then Anna wet her hairbrush, brushed the vomit out of Jody's hair and pushed it back with a hairband she found at the bottom of the bag. 'Now, pet, you're all clean.'

'All keen,' Jody repeated.

Anna looked at the little girl's pale face and bent down to kiss her. Jody put her arms around Anna's neck and snuggled into her shoulder. Anna felt something shift inside her. The feel of the child's hug reminded her of holding Hope. It was as if her heart had begun to beat again, slowly but steadily.

She carried Jody out and sat down on a chair outside the bar that had been vacated by someone running to be sick over the rail. Jody could see her mother through the glass doors of the bar. Anna saw her flirting animatedly with the barman. She was swaying on her stool.

Jody cuddled into Anna and laid her head on Anna's chest. Anna took Jody's sandals off and began to play 'This Little Piggy Went to Market' with Jody's toes. Jody squealed with delight. They played 'Round and Round the Garden' and Jody giggled uncontrollably when Anna tickled her neck. Anna sang songs to her – Jody knew 'Twinkle, Twinkle' and sang along as best she could.

Anna was singing 'Baa Baa Black Sheep' when it happened. Through the door of the bar, she saw Jody's mother slump down on the counter and pass out. The barman looked at the girl in alarm. She watched as he shook her arm gently and then a bit more urgently. It was useless: the girl was out cold.

A voice announced that they were docking in twenty minutes and asked all drivers to go to their cars. Anna looked at Jody. The little girl's blue eyes stared back into hers. Anna's heart began to pound. I can't do it, she thought. I can't let another child's life be ruined by a useless drunk for a mother. She'll end up on the streets or in prison or drinking like her mother. I've seen hundreds of children's lives destroyed and shattered. I've seen it happen so many times. I was only ever able to help those children for a year while they were in my class, but this time . . . this time I can do something. I can help this child. I can save this child. I can give her a wonderful life. I can be a good mother. I know I can love this child and cherish her. That drunk in there will destroy her. I can do it, I can do it . . . I *have* to do it.

Anna stopped thinking and went with her primal instinct. She picked Jody up, and as she was walking towards her car, she dropped Jody's red sandals discreetly over the side of the boat. Jody nuzzled into her neck and sighed contentedly.

Anna walked to her car and didn't look back.

PART 2
Now

12

Sophie

London, June 2011

Holly jumped up, pointed to the TV, and stuttered, 'But – but, Sophie, the artist! She's the image of you! She *is* you!'

Sophie was frozen to the spot. She stared at the television, at the woman who looked so like her. What the hell? Who was she? While her brain did somersaults, the interview ended and the artist was gone.

Holly was pacing up and down beside her. 'OK, what does this mean? Let's not freak out. We need to analyse it calmly.'

Sophie looked at her best friend and opened her mouth but no sound came out. Her mind was in overdrive. It was too weird, completely freaky. All she could see was red, bright, piercing red – her colour for panic. Her head throbbed.

Holly sat down and grabbed her hand. 'Oh, my God, Sophie, she looked so like you and she sees colours like you do.' She chewed her lip. 'She must be, like, an aunt or something. Maybe your mum fell out with her and they haven't spoken for years and that's why she looks like you and has your weird colour thing.'

She could be right, Sophie thought.

'Hang on, what about the baby thing? Her disappearance,' Holly mused.

Sophie found her voice: 'Maybe that's why my mum never talked about this aunt because she thought she was a bit mad, thinking her kid was still alive when she'd drowned.'

'That must be it. You always said your mum's incredibly secretive about her past and Ireland and all that.'

'And about who my dad is.'

Holly jumped up again. 'I've got it! She must be your dad's sister, which would explain why you look nothing like your mum and obviously are the image of your dad. And maybe your mum had a fight with her when your dad buggered off and that's why she took you to come and live in London and cut all ties with this Laura person.'

'Damn, no, it can't be that. Mum said my dad was American.' Sophie could feel panic rising in her throat. Something about this artist felt . . . real . . . She felt connected to her. She shook her head vigorously to stop the doubts creeping into her mind.

'Well, maybe Laura is actually American but lives in Ireland.'

'She has an Irish accent,' Sophie pointed out. 'She didn't sound American at all.'

'Maybe she's lived in Ireland for so long that her accent has changed.'

It was all too confusing. 'But Mum said she didn't know my dad's second name. That they'd had a brief fling and then he went back to America. If she knew his sister, she'd be able to find him.'

Holly pushed her hair out of her face. 'Perhaps she lied because she didn't want to find him.'

'She couldn't do that to me. I don't believe she'd lie to me about not knowing who my dad is if she did know.'

'OK, let's just stick to the facts. This woman is the spitting image of you.'

'And she has synaesthesia,' Sophie added.

'Which is rare, right?'

She nodded.

'So you have to be related somehow. It's too much of a coincidence. Could she be your mum's cousin or something?'

Sophie shook her head. 'Mum always said she had no family left. She was an only child and both of her parents were, too.'

'That's a lot of only children. I thought people in Ireland had loads of kids.'

'It does seem strange.' Sophie began to feel really queasy. In the back of her mind a terrible thought was forming. 'What about Laura's missing baby?'

'I think Laura just didn't want to believe the baby drowned,' Holly said. 'Maybe she felt guilty for not watching her more carefully. Most women would go a bit bonkers if their child died. You'd wish for it not to be true.'

Sophie tugged at her T-shirt. 'But that's just it. Laura didn't seem mad to me. She seemed perfectly sane. What if the baby didn't drown? After all, they never found a body.'

'Well, that's just really sad. You don't think –' Holly's face reddened. 'You're not suggesting . . .'

The words tumbled out of Sophie's mouth: 'My mum has no baby photos of me. She told me everything got burned in a fire.'

'Fires happen all the time, Sophie.' Holly's voice sounded shrill.

'Isn't it all a bit coincidental?' Sophie stared at her friend. Holly was looking away, avoiding her gaze.

'Well, then, what? It couldn't be . . . No way. Not your mum.' Holly had her back to Sophie but suddenly she spun around, beaming. 'I've got it. Maybe you were Laura's little girl and then you fell overboard and washed up on a beach somewhere and your mum found you and there was no one around so she took you home and looked after you.'

'Babies can't swim miles to shore,' Sophie snapped. She wanted to throw up.

'OK. Maybe a dolphin or a whale carried you on its back like that movie *Whale Back Mounting* or *Humpback Rider* or whatever it's called.'

'It's *Whale Rider*, and I doubt that happened. Come on, Holly!'

'There's no need to bite my head off. I'm trying to help. Incredible things happen all the time. Look at that guy who was stuck on a mountain and sawed his arm off with a blunt penknife or a razor or his teeth or something and survived.'

Sophie threw up her hands in exasperation. 'He was thirty-three years old!'

'I'm just saying it shows that humans have survival instincts. People are always getting mauled by tigers or attacked by killer sharks but they survive.'

'We're talking about a baby girl, not a bloody fish. She couldn't have swum miles in the sea to safety. She'd have died after a minute in the freezing water.'

Holly leaned forward and poked Sophie in the chest. 'Well, maybe the boat was almost at the dock. Maybe it happened in the South of France in the summer and the water was shallow and warm. Maybe Laura took her daughter to mother-and-baby swim classes in preparation for the holiday in France so she did know how to swim!'

'And my mother just happened to be strolling along the crowded beach in St Tropez in the height of summer at the exact moment when a mermaid child came out of the water and no one else noticed?'

'I didn't say St Tropez.' Holly crossed her arms defensively. 'I was thinking more Antibes or Saint-Raphaël.'

Sophie shook her by the shoulders. 'What difference does it make where it was? It's a ridiculous theory!'

Holly stepped back. 'It's a lot less ridiculous than implying that your mother's a kidnapper.'

Sophie sighed. 'I'm sorry. I'm freaking out here.'

'We both need to keep calm. Let's go back to the beginning. What exactly has your mum told you about being born and stuff?'

Sophie closed her eyes. Everything was bright red. 'All she ever says is that my dad was an American architect. She had a very brief relationship with him and he went back to New York. Then she realized she was pregnant and she didn't even know his second name so there was no way to trace him. She never heard from him again.'

'I can't imagine your mum having sex with a guy she barely knew,' Holly said.

'It does seem strange. But she said she was over the moon

when she found out she was pregnant because she was almost forty and she really wanted to have kids.'

'And then she came here, to London, when you were about two, which was when I met you.'

'Mum said that when her mother died, she had no other family or ties to Dublin so she decided to get away and start a new life in London.'

'And you've never met anyone from her past?'

Sophie shook her head. 'No one except Joe. He's her only friend from back then.'

Holly frowned. 'When you think about it, it is a bit strange. My mum has loads of friends and cousins and aunts and uncles. How can yours have no one?'

Sophie shrugged. 'She was an only child and her parents are dead so there is no family.'

'But what about school friends or college friends or work colleagues? I mean, she lived in Dublin for, like, forty years so how can she only have one friend?'

'She just does. She's not that sociable. Even here she has just a handful of people she's friends with.'

'I suppose you're right. It just doesn't seem . . .'

'. . . to add up.' Sophie finished Holly's sentence.

It really didn't add up. Anna never talked about Ireland. When Sophie asked about where she was born – which hospital, who was there, what did her granny say when she saw her, where was she christened, when did she take her first step – Anna was always vague and keen to change the subject. Something had never seemed quite right. And how could no baby pictures of Sophie have survived? She had asked Joe once when he'd come over to visit if he had any photos of her as a baby. He had stared at Anna, who had cut across him and said that of course Joe had no pictures of Sophie because he had been too busy taking pictures of his own baby, Mark.

And Sophie looked nothing like her mother. And Anna didn't have synaesthesia. It had taken her ages to figure out what was going on when Sophie kept describing how she saw emotions, numbers and words as colours. The doctor told them that it was usually passed down in families, most commonly from mother to child, but Anna had never even heard of it. She'd thought Sophie was making it up at first, but after a few months she had begun to worry that there was something wrong with her daughter. She said it was a huge relief to know that it was just the way Sophie saw the world.

She had never taken Sophie back to Ireland, even though Sophie had begged her to. Joe invited them all the time, but Anna refused to go. She said she had bad memories of her parents dying and she didn't want to go back there and relive sad times. When Sophie was about fourteen she kept asking her mother and pushing her to take her. Anna eventually lost her temper, which she rarely did. She had shouted, 'There is nothing for us there. I don't ever want to set foot in that place again. It will never happen.' She seemed so upset and furious that Sophie never asked again.

Holly interrupted her thoughts: 'Duh, we're so stupid. What we need to do is Google this Laura woman and find out more. We need more information.'

She grabbed her laptop and they Googled 'Laura, artist, Ireland', and Sophie added 'synaesthesia' to narrow it down. Her name came up – Laura Fletcher, artist. They went into her website.

Holly gasped when she saw her picture again. 'God, Sophie, it's like looking at you but older. Freaky.'

Sophie clicked on to Laura's bio page and scrolled down. There was a paragraph about her baby. It said that her daughter had been lost at sea on 14 August 1994.

'You moved here in August 1994,' Holly reminded her. 'I have pictures of you at my second birthday party on the twenty-ninth and you'd only been living next door for, like, a week or two. My mum was thrilled when you arrived because she had a playmate for me right next door.'

Sophie began to feel sick again.

'There's a pictures folder.' Holly pointed to the link.

Sophie clicked on it. There were pictures of Laura at various art galleries and exhibitions, and then there was one that said 'Jody 1994'. She opened it . . .

'Are you OK?' Holly asked, as Sophie threw up into the toilet for the sixth time. She was holding her friend's hair up and rubbing her back. 'Look, maybe it's just an incredible coincidence.'

Sophie wiped her mouth with a towel. 'Holly, the picture of me is identical to the pictures Mum has of me as a toddler, and the final proof is the blanket I'm holding in Laura's picture. It's the same one I had as a kid.' She had to stop talking and vomit again.

'Oh, my God, Sophie, what are we going to do? This is huge. This is the kind of thing you see on *Oprah*. What does it mean? Are we actually saying your mum . . . nicked you? Abducted you?'

Sophie groaned and threw up again. Everything was red now, bright red.

Holly handed her a tissue. 'She couldn't have – she's so serious and upstanding and honourable. She's a headmistress, for goodness' sake. My mum says your mum is the most trustworthy person she's ever met. She always says, "You can tell Anna Roberts anything and it will go no further. She's the soul of discretion." Someone like that wouldn't nick a baby.'

Sophie stood up and rinsed her mouth. She had to steady herself on the washbasin because her legs felt like jelly. 'Well, it looks as if she did something bad. Really bad. Illegal, unthinkable, incomprehensible and just wrong.'

'Hold on – don't jump to conclusions until we have all the pieces of the jigsaw.'

'You saw the baby photo.'

Holly chewed a fingernail. 'It's pretty damning evidence but we mustn't judge yet. We still need more info.'

Sophie sat on the side of the bath and sobbed. 'Who am I, Holly? If I'm not Sophie Roberts, who am I?'

Holly rushed to her. 'You *are* Sophie Roberts, my absolute best friend in the world. Wonderful, clever, creative, kind, beautiful . . . and soon to be extremely skinny if you keep throwing up like that. I wish I could throw up! I'm the one who needs to lose weight.'

'I can't handle this – it's too much. It's not right . . . It's crazy! It's madness!' Sophie cried. 'All I can see is red – everything is red.'

Holly took her friend's hand and led her back to the living room, where she sat her down on the couch. 'Breathe in and out . . . Come on, Sophie, there you go.' She patted Sophie's back as she began to calm down. 'We'll get to the bottom of it. We just need to be calm and think of a plan. Sophie, you're the mature, clever one in this friendship – as my mother constantly reminds me – so I need you to think clearly.'

Sophie could feel her heart racing. Her head ached. She willed herself to breathe slowly and try to make sense of what was happening around her. Her mother an abductor? She couldn't be. Holly was right: Anna was the most conservative, strait-laced, law-abiding person in the world.

Holly poured her friend a glass of wine. 'Drink this – you need it for the shock.'

Sophie knocked it back and felt it burn her throat.

'You don't look like a Jody,' Holly said, examining the website again. 'I think you're much more of a Sophie. Although I could imagine you being a Katie too.'

Jody Fletcher. That was Sophie's name. Her other name. Her baby name. Her mother was not her mother. Her identity was not her identity. Who was she? What was she?

'Sophie.' Holly turned Sophie to face her. 'My mum'll be back soon so we have to decide what to do.'

Sophie stared at her blankly.

'OK, I can see you're going to be no help at all. You may be smarter than me and more mature, but you don't handle shock well. OK, Sophie/Jody, you are going to have to try to behave normally. If your mother sees you in this state, she'll know something's up. Come on, snap out of it.' She clicked her fingers in front of Sophie's eyes. 'I'm going to walk you home and you're to go straight to bed and turn off the light. In the morning I want you to stay in bed. Tell your mum you feel a bit off, and when she goes to work, I'll come over. We'll have a snoop around your house and see if we can find any clues.'

Holly pulled Sophie to her feet. 'Now, one foot in front of the other.' She marched her out of the door, down the path and to her house next door. 'Sophie, I need you to get some sleep. Our heads have to be clear tomorrow when we're looking for evidence. I may not be Carol Vorderman at numbers but I'm turning out to be quite the Miss Marple. Maybe I should go to detective school instead of doing the horticulture, landscape and sports turf management course, which was the only thing I could get into.'

'You'll be great at it,' Sophie muttered, longing for bed. She needed sleep.

'Don't fob me off. We both know it's a ridiculous thing to study. What the hell is sports turf anyway? I hate sports and I didn't even know what turf was when I applied. I read it as "sports surf" and thought there'd be lots of gorgeous guys in wetsuits but it turns out it means mud! I'm going to study sports mud with a bunch of wellington-wearing muckers. Argh!'

Despite everything that had just happened, Sophie began to laugh. It felt wonderful. She laughed until her cheeks hurt, her sides ached – and she realized that she was crying. Everything turned light green, her colour for pain.

Holly hugged her. 'It's OK, I'm here for you. You haven't lost me to the country bumpkins yet!'

'Thanks. I need you, Holly – you're the only person I can trust.'

'Luckily for you, it looks like I'm going to be an excellent sleuth.'

13.

Laura

Killduf, June 2011

Laura put on her makeup slowly and deliberately. She wanted to look as if she had made an effort but she knew that if she put on too much it would be commented on. She felt sad and tired. It was a beige day. She wished things were different, better. She knew this celebration would be fake and hollow. She longed to be in her studio, alone, listening to music and painting. It was the only time her mind switched off. The only time she got away from it. The only time she felt any sense of peace.

Laura smoothed down her black dress. She had opted for a conservative look. She knew her more Bohemian 'arty' clothes would be criticized and she wanted to avoid any kind of confrontation.

Frank had organized dinner in a fancy restaurant in Dublin. There would be just the four of them. Laura willed herself to be calm and cheerful. She didn't want to argue; she didn't want to get upset. She really wanted it to go well. She desperately wanted to bridge the divide between herself and Joan, but there was an ocean of blame, anger, guilt and heartache between them.

She looked at her watch. Damn! It was a quarter past seven already.

'Mandy, are you ready? We need to go,' she called up the stairs. Silence.

'Come on, you know how much Joan hates anyone being late. The traffic could be bad. I really don't want to give her an excuse to be cross.'

She heard a door slam. 'Chill out, I'm coming.' Mandy stomped down the stairs. 'Jesus, Mum, you're such a Hitler.'

Her sixteen-year-old daughter was wearing skin-tight ripped black jeans and a black T-shirt with *Queen Biatch!* on it.

Laura chose her words carefully. She knew that if she openly criticized Mandy's clothes a massive row would ensue. Mandy was very touchy, these days, and Laura was finding her teenage moods difficult to navigate. Everything Laura said was wrong, 'lame' or ignored. 'It's a nice restaurant, Mandy. Can you at least put a cardigan or a jacket over the T-shirt?'

'This T-shirt rocks.'

'I don't want to argue with you, but please just put on a jacket.'

'Fine, whatever, but I'm not doing it for you. I'm doing it for Gran.'

Laura drove to the restaurant. Mandy sat beside her, texting. In the time it took to get there, barely a word passed between them. She wondered if all mothers struggled with their teenagers. Mandy had been a very sweet baby, but by the time she was three her stubborn streak had made itself known and had gone from bad to worse. She was constantly pulling away, trying to assert her independence, while Laura was desperate to rein her in. She knew she was an over-protective mother – but how could she not be with her history, her fatal mistakes?

When they arrived, Joan was sitting alone at a table discreetly tucked away at the back of the restaurant. They could hardly see her behind an enormous bouquet of Happy 60th Birthday balloons. Her face was like thunder.

'Late! You're all late! Some birthday this is. I'm sitting here like a fool on my own with these ridiculous balloons announcing to the world what age I am.'

'Chill, Gran, it's eight oh three. We're only a hundred and eighty seconds late.' Mandy sat beside her grandmother.

'Sorry, Mum. I organized the balloons, I thought they'd be cheery for the table.' Laura leaned down to kiss her mother's cheek.

Joan turned to her granddaughter. 'What type of an outfit do you call that?'

'It's called a young person's outfit. It's 2011, Gran, not the nineteen hundreds. Sorry to tell you, but we don't wear white gloves and hats with nets any more.'

'You cheeky lump.' Joan smiled at her. 'How do I look?'

'Like a sixty-year-old.' Mandy grinned.

'You look lovely, Mum,' Laura said. Her mother was wearing a very stylish blue shift dress. 'That's gorgeous. Is it new?'

'I treated myself to it.'

'It really suits you.'

Joan attempted a smile. 'Thank you.'

'Would you like to order a drink? Why don't you have a glass of champagne to celebrate?' Laura suggested.

'Can I have one too?' Mandy asked.

'No!' Joan and Laura said in unison.

'For God's sake, it's like being in prison around you two,' Mandy grumbled.

Laura ordered one glass of champagne and two Sprites.

When the drinks arrived, she raised her glass and toasted her mother: 'Cheers to you, Mum. I hope the next sixty years bring you happiness and health.'

'Well, they couldn't be worse than the last sixty, could they?' Joan sipped her champagne.

Laura willed herself to be calm.

Mandy's stomach throbbed.

Joan shook her head. 'I can't believe I didn't die of a broken heart after Jody. Thank God for you, Mandy. You saved me. You're the only reason I'm still alive.'

Mandy blushed. 'Am I really?'

Joan squeezed her granddaughter's hand. 'Yes, pet, you are.'

Mandy hugged Joan, and Laura felt a pang of jealousy. She wanted to scream, 'I suffered too, I need a hug too, I'm a person too,' but she wasn't allowed to. Joan had taken ownership of the grief. Laura wasn't allowed to grieve in front of her because it was *her* fault, *her* neglect, *her* drunken, irresponsible behaviour that had led to Jody's death. If you cause something, you can't complain about it afterwards.

The only kind thing Joan had done was not tell Mandy that Laura had been drunk when Jody disappeared. She had at least spared Laura the humiliation of Mandy knowing what a wretched human being she was.

Laura was glad that Mandy got on with Joan but she was envious of how relaxed they were together. There was no awkwardness between them. Mandy never hugged, kissed or even let Laura touch her. If Laura tried to put an arm around her, Mandy shrugged her off. She longed to be closer to her, but all they seemed to do these days was fight. As for Joan, their relationship had been destroyed after Jody's disappearance. Joan could barely be in the same room as Laura: she hated her daughter for what she had done.

Unable to cope with the grief and guilt, Laura had crawled into a bottle of vodka and blacked out the months that followed. She remembered almost nothing. If she hadn't got pregnant with Mandy she would have killed herself. Mandy had saved them both.

'Sorry I'm late.' Frank arrived to the table with a tiny, doll-like woman wearing a hat, pulled very low over her eyes, and large sunglasses. 'Happy birthday, Mum. I brought a guest with me.'

Frank's friend took her hat off and shook out a mass of blonde hair. She took off her glasses to reveal a deeply tanned face. She had four-inch nails, and underneath her coat she was wearing a very short, tight white dress.

'Oh, my God!' Mandy's mouth hung open. 'Are you Lexie Granger?'

The doll smiled, almost blinding them with gleaming veneers.

'Who?' Joan demanded.

'Lexie is the soon-to-be-ex-wife of Dougie Granger. He's probably the most famous footballer in England right now,' Frank informed his mother.

'In the world,' Mandy added.

'Never heard of him,' Joan said.

'My mother Joan, the charmer.' Frank laughed.

Lexie offered Joan a hand. 'Many happy returns, Joan.'

'And this is my sister Laura, the artist, and her daughter Mandy.'

'I'd like to see your paintings. Frank says you're brilliant. When the divorce is finalized, and Dougie gets his bloody finger out and pays up, I'll buy one,' she promised.

'Thanks.' Laura smiled at her. It was a relief to have outside company. Suddenly the night ahead didn't seem so daunting.

Lexie pulled out a chair and sat down beside Mandy.

'But what on earth are you doing in Dublin?' the starstruck teenager asked.

'It's like this, darlin'. After Dougie and I broke up, your uncle Frank here called me up, told me he was a literary agent and wanted to talk to me about writing a book. Reckons he can get me half a mill for it. He offered to fly me over here to write it. To be honest, I was glad to get away from the paparazzi for a while so I hopped on a plane. Frank got me the hat and coat and, so far, no one's spotted me. It's nice to be away from the madness for a bit. Some of the photographers are total scumbags.'

'Wow, that's amazing,' Mandy drooled.

'What kind of a book? Memoirs?' Laura asked.

Lexie nodded. 'It's going to be a kiss-and-tell, innit, Frank?'

Frank grinned. 'I like to think of it more as an in-depth and revealing memoir of your life. With heavy emphasis on your years with Dougie.'

'Memoir!' Joan snorted. 'She's a child.'

'Nah, that's the Botox, Joan. I'm twenty-six, love. That's considered very old in WAG circles.'

'WAG?'

Frank filled his mother in: 'It's a term used for footballers' wives.'

'How do you stay so thin?' Mandy was staring at Lexie's minute waist.

'I don't eat, and if I do, I stick my fingers down my throat. In my world, you have to be fit or you're out.'

'I wish I was thinner,' Mandy said.

Laura jumped in: 'You're perfect.'

Lexie laid a manicured hand on Mandy's arm. 'Darlin', if I came from a nice family like this, I wouldn't have to starve myself.'

'Where do you come from?' Laura asked.

'East London. I grew up in a council estate where people got stabbed or mugged every day.'

'Good Lord, how did you get away?' Joan sounded concerned.

'The only way I could, Joan. I got my tits out.'

'What?' Joan was horrified.

'Keep your hair on. These boobs were my passport out of that hell-hole. I got a boob job at sixteen, was on the *Sun*'s page three at seventeen and met Dougie a couple of years later. By twenty, I was married, living in a mansion, driving a Porsche and wearing designer clothes. All my dreams came true.'

'It's like a fairytale,' Mandy marvelled.

'It was, until I found out Dougie was sleeping with everything that moved behind my back.'

'You certainly have the material for a good story,' Laura whispered to Frank.

'This book will be dynamite.' He chuckled.

'You didn't have to flash your breasts to get on in life. You could have studied and gone to college and had a respectable job and married a nice man,' Joan suggested.

'You must be joking! I left school at sixteen and I'm dyslexic – I can barely read, love.'

'How on earth do you propose to write your memoirs?'

Lexie threw her head back and whooped. 'Write? Oh, no! I talk into a little recorder and some clever person turns it into a book. What do they call it, Frank?'

'Ghost writing.'

'Yeah, that's it. I've got a ghost.' Lexie grinned.

'What did you do when you found out about Dougie cheating on you?' Mandy wanted to know.

'I cut up all his favourite suits – all the fancy Savile Row ones. Then I smashed all the windows on his Ferrari, pawned his watches and diamond earrings and changed the locks on the front door.'

'Good for you,' Joan said.

'What did he say?' Laura asked.

'He didn't say nothing. He went out and shagged my sister.'

'*What?*' they exclaimed in unison.

Lexie shrugged her tiny shoulders. 'She's my half-sister and a right slapper. We're not close, but it still bothered me, as he bloody well knew it would.'

'You couldn't make this stuff up.' Frank winked at his sister.

'What did you do to her? Did you not kill her?' Mandy was aghast.

'I put her mobile number in the local paper under "escorts". Apparently her phone hasn't stopped ringing.' Lexie giggled.

'Cool.' Mandy was awed.

'It doesn't really matter, though. She didn't change anything. Me and Dougie was over anyway. It's a pity. In the beginning the marriage was great. But he couldn't keep it in his trousers and you can only ignore so much.'

'He must be a blind fool. You're stunning,' Mandy gushed.

'Thanks, babes. Now, that's enough about me. Let's talk about you lot. What's the story with Frank here? Why's he not hitched?'

'Frank is the eternal bachelor.' Laura laughed.

'He'll never get married – he doesn't like being told what to do,' Mandy added.

'I'd love to see him settle down and have a family.' Joan sighed. 'He's had lots of lovely girlfriends and some not so lovely ones, but the minute they start looking for commitment he's gone.'

'I like my life the way it is,' Frank said.

'Fair enough. At least you know what you want and you're honest about it. That's what I said to Dougie – "Why get married if you wanted to mess around?" He said his manager'd told him to get married, that it was good for his image. Charming! What about you, Laura? Are you married?'

Laura shook her head. 'I never met the right person.'

Lexie pointed a pink nail towards Mandy. 'What about her dad? No good?'

'She didn't have time to get to know him.' Joan sniffed.

'I'm the result of a one-night stand.' Mandy pouted.

'Most people are, darlin'.' Lexie patted her hand.

Laura blushed. 'Mandy's dad, David, is a great guy, but we met when we were very young and it just didn't work. He's married to Tanya now and has two other daughters.'

'Do you like your sisters?' Lexie asked Mandy.

'They're only seven and six but they're cute. The problem is Tanya, my stepmother. She hates me. She's always in a bad mood when I go to see Dad. She can't stand her perfect unit being ruined by me.'

'She sounds like a Queen Biatch!' Lexie pointed to Mandy's T-shirt and they both giggled. 'What about you, Joan? Any love in your life?'

Joan bristled. 'I was widowed twenty years ago and no one could ever replace my Harry. He was a wonderful husband. We had twenty-three very happy years together.' Her hand shook as she took a sip of her drink.

'He was a fantastic dad too,' Laura added.

'They don't make 'em like they used to,' Lexie said. 'My grand-dad was great, straight up, no funny business. He was a milkman and proud of it. My dad, on the other hand, is in the nick, doing a ten-year stretch for armed robbery. It's a wonder I'm normal at all.'

'Don't forget to put that in the book,' Frank said.

Lexie glugged some wine. 'Don't you worry, Frank, it's all going in there. It's like my therapy, this book is.'

'That's how I feel when I paint. I get a lot of emotions out,' Laura told her.

'Do you paint, Mandy?' Lexie asked.

'No, I'm not creative at all. I'm crap at art.'

'But she's brilliant at the guitar,' Laura said.

'No, I amn't,' Mandy snapped. 'God, Mum, you always exaggerate everything.'

'That's because she's proud of you,' Lexie said. 'I'd love to have kids. Would you like more, Laura?'

Everyone froze.

'What did I say?' Lexie looked alarmed. 'Flippin' hell, you could get frostbite in here, the temperature dropped so fast. Did I put my foot in it?'

'Laura had another little girl,' Frank said, 'but she –'

'Drowned almost seventeen years ago.' Joan's eyes welled. 'Her name was Jody.'

Lexie's hand flew to her mouth. 'Oh. Laura, you poor thing, that's terrible. I'm so sorry, darlin'. How did you cope?'

'Not very well,' Laura admitted.

'There was a lot of guilt involved,' Joan said tightly.

'Mum!' Frank warned.

'A child doesn't drown if its mother is looking after it properly,' Joan snapped.

'Bit harsh, Joan,' Lexie said.

Mandy stopped eating.

'No, she's right. It was my fault – completely my fault.' Laura tried to control her emotions. Even after all this time, the pain took her breath away.

Lexie reached over to hold her hand. 'We all make mistakes, darlin'.'

'Not like that one,' Joan muttered.

'I live with the guilt every day, Mum.' Laura's voice quivered.

'And I live with a broken heart. I loved that child like my own.' Joan wiped her eyes with a handkerchief. 'How could you –'

'Mum, not now,' Frank interrupted.

Mandy held her breath. She hated Jody being mentioned. She wished everyone would stop dragging it up. It had happened years ago and they needed to move on. It was like living with a ghost. Her stomach curled into a tight knot.

'Right. Come on, everyone, we need a stiff drink.' Lexie handed a glass of wine to Laura.

'No, thanks. I don't drink.'

'Really?'

'She's a boring Pioneer.' Mandy rolled her eyes.

'She gave up shortly after Jody's accident,' Frank explained.

Lexie put the glass down. 'Probably wise – you might have ended up drowning your sorrows in a bottle of gin for the rest of your life. I can't have kids. I had an abortion at sixteen that went wrong. But I reckon I'll adopt a black one, an Asian one and a white one, mix it up a bit.'

'Children are not dolls,' Joan carped. 'I'm sick of celebrities adopting children of all races and parading them about as if they were a badge of honour. Motherhood is hard. It's a never-ending roller-coaster. Your children let you down, hurt you, break your heart. It's not all trips to the park and Christmas stockings.'

'Come on, Joan, what about the good times, the happy memories?' Lexie asked gently.

Joan looked directly at Laura. 'I have to block them out. It's remembering the good times that kills you. It's too much pain. Jody was such a beautiful baby . . .' She began to cry.

Lexie turned to Frank. 'It looks to me like you've got a book of your own right here. You've got more skeletons than I have.'

Laura was quiet on the way home in the car. The things Joan had said had stung, as they always did. Seeing her mother just reminded her of the pain she had caused. It ate her alive to see Joan's broken spirit. Their relationship would never mend. She could see that now.

She wished they could comfort each other in their shared grief, but it wasn't possible. She had tried, she continued to try, but Joan didn't want to know. Every year on Jody's birthday Laura fell apart. She knew it was hard for Joan, too, so she always called her, but Joan never answered the phone. Laura left messages saying she was thinking of her and begging her to forgive her, but Joan couldn't. A part of Joan had died on the day Jody had disappeared. Grief had changed her. It had aged her and crushed her spirit.

If it hadn't been for Frank, Laura thought, she wouldn't have got through those black days. He always called into her on Jody's birthday and, even more importantly, on the anniversary of the day she had disappeared. He let her cry and scream and eat herself alive with guilt. But after a while he'd make her focus on the good memories. They'd look at photos and remember the cute things Jody had done – her funny wobbly walk and her infectious giggle – and Laura's heart would ease, not much but just enough to get her through the day.

She knew she'd been a terrible mother. She knew that she hadn't spent enough time with Jody, getting to know her, loving her, being her mother. The precious little time she'd had with Jody she had wasted in going out and partying while Joan had cared for her child. She felt sick every time she thought about it. It was after Jody had disappeared that Laura had fallen in love with her. It was after she lost her baby girl that she had realized how much she meant to her. Hindsight is cruel.

Frank was the only person Laura could talk to about her conviction that Jody hadn't drowned. Over the years she had gone to countless fortune tellers, mediums and psychics. Some had told her they could see Jody's spirit on the other side. Others had said nothing. A few had asserted that Jody was alive. Most had been quacks, Laura knew that, but she needed to try, to hope . . . Eventually after a lot of money and mixed, confusing signals, she had stopped going and kept her belief to herself. She knew she was clinging to straws but, deep in her soul, she knew Jody was out there.

'MUM!'

Laura was startled. 'What?'

'I've been talking to you for the last five minutes and you've been staring into space.'

'Sorry, what were you saying?'

'I was telling you about next Saturday. It's Nina's seventeenth birthday party. Her dad's hired a room in Chic nightclub. Everyone's going. It'll be amazing.'

Laura shook her head. 'I don't want you in a nightclub. You're only sixteen.'

Mandy's face clouded. 'Everyone in my class is going. There's no way you can stop me. I'm sick of being a prisoner in my own house.'

'I'm not trying to stop you having fun or imprison you. I just think you're too young for nightclubs. If she was having a party in her house it would be different. But that nightclub has a bad reputation – there was a knife fight there only about a month ago.'

Mandy thumped the dashboard in frustration. 'I knew you'd bring that up. You always have to look for the worst in everything. It was the only bad thing that's ever happened there and neither of the guys got hurt. They were thrown out straight away.'

Laura glanced at her furious daughter. 'The fact is that the people who go to that club are obviously aggressive and dangerous and I don't want you in that environment.'

Mandy rounded on her: 'It's always the same. You never want me to do anything. When I go out with my friends, you stalk me on my mobile. If I don't answer it after three rings you freak out. It's hell living with you. I hate it. I'm sick of being treated like a child. I'm sick of never being allowed do anything, go anywhere, be a normal teenager. I'm sick of paying for Jody. I'm *not her*!' she screamed.

Laura gripped the steering wheel and tried really hard not to cry. She willed herself to remain dry-eyed, but it was impossible. The night had been so tense and now Mandy was screaming at her . . .

'Oh, great!' Mandy exclaimed. 'Now you're crying and I feel like crap. Forget it, Mum, I won't go to the party. Forget I mentioned it. I didn't mean to upset you.'

Laura felt awful. It wasn't fair on Mandy. Jody's shadow did loom over their lives. She leaned across briefly to touch Mandy's hand. 'No, you're right, I am too protective. You can go, but I'll be picking you up at twelve thirty.'

'One, please, Mum. I'm not Cinderella.'

'Twelve forty-five is my final offer.'

'OK.' Mandy suppressed a grin.

When they got home, Mandy went straight up to her bedroom. Laura boiled the kettle and made herself a soothing cup of camomile tea. She curled up on the couch in the lounge and watched the moonlight dancing on the water. Every room in the house had floor-to-ceiling windows so the sea was ever present in their lives and Laura found it immensely calming. She sipped her tea and tried to clear her mind. She was awash with orange after seeing Joan and tried to fight it.

Her phone rang. It was Frank.

'Hey, sis, you OK?'

'Bit wobbly.'

'Orange night?'

'Afraid so.'

'She doesn't mean to upset you,' Frank defended Joan.

Laura rested her head on her hand. 'I know. It's not her fault. I don't blame her. It's just hard. I'll be fine.'

'Well, if you need to offload, call me.'

'Thanks.'

'Actually, I've got a favour to ask you that will be a good distraction for you.'

Laura was delighted to help. Frank had done so much for her over the years, spending time with Mandy, building bridges with Joan, encouraging her in her art . . . 'Of course. What do you need?'

'It's Lexie. I need to hide her somewhere quiet, remote, where the paparazzi won't find her.'

Laura smiled. 'And my house is about as remote as it gets.'

'It would be for a couple of weeks, just until she finishes her book. She's going to record everything on tape for the ghost to write up.'

Laura was worried about Mandy. How would she react to having a stranger in the house? Lexie had seemed nice, but would she be a bad influence? It didn't matter. There was no way she could refuse Frank. 'No problem. I'd be happy to have her.'

'Are you sure?'

'Of course.'

As if he had read her thoughts, Frank added, 'And don't worry about Mandy. Lexie is the most sensible person I've ever met. She's not a traditional role model, I grant you that, but she's a rock of sense once you get past the boobs and the peroxide hair.'

'She seems lovely.'

'Thanks, sis, I owe you for this.'

Laura sat up. 'Frank, you owe me nothing. If it wasn't for you I'd be in a strait-jacket, locked up in a psychiatric hospital. You've kept me sane through all the grief and despair. I'd be lost without you.'

Frank was silent.

'Frank?'

He coughed. 'I'm here. I just wish none of this had happened. It's been so hard on you and Mum.'

'And you,' Laura whispered.

'On all of us,' he said quietly.

Laura exhaled deeply. 'Frank, do you think it's stopping you having kids? I know how attached you were to Jody. I just think sometimes maybe her disappearing has made you afraid to have kids of your own. But look at Mandy – it worked out for me the second time.'

'Come on, Laura, you know me better than that. I was mad about Jody and Mandy's fantastic. But the reason I don't have any of my own is very straightforward. When I see my old college mates and how their lives have turned out, I don't envy them or want anything similar. It's not for me. I used to have great fun with Danny and Andrew, but now when we get together all they do is moan about how tired and fed up they are. They complain about having to get up six times a night with their small kids and that their wives nag them all the time. They never stay out late because they have to get up at five with the kids. They rarely come to rugby internationals because their wives won't let them. Marriage sounds worse than prison. And to top it all off, none of them seem to be having sex! Where's the sales pitch? It looks like hell to me.'

'Is Danny really not having sex?' Laura probed.

'Apparently since the last child was born . . .' Frank paused for effect '. . . eight months ago, he's had it twice – once was on his birthday. He says Amber's always tired or has a headache.'

Laura grinned: she had been very jealous when Amber had married Danny. 'Is it incredibly immature of me to be thrilled to hear that his sex life with Amber is non-existent?'

'Yes, but I forgive you. Apparently she nags him incessantly too.'

'Poor Danny, he should have taken me and my baggage.'

'He never would have. He was always too conservative for you.'

'I know. So, you're determined to continue as the happy bachelor.'

'Yes, and the key to it is the happy part. I like my life just the way it is. I love being an uncle but I don't fancy being a dad. Not now, anyway. I'm happy, my mates are miserable. Besides, I've met great people through work. Thank God I got out of that dead-end marketing job and set up my agency. At least this way I get to meet really interesting and diverse people.'

'Opening the agency was a brave move, but you always had a brilliant personality and incredible powers of persuasion. I'm not surprised you're doing so well.'

'Thanks. I'm hoping to get an auction going for Lexie's book. I reckon it's going to make me and her a lot of money.'

'She's certainly led a colourful life!'

'That's what sells best these days.'

'Frank, don't rule out being a dad.'

'I won't, but for now I'm having too much of a good time. Maybe when I'm fifty I'll decide to settle down with someone but she'll be young, energetic, have a big sex drive and never nag. Actually, maybe someone who doesn't speak English – being nagged in Italian probably sounds quite sexy. Maybe a hot young Italian author . . .'

'You're impossible!' Laura scolded.

'I'll take that as a compliment. OK, better go, thanks for agreeing to have Lexie as a house guest. I'll drop her down over the next couple of days. I'll call you.'

'Goodnight, Frank.'

'Goodnight, Laura. Try to sleep, and remember that Mum doesn't mean to be cruel. She's just unhappy.'

'I know, but it's hard. I miss Jody too.'

Laura hung up and spent the next three hours staring at the moonlight while her mind wandered into very dark places.

14.

Anna

London, June 2011

Nancy knocked on the door. 'Come on, I know you're in there.'

Anna let her next-door neighbour in. Nancy twirled. 'What do you think?'

Anna didn't know what to say. Nancy was wearing a low-rise sparkly turquoise gypsy skirt and a short belly top. The outfit didn't show her at her best.

Nancy followed Anna's eyes and laughed. 'I'm aware that my flabby stomach is on show but I really don't care. It's liberating to let it all hang out.'

Anna smiled. 'Good for you. That colour's lovely on you.'

Anna had opted for tracksuit bottoms and a T-shirt. 'It did say that we could wear ordinary clothes, didn't it?'

'Yes, but you look like you're going for a jog. Here, put this on.' Nancy tied a glittery pink scarf around Anna's waist. 'I have a pair of spangly leggings, if you want to borrow them?'

'I'm fifty-seven, Nancy. I'd look ridiculous.'

Nancy wagged a finger. 'Come on now, Anna, you promised you'd get into the spirit of this. Besides, fifty is the new forty.'

Anna laughed. 'That's easy for you to say when you're ten years younger than I am.'

'And two stone heavier.'

'You look lovely.'

'I look like a big fat forty-seven-year-old stuffed into a belly-dancing costume that's too small for her. But I can feel the menopause knocking at my door and I need to let loose. And you, my lovely but far too serious Irish friend, need to get out of the house and have some fun, so let's go!'

Anna really didn't want to go to belly-dancing classes. But Nancy had insisted and wouldn't take no for an answer. Eventually Anna had given in. Nancy was right: Anna didn't get out much. Between work and looking after Sophie, she rarely went anywhere. But she was happy: she didn't miss having a social life; everything she wanted was at home.

As they were climbing into Anna's car, Nancy's thirteen-year-old son, Gordon, and three of his friends cycled past. 'Dude, isn't that your mother?' one of the teenagers asked, pointing to Nancy.

Gordon went purple.

'Yoo-hoooo! Hello, Gordon – do you like my outfit?' Nancy wiggled her hips, highly amused by her son's mortification.

He threw down his bike and marched over. 'What are you doing?'

'Going to belly-dancing class.'

'Where's your top?'

'This is what you wear for belly-dancing. You're supposed to see the stomach.' Nancy ruffled her son's carefully gelled hair.

'Don't you have a jacket or something?'

'It's twenty-five degrees.'

'Seriously, Mum, it's way too much information. Women your age should cover up. It's embarrassing.'

'Inside, I'm still fifteen,' Nancy confessed.

Gordon glanced back at his friends, who were all wolf-whistling. 'You look a bit . . . well . . . desperate,' he whispered. 'Why can't you wear proper clothes like Anna?'

'Because Anna is sensible and I'm not. Because Anna gets to go to work and be with adults during the day and I don't. Because staying at home to raise three children has driven me potty. Because I refuse to become middle-aged. Because I intend to grow old disgracefully.'

'Why can't you be more, you know, normal?' Gordon said. 'Why can't you do gardening or jogging like other mothers?'

'Because they're boring and I need some fun in my life.'

Gordon looked at her pleadingly. 'Boring can be good.'

Nancy kissed her son's hot cheek. 'Gordon, I was put on this earth to mortify you. So you'd better get used to it. Now, there's a steak and kidney pie in the oven for you and your friends. And I bought those ice-creams you like. I'm off to make a complete fool of myself. See you later.'

Gordon slunk back to his friends while Nancy and Anna drove away.

When they got to the church hall, Anna stood at the back, surveying the group. There were eleven women in total, all ages, shapes and sizes. There was at least one woman who looked older than her, which was a relief.

The teacher clapped her hands and asked them to stand in a line. She introduced herself: 'My name's Sakhmet. I'm from Croydon.'

Nancy snorted. 'Sack of meat from Croydon! Not very exotic.'

Sakhmet was wearing a bright orange sparkly skirt with coin belts around her rather large stomach. It all looked tight and uncomfortable. Her top was little more than a bra with beads hanging down from it. The fake tan she was wearing was the same colour as her outfit.

'I thought this was supposed to tone you?' Anna whispered to Nancy.

'I know! Her belly's as big as mine!' Nancy groaned. 'I expected an exotic girl from Cairo, with long, firm limbs and a tiny waist that I could aspire to.'

'I've been dancing for ten years,' Sakhmet told them. 'Belly dancing is fantastic for your posture and for tightening up your muscles.'

'Which ones?' Nancy whispered. Anna tried not to laugh.

Sakhmet stared at Nancy and asked for silence. 'Belly dancing has been around for ever. It originated in Egypt and it's quite posh over there. All the really classy weddings have a belly dancer to entertain the guests. You can actually make a lot of money. Top belly dancers can make up to two or three thousand pounds for a forty-five-minute performance.'

Anna nudged Nancy. 'It could be a lucrative career for us. If you did four performances a week, you could make twelve thousand pounds for three hours' work,' she calculated. 'I wish I'd taken this up when I was younger – it pays a lot better than teaching.'

'Can you be quiet over there?' Sakhmet frowned. 'Now, Islam has not been kind to belly dancers. The fundamentalists burned down a lot of the nightclubs in Egypt where it took place. A lot of dancers have given it up because of pressure from those bastards.'

'Bloody fundamentalist party poopers,' Nancy whispered.

Sakhmet waved her arms. 'These people are ruining a time-honoured tradition. The famous Egyptian dancer Hala Safy gave up dancing after seeing a vision and started wearing a veil. She used to earn up to a grand a day – the average civil servant in Egypt earns fifty quid a month.'

'That's it! We're moving to Egypt. I could make a fortune,' Nancy said. 'They clearly need more dancers if the others are all hiding behind their *burkhas*. We'd be famous and wealthy in no time.'

'I might be a little old to do shows. I think they'd pay me a thousand pounds to go away!' Anna laughed.

'Those Islamic men are mad for Western women underneath it all. I think we could be on to something here.' Nancy grinned. 'I could call myself Fatyarse.'

Sakhmet raised her voice: 'No respectable Egyptian family wants their daughter to become a dancer because they have low social status unless they become famous. But the top dancers are icons, and often end up on TV or in the movies.'

'We could be judges on the Egyptian *X Factor*.' Nancy giggled.

'Or movie stars,' Anna mused.

Sakhmet glared at them. 'As I was saying, the upper classes would never allow their daughters to dance. Calling someone "son of a dancer" is like us saying "son of a bitch". It's a terrible insult.'

'That's what Gordon's friends are currently calling him.' Anna chuckled.

Nancy snorted. 'Hilarious.'

'Thankfully, in the Western world we don't have any of these prejudices and women enjoy the freedom to show off their tummies and dance whenever they want. So come on, ladies, let's get you started. Right, follow me, put your feet hip distance apart, knees soft, stomach muscles engaged.'

'Engaged in what? Wobbling about?' Nancy asked loudly.

Sakhmet eyeballed her. 'Concentrate, please. Now, ribcage lifted, shoulders back and relaxed.'

Anna tried to follow the instructions. Sakhmet came over to her to adjust her posture. 'Relax your shoulders,' she said.

'I'm trying,' Anna assured her.

'Come on, back and down.' Sakhmet tugged at her. But Anna couldn't do it. 'You hold a lot of tension in your shoulders,' Sakhmet noted. 'They're as stiff as bricks. You need to relax.'

If only you knew how wonderful that would be, Anna thought. To relax, to feel relaxed, calm, loose, light . . .

'Engage your stomach,' Sakhmet told Nancy.

'I'm trying,' Nancy replied. 'There's just a lot of it.'

Sakhmet went back to the front of the class.

'My God, her fake tan smells appalling. I feel ill.' Nancy wrinkled her nose.

'Now, ladies, watch me. Arms up and down like this.'

'Excuse me.' A girl of about twenty-five spoke up. 'Can you show us the Shakira hip wiggle. That's why I'm here. This arm stuff is dead boring.'

'Does a baby run before it crawls?' Sakhmet asked. 'Do you eat food before it's cooked? Do you put your shoes on before your trousers? Do you put your makeup on in the dark?'

'It certainly looks like it,' Nancy muttered, and suddenly Anna was laughing uncontrollably.

Anna parked the car outside her house.

'At least we had a good laugh,' Nancy said. 'Maybe we should try pole dancing next.'

'You're on your own there,' Anna warned her. 'No amount of

pleading will get me to entertain that idea or any others. I'm sticking to yoga.'

'What about salsa?'

'Goodnight, Nancy.' Anna closed the front door behind her and went up to Sophie's bedroom, but the door was shut and the light was off. She opened the door gently and peered in. Sophie was safely tucked up in bed, asleep. Anna said a silent prayer of thanks, as she did every night, for the gift of motherhood.

As the early-morning sun streamed through the window, Anna finished her ten minutes of meditation. She loved this time of day when the world was still quiet and she could escape from the stresses and strains of everyday life. Her meditation always started with gratitude for Sophie. Her beautiful baby girl with the golden ringlets had grown into an incredible adult. She was the love of Anna's life.

Anna lay back on her mat and stretched like a cat. She couldn't believe Sophie was eighteen. She was so grown-up for her age. Anna supposed it was because she had no siblings and it was just the two of them. Sophie had only ever known adult company at home. Anna had worried that it was lonely for her, but Sophie spent a lot of time at Holly's house where there was always plenty of action. Anna was so proud of her daughter: apart from the very occasional teenage tantrum, Sophie had been a dream. Anna dealt with so many troublesome teens at her school that she knew how lucky she was with Sophie. She was one in a million. A gift from God.

Anna got up and went into the bathroom to brush her teeth. She stood sideways and sucked her tummy in. She wasn't bad for someone three years from sixty. She had put on some weight over the last few years but it hadn't been a bad thing: she'd been too thin. It suited her face to carry more weight. She looked less gaunt. She examined it. Lined, but not overly so. Parents often commented that she looked younger than her age. The mums said it was because she wasn't married – 'Husbands give you wrinkles,' they said.

One of the fathers who always flirted with her told her she looked like Susan Sarandon. She had Googled her when she got home and discovered that the actress was seven years older than she was! Sophie had said it was rubbish and that she looked like Geena Davis, which was a lie but a sweet one.

Anna hummed as she brushed her teeth. Her holidays would start soon and she'd have a blissful six weeks off. She looked forward to it. Being a headmistress was tiring. You had to deal with everyone's problems, issues and complaints – teachers, parents, students. It was never-ending. Most of the time Anna didn't mind because she liked problem-solving. But some people were never happy and it required a lot of patience and diplomacy to keep things running smoothly in a big school. It would be nice to have a break from it all.

She was looking forward to spending three weeks in France with Sophie. They had booked a week in Paris, a week in Provence and then a final week walking in the Alps. Joe was going to join them for a few days in Provence. Anna was looking forward to it. It was nice for Sophie to have a positive male role-model in her life, and although they only saw Joe once or twice a year, it was always fun to have him around.

Anna knew that this would be her last big holiday with Sophie. From next year she'd want to go away with her art college friends, travelling the world. Anna was determined to make it a really special, memorable trip.

She got dressed and went to check on her daughter. She was awake and staring at the ceiling when Anna went in.

'Morning! I thought you'd still be asleep now that your holidays have officially started.'

'Well, I'm not.'

Anna sat down on Sophie's bed. 'You look a bit peaky. You must be worn out after all those exams. Are you feeling OK?'

Sophie rolled over, turning her back to her mother. 'No, I'm not. I feel awful.'

'Let me check your temperature. I hope you're not coming down with something.'

'I'm fine. Leave me alone. I just need to stay in bed.'

Anna frowned. 'You seem quite bad. Maybe I should take you to the doctor.'

'Stop fussing. I'm not a child. Go to work. I'll be fine,' Sophie snapped.

'Well, you don't seem fine. I'll go to work later. I don't want to leave you like this.'

'For God's sake, Mum, just go. I don't need you.'

Anna flinched. 'All right, I'll leave you for now, but if you feel any worse, call me. I'll come back at lunchtime to check on you, and I'll ask Nancy to pop over in an hour.'

'No!' Sophie sat up in her bed. 'Holly's coming over later. I don't need her mother coming too. If I feel worse, I'll call you. Now just go, I want to sleep.'

'Can I get you anything before I go? Some paracetamol or a cup of tea?'

'No.'

'Is it a green day? Are you feeling pain?'

Silence.

Anna bent down to kiss her unusually grumpy daughter, but Sophie's head was tucked under the duvet. Anna left her alone and headed to work. She felt uneasy. Her ulcer began to throb. Sophie was rarely sick and she didn't like leaving her alone. She decided to pop in to Nancy.

Her friend answered the door in her dressing-gown, hair askew, and ushered Anna into the kitchen. 'Please ignore the mess, I'll get around to cleaning it some day. Coffee?'

Anna propped herself against the kitchen counter. 'No, thanks. Look, Nancy, I'm sorry to call in so early but I'm worried about Sophie.'

Nancy smiled. 'Anna, you're always worried about Sophie. You're going to worry yourself into an early grave.'

Anna threw her hands into the air. 'Guilty as charged. I can't help it. Anyway, this morning she said she wasn't feeling well and she seems very out of sorts.'

'She's probably just tired after the exams.'

'I think it's more than that,' Anna worried. 'She looked very pale. I offered to take her to the doctor but she said she just wanted to sleep. She mentioned that Holly is due over this morning. Could you ask her to call me if she thinks Sophie's getting worse?'

Nancy patted Anna's arm. 'No problem at all. I'll talk to Holly when she wakes up and I'll check on Sophie myself later. Don't worry, we'll make sure she's OK.'

'Thanks, Nancy. Poor Sophie, the last thing she needs is to get sick now, just after finishing her exams when she should be relaxing and enjoying herself.'

'I know, and she worked so hard, unlike my jack-in-the-box who couldn't sit at her desk for more than ten minutes.'

Anna smiled. 'Holly will be fine. She's a great girl.'

Nancy put her coffee on the table. 'Holly needs to channel her energy into more than music and boys. She's totally distracted. I found her application form for a summer job in the pizzeria and she had written, "Am great with the pubic." Honestly, Anna, she's a ditz.'

Anna laughed. 'She's just a normal teenager. Their attention to detail is never good. She's a sweetheart and she's been such a wonderful friend to Sophie. Honestly, moving in next door to you guys was a blessing.'

'We did better out of it. Sophie's such a steadying influence on Holly. Thank God my scatterbrained daughter at least had the sense to befriend someone much more responsible and level-headed than she is.'

'They complement each other. Sometimes I worry that Sophie's old beyond her years. I think it's a bit quiet for her with just the two of us. She loves the hustle and bustle in this house.'

'She must be mad – the kids are so boisterous! Sophie is so calm and polite, not like my unruly lot. You've done an amazing job, Anna. You should write a manual on child-rearing – us demented mothers need tips.'

Anna loved hearing Nancy say this. It made everything worth-while to know that people thought she had done a good job in raising Sophie. 'I was blessed with Sophie. I've been so lucky.'

Nancy put her hand on Anna's shoulder. 'Sophie's the lucky one. I spend all day shouting at my children. I don't think I ever speak to them in a normal tone. You're always so poised and together. In all these years I've never heard you shout at her or lose your cool. I don't know how you do it. No wonder you became the headmistress at St Catherine's so quickly – you're the only person I know who could run a school and not be on Prozac!'

Anna roared laughing. 'Believe me, there are days when I con-sider taking it. You need to stop putting yourself down! You're a brilliant mother. I have one child to look after, you have three. There's a world of difference. Your children are lovely, and Holly is the sister Sophie never had.'

'You're a good liar and a good neighbour for not reporting me to Social Services for verbally abusing my children on an hourly basis.'

Suddenly they heard a huge bang as Gordon came flying through the kitchen door backwards, followed by his sister Jessie, who dived on top of him and began to thump him.

Anna jumped out of the way while Nancy grabbed fifteen-year-old Jessie by the ponytail. 'STOP TRYING TO STRANGLE YOUR LITTLE BROTHER, YOU WITCH!'

'He took my phone and read my texts.' Jessie kicked out at him.

'For God's sake, ignore him,' Nancy said.

'You fancy Oliver, you fancy Oliver,' Gordon taunted.

'Yeah, well, you're a loser with a face full of zits,' Jessie shrieked.

'You're a – a LESBIAN!' Gordon bellowed.

'If I like Oliver, I'm hardly a lesbian, you idiot,' Jessie sneered.

Gordon's face turned bright red. 'WANKER!'

Nancy looked at Anna. 'I imagine breakfast in your house doesn't normally include physical violence and verbal abuse?'

The door flew open again. 'For God's sake, I'm trying to sleep.' Holly stomped into the kitchen.

'Hello, Holly,' Anna said.

Holly swivelled around and blushed. 'Oh, hi,' she said, looking down at the floor.

'I was just telling your mum that Sophie's not feeling well and I was a bit worried about her. Would you mind keeping an eye on her today?'

Holly crossed her arms. 'I was planning on spending the day with her anyway. We have *lots* to talk about.'

'OK. Well, call me if she seems worse or if she wants to go to the doctor or anything.'

'Of course she will, won't you, Holly?' Nancy prodded her daughter. Holly nodded without enthusiasm. 'Right, then. Anna, go to work and don't worry about a thing. I'll call you later to give you an update on Sophie.' Nancy walked her to the door.

'Dickhead!' they heard Jessie shout at her brother.

'I'm going to rip your head off and your leg and – and – and –' Gordon stalled.

'Feed them to hungry sharks?' Holly suggested.

'Yeah! Yeah, that!' Gordon jumped up and down.

Nancy rolled her eyes. ''Bye then, Anna. I hope you have a nice civilized day, not like mine here at the human zoo.'

Anna smiled to herself as she climbed into her car. She loved Nancy but she didn't know how she put up with the madness. Nancy's house was chaotic, yet she was always so good-humoured and welcoming.

Nancy was the first person Anna had met when she moved to London. She had called over with Holly, an apple tart and a bottle of wine on the day Anna and Sophie, her daughter's new name, had arrived. Nancy had made moving to London easy. She had embraced Anna and Sophie and introduced them to everyone. She had lent Anna beakers and nappies and pyjamas for their first night because Sophie's things had 'got lost' in the move from Dublin. She had taken Anna under her wing and shown her all the best parks and playgrounds, the best shops, restaurants and playgroups to go to and, even better, she had offered to look after Sophie while Anna was at work. She had been her child-minder for that first year until Sophie had gone to kindergarten. It was there that Holly and Sophie had formed their lifelong friendship.

When Nancy eventually asked about Sophie's dad, Anna had said that she was the result of a very brief fling with an American who had been passing through Dublin and that she had never seen him again. Nancy had accepted the story and never asked about him after that.

Anna had taught Holly and Sophie together when they came to St Catherine's at five years of age and she had watched Holly's sister Jessie and brother Gordon grow up on her doorstep. They were a lively bunch, and she was incredibly fond of them all. They were her surrogate family. Kevin, Nancy's husband, was always on hand to help when Anna's washing-machine broke down or her pipes leaked. He said he liked coming over to help: it got him out of the madhouse he lived in. Anna was always very careful not to overstep the mark. She was friendly to Kevin, but never overly so. She didn't want Nancy to worry that she was flirting with him or trying to steal him, although Nancy never seemed to feel threatened by Anna's being single. But lots of women had been. Anna had seen the way some of the mothers glared at her when she talked to their husbands. A single woman was considered dangerous. Some mothers had confronted her about her status: why was she single? Where was Sophie's father? Why did she never date? Anna was shocked at first that people could be so assertive. But she had learned to deal with it. She said her life was full enough with raising a daughter and running a large school. She had no time for men, no time for relationships. She knew there had been rumours that she was a lesbian. Some people – a minority, thankfully – seemed to find it very odd that she had no man in her life.

She had gone on a few dates, but never followed up. She knew that she couldn't be in a relationship. She wanted Sophie all to herself. There was no way she was going to let some man walk into their lives and become Sophie's 'dad'. She had made a pact with God: if I get to keep this child, I will devote my life to her. And that had been that. It was unbreakable and had been surprisingly easy to keep. Anna's life was busy and full and she was content. And as for sex . . . Well, that was where Joe came in. When he visited, and Sophie was fast asleep, he would sneak into Anna's room. But she always asked him to leave before dawn. She didn't want Sophie to think anything was going on, to know that her mother was sleeping with Joe. He was their friend, their buddy, not Anna's occasional lover.

Anna had resisted Joe at first, but when he had told her his marriage was over in all but name, she had given in. That had been six years after she'd run away. Six years after she'd found Sophie. Six years without the touch of a man. Six years without love, six years without looking back, six years of forgetting her past, six years of only looking forward.

Joe had insisted on coming to see her. She had put him off for all those years, only speaking to him on the phone, but then he'd said he was coming to a conference in London and was going to track her down if she refused to meet him. So she did and she told him she had a daughter now. A little girl had come into her life soon after she'd arrived . . . She explained to Joe that initially she had offered to foster a neglected child, but when the child's mother had continued to drink and had shown no interest in raising her, Anna had adopted the little girl. However, Anna told Joe that she didn't want Sophie ever to know about her awful mother, so she had told her she was the result of a fling with an American man. She wanted Sophie to feel secure and loved and didn't want her traumatized by knowing her birth mother had chosen drink over her own flesh and blood.

Joe had been taken aback by her reasoning, and told her so. He argued that lying about Sophie's origins was a bad idea. 'Lies always come back to haunt you,' he reminded her. He believed that Sophie deserved to know the truth. Anna was furious, and threatened to sever all ties with him if he went against her on this. It was her decision to protect Sophie from the awful truth and she was sticking to her story – and Joe would have to as well, if he wanted any place in her life. She demanded that Joe never mention her marriage to Barry or Hope or anything else about her past life in Ireland. As far as Sophie was concerned, none of that had ever happened: she was Anna's first and only child.

'You can't erase your past,' Joe had insisted. 'She'll find out some day and she'll be so angry with you for lying.'

Anna was fiercely determined. 'Joe, you have a choice here: you agree to stick to my story or I can't ever see you again. It's as simple as that.'

Joe realized she was completely serious about it, so he had reluctantly agreed to keep her secrets. In his heart he knew that what Anna was doing would lead to hurt, but he loved her, and he couldn't bring himself to break off his relationship with her. So he had always done things her way.

Joe had asked to meet Sophie, but Anna said no. Not yet. Not now. The next time. So he had come back six months later and met Sophie. At first she had been shy with him. He was the only friend from Ireland, from her past, her mother had ever introduced her to. But Joe had a way with people, a natural ease that had served him well as a GP. He'd soon had Sophie eating out of his hand.

But Anna didn't want Joe in her house, meeting Nancy and other local parents. She didn't want questions asked, rumours started, so they had agreed to go on holidays together every year. Sometimes Joe brought Mark along. Sophie loved it when he came: he was fun to have around. Things had worked out, life was good, Anna was happy. Joe had stuck to their agreement and never mentioned Anna's marriage or Hope.

Over time, Anna accepted that she could trust Joe, that he would never betray her. He could see how happy Sophie was and he'd never do anything to ruin that. Anna's secrets were safe.

★

Nancy phoned to say that she had checked on Sophie, who seemed better. She was up and about, looking pale and tired but not unwell. Anna was relieved.

When she got home, Sophie was in bed. 'Hello, darling, how are you feeling now?'

Sophie turned away from her. 'Not good.'

Anna went over and tried to feel her daughter's forehead, but Sophie buried her head in the pillow. 'Will you come down for dinner? I'm making your favourite tonight, lasagne.'

'I'm not hungry.'

'Come on, Sophie, you have to eat something.'

'I said I'm not hungry.'

'I'm worried about you, pet. What's the matter? Do you feel sick? Nancy said there's a tummy bug going around.'

'Leave me alone.'

'Sophie, has something happened? Are you unwell or are you worried about something?'

'I'm just tired, OK? I'm not hungry, and I don't have a temperature or a stomach bug. I just want to be left alone so I can sleep.'

'It's not like you to be so upset. I think I should call a doctor.'

Sophie sat up. Through gritted teeth, she barked, 'All – I – want – you – to – do – is – go – away – so – I – can – sleep!'

Anna stood up, feeling hurt and rejected. Sophie was never like this. 'All right, I'll leave you. I'll make the lasagne in case you feel hungry later. If you need me at all during the night, wake me up.'

'Fine.'

'Goodnight.' Anna closed the door gently and felt her stomach burning. She stumbled into her bedroom. The searing pain of her ulcer was making her dizzy.

15.

Laura
Killduf, June 2011

Sarah McLachlan's haunting voice filled the studio. Laura swayed to the music as she painted. She let herself go, escape, disappear into the moment. It felt wonderful. She felt lighter, cleaner, freer. She savoured the moment of peace.

Joan's birthday dinner had thrown her into a black hole. For days her head had been awash with orange for pain, white for shame and, most of all, pink for guilt. She had spent seventeen years seeing mostly pink and orange. Whenever Joan looked at her, all Laura could see in her eyes was anger and resentment. Her mother hated her. Laura understood it: she hated herself. She had broken her mother's heart.

Every day when she woke up, Laura cried for her lost baby. For the child she had let go. The child she had neglected. She'd stare at pictures of Jody and ache to hold her, to feel her soft cheek against her own. She yearned, more than anything in the world, to be a good mother to her, to show Jody that she did love her and to beg her forgiveness. But she was gone, and Laura would never be able to tell her how sorry she was. Why, oh, why had she not cherished every second? She'd been so stupid, so immature and selfish. She despised her teenage self.

There was a knock on the door. 'Mornin', darlin'. Not disturbing you, am I?' Lexie came in, wearing a very short, plunging black silk négligée. She was carrying two cups of coffee and a bundle of letters. 'The postman come and delivered these for you.'

'Lexie! You're not supposed to be opening the door. You're in hiding, remember? Frank told me yesterday that I was to keep you away from all other humans until the book is finished. How did you sleep? Is your bedroom OK? You're probably used to five-star hotels. It's pretty simple here in the country.'

'Laura darlin', I grew up in a two-bedroom flat with five brothers and sisters. This is luxury. The only problem here is nature. All them birds twittering and cows mooing – such a racket. I woke up early. You wouldn't normally see me before eleven. Anyways, I seen the postman coming and I fancied some company, so I invited him in for a cuppa.'

Laura grinned. 'Did you have a dressing-gown on?'

'No, just this. I did catch him staring at my boobs a lot.'

'I've no doubt. Poor Sean hasn't seen the likes of those in his life. This is a quiet country village, Lexie. We don't get glamorous women like you passing through.'

'Well, he was very nice. He told me he's been married to his wife for forty years. Imagine that!'

'It's good going.'

'Me and Dougie only lasted four. Bit sad, innit?'

Laura rinsed her paintbrush. 'It's hard to stay with a man who's being unfaithful.'

'I know, but we did have some good laughs.'

'Did the postman ask you what you were doing here?'

Lexie nodded. 'I told him I was your accountant.'

Laura burst out laughing. 'Brilliant.'

'He looked a bit surprised but he just said I was a great girl to have such a solid career.'

They giggled.

'So, how's your morning going?' Lexie asked, sipping her coffee.

Laura put down her brush. 'Good, thanks. I'm working on a new piece.'

'Do you mind if I have a look at your pictures?'

'No, not at all.'

Lexie walked around the studio. 'I wish I had a talent like this. All I know is getting my tits out. Not much for my future kids to be proud of, is it?'

'You'll be a great mum.'

Lexie moved to the corner of the studio. 'Oh, Laura, I love this one.' She was standing in front of a painting of a little blonde girl.

'Thanks,' Laura said shortly.

'It's her, isn't it?' Lexie asked. 'The little girl you lost.'

Laura nodded and, despite her best efforts, began to cry. Lexie rushed over to comfort her. 'There there. You poor old thing – what a shitty thing to happen. What are the chances? It was such bad luck. I bet you was a brilliant mum an' all. You're so calm, not like me, all wound up and mouthy. She was lucky to have you.'

Laura pulled away. 'I was a terrible mother. I was the worst.'

'Don't say that. Accidents happen all the time.'

Laura buried her face in her hands. 'It wasn't an accident.'

'Course it was – people drown every day. And kids are impossible to watch all the time. No one could ever blame you.'

'Yes, they could. I was drunk.'

Lexie stared at her. 'Drunk? As in pissed?'

Laura looked up, tears streaming down her face. 'Yes, out-of-my-mind drunk. I was so drunk I passed out at the bar and let my baby daughter wander off. How's that for Supermum? When the police questioned me I couldn't remember anything. I vaguely remembered a woman taking Jody for milk, but I couldn't describe her, too drunk to remember. And then they found Jody's sandals floating in the water and that was it. Case closed, mystery solved – Jody was dead. Everyone stopped asking questions. She drowned, end of story.'

'What about the body?'

'Never found.'

Lexie studied Laura's face. 'You still think she's out there, don't you?'

'Yes, I do.'

'Do you think that woman took her?'

'Yes.'

'Crikey, Laura! I thought my family stories were bad. That's the worst I ever heard. But you've got to stop beating yourself up – everyone gets pissed. It wasn't like you hit her or abused her. You were stupid, really stupid, but you was only a kid yourself. How old was you?'

'Twenty. Old enough to know better.' Laura sobbed. 'Oh, Lexie, I wasn't nice to her at all. I never told her I loved her. I never told her how wonderful she was. I was so wrapped up in myself and she was so sweet and beautiful.'

Lexie hugged her again. 'You poor thing, the guilt's eating you up inside, I can see it. But you have to forgive yourself, Laura.'

'I know she's out there, Lexie, I feel it. A mother knows when her child is dead and my instinct tells me Jody's alive. At first everyone thought I was saying it to make myself feel better, but I still believe it. I believe in my heart and soul that she's out there somewhere.'

'Weren't there any clues?'

Laura looked out of the window at the sea. 'Nothing. She vanished into thin air. The boat was packed, it was summer, there were kids running around everywhere. No one remembers seeing her. And when they found her sandals . . .'

'How did you get through it?'

Laura smiled ruefully. 'I drank. From when I woke up in the morning until I passed out at night. And then I started to cut myself. Feeling physical pain helped ease the agony for a minute or two and then it would come back again, stronger, so I'd cut myself again, a little deeper every time.'

Lexie understood. 'Oh, babe, my sister used to self-harm. Not the sister that shagged Dougie, my real sister. She did it when my dad went to prison. Her arms was like train tracks. Did you do it for long?'

'Not very. About six weeks after Jody disappeared, Frank found me one night, drunk, in a pool of my own blood. He went crazy. I've never seen him so angry.'

'I can't imagine Frank losing it.'

'He lost it, all right. He smacked me across the face, and called me a selfish bitch. He was furious with me. But then he bandaged my arms and made me coffee and sandwiches to sober me up.'

'Bless him. I wish I had a brother like that.'

Laura went on, 'He said I didn't get to opt out. He said our family had suffered enough. He couldn't take any more and neither could Mum. He said he loved Jody too and he missed her terribly and then he broke down . . . I was so wrapped up in my own grief that I didn't realize how bad it was for him, too. He really loved Jody. He was amazing with her. She adored him. He sobbed his heart out – it was horrendous to see his pain.'

Tears ran down Lexie's face. 'It's all so flippin' tragic. Poor you and poor old Frank. He's a big softie underneath it all, isn't he?'

She nodded. 'Yes, he really is. I'd die without Frank. He's my rock.'

Lexie blew her nose. 'What about Joan, then? I could see the tension between you two at dinner. You could have cut the air with a knife. It was like the time when my dad told my mum he was leaving her for the tart down the road. She excused herself, came back in with a saucepan and smacked him over the head with it. Knocked him unconscious, she did. Then she dragged him outside and hung a sign around his neck saying, "He's all yours."' Lexie sighed and took a sip of her coffee. 'Happy families, hey! Now, tell me about Joan.'

Laura took a deep breath. It was hard for her to talk about Joan. 'My mum spent most of those first months in bed. I honestly think she was paralysed by grief. She couldn't look at me. Every time I went in to see her, she'd scream, "Murderer."'

Lexie looked shocked. 'Bit harsh.'

'She was heartbroken. You have to understand – Jody was like her own daughter. She worshipped her. If I'm being honest, Mum was the one raising her, not me. She just adored her granddaughter. For the first few weeks the doctor had to sedate her on a daily basis. After that she started taking sleeping tablets. Sometimes she slept for days.' Her mother had stopped eating and turned into a shell of her former self. A woman with no will to go on . . . and all because of Laura.

'It must have been hard for you to see that. Even more guilt, right?' Lexie asked.

Laura stared into her coffee cup. 'Seeing the pain I'd caused her and Frank was just too much to bear. I couldn't stand it so I decided to kill myself. It was the only solution. I had to make it stop. I thought it would be easy. I was used to cutting myself. I'd just have to cut my wrists a bit deeper and then all the pain, the hurt and the guilt would go away.'

Lexie wiped her eyes. 'You poor thing, you was only a kid. Thank God you're still here. What happened to change your mind?'

Laura smiled. 'I discovered I was pregnant.'

'Of course! Mandy!' Lexie whooped. 'Babes, this is way more interesting than my book. You should write your own life-story. It's incredible! It's got everything, drama, grief, family feuds, death, life . . . It'd be a bestseller. Now, tell me, how the hell did you get pregnant between drinking yourself into a coma and cutting yourself? Where did you fit in time for sex?'

Laura told Lexie about David.

About two months after Jody's disappearance on the boat, Laura had gone out with Chloë and Hayley. They'd gone to a bar, sat in a dark corner, cried and got drunk. It was the only thing they could think to do. After a few hours some guys from Hayley's economics class in college came over to talk to her. They stopped in their tracks when they saw Laura in the corner. No one knew what to say.

''S OK, sit down. I'm not infectious. At least, I don't think I am,' Laura had slurred.

The guys had sat down, one of them, David, beside Laura. He was geeky, with glasses and curly hair – not the type Laura would ever go for.

He had pushed his glasses up on to the bridge of his nose. 'I'm sorry about your little girl.'

'Thanks.' Laura tried not to cry.

'Can I get you a drink?' he offered.

'Double vodka.'

They'd got drunker and drunker, and somehow Laura had ended up back in David's apartment, listening to music and smoking joints. She had made the first move: she leaned over and kissed him. It had been completely spontaneous and had taken her by surprise. Suddenly she had wanted desperately to be kissed, to feel something, anything, other than pain. She had ripped her clothes off. She needed to feel loved. She needed sex. She needed a man to want her. She needed to feel like a person. She needed to feel something else, something other than grief . . . to see some other colour than orange.

When she had woken up the next morning, he was fast asleep beside her. She had grabbed her things and run. She'd felt ashamed. She'd wanted never to see him again. How could she have slept with a stranger? Had she learned nothing from her past mistakes? What was wrong with her? She was a useless human being. She stayed in, refusing to go out, afraid of her actions, afraid of herself, wanting only to die . . .

'When did you find out you was pregnant?'

'About six weeks after that night, Joan woke up one morning, went into Jody's bedroom and packed all of her things into boxes. I could hear her wailing as she folded her little dresses and vests. I swear, Lexie, it was like a knife piercing my heart. I just couldn't handle it so I decided to commit suicide. I spent the day planning what to do, but I kept having to run to the bathroom to be sick. I thought I had a bug or something so I went to bed to rest for a few minutes and ended up falling asleep. I didn't wake up until the next morning. I still felt awful, really sick and tired. I didn't have the energy to kill myself. I stayed in bed and drifted in and out of sleep. When I finally got up later that day, I threw up again. Frank came into my bedroom to check on me and his aftershave made me run to the bathroom again – and that was when it hit me. Nausea, vomiting, sensitivity to smells and no period.'

'You was pregnant!' Lexie cheered. 'I felt like that when I got pregnant, sick as a dog I was. Didn't understand how any woman could carry a child full term feeling that bad. Anyways, I had my abortion then. I was nine weeks gone. I regret it because it's made me barren, but I couldn't have handled a baby at sixteen, no way. It would have ruined my life – well, that's what I tell myself, anyway.' She smiled grimly.

'I'm so sorry. But you really should think about adopting. You'd be a lovely mum.' Laura squeezed Lexie's hand.

'I will, when I get my money from that cheating snake. Now, back to you. You must've been delighted when you found out you was expecting?'

Laura watched the waves breaking on the sand. 'My immediate reaction was joy. I was happy, hysterically so. But then I felt incredibly sad, guilty and scared.'

'Why? In case you messed up again?'

'Yes.'

'I reckon it was God's way of telling you to move on, to forgive yourself and get on with your life. The way I see it is that you only get one life, so when something knocks you sideways, you have to dust yourself down and keep moving forward. If I hadn't had my boobs done, I'd be either dealing crack or stuck in some dump with six kids and a husband who beat me. We're survivors, Laura, you and me, survivors.'

'Mandy saved my life.'

'Good old Mandy.'

'And you're right. It was a sign from God. It was a gift, actually, the gift of a second chance. So I stopped drinking and have just tried to be the best mum I can be. I'm determined to make up for my sins of the past. Since Mandy was born I've done everything I can to make her happy and keep her safe. I know she finds it claustrophobic, but I need to know where she is all the time. I can't let her out of my sight. She's my miracle.'

Lexie's eyes filled again. 'She's a lucky girl. To be loved like that is very rare. I'm going to love my kids like that. I was thinking I'd adopt them on my own.'

'You should,' Laura encouraged her.

'Now I just need to write my book, make a shedload of cash and then go to Africa or Asia or whatever to get the babies. When I come back I'll do a big magazine spread in a bikini, talking about how happy I am. I'm going to make Dougie sick with jealousy.'

'It sounds like you have it all planned out.'

'Too right, Laura. I'm going to make as much money as I can before my tits start dragging along the ground with my arse. My kids are going to have everything. I want them to go to good schools so they don't have to do what I did to earn money. I want them to have proper jobs and be respectable.'

'Good for you.' Laura smiled at her.

'I may be common, but I'm not thick.' Lexie chuckled. 'Now, tell me more! What did Joan say when she found out you was pregnant with Mandy?'

Laura winced at the memory. 'She freaked and called me a slut and accused me of trying to replace Jody and erase the past. But she came around when she saw Mandy.'

'She's hard, is Joan. You can see she's suffered a lot in her life. What about David? Did you give it a go with him? I know he sounds a bit of a nerd but sometimes they make good partners. The flash bastards like Dougie are the ones to stay away from.'

Laura shook her head. 'No, I told him about the baby and he very sweetly offered to go out with me, but it would never have worked. I was a train wreck. I was still only half a person. I sometimes still think I'm not whole. Part of me died when Jody disappeared. But I was really lucky with David. He's been a brilliant dad.'

Laura hugged her knees as she told Lexie about the day Mandy was born. It was a warm autumn day, and David had been there to witness her arrival. Frank had waited outside, pacing the corridor nervously. Joan had refused to come to the hospital or to have anything to do with the baby.

Laura hadn't uttered a sound throughout the labour. She had refused all pain relief. The pain *was* her relief. She had embraced it, willed it. Every contraction was a joy to her. Life: she was creating it, not destroying it. She wasn't completely worthless. She had a reason to live.

But when Mandy had been born and the doctor had told her it was a girl, a sound came out of Laura's mouth that made everyone stop. It was a primal scream, a howl, a broken-hearted wail for her lost baby. A calling, a yearning for what should have been, what could never be, a plea for forgiveness, a farewell cry.

Mandy was placed in her arms. Laura had held her close, looked into her eyes and whispered, 'I'll keep you safe. I won't let you down. I promise I won't. I'll be a good mum this time.'

Both Frank and David had cried when they held her. Joan had come in the next day. She had ignored Laura, walked past her bed, and gone over to the cot where the baby was sleeping.

'I'm calling her Mandy after Dad's mum, Amanda,' Laura had said.

Joan didn't react. Mandy wriggled, stretched her arms over her head and yawned. Then she opened her eyes and stared straight into Joan's. Laura saw her mother flinch.

Joan had put her bag down slowly and reached into the cot. Her hands were shaking. She picked the baby up and slowly, with quivering fingers, held her tiny face to her cheek. Laura had watched as Joan cried the silent tears of a broken woman who had begun to hope anew.

Lexie dried her tears. 'I swear that's the most heartbreaking story I ever heard. Babes, you have been through the wringer! I can't believe you're so normal.'

'I don't know that I am,' Laura said.

'Believe me, I know a nutter when I see one. And look at all this.' Lexie gestured at Laura's studio. 'You're so talented and successful.'

'The success was slow in coming. I only started making good money in the last few years. But painting is my haven. I come in here and let my imagination run free. My emotions dictate the colours and my subconscious moves the brush.'

'Wow, that's amazing. So you never plan what you're going to paint?'

'I've tried to but it never works. My painting comes from in here.' Laura pointed to her stomach. 'The inspiration is buried somewhere deep down and I just have to surrender to it and let it lead me where it wants to go.'

'That's genius, that is.' Lexie was impressed.

'I don't think so, Lexie. But I do know that art has been my escape. Painting has kept me sane. It's kept me from spiralling into a black hole. This studio is my safe place. My switch-off.'

'I'm not surprised. It's a lovely space and the views are incredible. I could sit here all day looking out at the sea. It's very soothing, innit?'

'Yes, it really is. After Mandy was born, I had to get away from Dublin. I wanted to live in a small village where no one knew me or my story. Somewhere life was quiet and calm. I needed to get away from all the Jody memories and the accusing eyes and start afresh. There were only the two of us, so I wanted somewhere small. I couldn't be too far from Dublin, so Mandy could see her dad and Frank and Joan whenever she wanted, and it had to have views of the sea. When I saw this property, I knew it was perfect. It was only forty minutes from Dublin and it had the quaint three-bedroom house with a separate garage that I converted into this studio.'

'It's perfect,' Lexie said. 'How often does Mandy see her dad, then?'

'It used to be every second weekend, but since David got married eight years ago, it sometimes stretches to every third weekend. I've tried really hard to warm to his wife, Tanya, but she's very cold.'

Lexie rubbed her hands together. 'Oooh, go on, tell me all. I like a good bitch.'

143

'She's a terrible snob. David's a lawyer and he's doing very well. They live in a very big house in Dublin and their children –'

Lexie exclaimed, 'Oh, yeah, I forgot he had other kids. Two girls, innit?'

'Mya and Lola. They're seven and six. They seem like sweet kids. I've only met them a few times, but Mandy dotes on them. Tanya has them in a very expensive private school and seems to spend all her time having coffee with equally socially ambitious women. The only things she cares about in life are herself, David and her daughters. She can't stand me. I'm a blot on her perfect life. The drunken freak who let her own daughter drown. I really don't care what she thinks of me but it bothers me that she's not very nice to Mandy. She tolerates her because she has to. She came with the David package. But you can see she doesn't like having Mandy around, and Mandy feels left out.'

Lexie clicked her tongue. 'That's it. I hate this Tanya already. So what about David? Is he still a good dad or is he all about the other two kids now?'

'No, he's still great, but he works incredibly long hours and he tries to keep everyone happy, which is impossible. He really loves Mandy but she hardly ever sees him on his own any more, which is hard. Now when they're all together she only gets a little bit of his attention, and for the first eight years of her life she had him all to herself.'

'It's a pity he met this Tanya.'

'I'm glad for him that he got married and had other children. I just wish he'd chosen someone nicer.'

'Poor old Mandy, but at least she has a mum and dad who love her. Families are always complicated. I know I'll hate whoever Dougie ends up with. It's bound to be some gold-diggin' slapper.' Lexie stretched her arms up and yawned. 'Crikey! Look at the time!'

Laura glanced at her clock. It was almost one. They'd been sitting there for hours. 'God, sorry, Lexie, I've completely bent your ear off.'

'Babes, it was fascinatin', and I feel as if I really know you now. I'm glad Frank hid me down here. I was a bit nervous arriving yesterday, seein' as I'd only met you once, but you've been so nice and welcoming, I feel really at home. I hope Mandy won't mind having a house-guest for a week or two.'

'She'll be thrilled. She thinks you "rock". She should be home soon – David's due to drop her back at lunchtime.'

'I'd better get dressed, then. I don't want to shock your ex.'

While Lexie got dressed, Laura tidied up her paints and went into the house to make lunch. She'd been a bit reluctant when Frank asked her to put Lexie up, and now she was pouring her heart out to the doll-like woman. She smiled to herself. Never judge a book by the cover. Lexie was one of the most sympathetic, smart, sensible people Laura had ever met. Having her around was lovely.

Half an hour later, the kitchen door banged open. Mandy stomped in, flung her bag in the corner and threw herself down on the nearest chair. She was followed by Tanya, who looked furious. Laura put down the salad leaves and wiped her hands on a tea-towel.

'Hi, Tanya, hi, Mandy.'

'Laura, I've had enough of this,' Tanya snapped. 'Your daughter is out of control. You need to teach her some manners or she's not welcome in our home again.'

Laura looked at Mandy. She could see from her daughter's set jaw that she was upset but pretending not to be. 'What happened, Mandy?' she asked.

'I'll tell you exactly what happened.' Tanya stood in front of Laura, shaking a manicured nail in her face. 'Your daughter humiliated me in front of my friend and I won't have it.'

'What do you mean?'

'David had –' Tanya abruptly stopped talking and stared over Laura's shoulder.

'Lexie?' Mandy jumped up. 'What are you doing here?'

Laura turned. Lexie was wearing skin-tight white jeans with a very low-cut red Sequence vest and sky-high red suede shoes.

'All right, Mandy, how are you, darlin'?' Lexie gave the teenager a hug. 'I've come to stay for a little bit. I'm hiding from the paparazzi.'

'Would someone like to fill me in?' Tanya demanded.

'Sorry, Tanya, this is Lexie. She's a client of Frank's. She's going to be staying with us while she finishes her autobiography.'

'Are you Lexie Granger?' Tanya asked.

'The one and only.' Lexie tapped the side of her nose. 'Now, darlin', mum's the word. I don't want you tellin' anyone I'm here. Frank's sent me to Laura to finish my book and stay out of trouble. So you never saw me, *capisce*?'

'I beg your pardon?' Tanya frowned.

'You know, *"capisce"* – it's like in *The Godfather* when Marlon Brando tells everyone, *"Capisce,"* and if they rat him out they get shot.'

'Are you threatening me?' Tanya asked.

'No, darlin', just warning you.' Lexie roared laughing.

Tanya flicked back her freshly blow-dried hair and pulled her beige suede jacket around her. 'I can assure you that no one I know would be remotely interested in your whereabouts.'

'Easy, Stepmum, no need to get your claws out.' Lexie winked at Mandy, who was staring at her adoringly.

Tanya looked at her diamond-encrusted watch. 'I haven't got time for this, and I really don't think someone who bares her breasts for a living is in any position to criticize other people.'

'Relax, babes, I'm just havin' a laugh.'

Tanya scowled at her. 'I'm afraid our sense of humour is very different.' She spun back to face Laura, who was thoroughly enjoying this. 'As I was saying, David had to go into the office so he couldn't take the girls out for the afternoon, as he had promised. I was having the head of the school parents' association over for lunch, so I asked Mandy to watch Mya and Lola for me.'

'Which I did,' Mandy piped up.

'Putting a DVD on does not make you Supernanny,' Tanya retorted.

'She's not their nanny, she's their sister,' Lexie reminded her.

Tanya glared at her. 'Halfway through lunch, Mandy came into the kitchen, when I had specifically asked her not to.'

'Because she doesn't want her "friend" to meet the freaky step-daughter.' Mandy scowled.

'So what happened that was so awful?' Laura enquired.

'My friend, who is an incredible cook, was complimenting me on my delicious quiche and I –'

'She was lapping it up, pretending she'd made it so I fished out the box it came in and started waving it around.' Mandy smirked. Lexie burst out laughing again, while Laura tried to keep a straight face.

'I was mortified!'

'Bit sad to be lying about cooking at your age, love,' Lexie said.

'What I do or do not do is no one else's business.' Tanya folded her arms defensively.

'Well, I'm sure Mandy just thought it was best to be honest.' Laura tried to smooth things over.

Tanya's eyes narrowed. 'Oh, but it gets worse. My friend is very anti-television. She was complaining about the rubbish children watch and how it affects their progress. I was agreeing with her. I don't allow the girls to watch too much TV, just an occasional programme here and there.'

'So I said, "Then how come they've already watched three hours of cartoons this morning?"' Mandy giggled.

'My mum had the telly on mornin', noon and night. I'm surprised I don't have square eyes. Didn't do me no harm. Mind you, my sister's a bit mental but I think that's because she was dropped on her head when she was little, not because of the telly.'

'Can you please stay out of this?' Tanya was getting exasperated with Lexie's constant interruptions. 'The point is, Mandy humiliated me in front of a very important person.'

'Sounds like she was just tellin' the truth to me. You made your own bed, babe, and you had to lie in it.'

'Look, Lexie, or whatever your name is, this is a private conversation between Mandy, her mother and me.'

'No need to get your knickers in a twist.'

Tanya turned to Laura. 'Because of Mandy, this woman now thinks I'm a fraud and a bad mother. My reputation in the school will be ruined. I will not be made a fool of in my own home. I don't think Mandy should visit for a while. She needs to learn how to behave properly.'

'Now, hold on a minute.' Laura was seething. 'All Mandy did was tell the truth, which is what David and I brought her up to do. There is no way you are going to stop her seeing her dad over something so ridiculous.'

Mandy jumped up. 'Dad won't let you keep me away, you freak. No matter how hard you try and how much you wish I'd piss off and disappear, it's never going to happen. I'm going to be around for ever. So get over it.'

'Mandy, language,' Laura scolded.

'Language! Is that all you have to say?' Tanya was incredulous. 'She's a brat. You should start disciplining her before she ends up in prison.'

Lexie shrieked, 'Prison? You need to get out more, darlin'. Half my relations are in prison. I know bad people, and Mandy here is a good girl. She's just windin' you up because your head's stuck up your arse.'

'How dare you speak to me like that?'

'Easy, tiger. I'm just being honest.'

Tanya's eyes narrowed. 'Well, if you value honesty so much, let me tell you this. Mandy is going to end up a delinquent unless Laura does something about it. Her exam results are getting worse each year, she doesn't have any interest in sports, and she's permanently angry and sulky. These are not good qualities and I won't have her dragging my family down. Laura needs to start parenting properly and not indulging her all the time.'

Laura shook a wooden spoon in Tanya's face. 'Don't you dare criticize my daughter or my parenting skills. I'm doing the best I can, and Mandy's a great girl. Like any teenager she has her moments, but that's normal.'

'Normal! There's nothing normal about her or you. Dysfunctional is what you all are.'

Lexie tottered over to Tanya. 'Oi, I won't have you talkin' like that to my Laura. Bloody amazin' is what she is. Brave and strong and kind. You should be thankin' your lucky stars you know her. I've met a lot of people in my day and she is one special lady.'

'Thanks, Lexie.' Laura was touched.

Tanya rolled her eyes. 'I'm leaving now but Mandy is not stepping inside my house until she apologizes for what she did.'

'You don't apologize for honesty.' Laura glared at Tanya. 'Go. I'll discuss this with David.'

'Of course you will because David's a walk-over.'

'No, because David is her father. Goodbye, Tanya.'

Tanya stormed out, almost taking the door off its hinges as she slammed it.

'Blimey, she's a piece of work.' Lexie exhaled.

Mandy exploded, 'I hate her. She's so fake and ridiculous. And she makes me feel unwelcome all the time.'

'She just finds it difficult being a stepmother to a teenager,' Laura soothed her.

'That's her problem, not mine. He was *my dad* before she met him.'

'I know, and he'll always be your dad so you don't have to worry about that.'

Mandy snorted. 'I'm not worried. I just think he has shit taste in women.'

'Hang on a minute, he won the flippin' lotto with your mum,' Lexie reminded her.

'Well, she should have tried to make it work. She should have been nicer to him,' Mandy said.

Laura placed the lettuce in a salad bowl. 'Your dad and I would never have made it as a couple but we've always got on very well as friends.'

Lexie wagged a long red fingernail at Mandy. 'Now you listen to me, darlin'. You're lucky that your parents get on so well. My old pair used to go at it like alley cats, day and night. It was a relief when my dad got put in the nick.'

'Well, I don't feel very lucky. I have a mother who never lets me out of her sight. Who follows me around all the time asking me where I'm going and what time I'll be back, like some kind of prison officer, and a father who's too busy with work and his other kids to give me the time of day.'

'Feeling sorry for ourselves, are we, babes? Let me tell you something. You are a very lucky girl. When I was growin' up, no one gave a damn where I was, who I was with or what I was doing. When the school rang to say I hadn't turned up, my mum said it wasn't her problem. I'd have loved to have a mother who gave a shit and a dad who worked hard instead of one who went around robbin' people at gunpoint. So stop your boo-hoos and start realizing how good you have it.'

Laura could have kissed Lexie, but Mandy looked furious.

'You don't know anything. I hate my life!' she shouted, and stomped up the stairs.

Laura followed her, but by the time she got to her daughter's bedroom, Mandy had locked the door. Laura sank down to the floor. All she wanted was for Mandy to be happy. She felt that was her job. She had let Jody down in the worst way so she wanted Mandy's life to be as perfect as she could make it. When Mandy wanted something, she usually got it. Laura knew she was indulgent, but how could she not be? How could she deny this child anything? She loved her to distraction. Mandy was her life. Mandy was her second chance, and she had made a pact with God to devote herself to her child and make her life as wonderful as she possibly could.

Lexie came up and sat beside her. 'Teenagers are hard going. I was running wild and pregnant at her age.'

'I wasn't much better myself,' Laura admitted.

'She'll be all right. She's got a good family around her.'

Laura leaned her head back against the wall. 'I hope so.'

'It's hard doin' it all on your own. Didn't you never meet any men after David?' Lexie asked.

Laura shook her head. 'No. When Mandy was born I swore I'd be there for her. I didn't want a man to come in and make her feel left out or marginalized. When I saw how difficult she found it after David married Tanya, I knew I was right.'

'Yeah, but you're a gorgeous woman with your whole life ahead of you. Don't rule out love. You deserve to be happy too.'

Laura smiled ruefully. 'I *am* happy, in as much as I'll ever be. I got a second chance. I won't let anyone come between me and Mandy. Ever.'

'You're a saint.'

Laura's eyes were moist. 'Saints don't wake up every day sick with guilt. Only sinners do.'

16.

Sophie

London, June 2011

Holly knocked on the door. 'It's me, open up.'

Sophie let her friend in. She was still in her pyjamas and felt awful. She had spent hours tossing and turning, and when eventually she'd fallen asleep she'd had terrible nightmares. Red was the colour again today – panic. It was so bright it was making her feel nauseous.

Holly was breathless. 'Oh, my God, Sophie, when I woke up I thought I'd dreamed it all but when I walked into the kitchen your mum was standing there talking to mine and it all came flooding back. I nearly fainted when I saw her. I couldn't look her in the face. I just kept thinking, Baby-snatcher. And then I felt bad about it because maybe she didn't steal you. Maybe we got it all wrong.'

Sophie sat down on one of the kitchen chairs. Her legs felt unsteady. 'I don't know what to believe either. I couldn't look at Mum and she kept hovering about in my bedroom, asking if I felt OK. I couldn't bear her to be near me. I just wanted her to go away so I could think.'

Holly put the kettle on. 'She's really worried about you – she thinks you're ill. I said I'd call her later to tell her how you were. You do look sick but I expect that's normal after finding out your mother isn't your mother, that she's actually a stranger who kidnapped you.'

'Thanks, Holly, that's really helpful. Could you be any more insensitive?'

'Sorry! You know me. I was born with foot-in-mouth disease. I promise to tread more carefully. But we need to get to the bottom of this today.'

Sophie could feel her body beginning to shake. 'I don't know if I can handle it. I wish I'd never seen that Laura woman. I wish I didn't know any of this.'

Holly threw her arms into the air theatrically. 'But the truth will set you free.'

'What?'

'You know, Father Boyle was always saying it at school masses. The truth will set you free. I think Jesus or one of his apostle guys said it. It's true, though, it will set you free.'

Sometimes Sophie wondered if Holly was a bit mad. She seemed to live in a parallel universe. She was beginning to annoy her. This was serious: this was her life they were talking about. 'Are you completely insane? How exactly is finding out my mother abducted me going to set me free?'

Holly popped a handful of cornflakes into her mouth. 'Because you'll no longer be living a lie.'

'But I didn't know I *was* living a lie. I was perfectly happy with my life. I didn't have guilt or fear or worry. I was just a normal girl.'

'Nobody wants to be normal. It's boring. I'm not saying that this whole situation isn't terrible for you or that it will be easy to accept, but isn't a tiny bit of you thinking, Wow?'

'No, Holly, not at all!'

Holly put the cereal box down and sighed. 'You don't have to jump down my throat. I'm just trying to cheer you up by seeing the less gloomy side of it. You know, every cloud has a silver lining and all that.'

'This is my identity we're talking about, not some movie.'

'Speaking of movies, though, I could definitely see a film of this being made. I think Scarlett Johansson could play you and Keira Knightley could play me.'

'What? You don't look anything like Keira Knightley.'

Holly bristled. 'Who do I look like?'

Sophie decided to annoy her. 'America Ferrera.'

'Ugly Betty?'

'She's not ugly.'

'The whole programme is named after how ugly she is. You are such a bitch. I'm going home. Good luck finding out who you are!'

Sophie grabbed her arm. 'Come on, Holly, you know you're gorgeous. I was only joking. I was being a bitch because you weren't taking my situation seriously enough. It's not funny to me. Not one bit.'

Holly hugged her. 'I know, Sophie, and I do understand. But you looked so terrified when I came in that I thought I should try to distract you so you didn't have a heart attack or something.'

Sophie smiled. Holly's intentions were always good, even if she tended to go off on tangents.

Holly clapped her hands. 'Right. What's our plan?'

'I think we should start by trying to find clues or evidence.'

'Let's get snooping. Where does your mum keep her papers?'

Sophie had been thinking about it all night. Where did her mother keep her private things? When she was younger she used to sneak into Anna's bedroom and look in her drawers. She didn't know what she was looking for. But the only thing she'd ever found were some photos of her mother's parents and one of her mother with a man, standing arm in arm in front of a house. She'd looked very young and happy. The only thing written on the back of the photo was 1987. It wasn't much to go on.

'I don't know,' Sophie admitted.

'Well, my mum keeps her cigarettes hidden in the back of her wardrobe in an old shoebox, so let's start with your mum's wardrobe,' Holly suggested.

They went upstairs and locked the bedroom door in case Anna decided to come home to check on her daughter.

'You know what you should do?' Holly said, as she opened the wardrobe doors. 'You should text your mum to say you're feeling better so that she doesn't come back.'

'Good idea.' Sophie sent her mother a short text. She received one back immediately – *So glad to hear it. See u later. Call if u need anything. Mum Xx.*

'Excellent. She's off the scent,' Holly said. 'We're free to nose around.'

They spent some time opening and closing shoeboxes, carefully replacing them exactly as they had been.

'Your mum is so tidy!' Holly exclaimed. 'My mum's clothes are thrown everywhere. It would be difficult to hide anything in here.'

'Maybe we're wasting our time. I doubt Mum would leave any clues lying about,' Sophie said.

Holly stood up, hands on hips. 'Excuse me, did Nancy Drew ever give up? Or Sherlock Holmes? Or –'

'OK, I get it, we need to keep going.'

Holly dragged the chair from Anna's dressing-table across to the wardrobe and climbed up to check the top shelf. 'Aha, I've got something!' She pulled a heavy, dusty old box down and handed it to Sophie.

They sat on the floor opposite each other. 'This is it,' Holly said. 'I can feel it in my bones. This box contains the answers.'

With trembling hands Sophie pulled back the cardboard flaps. Inside were photo albums, at least fifteen, and several folders bulging with papers held together with elastic bands. Holly took out one of the albums and opened it. 'Oooooooh!' she said.

'What?' Sophie shut her eyes, afraid to look.

'It's you at my party. You're so cute.'

'*What?* I thought you'd found something terrible.'

Holly turned the photo album towards her friend. 'No, this is just loads of photos of you as a kid.'

Sophie sat beside Holly and they flicked through the pages of album after album. They were filled with pictures of Sophie, hundreds of them. Everything she had ever done had been recorded by her mother and lovingly placed in the albums – Hallowe'ens, Christmases, birthdays, holidays, her first day at St Catherine's, making her Holy Communion with Holly beside her . . . swimming, tennis, hockey, lacrosse . . . trips to museums, art galleries, plays . . . the beach, the countryside, the mountains . . .

'What are these?' Sophie picked up the folders. She opened one. It contained all her old school reports, medical records, essays she had written, paintings she had done, ticket stubs from the first movie they'd been to, from her first trip to Madame Tussaud's, her first plane ticket . . .

'Seriously, Sophie, this is incredible,' Holly said, leafing through the paperwork. 'My mum throws all our stuff out. She says it clutters the house. This box is a shrine to you. Look at how carefully she kept everything. It's so nice. Your whole life is here in front of you. I don't know anyone else whose mother would do this.'

Sophie began to cry. Holly was right: who else would care about these details? Who else would keep a ticket from her first movie? Who else would take hundreds of pictures of her and file them away so carefully?

Holly leaned over and gave her a hug. 'Whatever she did to get you, she's been a devoted mother.'

Sophie nodded, blew her nose and wiped her eyes.

Holly sighed. 'There's no question that she adores you. You're her whole life.'

'I know, but if she took me, that's wrong.'

'Yes, it's the Eighth Commandment.'

'What?'

'Didn't you listen to anything in religion class for the last thirteen years? The eighth commandment is "Thou shalt not steal."'

'Since when did you get so holy?'

'Since Father James taught us. You know I fancied him.'

'Urgh, Holly, your taste in men is so weird. He's so old – he must be thirty-five.'

Holly shrugged. 'I can't help it. Older men do it for me.'

'He's a priest!'

'That's the whole point. He's unavailable. I want to use my sexual powers to tear him away from his vows.'

'Seriously, Holly, you're watching way too much TV. You sound like a bad reality-TV star.'

She jumped up. 'Take that back!'

'You do! And reality TV is such rubbish.'

'I love the Kardashians. They feel like friends to me now.'

Sophie groaned. 'That is so sad.'

'I can't help it. I love the show.'

Sophie sighed. 'Is there any chance we could get back to my reality now? I need you to focus on this.'

Holly sat down again. 'OK. We think your mum did something bad but we can't find any proof. All we have here are the signs of a devoted mother.'

Sophie felt her heart beginning to lighten. 'And if the baby pictures did burn in a fire, then maybe this is just a mix-up. A case of two babies who just happen to look like each other.'

'Exactly,' Holly agreed.

Sophie fished in the box to see if there was anything else at the bottom. That was when she pulled it out. The blanket. The pink blanket with the elephant on it. The same blanket the child was holding in the picture on Laura's website. She gasped.

Holly grabbed her by the shoulders. 'Don't panic, Sophie. We need to get your laptop and look at that picture again. We may have been mistaken. Lots of baby blankets look the same.'

Holly unlocked the door, ran into her friend's bedroom, grabbed the laptop, came back in and relocked the door. They logged on to Laura Fletcher's website and looked at the picture. The child in the photo was the image of Sophie. The two friends examined the blanket the child was holding. It looked the same: pink with an elephant. The little girl was sucking the corner of it, just like Sophie was in the photo of her at Holly's second birthday party. There was no denying it: this child was Sophie and Sophie was this child.

They sat in silence, staring at the screen.

'You could have been switched,' Holly suggested. 'I saw this movie where the babies had been switched by mistake when they were born, and years later one of them got sick and then they realized that her blood type was different from her parents' and that she was someone else's kid.'

Sophie put her hand up. 'Holly, there is no other baby. There's just me. I can't have been swapped. I'm the same person.' She began to hyperventilate.

Holly held her hands. 'Look at me, Sophie. Please don't have a panic attack. Breathe slowly in and out . . . there you go. We need to think clearly. We need to be very careful.'

'It explains so much,' Sophie puffed. 'Why Mum is always so overprotective. Why she never went back to Ireland. Why my dad was always this shadowy figure, who actually never existed. Why she has no baby pictures. Why she didn't understand my synaesthesia. Why she never stayed in touch with anyone from her past, except Joe.' She sat upright. 'God, I wonder if Joe knows. How could he? How could he keep a secret like this?'

'Maybe he doesn't. Your mum is very secretive. But I must say it does explain why she used to go so crazy if you were even five minutes late coming home. I asked my mum about it one day and she said, "Anna's just like that because Sophie is all she has. Her life would fall apart if anything happened to Sophie. Whereas if one of you died I'd still have two left." Then I asked her which child she'd mind dying the least and she refused to answer, but she did smile when I said I bet it was Jessie.'

Sophie paced the room, up and down, up and down. She couldn't think straight. 'How could my mum do this?'

'I'm even more shocked than when you told me Ricky Martin was gay. I'd always fancied myself as Mrs Holly Martin, wife of the very famous, very sexy and incredibly rich Ricky. Besides, your mum is such an upstanding citizen. She's the headmistress of a Catholic girls' school, for goodness' sake. She couldn't be any more conservative! There has to be a good explanation.'

Sophie wrung her hands. 'Well, what is it, Holly? Tell me, why would she do such a terrible thing?'

'Mum always says when someone behaves out of character, there is a definite reason for it. Something must have happened or she saw a bad thing or, I don't know, maybe Laura beat you or was a bad mother. Maybe she was too busy painting to raise you or had no money or something.'

'I have to find out. I have to know what's going on. Oh, God, Holly, who am I? What am I? A fraud? Everything's –'

Holly stood up and stopped Sophie in her tracks. Looking directly into her eyes, she said, 'You are you. You're still Sophie, the same person you were yesterday, just with a slightly psychotic mother . . . or mothers.'

But Sophie wasn't the same person. She was confused, terrified, furious. All she could see was a rainbow of colours, all mixing together – red and orange and yellow. She glared at Holly. 'I have to know the truth. I have to know what happened. I'm going to get in touch with Laura.'

Holly squealed, 'Have you lost your mind? You can't just call her up and say, "Hey, Laura, how are you? It's your daughter here, the one everyone said drowned." The woman will die of shock on the spot. Besides, you don't know what kind of person she is. She could be a terrible human being.'

'I'm going to send her an email. There's a contact email here for her studio.'

'What are you going to say?'

Sophie bit her nail. 'I don't know. Help me, Holly. I need to word it carefully.'

'You're the clever one!'

Sophie took a deep breath. 'I'll just –'

Holly screamed. Someone was trying to push the door open. Sophie grabbed the box and flung it behind the bed.

'Mum, is that you?' she called.

'What are you weirdos doing in there? Are you lesbians? Are you having lesbian sex?' Jessie asked.

'You little shit, you almost gave me a heart attack.' Holly let in her younger sister.

Jessie looked around suspiciously. 'Why was the door locked?'

'Excuse me,' Holly poked her in the chest, 'I'll ask the questions. What the hell are you doing in this house? How did you get in?'

'Mum told me to come and check on you. The back door was open so I walked in. You're lucky I wasn't some serial killer or rapist.'

'Go home. Tell Mum we're fine.'

'You don't look fine. You look all guilty and secretive. Have you been drinking in here? Can I have some?'

Sophie finally found her voice: 'No, we haven't. Now, Jessie, please go. Tell your mum I'm fine and Holly's fine. We're just doing some work on my computer.'

'So why did you lock the door? Are you looking at porn? Are you on lesbian porn sites?' Jessie lunged for the laptop. Sophie snapped it shut on her chubby fingers.

'Ouch. You really hurt me, Sophie. I think you've broken my finger.'

'Sorry, but you shouldn't be so nosy. It's rude.'

'I've obviously touched a nerve. I always knew you were lesbians.'

'Shut up, you fat, ugly cow. The only lesbian here is you because no guy will go near you,' Holly snapped.

Jessie lashed out, 'At least I'm not stupid. At least I'm not going to university to dig fields.'

'At least I'll have a social life that doesn't revolve around eating pies,' Holly told her.

'You bitch! I've lost two pounds.'

'Bravo. Only three stone to go.'

'I'd rather be a tiny bit overweight than thick.'

'A tiny bit overweight?' Holly shrieked. 'You need to staple your mouth shut.'

Jessie jumped on top of her sister. 'I'm going to kill you.'

'Help me, Sophie! She'll crush me to death,' Holly pleaded.

Sophie pulled Jessie back.

Jessie was livid. 'I'm going. You two are being total psychos.'

'Goodbye,' Holly said, and pushed her sister out of the door, which she locked again.

'I'm going to tell Mum you're up to no good,' Jessie shouted, from the landing.

'Oh, really? Well, I'll tell her about the cigarettes I found under your mattress,' Holly retorted.

'I hate you!' Jessie shrieked.

They heard her stomping back down the stairs.

'God, my heart.' Sophie sat down on the bed. 'I thought it was Mum!'

'It was a very close call. Look, if you want to send this email we'd better hurry up. It's almost three and she'll be home from school soon.'

'How about "Dear Ms Fletcher, this email may come as a surprise to you but I think I may be your lost daughter, Jody."'

Holly started giggling hysterically.

'It's not funny!'

'Sorry, it's all just so . . . bizarre and crazy. Why don't you say something like "Dear Ms Fletcher, Guess who? I'm alive!"'

'Stop it!' Sophie was laughing despite herself.

'It's nervous hysteria.'

'You're supposed to be supporting me. Your job here is to be the strong, sensible one. I'm the one who should be hysterical.'

'You're right.' Holly went into Sophie's bedroom and came back with the scanner. She sat down, pulled the computer on to her lap and began to type. 'OK, I think you should say this: "Dear Ms Fletcher, My name is Sophie Roberts, I'm eighteen years old and I live in London. I saw your interview on BBC TV yesterday and was shocked by how similar we are. I have synaesthesia too. When I heard about your baby daughter who went missing and saw her picture I got a fright because it looks so much like me when I was a baby. I don't know what this means. I'm very confused. I am attaching a picture of me when I was almost two. I think if you look at the photo you'll understand why I felt I had to get in touch. You'll see even the blanket is the same. I haven't said anything about this to anyone, I'm too freaked out. Please don't think I'm a stalker. I'm just a normal girl who had a normal life . . . until yesterday."'

Holly finished typing and looked up.

Sophie patted her friend's shoulder. 'It's perfect. Thanks, Holly.'

'See? I'm a good friend, detective and partner in crime. I just have a tendency to giggle when I'm nervous but I'll work on that.'

'Should I send it?' Sophie was having second thoughts. What if Laura was a nutter, an abuser, an alcoholic, a drug addict, a liar, a murderer even? There had to be a reason why her mum had taken her. But when she had seen Laura in that interview she had felt a strong connection with her, and she had seemed normal.

'Yes,' Holly said, scanning Sophie's baby photo in so they could attach it. 'You have to send it. You can't ignore it. You need to know. Are you ready?'

Sophie nodded and pressed send.

17.

Anna

London, June 2011

When Anna got to school the next day there was a pile of messages on her desk. Mrs Kirkwood, the infants teacher, popped her head around the door to remind Anna that she was due to speak to the class at ten.

Every year, before school broke up for the summer holidays, Anna went to speak to all the classes individually, from the infants to the final-year students. It was a tradition she had started when she first became headmistress. She liked seeing the girls in small groups to have a chat about their year in school and wish them well on their long summer break.

She knocked on the infants' door and walked into the classroom. Sixteen little girls looked up at her.

'Now, girls, as a special treat, Mrs Roberts has come to talk to you all about how you got on this year and what you're going to do in the summer holidays,' Mrs Kirkwood informed them.

Anna smiled at their expectant faces and asked them to come and sit on the floor with her in a big circle.

'Well, girls, how has this year been for you? It's not easy starting big school and having to wear a uniform, is it? And the school day can seem long sometimes, can't it?'

They all nodded.

'Let's go around the circle and ask everyone to talk about what they thought of school this year.' Anna looked at the little girl to her right. 'I'll start so you can see what I mean. My name is Mrs

Roberts and this year was a good year for me but very busy. I'm glad the summer holidays are coming up because I'm tired and I'm looking forward to a break. I'm going on holidays with my daughter Sophie – you may know her. She's one of the final-year students here.'

Anna looked to the little girl on her right. 'Now it's your turn.'

'My name is Georgiana and I'm five and three-quarters and I'm very happy to have holidays soon. I'm going to France with my mummy and my brother Johnathan. He's seven and he's mean to me – he pulls my hair quite a lot. Mummy says it's all the testostreown in his body and that I must ignore him but it's hard when he hurts me. Daddy was supposed to come to France too, but he moved into a new house with Jenny, who used to be his secretary. Mummy has sad eyes all the time now and when she sees Daddy she keeps shouting about Jenny being a tart.'

'Like an apple tart?' another little girl wondered.

Georgiana shrugged. 'I'm not sure. It could be rhubarb. Mummy hates rhubarb.'

Anna thanked Georgiana and moved on to the next child. 'My name's Clara and I'm five and a half and I don't like school because it's too long and boring. I'm going to Spain with my family and our au-pair. Her name is Natasha and she comes from a country that sounds like the Crane.'

'Ukraine?' Anna asked.

'Yes, that's it. Mummy says Natasha needs to pull up her socks because otherwise she'll have to go back to the Crane. I pull up my socks every morning when I get dressed because I don't want Mummy to send me to the Crane with Natasha.'

'Good for you.' Anna tried not to laugh.

The next girl spoke up: 'My name is Nathalie and I speak French at home and English in school. We are going home to France for the summer. Maman says that she can't wait to get back to Bordeaux. She thinks English people are very strange because they talk about the weather all day. Maman says it's boring to talk about the weather. She says we should be talking about filo-sophie and litter-ture. She says the women here put on too much lipstick and clothes that are very tight so they can't breathe and shoes that are too high so they can't walk. Maman says that English women are not chic. She says they are very show-offy and wear all their jewels all the time, even at breakfast! Maman says that it's vulgar.'

'I see. Well, that's a very interesting insight.' Anna exchanged glances with Mrs Kirkwood, who was chuckling behind her hand.

'My mummy says that your mummy is rude,' a little girl with plaits piped up.

'Rebecca, no telling tales,' Mrs Kirkwood warned.

'I'm not telling tales. My mummy said that Nathalie's mummy is very condersending and that she needs to remember that the French are a bunch of cheese-eating sur-ender monkeys.'

'Maman is not a monkey! And monkeys eat bananas, not cheese, you idiot.' Nathalie pouted like a true Frenchwoman.

'I am not an idiot –'

'Let's move on, shall we?' Anna suggested, pointing to the next girl.

'My name is Amelia and we're not going on holiday this year because my daddy was made dundant.'

'What does that mean?' Georgiana asked.

'Um, well, Mummy said that he doesn't have a job any more and that his cheeks are bouncing all over the city.'

'Bouncing cheeks? That's funny.' Clara giggled.

'Mummy said if Daddy doesn't get a new job soon I'll have to go to a coppenhensif school.'

'Ooooooooooh.' All the girls looked horrified.

'The children in those schools are crazy,' Georgiana said.

'Now, girls,' Anna interrupted, 'comprehensive schools are perfectly good. But, Amelia, I don't want you to worry about going to a new school. You will always be welcome here. I'll talk to your mummy.'

'A boy got killed in a coppenhensif school,' Clara said. 'Another boy got a knife and killed him in the classroom and there was blood everywhere and the police came and put the other boy in prison for infinity days.'

'I don't want to go there.' Amelia looked terrified.

'And the girls pull your hair and kick you and punch –'

'That's enough, Clara,' Anna said firmly. 'Most comprehensive schools are very good, and that was just a most unfortunate incident. Anyway, as I said, Amelia doesn't have to worry about going to one next year.'

'I'm going to Ireland on my holiday,' a sweet little girl with long black hair announced.

'That's nice.' Anna smiled at her.

'I hate going to Ireland,' the little girl admitted.

'Why?' Anna asked.

'Because my granny lives in a little village and all the kids make fun of how I talk and my granny makes me eat yucky food, like cabbage and pudding.'

'I love pudding!' Amelia said.

'It's not pudding like we have here. It's like a long lumpy black sausage and my cousin told me it's made from pigs' blood!'

'Yuck.' The little girls made gagging noises.

Anna laughed. 'My mother used to try to get me to eat black pudding but I never liked it either.'

'It makes me want to be sick but my granny gets really cross with me if I don't eat it. She says that millions of people in Ireland died because they had no food when the potatoes went all black and I'm lucky to have food to eat and that it's a sin not to eat it.'

'Maybe you should talk to your mummy about it?' Anna suggested.

'I did, and she said she thinks it's yucky too and she wishes Daddy was from France and not Ireland so that we could eat *foie gras* and have sunny days.'

'My granny's Irish and she gives me sweets and chocolate and never makes me eat yucky food,' another girl said. 'But Mummy was cross with her after the last holiday because I had to have a filling in my tooth when I came back.'

'Oh, no, poor you.' Anna was sympathetic.

'Mummy was furious and said Granny was naughty because Mummy asked her not to give me sweets. Then Granny said she was only trying to be nice and Daddy told Mummy to leave Granny alone, and Mummy told Daddy to crawl back under the rock he came from, which is funny because babies come from their mummies' tummies, not rocks, don't they?'

'Yes, pet,' Anna agreed.

'No!' A tiny little girl jumped up. 'If you're adopted, like me, then you come from Vietnam. My mummy and daddy got me in a special hotel where God keeps all the best babies in the world. When they saw me they knew I was their heart baby. Mummy says it's better to be adopted because you're more specialer than other children.'

'Well, that's a lovely way of putting it.' Anna beamed at her. She was right, because that was exactly how she felt about Sophie: she was her heart baby.

When Anna got home, she found Sophie in her bedroom on her laptop. She slammed it shut when Anna walked in.

'God, Mum, you gave me a fright.'

'Sorry. How are you feeling?'

'Better.'

'Good. Are you hungry? I could heat up the lasagne from last night.'

'OK.'

Anna and Sophie went down to the kitchen. Sophie set the table while Anna heated the lasagne and made a salad.

When they sat down to eat, Anna asked Sophie what she had done all day.

'Why?'

'What do you mean "why"? I'm your mother. I'm interested in knowing what you spent your day doing.'

'Nothing. Holly came over and we just hung out.'

'Good. You needed a day resting.'

Sophie didn't answer.

'Well, only ten days to go and we'll be in France. I can't wait.' Anna smiled at her daughter.

Sophie prodded her lasagne with her fork. 'You know the fire?'

Anna frowned. 'What fire?'

'The fire in which all my baby photos were burned.'

Anna stared at her. Where had this come from? She took a breath. 'Yes. What about it?'

'Where was it?'

'In Dublin.'

'I know that, but where?'

'I told you. In the house I lived in, close to the centre.'

'So did the whole place burn down?'

'Yes.'

'How come you've still got the photos of your mum and dad?'

Anna could feel her ulcer burning. 'Because I had them in my bag. Why are you asking all these questions?'

'Because I'm interested. I want to know more about my past. What's so strange about that?'

'Nothing.'

'Why do you not like me asking questions?'

Anna knew it was imperative that she stay calm and appear unfazed. 'I don't mind at all. It's fine.'

Sophie speared a piece of cucumber. 'Why do we never go back to Ireland?'

'I've told you before. I don't have anyone to go back to and it just reminds me of my parents and their loss.'

'I'd like to visit their graves. I'd like to see where you grew up and went to school and all that.'

'It's not important and a graveyard is no place for a young girl. They're very gloomy and depressing. Now, come on, eat up.'

Sophie ignored her. 'But you must have some friends in Ireland that you'd like to see.'

Anna put her fork down. 'I have Joe.'

'Apart from Joe.'

'Look, Sophie, I left Ireland because I was unhappy. I came to London to get away from it all and I've been incredibly happy here. I don't see the point in going back. My life is here, with you.' She reached out for Sophie's hand, but her daughter pulled away.

'Who was there when I was born?'

Anna's ulcer blazed. 'I told you, just my mother.'

'Why did you call me Sophie?'

'You know it's because it was my mother's name. What is all this about?'

Sophie glared at her. 'What's wrong? Can't I ask a few questions about my life and my childhood without you freaking out?'

Anna gripped the table. 'I'm not freaking out,' she lied.

'Good, because I have more questions for you.'

'Fine.'

'What did my dad look like?'

'He looked like you. Blond, blue eyes, pale skin.'

'What else?'

'I've said this before, Sophie. I'm not proud of it but my relationship with your father was just a fling.'

'A one-night stand?'

'Well, yes.'

Sophie rapped her fingers on the table. 'Weren't you surprised that I didn't look anything like you when I was born?'

'Lots of children look like their fathers or vice versa.'

'What about my synaesthesia? Isn't it strange that no one in your family had it?'

'Not really. You obviously got that from your dad too.'

Sophie shook her head. 'You have answers for everything, haven't you, Mum?'

Anna wanted desperately to ask where this was going, where it had come from and what had sparked it, but she was too scared. Why was Sophie behaving like this? Why was she suddenly so interested in her past? Her ulcer flared and scorched in her abdomen.

Despite her best efforts to remain poised, tears sprang to her eyes. 'Sophie, pet, all I can tell you is that, despite being the result of a brief affair, you are the most wonderful thing ever to happen to me. I thank God every day that I met your dad. I'm the luckiest person in the world. You mean everything to me.'

Sophie stood up. 'Stop it, Mum – OK? Just stop it.'

'What?'

'It's too much. I can't breathe. You're smothering me.' Sophie stormed out of the kitchen, ran upstairs to her bedroom and locked herself in.

Anna rushed up after her. She leaned her head against the door. 'Sophie, darling, I love you. That's all you really need to know. I'm sorry I can't tell you more about your father, but I've tried to be the best mum I can be to make up for him not being around.'

Silence.

'Sophie, are you OK? Please talk to me. You're scaring me, you seem so stressed.'

'I'm fine. I need sleep – I'm exhausted.'

'Is there anything I can do to help?'

'Please just go away.'

'I'm worried.'

'I'm fine. I'm OK. Just go.'

Anna stayed at the door for a while. There were no sounds from inside. She went into her bedroom and took some tablets to help the piercing pain in her stomach.

She lay down on her bed and forced herself to breathe slowly. What was going on? Why was Sophie behaving like this? Could she have found something to make her suspicious? Anna had been so careful. It must be about her dad. Maybe now she had finished school and was about to go to college she wanted to know more about who she was. Anna hoped she wasn't going to interrogate her regularly – she couldn't handle it. She had suppressed the doubts and the worry. They were buried deep inside her and that was where they needed to stay.

Her phone rang and she jumped. It was Joe. 'Hey there! How's it going? I'm calling to finalize our holiday plans. I've finally got Mark to commit. He's going to come for the week in Provence.'

'Oh, right, yes.'

'Anna, could you try to sound enthusiastic?'

Anna peeled her eyes away from Sophie's locked door. 'Sorry, I'm thrilled, honestly. I'm just having a bad day.'

'Is your ulcer playing up?'

'Horrendously.'

'What happened?'

'It's Sophie,' she whispered. 'She's been acting strangely the last day or so and tonight at dinner she started interrogating me.'

'About what?'

'About my past and why I never go back to Ireland and why I have no baby pictures of her and a lot about who her dad is.'

Joe exhaled deeply. 'I told you this would happen, Anna. All kids eventually want to know more.'

Anna closed her eyes. So many lies, so much deceit . . .

'I know you're sick of me saying it, but you really need to tell her the truth. She has to know that she was adopted. I knew this would come back to haunt you. You may believe that keeping the truth from her was for her benefit, but it doesn't make it right. She's old enough to know what really happened.'

Anna began to cry. 'She's mine, Joe. She's not someone else's, she's mine. I saved her. I gave her a good life. I'm her mother.'

'Of course you are,' Joe soothed. 'You're the only parent she's ever known. You're not going to lose her by telling her she's adopted. I know it's frightening for you – all adoptive parents feel this way – but you mustn't get yourself into a state. I've seen the way Sophie looks at you and she adores you.'

Anna wiped away mascara-streaked tears. 'I love her so much, Joe. I don't want anything coming in and interfering with our lives.'

'Whatever happens, she'll never stop thinking of you as her real mother. You're the one who changed her nappies and nursed her when she was sick and kissed her when she fell over. You're her mum in every way, so stop worrying.'

Anna's head pounded. She couldn't think straight. 'Thanks, Joe. Look, I'd better go. I'm so glad Mark's coming on holidays – Sophie will be thrilled. I can't wait to see you both.'

'Hey, look after yourself and don't worry too much – you'll aggravate the ulcer. Call me anytime, day or night, if you're worried about Sophie. I'm here for you, Anna, you know that.'

'Thanks, Joe. That means a lot.'

'Get some rest. See you in two weeks.'

''Bye, Joe.'

Anna hung up. Her mind was racing. She needed to banish the fears: she had to distract herself, calm down. She did what she always did on bad days: she got the box down from the top of her wardrobe and looked at the photos.

As she turned the pages of the first album she felt her heart rate slowing. It was like magic. She looked at Sophie's smiling face, radiating out from the pages, a happy, contented, cherished child.

My Sophie. My baby girl. My daughter. Mine.

18

Laura

Killduf, July 2011

Lexie sat cross-legged in front of Mandy. They were in the lounge. Laura was sitting at her computer, under the arch in the kitchen, looking through a pile of paperwork and a long list of emails.

'Go on, darlin', I'm all ears.' Lexie was urging Mandy to sing.

'I'm too embarrassed. My stuff's crap.'

'I bet it's brilliant. Your mum said so.'

Mandy threw her eyes to the ceiling. 'Mum says everything I do is brilliant. It doesn't mean anything.'

'My mum told me I'd never amount to anything. I'd have liked a bit of praise. Now, go on, don't make me beg.'

'All right, but don't laugh, OK? Promise?'

'Mandy, I got me boobs out for a living. I'm in awe of anyone with a real talent. Get on with it before my arse goes numb.'

Mandy bent over her guitar. Her fringe fell over her eyes, hiding them from her audience. Laura peeped around the corner and smiled. Good old Lexie. She was brilliant with Mandy, bringing her out of herself and reminding her constantly how lucky she was. Laura had half a mind to ask her to move in permanently.

'This song is called "Trapped In A World I Didn't Create And Want To Dissipate".'

'Sounds like a barrel of laughs,' Lexie remarked.

Laura stifled a giggle.

'It's about my life,' Mandy mumbled.

Lexie clapped her hands. 'I can't wait to hear it. Off you go.'

Mandy closed her eyes and began to strum . . .

I was born into a family of dysfunction, it's hard to function.
Sometimes I feel as if I'm in a prison, new thoughts arisen.
I long to break away and start a new day.
But my mother stalks me, she lost my sister see,
She can't let go of me, it's family history.
But I'm sick of paying,
The stress is weighing me down.
Oh yeah, oh yeah, weighing me down,
Oh yeah oh yeah, down down down.
Until my forehead is nothing but a frown,
Oh no oh no, nothing but a frown.
Wait for this, it gets more glum,
You see I've got a stepmum.
She's a selfish be-ach and I wish she would catch
A horrible disease that would make her wheeze
And stop breathing and die. I wouldn't cry.
I'd be over the moon, it couldn't happen too soon,
I dream about it all the time, her living is a crime,
Her death will come, she'll be nothing but a crumb,
Oh yeah oh yeah, nothing but a crumb . . . crumb . . . cruuuuuuuuumb.'

Mandy howled out the last word.

'Well I never!' Lexie exclaimed. 'You don't hold back, do you? Poor old Tanya, I almost feel sorry for her.' She chuckled. 'I'd say her ears are burning. Have you played this song for your dad?'

'No, he'd kill me. For some reason he thinks Tanya's great.'

'There's no accountin' for taste. Maybe I should write a song about Dougie being a cheatin' tosser. Do you get a lot of anger out when you sing? You was really gettin' into it there, shoutin' out the words and all.'

Mandy flicked her black fringe out of her eyes. 'Yeah, I do. I guess it's a form of therapy for me.'

'That's great, darlin'. People should do whatever makes 'em feel good. That's my motto.'

Mandy lowered her voice. 'I'm hoping to do this full time

when I finish school. I haven't told Mum or Dad yet. They'll freak. But I really feel that music is my destiny.'

Laura winced. Mandy's future definitely did not lie in music. And there was no way in hell she was going to be allowed to miss out on college. Both she and David wanted her to have three years in university to study, grow up and mature before heading out into the world. Laura couldn't even think about Mandy leaving home without feeling nauseous.

Lexie nodded slowly. 'Right, I see. It might be a good idea to have a back-up plan, though, just in case it don't work out. It's tough out there, babe.'

'I know, but true talent always succeeds,' said the confident musician.

'Yes, but sometimes people don't recognize talent straight away. So maybe you should go to university and keep singing on the side.'

'It's a waste of time. Why should I spend three years studying something that I won't need when I could be changing the world with my music?'

'What about doing a business course so you don't get screwed by your record company?'

Mandy smiled. 'I've thought about that. I'm going to get Frank to be my manager.'

Laura chuckled to herself. Frank would insist that Mandy go to college before he'd consider representing her.

'It seems like you have it all sorted.' Lexie was running out of ideas. 'Have you recorded yourself yet? Have you actually heard yourself singing?'

Mandy shook her head. 'Not yet. I need to get the songs finalized first.'

'Might be an idea to do it. It'll give you a feel for what you sound like. You might find you want to tweak it a bit.'

'Maybe, but I doubt it. I'm happy with my sound. I feel it's unique,' Mandy explained.

'Oh, it's unique, all right, darlin'. I never heard anything like it.

Is it just you on your own?' Lexie asked. 'No other band members?'

'My friend Caroline was with me for a while, but she kept wanting to write happy songs about being in love and fancying boys. It was really fluffy, upbeat stuff that no one wants to hear. Who does she think I am? Kylie?'

Lexie tried not to laugh. Mandy looked about as different from Kylie as you could get. She was tall and athletic, except she hunched over all the time, as if she was ashamed of her height. She had jet black hair cut into a short, jagged bob and brown eyes, constantly rimmed with black eyeliner.

'I got into music to write songs that other people can relate to. Deep songs about life,' Mandy explained.

'And disease and death,' Lexie noted.

'Totally. Things that matter.'

'I wish you the best of luck with it all.' Lexie smiled at the intense teenager. Mandy was just a big bundle of hormonal emotion. 'Can I give you one little piece of advice?'

'Of course.'

'All successful musicians write about love. It's the most powerful emotion of 'em all. Just think about it.'

Mandy nodded. 'I will. Thanks.'

'Haven't you ever been in love? Fancied a boy in your class or in the village or something?' Lexie wondered.

Laura held her breath. She wanted to hear this.

Mandy blushed. 'Well, not really. I mean, kind of.'

'Go on, tell your auntie Lexie.'

Mandy squirmed. 'There's a guy in my guitar class who's kind of cool.'

'What's his name?'

'Johnny.'

'Details, please. Blond or dark?'

'Blond with blue eyes, which is so not my type. I always fancy dark, broody guys.'

'I always liked the blonds myself. Go on, what's he like?'

'He's really friendly.'

'Oh, is he, now?' Lexie giggled.

'Not just to me, to everyone,' Mandy said. 'He's like that, you know, friendly.'

'He sounds lovely.'

'It's weird, though, because he's the opposite to what I normally go for. He's very smiley and happy. I usually like moody outsiders, you know – tortured souls –'

'Now you listen to me,' Lexie interrupted. 'I grew up surrounded by tortured souls and they are a world of trouble. All they think about is themselves. They'll suck you dry and spit you out. Mark my words, you want a nice, happy chap who'll make you laugh. Life is difficult enough without some grumpy dickhead with a chip on his shoulder dragging you down. This Johnny sounds perfect. Now, you need to go easy on the black eyeliner and smile a bit more or you'll scare him off. You're very pretty when you smile. You remind me a bit of that actress – you know, the one who was in that film with Johnny Depp where his hands was scissors.'

'Winona Ryder?' Mandy gasped.

'Yes, that's the one. You look like her.'

'Really? Or are you taking the piss?'

'No! I'm deadly serious.' Lexie took her hand. 'Come upstairs with me. I want to do your makeup for you. If we scrub off some of that black liner, you might be able to see your lovely eyes. I'll also give you a few tips on how to hook a man. Rule number one: eye contact. We might have to trim that fringe of yours an' all.'

Laura sat back down at her desk and smiled. Lexie was so good for Mandy. She was able to draw her out and say all the things Laura longed to say. Somehow everything Laura said just seemed to irritate Mandy instead of helping her. This Johnny sounded lovely. She'd have to make up some excuse to go in with Mandy to her next guitar lesson and have a look at him.

Beep. Another email came into Laura's inbox. It was time to

tackle all the messages and the bills she had let pile up. Laura hated all technology. She knew it was a necessary evil, but she found mobile phones, computers and video games very noisy. She liked peace and quiet. She liked calm. She liked to hear the sound of the waves lapping on the sand, not the pinging of her computer when she received new emails or her phone blaring out the awful ring-tone Mandy had changed it to. When she was in her studio she left her laptop and her phone in the house. She had a land line in there for emergencies, but only three people had the number: Mandy, Frank and Joan.

Laura's days were spent painting to the sound of nature or gentle, soothing music. But every Friday afternoon she forced herself to deal with her emails. Otherwise they backed up and then she found herself spending hours trying to answer them all. Frank told her to keep on top of them. He said she had to get back to people without too much delay. He reminded her that she wasn't just an artist, she was also a self-employed business-woman, who had to reply to queries from galleries, potential clients or investors.

While Mandy and Lexie were upstairs occupied with makeup lessons, Laura forced herself to plough through her inbox, answering requests for interviews, giving advice to aspiring artists, updates to clients, and replying to the nice ones from galleries telling her they had sold her work. She was about to log out when one final email came through: Sophie Roberts. It was bound to be another aspiring artist looking for advice. Laura was tempted to leave it until next week. She glanced at the clock: she had plenty of time before starting dinner. She opened the email . . .

Her coffee cup smashed into a thousand pieces on the floor.

She stuffed her hand into her mouth to stop herself screaming. Her body went into shock. The picture attached to the email was of Jody, her baby, her little girl, her angel, her firstborn, her lost child. Jody with her blanket. The blanket Joan had bought her with the elephant on it. She was sucking the corner. Jody! Same hair, same eyes, same mouth, same chubby fingers. It was her. It was Jody. What was this girl's name – Sophie? Oh, my God, was this it? Was this the day she had been waiting for, praying for? Was this girl Jody? Or did she just have a picture of her?

Calm down, she ordered herself. Read the email again. No, it wasn't a hoax. It was real. She knew it – she'd always known it. Blue: all she could see was bright aqua blue. Oh, the joy!

But how? Who? The girl said London. Who had taken her there? Was she OK? She sounded OK. Oh, Jesus. Laura's heart was pounding. She had to call someone. She needed help with this. There was only one person: Frank.

She dialled his number with trembling fingers.

'Frank!' was all she said.

'What's wrong?'

'I have to see you.'

'Are you sick?'

'No.'

'Is it Mandy?'

'No, no, we're fine, I can't explain. Meet me in Johnston's Hotel – it's the nearest place to both of us. Drive as fast as you can. Bring your iPad.'

Laura printed the email out and made sure to turn her computer off. She wrote a note but her hands were shaking so much it was almost illegible – *Back in an hour or so*. She ran out to her car, drove like a maniac to the hotel and waited impatiently for Frank.

While she waited, she read the email over and over again, devouring every word. Trying to read between the lines. Trying to understand. The girl sounded so polite, and she said she had synaesthesia too. How amazing was that. Jody had synaesthesia. Or was it Jody? Could it really be her? Laura was too scared to believe it, too afraid to hope. The girl had said she hadn't told anyone – who did she mean? Was she in an orphanage? A home? Did she have parents? Was she being looked after?

She'd said she had a normal life. What did that mean? What's normal? Oh, God. Laura's head was whirling. Colours were flashing in front of her eyes, orange, green, beige and blue – beautiful, joyful blue.

Frank's car hurtled to a stop outside the hotel. Laura ran out to him. She grabbed his arms.

'JODY'S ALIVE!' she shouted. 'SHE'S ALIVE!'

Frank stopped in his tracks. 'WHAT? Laura, calm down, talk to me. What's going on?'

Laura laughed wildly. 'I haven't gone mad. It's true, Frank.' She pulled him into a corner of the hotel lobby and handed him the email.

Frank read it. 'Jesus, Laura, this doesn't mean anything. She could be some nutter. You must calm down.'

'No no no no!' Laura was becoming hysterical. 'Look at the picture, quickly, open up my email. You'll understand when you see it. Hurry, Frank, hurry. It's my baby, it's my Jody.' Laura fell back on to a couch and began to sob as the magnitude of the news sank in.

Frank took out his iPad and logged on to Laura's Hotmail account. He opened the photo attachment. The child was the image of Jody. He read the email again.

Laura was gripping his arm. 'You see, Frank? You see?'

'OK, hold on a second. We mustn't jump to conclusions.' He tried to remain calm. Laura was hysterical. He needed to be measured, careful. This was explosive news. He had to protect Laura. It could be a hoax.

'It's her, Frank, I know it is. Didn't I tell you? Didn't I always tell you she was alive? I knew my Jody didn't drown. She's come back to me! She's come back!' Laura buried her face in her hands. She was completely overwhelmed.

Frank leaned over and hugged her tightly. She sobbed into his shoulder. 'Hey there, it's OK. You've had a huge shock. Now, listen to me, we're going to take this slowly. One step at a time. We need to make sure that the picture isn't false. We need to verify that it's not someone messing with your head. I know you want to believe it but you mustn't rush into anything. We need to reply to her and ask for more information.'

'I can't do it – you do it. I don't know what to say.' Laura was shaking.

Frank ordered a strong coffee with lots of sugar for Laura and a whiskey for himself. 'OK, let's decide on the wording . . .'

He took out a pen and began scribbling on a napkin. Laura sat beside him, fidgeting.

'How about this? "Dear Sophie, I received your email this morning and was obviously shocked by the information. Can you please send me further photos of you as a child and more recent ones of you now? I would also like more information about your background –"'

'Stop!' Laura laid her hand over Frank's. 'I'm not writing that. I'm not being stiff and formal with my girl. I know you're trying to protect me but this is Jody. I can feel it with every nerve in my body. I knew this would happen some day. I knew she was alive. I can't write a letter full of demands to this poor, confused girl. I'm going to write from my heart.'

Laura took his iPad and began to type: 'Dear Sophie, I can't tell you how glad I am that you got in touch. I understand how con-fused you must be. I'm confused too. I really want to meet you face to face to talk about all of this. I'm going to come to London to see you. I think you're my Jody. I feel it. I know it.'

Frank frowned: it was too accepting and too gushing. This girl could be a gold-digger. It might not even be a girl: it could be some creep messing with his sister's head. But before Frank could stop her, she'd sent it.

'There, it's done.' Laura laughed through her tears.

The waitress arrived with their drinks and discreetly ignored Laura's obvious distress. Frank tipped her generously and turned back to his sister. 'Laura, please don't get your hopes up yet. We don't know who this person is. Photos can be tampered with. I know you want to believe it but I'm begging you not to rush into it. I don't want you to get hurt by some freak playing a trick on you. You've been in the media a bit recently with the sale of your painting to Hank Gold. There are weirdos out there who might be just messing with you. Please don't jump to conclusions. Wait until we have concrete evidence.'

Laura shook her head. 'There's nothing you can say, Frank. I'm her mother and I know it's her. I knew she was alive. I prayed for this day to come. I can't believe it's finally happened. My baby's back.' Laura began to sob. Frank did his best to soothe her.

Twenty minutes later, having gone around in circles trying to work it all out, Frank ordered another coffee and whiskey. As the waitress set the drinks down on the table, Laura's email beeped.

They froze . . .

19

Sophie

London, July 2011

Sophie stared at her computer willing there to be an email from Laura. It had been four days and nothing. By Friday afternoon she was beginning to give up hope. Holly called in after her shift in the pizzeria with a large pepperoni supreme for them to share.

Unfortunately Jessie saw her and came running in. 'Can I have some pizza?'

'No. Bugger off,' Holly said to her sister.

'You're such a bitch. Just one slice.'

'Have you seen your arse lately?' Holly asked her. 'More salad and less pizza, Jessie.'

'At least I'm not thick and I can spell. At least I didn't say I was good with the *pubic* on my application form. You loser.'

Holly waved the pizza box in her sister's face. 'The manager didn't seem to mind too much – he gave me the job. You'll never get a job in a restaurant because they want you to serve the food, not eat it.'

'Spell pepperoni, Holly – come on give us a laugh,' her sister sneered.

'Go and glue your mouth shut, Fatty.'

'Beauty is from within,' Jessie spat.

Holly shrieked with laughter. 'How's that going for you? Kissed any boys lately? Do you think Oliver looks at you and thinks, Wow! Underneath her five chins is a really beautiful person?'

'At least I'm not a lesbian!'

'Believe me, girls wouldn't want you either.'

'Stop!' Sophie cut across their bickering. 'I can't listen to any more of this. Holly, I need your help with something. I'll see you later, Jessie.'

She pulled Holly through the front door and closed it before Jessie got any ideas about coming in too.

Holly looked at Sophie. 'P-e-p-a-r-o-n-i, right?'

'P-e-p-p-e-r-o-n-i.'

'God, I am stupid.' Holly blushed.

'No, you're not.'

'Yes, I am. I just wish I was dyslexic so I'd have an excuse.'

'Holly, you may not be a brilliant speller, but you're street smart. You're going to be a huge success at whatever you do.'

'Digging ditches with a bunch of farmers?'

'You'll figure a way to make it work for you. I know you will.'

They went up to Sophie's bedroom. Holly plonked herself down on the crisp white bed linen and put her pizza box on her knee. She opened it and the smell of warm pizza filled the room. Sophie opened the window. She didn't like strong smells: they crowded her mind with colours. She only ever wore very light scents. The strong ones were too much for her senses.

'Sorry – is it very smelly? I'm so used to the smell from working that I'm immune to it.'

Sophie smiled. 'It's OK. Thanks for bringing it. I'm starving.'

Holly offered her the box. 'Any news?' she asked.

Sophie picked up a slice of pizza. 'I just can't believe she didn't write back,' she said, for the millionth time.

'Are you sure the email was sent?' Holly asked, yet again.

'Positive.' Sophie chewed a piece of cheese.

'She's obviously not your mother, then.' Holly wiped her hands on a napkin. 'We were wrong. It was just a coincidence. Anna is your mother.'

Sophie refused to believe it. 'She isn't. I just know it.'

'Look, Sophie, you have to let it go now. It's not healthy to obsess this much about anything. I should know. Remember when I was fourteen and I was so obsessed with Carl Jackson that I refused to believe he was gay? All the signs were there – he liked musicals, he spent all his time in my house but he never wanted to kiss me, he liked looking at fashion magazines and helping me choose what to wear and he loved dancing. I thought he was perfect. The only thing that annoyed me was that he was always wanting to watch football with my dad.'

They both giggled.

'Everyone knew he was gay,' Sophie said.

'I know! It's so embarrassing. I obviously have a very bad gaydar. I never picked up on it.'

'Your dad did, though.' Sophie laughed.

'Oh, God, poor Carl, he nearly died when Dad told him to stop hugging him every time someone scored.'

It was while they were laughing that Sophie's email pinged. She leaped across the bed, upending pizza all over her sheets.

Laura Fletcher. OH, MY GOD!

'It's her! Holly, she wrote back to me!' Sophie stared at the email, too afraid to open it. Holly scrambled over beside her.

They stared at the name. Sophie was having difficulty breathing. Holly turned to her. 'Do you want me to do it?'

Sophie nodded.

Holly clicked it open. Sophie leaned forward and tried to read the words but her eyes were swimming. Holly read it out. 'Oh, my God, Sophie, she thinks you're Jody. She's coming over to meet you.'

They screamed and jumped up and down. Sophie was seeing light green but also pink, which was her happy colour. She felt so relieved. Laura had written back! She didn't think Sophie was mad. She thought Sophie was her Jody. Her daughter. Her abducted –

'Holly! This means that my mum did steal me.' Suddenly Sophie felt sick.

Holly's cheeks were flushed. 'Sophie, do you realize that this is, like, the biggest story ever? When the media get hold of it you're going to be so famous. They'll do a book and a movie and maybe even a mini-series. You'll be on *Oprah* and *Ellen* and *Graham Norton* and all the other talk shows.' She clapped her hands together. 'Can I be your personal assistant? I'd love it. I can help style you and deal with the media. We should probably call Max Clifford now. He's the most famous publicist around. I bet he'll get you millions for your story. It's going to be fantastic. Now I won't have to go to stupid horticulture and turf college with a bunch of wellington-wearing bumpkins whose idea of fun is skinning rabbits. I can hang out with you and all the other stars on the talk-show circuit. This is going to be so much fun.'

'Holly! There won't be any publicity. Do you understand? You are not to say a word to anyone. I swear if you tell a soul I'll kill you. I need to get it all straight in my head. I've got to meet Laura and see if it's really true.'

'OK! I'm just telling you what's going to happen. You need to be prepared. It'll be the biggest story since – since the royal wedding.'

Sophie grabbed her friend's hands. 'Holly, I'm serious. Promise you won't say a word.'

'I promise, and you know I never break my promises. Except that one time when I told Jason you fancied him. But I only did it for your own good and you did end up kissing him. It wasn't my fault he was a terrible kisser and kept licking your face like a thirsty dog.'

Sophie laughed despite herself. 'OK. Now, come on, focus. What am I going to write back? Laura can't come here. She can't come to London – it's too risky. Mum already suspects something's up. Today's her last day at work before the summer holidays. She's going to stalk me for the next week until we go to France. She's really paranoid at the moment because I keep asking her questions about the past.'

'She should be too, considering she's a criminal!' Holly was indignant.

Sophie chewed her fingernail. 'I'll have to go to Ireland and meet Laura there.'

'What? Are you mad? Your mother will go completely bonkers.'

'Obviously I'm not going to tell her. I'll leave her a note or send her a text, but I won't say where I've gone. I need a couple of days to meet Laura and figure out what happened and who the hell I am.'

'You could say, "Gone to find myself." It's true and it doesn't give anything specific away,' Holly suggested.

'When Mum finds out I've gone, she'll come over and interrogate you,' Sophie warned Holly.

Her friend looked a bit frightened. 'Your mum can be scary but I won't break. I promise. I'll be like one of those spies in the war when the Nazis tried to get them to give up their friends and they refused. They stood up straight, shoulders back, and hummed the national anthem while their nails were being extracted.'

'Earth to Holly, all I need you to say is that you don't know where I've gone but you're sure I'm fine. I'll text her every day so she doesn't think I'm dead.'

'Maybe you shouldn't text her at all so she understands how poor Laura felt all those years ago when she thought Jody was dead.'

Sophie softened. 'I couldn't do that to her. She's my mum.'

'But that's the whole point, Sophie. Anna isn't your mum.'

Technically Holly was right, but Anna was the only mother Sophie had ever known. She couldn't let her think she was dead. It was too cruel. 'I'll have to pretend I'm going to the movies with you and instead go to the airport.'

'Why don't I come with you?' Holly offered.

Sophie was tempted. It would be nice to have Holly there, but she had to do this alone. She needed to figure it out by herself. 'No, thanks. I'll be fine. But thanks for offering. If it all goes wrong I can call Mark – I have his address in Dublin. I won't be stranded.'

'All right. Let's look up flights.'

Holly found a flight from Heathrow to Dublin at three o'clock the next day. Sophie used the emergency credit card Anna had given her to book it. It was the only time she had ever used it.

'Done!' Holly looked up at her, beaming. 'Your adventure begins now. This is the most exciting thing to happen . . . ever.'

Sophie's eyes were like saucers, and adrenalin was pumping through her veins. 'Now I need to send Laura an email and tell her I'm coming. What shall I say?'

Holly began to type:

Thank you for your email. I would very much like to meet you too. But it's better if I come to Dublin. So I'm flying in tomorrow. My flight lands at four fifteen. If you tell me the best place to meet you I'll get a taxi there.

'Perfect. Thanks, Holly. Send it before I change my mind.' Holly pressed send.

'Right, we need to find you something fabulous to wear. I'm not sure what the dress-code for long-lost-mother-daughter reunions is. Let's Google it.' Holly typed in 'long lost mother and daughter reunions': 270,000 results. 'My God, Sophie, you're not alone. Loads of people haven't seen their mothers in years because they were stolen.' Holly scrolled down the page. 'Oh, my God, some of them have had terrible lives. You've been lucky. Anna's a good mother. Look at this poor girl who was beaten up by the woman who stole her – and this one was taken and sold as a sex slave! Wow, things could have been a lot worse. You could have ended up in Thailand as a prostitute. Anna seems almost normal!' Holly continued to scour the pages. 'Lots of sad stories, but no information on what to wear. We'll have to figure it out ourselves.'

She opened Sophie's wardrobe and began to pull things off hangers and down from the shelves. Sophie sat on her pizza-stained bed, too overwhelmed to argue.

'What look do you want to achieve?'

Sophie gestured helplessly. 'Holly, I can't think straight. I have no idea. I just want to look like me.'

'Mm. Well, you can be a bit conservative at times and Laura is an artist, so I think you should try to shake it up a bit. On the other hand, you don't want to look too desperate, too young, too old, too tarty or too square . . .'

'Why can't I just wear jeans and a T-shirt?'

Holly sighed. 'Because, Sophie, this is the most important meeting of your life.'

She had a point.

'And you want to look perfect. You want Laura to fall in love with you all over again. Thankfully, God gave you good genes so it's not going to be difficult to make you look gorgeous. What about this red dress with the yellow scarf and these nude shoes?'

'I've never really liked that dress. Red is my colour for panic. Besides, those shoes are really high and uncomfortable. They're sitting-down shoes, not walking-around shoes.'

Holly waved them at her friend. 'Sometimes you have to suffer for fashion.'

'I'm not wearing them. I need to be comfortable. I don't want to fall over on ridiculous heels when I meet Laura.'

'It's kind of like a first date,' Holly said. 'It's important you look your best.'

Sophie got up and walked over to the wardrobe. She pulled out a pink sundress with white daisies on it. Pink was her happy colour. 'What about this?'

Holly's brow furrowed. 'It's a bit girly. And apparently it's always freezing in Ireland. My aunt Hannah went over there for her summer holiday once and said it was cold and rainy even in August.'

'I'll check the forecast.' Sophie looked up the weather on her laptop. 'It says it's going to be twenty-three degrees and sunny tomorrow.'

'All right. Well, wear these wedges with it. They'll make it a bit edgier.'

Sophie tried on the dress and shoes.

Holly looked her up and down and made her twirl around. 'It's a good look. Young, fresh, but not innocent, and the shoes give it a cool element. Now, what are you going to travel in?'

'It'll have to be jeans, a T-shirt and ballet pumps. I can't get too dressed up to go to the cinema with you or Mum will suspect I'm lying.'

'OK, wear your Seven jeans. They look really good on you. And you'd better take pyjamas and some extra T-shirts in case you end up staying a few days. You never know what might happen.'

Sophie hadn't thought of that. All she'd been thinking about was meeting Laura. But what if it went well and she wanted Sophie to stay for a few days so they could really get to know each other? Holly was right: she needed to be prepared. But she could only take a small bag or Anna would know something was up. She was already watching her more closely than usual.

'I know what you're thinking.' Holly smiled. 'Inspector Morse, a.k.a. Anna, will suspect something if you leave the house with a big bag. You can give me some clothes and I'll put them in my backpack. I use it all the time for my pizza uniform so my mum won't suspect anything.'

Sophie squeezed her friend's hand. 'Thanks, Holly. I don't know what I'd do without you.'

'Don't get emotional. You'll only start me off. Right, come on, give me some T-shirts, a spare pair of jeans, some makeup, knickers and bras.' Holly neatly folded the clothes and stored them in her backpack.

An email came in. They both jumped and ran over to read it. It was from Laura: 'I'm thrilled! I'll be at the airport waiting for you. Don't worry, I'll recognize you. Thank you for coming over. I'm beyond happy.'

'Oh, my God, Sophie, it's real now. This is really happening.' Holly looked a bit shaken. It was as if she had suddenly understood the magnitude of what her friend was about to discover.

'Holly! This time tomorrow I'll know who I am.' Sophie felt afraid. She began to cry.

Holly hugged her. 'It'll be OK . . . It'll all work out.'

'I hope so, I really hope so. I'm so confused.' Sophie had a splitting headache. 'I need answers. I need to know the truth.'

'Of course you do, you poor thing. This has been such a shock for you. But, Sophie, I think you need a plan B,' Holly warned her. 'Just in case things go wrong, in case Laura isn't who we think she is. She could be high on drugs when she collects you. Some people can function for years with serious drug habits. I saw this programme once about a singer. I think it was –'

'Holly, if I need help when I get to Dublin, I can get in touch with Mark. I'll only call him if I need him, though. Joe will be the first person Mum rings when she finds out I've disappeared. And Joe will call Mark and I don't want Mark to have to lie to his dad for me. I'll see how it goes with Laura first.'

'No,' Holly said firmly. 'You have to speak to Mark before you go. You need someone over there who knows where you are and who can come to your rescue if anything goes wrong. This may not work out the way you hope. You may find out that Laura's not your mum, or that she is but she's a nutter.'

Sophie looked at her friend, tears welling in her eyes. 'Oh, God, what if she is mad? What if she's a terrible person? She probably is, otherwise why would Mum have taken me?'

Holly hugged her. 'If you have any doubts, don't go.'

'I have to. I have to figure it all out. Otherwise I'll spend the rest of my life wondering who I am. It's already driving me insane and I've only known for a few days. I'll end up in a strait-jacket if I don't get answers to my questions.'

'I'd be the same if it was me. Although there's no doubt that I'm my mother's flesh and blood – we have the same hazel eyes, mousy brown hair and big breasts. If it wasn't for good hair dye and underwear, I'd be very lonely.'

'You're gorgeous.'

'No, I'm attractive on a good day with a lot of effort. You, on the other hand, wake up looking like Scarlett Johansson. Now, I'll have my phone on, and in credit, twenty-four/seven. If anything happens, call me. Even if nothing happens, call me. I'll be desperate for all the details. And if you need me to come over, let me know and I'll be on that plane like a shot. I'm making tons of tips at the pizzeria, the up-side of having big boobs, so I could even pay for a hotel in Dublin for us.'

'Thanks, Holly.'

Holly grinned at her. 'Do you realize that this is like our own amazing reality-TV show? The Kardashians have nothing on us. I bet Piers Morgan wants the first interview. This could actually turn out to be an amazing adventure.'

'Or a total disaster,' Sophie said quietly.

Holly put an arm around her. 'Come on, Sophie, you've got the easy bit. I'm the one who has to deal with your mother when she finds out you've left the country!'

20.

Anna

London, July 2011

Anna was in the kitchen reading the paper when Sophie walked in. She was still in her pyjamas, enjoying a leisurely coffee on the first day of the summer holidays. The sun was beaming through the window, warming her toes. Anna loved the kitchen, which was painted a pale shade of lilac, Sophie's colour for calm and peace. It was the hub of the house, where they ate together, talked together and ironed out any problems that arose.

The kitchen walls had originally been magnolia. When Sophie was about five, Anna had painted them a pale mint, but when Sophie had seen it she had begun to scream. Anna thought she'd hurt herself but then she'd heard her say, 'No, Mummy, bad colour, change it.' That was the first time Anna had noticed the way Sophie linked emotions with colours.

Initially she had panicked and thought Sophie was autistic. But after months of seeing specialist after specialist they had finally discovered it was synaesthesia. It had been a learning curve for Anna as she had never heard of it before. But when she had researched it and begun to understand it, she had stopped worrying. Now she looked on it as a gift: Sophie was so special that she saw the world in a unique, artistic way.

'Morning.' She smiled up at her daughter. 'Are you hungry? Can I get you anything?'

Sophie was dressed in jeans, flat navy pumps and a pink T-shirt. She turned her back to her mother and opened the fridge door.

'No, thanks. I'm heading into town with Holly this morning. We're going to pop into Top Shop and then go to the cinema.'

Anna frowned. 'Which one?'

'The one in Putney.'

It was close by, and Anna breathed a sigh of relief. She didn't want Sophie going to the cinema in Leicester Square. Too many unsavoury characters hung around there. She'd heard stories of drug dealers and prostitutes. She liked to have Sophie within walking distance. Safe.

'So you're coming straight back out from Oxford Street after you've gone to Top Shop?'

'Yes,' Sophie said, still rummaging in the fridge. 'We're going into town early to avoid the Saturday crowds and then we're going to see the two o'clock showing of the new Robert Pattinson movie. It's supposed to be good.'

'Well, that sounds like a great plan. Will you come straight home afterwards, please? I want to take you out for dinner to celebrate the first day of the summer holidays and discuss the details of our trip to France.'

'Fine.' Sophie pulled out an Actimel, closed the fridge door and turned around. Anna was standing directly behind her. Sophie nearly jumped out of her skin. 'God, Mum, you gave me a fright.'

'Sorry, I just wanted to give you a hug. I've hardly seen you this week. You're either sleeping or with Holly. I'm looking forward to spending time with you in France without phones, laptops and your friends calling in all the time. Just the two of us. I can't wait.'

Anna put her arms around Sophie, who was rigid. 'Come on, Sophie, give your old mum a proper hug.'

Sophie forced herself to lift her arms.

'I love you, Sophie.' Anna kissed her daughter's cheek. 'I'm so proud of you.'

Sophie wriggled out of the embrace. 'I've got to go, Mum. Holly's waiting.'

Anna was hurt. Sophie usually laughed when she hugged her.

But now it felt as if she was allergic to her. 'All right, see you later,' she said, as cheerfully as she could.

As Sophie was closing the front door, she turned back to look at her mother, her expression serious. 'Goodbye, Mum.'

''Bye, darling, have fun.' Anna waved as the door closed. She felt very uneasy. Something didn't feel right. Her ulcer throbbed. This week had been strange and stressful. Sophie was avoiding her and being very secretive. What was going on? Was it a boy? Was she pregnant? Was she just trying to assert her independence? Or did she suspect something? Was she suspicious of her past? Had she found something? Anna went up to her daughter's bedroom. Everything seemed normal. If anything, it looked tidier than usual. She went across to her own bedroom, knelt down and pulled back the rug. She pushed up the false floorboard, which hid a small safe. Anna entered the combination and the steel door of the safe clicked open.

Her papers were all exactly as she had left them. Nothing had been tampered with. Hope's birth certificate – which she had used for Sophie's passport – was untouched. Her marriage and divorce papers were there too. So were her mother and father's death certificates and all the photos she had of her wedding day, honeymoon and the interim years – moving into the new house with Barry, birthday celebrations, holidays, Christmases . . . their whole life together. Anna could see the deterioration of her marriage in the photos. As the years had passed their smiles had faded and their eyes had lost their brightness as happiness had drained away.

She picked up some photos of her mother, looking healthy and happy on Anna's wedding day, then increasingly unwell as the years slipped by. Anna looked at the last picture she had taken of her mother and whispered, 'You'd love her, Mum. Sophie's wonderful. The two of you would have got on so well. I wish you'd known her. I wish she'd known you. You would have been a fantastic grandmother. I'm sorry I wasn't able to give you that.'

Anna then took out the photos of Hope and the soft pink

blanket that the hospital had wrapped her baby girl in. She buried her nose in it. The baby smell was long gone but it still made her feel close to Hope. She hadn't done that in ages. She had only allowed herself to look forward, not back. She held the blanket to her cheek and allowed herself to shed a tear for her lost baby.

She dried her eyes and scolded herself. She had no reason to feel sad when she *had* been given the gift of motherhood in the end. She *had* become a mother, after all, in spite of it all, because of it all.

Anna put everything carefully back into the safe. Nothing had been touched; her secret was secure. Maybe Joe was right and Sophie's curiosity was natural at her age. She was asking more questions about who her father was and Anna's past because she was an adult now and she wanted more information. Anna needed to stay calm. She had to stick to her story. She mustn't panic. It was normal: all children were inquisitive. Anna felt her tension ease.

Anna tried Sophie's number again. It was five thirty. The film Sophie had gone to see had finished at ten past four. Anna had called the cinema and checked. The walk home from there was only ten minutes. Where was she? Why was her phone switched off? Sophie knew Anna worried when she couldn't get in touch with her. They had an agreement that if Sophie responded to texts and calls Anna would try to give her more freedom. Anna tried Holly's phone. It was switched off too. Maybe they'd gone for coffee . . .

Anna knocked on Nancy's door.

'Hello.' Nancy was in her daily uniform of a Juicy Couture tracksuit. Today she was wearing her powder-blue one. She had them in eight different colours. She'd proudly shown them to Anna once. 'Stylish yet comfortable,' she'd claimed. Anna had nodded, but in fact she didn't agree at all. She thought Nancy would have looked so much trimmer and smarter in tailored trousers and a shirt.

'Come on in – I'm just making brownies. I could pretend they're for the kids but they're really for me. I'm not sure what my Weight Watchers leader would have to say about it. I'll have to skip my weigh-in this week. I think there are about ten million calories in every bite.'

The kitchen was a mess. The table was strewn with newspapers, magazines and unopened mail, now spattered with melted chocolate. Flour had spilled on the floor, along with some crushed walnuts that were now sticking to Anna's shoes. 'Nancy, is Holly back?' Anna asked.

'No, she's working at the pizzeria tonight.' Nancy turned around. 'I know that worried face. Is Sophie late?'

'Yes, very. It's six now and the film they were going to see ended two hours ago.'

'Oh, don't worry, she probably went to the pizzeria with Holly.'

Absentmindedly, Anna began to tidy the papers on the table. 'Maybe, but neither of them is answering her phone.'

The kitchen door swung open. 'Yum, brownies!' Jessie exclaimed, as she stuck a chubby finger into the mixture.

Nancy swatted her away with a wooden spoon. 'If you don't want to end up like me you need to stay away from brownies.'

'Well, you shouldn't make them. It's cruel. I'm going to report you to the NSPCC.'

'Go ahead. They're welcome to come and take you to a foster home so I can have some peace.'

'Come on, Mum, let me lick the spoon.'

'You can have one when they're cooked.'

'Jessie, have you seen Holly and Sophie?' Anna asked.

Jessie spun around, still licking brownie mixture off her finger. 'No, but they're probably looking at lesbian porn on their laptops.'

'What?' Anna was taken aback.

'Don't tell me you didn't know they were gay!'

'That's enough of your cheek,' Nancy scolded. 'Ignore her, Anna, she's just jealous because the girls never let her hang out with them.'

'I don't want to hang out with my sad older sister and her dorky friend, thank you very much.' Jessie stuck her finger into the bowl again. 'Why would I want to be associated with a pair of lezzers anyway? They're total losers.'

'So why do you follow them around like a lost puppy?' Nancy winked at Anna.

'I do not!'

'Yeah, you do.' Gordon came in bouncing a soccer ball. His jeans were hanging below his hips, revealing stripy boxer shorts. 'You're always trying to hang out with them. And it's never going to happen. Accept it, you're the short fat sister no one likes.'

'I'm not fat!'

'Sorry, I meant obese.' Gordon laughed.

'Stop that!' Nancy snapped. 'She is not obese or fat. She's beautiful.'

Gordon snorted. 'You need to go to Specsavers, Mum, pronto.'

Nancy sighed. 'That's enough. Anna's worried about Sophie because she's late home. Has anyone seen her?'

No one had.

'I'll bet she's gone to work with Holly. The pizza place never gets busy until seven. Holly probably asked her to keep her company,' Nancy suggested.

'I'll pop up and see if she's there,' Anna said, keen to do something.

'If I hear anything I'll let you know,' Nancy promised.

'Thanks.'

Anna peered through the window. She could see Holly in her uniform – red dress and white apron – talking to the barman. She went in and looked around. No sign of Sophie. Only two tables were occupied and a bored-looking waitress in the corner was filling salt cellars.

Anna walked over to the bar. Holly had her back to her. She was asking the barman about cocktails.

'Holly?'

Holly turned, saw Anna, and dropped her tray. Thankfully, there were no drinks on it. Anna bent down to pick it up and handed it to Holly, who had gone very red.

'I'm looking for Sophie. Is she here?' Anna asked.

Holly placed the tray on the bar. Her hands were shaking. 'Um, no, she isn't.'

Anna stepped sideways so she could see Holly's face. The barman moved away, sensing tension in the air. 'Where did she go after the cinema?'

'She, um, said she was going to have a look in the shops or go for a walk or something.' Holly was avoiding eye contact.

'Well, she hasn't come home. What time did you leave her?' Anna was really worried now.

Holly began to line up the bar stools. 'I guess about five.'

'It's almost seven now. The shops are closed and her phone is switched off.'

'I'm sure she'll be back soon,' Holly said, still avoiding Anna's eyes.

She seemed so nervous, Anna thought. Something was up. She willed herself to remain calm. 'Holly, you need to tell me where Sophie is. Is she with a boy?'

'Gosh, no.' Holly looked at Anna for the first time.

'Well, where is she?'

Holly looked at her watch. 'Right now, I can honestly say I don't know.'

Anna put a firm hand on Holly's arm. 'I'm worried about my daughter and I need to find her. Please don't lie to me.'

Holly pushed a stray hair behind her ear. 'I'm not. I really don't know where she is now.'

'All right. Where was she going when you last saw her?'

'Like I said, to look around the shops.'

'Holly, I don't –' Anna's phone beeped. She grabbed it out of her pocket. It was a message from Sophie: *I've gone away for a few days. Don't worry. Don't look for me. I'm fine.*

Anna gasped. She waved the phone in front of Holly's face. 'What the hell does this mean?'

Holly looked at the message but said nothing.

Anna's fingers trembled as she tried to call Sophie back but, once again, her daughter's phone was turned off. Something really bad was going on, she could feel it. She had sensed it this morning. She had to find out what it was. Sophie had never left home like this before. Anna felt sick. She grabbed Holly's arm again. 'You'd better tell me what the hell is going on or I swear I'll start screaming this restaurant down. Where is Sophie?'

'I can't say, I promised I wouldn't.'

Anna felt bile rising in her throat, and her ulcer was pulsing. 'Is she in danger? Did she go away with a strange man?'

Holly pulled her arm back and rubbed it. 'No. It's nothing like that.'

'So where is she?'

'I'm not going to tell you.'

Anna gritted her teeth. 'Oh yes you are.'

'No, I'm not.'

Anna pulled Holly out on to the street. She let the restaurant door slam shut. The barman followed them and poked his head outside. 'Is everything OK here, Holly?'

'It's fine, Alex, thanks. It's just my friend's mum. She's worried about her.'

'I'll be inside if you need me.' He stared pointedly at Anna.

When he had gone, Anna turned on Holly. 'If you don't tell me where Sophie is I'm going to drag you to the police station and let them interrogate you.'

Holly crossed her arms. 'I don't think that's a good idea.'

How dare she speak to her like that? Holly had never been rude to her before. What on earth was going on?

'I don't think you want the police involved in this.' Holly stuck her chin out defiantly.

'Is it drugs?' Anna's head was spinning. 'Is that what this is? Have you taken drugs? Did Sophie have a bad reaction? Is she in hospital?'

'Of course not! Come on, this is Sophie we're talking about!'

'Well, then, what?'

Holly took a deep breath. 'I'm just saying that it's a bad idea for you to get the police involved, considering.'

Anna narrowed her eyes. 'Considering what exactly?'

'Nothing. It doesn't matter.'

'It matters very much. What has Sophie got herself into?'

Holly glowered at Anna. 'It's not Sophie who got herself into it.'

'Who, then?'

'I'm not saying.'

'Is she in bad company?'

'That depends.'

Anna's blood was beginning to boil, her ulcer was blazing, and she wanted to smack Holly's defiant face. 'Depends on what?' she shouted.

'On lots of things.'

'Jesus Christ, Holly, stop talking in riddles. Is Sophie in danger?'

'I told you she's not.'

'Who is she with and where has she gone?'

Holly paused, then smiled. 'She's with someone who is close to her and she's gone somewhere that you know well.'

'WHAT?'

'I can't say any more.'

'That's it! I'm taking you to the police! I've had enough of your games. This is not funny, Holly. Sophie is my only child – she's all I have in the world. If anything happened to her I'd die. Do you understand? Die!' She began pulling Holly towards the police station across the road from the pizzeria.

'I'm not going to the police!'

'Yes, you are.'

'You'll be sent to jail!' Holly shouted.

Anna stopped. 'Me?'

'Yes, you.'

'For what?'

'For what you did.' Holly glared at her.

Anna's heart skipped a beat. 'What are you talking about?'

'You know exactly what I'm talking about.'

'No, I don't.'

'Sophie knows.'

'Knows what?'

Holly leaned in. 'That you're not her mother.'

Anna's legs crumpled. She only managed to stay upright because she was holding on to Holly. 'What do you mean?'

Holly supported her and steadied her. 'We know about Laura and Jody, her little girl on the boat, who everyone thought drowned. But she didn't drown, did she?'

Anna could barely breathe. 'How?'

Holly took a step back and buried her hands in her apron. 'It doesn't matter how. The important thing is that she knows and she's gone to Ireland to meet her real mother. How could you, Anna? How could you do that?'

The words came from Anna's lips like bullets: 'Don't you dare judge me. Don't you dare accuse me. You have no idea what you're talking about. You have no idea what happened. You don't understand anything. You have no idea of the person you're dealing with. You've sent Sophie into the arms of a terrible woman. An abusive drunk who treated her like dirt. My poor Sophie. Oh, God, what have you done?' Anna began to cry. Her body heaved with emotion. The shock of finding out that Sophie knew what she had done. Knew that she wasn't hers. Knew that she had taken her. Knew that she had lied to her. Knew that she wasn't her real mother . . . Oh, God. Anna bent over and retched as the pain of her ulcer ripped into her.

Holly crouched down. 'Are you all right? Anna, you look awful – do you need a doctor? Should I call an ambulance? I'm sorry – I didn't mean to make you ill.'

Anna put her hand on Holly's shoulder and heaved herself upright. The pain was excruciating. She gulped air into her lungs and tried to suppress the terror creeping up her body. Sophie knew the truth . . . Her worst fear had come true. Try as she might, she could not stop crying. Holly hopped from one foot to the other, apologizing and handing Anna paper napkins that she had in her apron. Her eyes were like saucers – she had never seen anyone in such distress.

'I'm so sorry, Anna. I'd no idea that Laura was a bad person. I was just trying to help my friend. Sophie's really upset and confused and I'm trying to be supportive. She wanted to meet Laura and she seemed so normal.'

'Well, she isn't!'

Holly began to sob. 'I swore to Sophie I wouldn't tell you where she was. I promised faithfully and now I've let her down, too. This is a total disaster. I don't know what to believe any more, and Sophie's going to kill me when she finds out I spilled the beans. Look, I'm sorry I was mean and rude – it just all seemed . . . well . . . wrong. I never meant to upset you so much,' Holly whimpered.

Anna clenched her fists and took a deep breath. She needed to calm the situation and take control. She couldn't let Holly go back to work hysterical and tell everyone what was going on. She had to get her to keep this information to herself, no matter what.

She laid a hand gently on Holly's arm. 'It's OK, Holly. Don't get upset. I'll sort this all out. It's a misunderstanding. I need to talk to Sophie and explain everything to her. In the meantime I need you to promise me that you won't tell another soul – not even your mum – about this. If she asks where Sophie and I have gone, just say we went on holidays early. I need you to promise me, Holly. Do it for Sophie. She needs time to process the information and to understand what actually happened. It's not what you think at all. I saved Sophie's life. I understand that it's confusing for you, and I promise I'll explain it to you later. But for now

I have to go and see Sophie. Do you know where this woman lives?'

Holly stopped crying and wiped her eyes with her hands. 'Her name's Laura Fletcher and she's an artist. There's an address on her website. Oh, God, is she a psycho? Is she, like, a stalker or something? Did we get it all wrong? Is Sophie really in danger now?'

Anna sighed. 'This Laura Fletcher is not a nice person. I need to get Sophie out of there. But remember, Holly, say nothing.'

Holly nodded vigorously. 'I swear on my life.'

Anna patted her shoulder. 'Good girl. Now, go back to work and try to forget about it. I'll fix this. I want you to stop worrying. It's all going to be fine. I'll have Sophie back home safely in no time.'

Before Holly could say anything else, Anna hurried away, trying to suppress the scream rising in her throat.

She turned on her laptop and Googled Laura Fletcher, Irish artist. It was a name she had never wanted to know. The web page sprang up. Anna stared at the picture of Sophie's mother. She was the image of Sophie. Anna felt sick. She went into Laura's bio page – it just said she was an artist and had one daughter. Then on a different page, she found a photo and a painting of the daughter as a toddler. Sophie.

She may look normal but she's a drunk, a useless, cruel, neglectful drunk, Anna thought. She had no right to look after that child – she couldn't look after it. She was incapable. She passed out. If it hadn't been for me, the baby would have drowned or been taken by some paedophile.

Sophie was lucky Anna had come along: she had saved her from a life of misery and neglect. She had been in mortal danger and Anna had had to help her. She'd had to . . .

Anna went into the bathroom and took four painkillers. Her stomach was agonizing and her head throbbing. She had to compose herself. She needed to think straight. First she must book an early flight to Dublin. She went online. She was too late to leave tonight but she could get on a plane at six thirty in the morning. She booked a seat, then went back to Laura Fletcher's website and took down the address of her studio. Anna didn't recognize the name of the village – Killduf. She looked it up. It was forty miles outside Dublin. She'd have to hire a car.

She needed help. She needed to talk to someone she trusted completely, someone who knew her, someone who wouldn't judge.

'Joe?'

'Anna, hi.'

'Help.'

'What's wrong? Is it Sophie?'

'Yes.' Anna's composure crumbled. She told Joe that Holly had just admitted Sophie had run away to Dublin. 'Did she call you? Or Mark?'

'No. Mark's here now. Hang on.' Joe asked his son if he'd heard from Sophie but he hadn't.

'What happened? Did you have a fight?' Joe asked.

'No. She's gone to Ireland to find her mother.'

'What? I thought you adopted her in England?'

'I did,' Anna lied, 'but her mother was Irish.'

'How did Sophie find her?'

'I don't know. Holly was vague on the details. She said Sophie flew to Dublin this afternoon to meet this woman and I'm scared, Joe.' Anna began to cry hysterically. 'I'm terrified. The woman is a drunk. Sophie has no idea what she's letting herself in for.'

'Christ, do you know where she lives?'

Anna's mobile beeped. 'Hang on, it's a message from Sophie.' Anna read it out: *'Holly texted you're coming to get me. DON'T. I'm fine. I'm with my real mother. I need space to think.'*

'Thank God she's all right,' Joe said.

Anna tried to call her back but Sophie had switched off her phone again. 'What will I do, Joe? I have to find her. I've booked the first flight over.'

'Don't panic. I'll pick you up from the airport and we'll figure out what to do. Maybe Sophie would talk to me.'

'Thanks. You're a life-saver. I can't bear my Sophie to be with some other woman. I'm her mother. I raised her. She's mine,' Anna sobbed out.

'Of course you're her mother,' Joe soothed her. 'But you have to let her find out where she came from. All adopted children are curious. It's natural, Anna. You have to let her meet her biological mother. It's a rite of passage. She's entitled to do it. I know it's difficult for you, but it's something Sophie obviously feels strongly about.'

'You don't understand . . . This woman is – is awful.'

'Why don't you try ringing the adoption agency and see if you can get a name and address for her?'

'I can't.'

'Why not?'

'It's complicated. It's not that straightforward.'

'Anna,' Joe's voice was serious, 'you did adopt her properly, didn't you? You didn't cut corners or dodge paperwork, did you?'

'I'll talk to you tomorrow. I'd better go. I land at seven forty.'

'I'll be there.'

'Thanks.'

Anna covered her face with her hands. She hadn't cut any corners: she'd bulldozed them down.

21.

Laura

Killduf, July 2011

Laura had been awake all night. Jody was alive! She was alive! She was going to see her in a few hours. It was a miracle, the one she'd been praying for every day for so many years. She tossed and turned, lurching from ecstatic joy to terror. What if Jody didn't recognize her, or like her, or want to spend time with her? What if she remembered Laura shouting at her and being a terrible mother? Oh, God, she prayed Jody wouldn't remember that. She had loved her so much in her heart since the day she had vanished. The day when Laura had finally grown up and realized – too late – that she had a precious daughter who had gone. Hopefully, Jody would sense that. Hopefully, she would feel Laura's love for her. Oh, the joy of seeing her baby's face again . . . of holding her in her arms . . . her precious girl . . .

Eventually Laura gave up on sleep and went downstairs to make herself a coffee. The house was quiet; everyone was asleep. She pulled on a cardigan and took her mug outside. She tiptoed over the dewy grass and sat on the bench in the garden to watch the sun rise over the sea. Usually something so beautiful would make her cry, but today it made her smile and laugh for pure joy. If anyone had been watching her they would have thought she was completely insane.

Eventually she went into the house and tried to meditate but her mind was racing. Too many memories flooded her brain. Lots of images of Jody giggling, her funny little wobbly walk, sleeping in her Minnie Mouse snuggle suit, clapping her hands when Joan sang 'If You're Happy And You Know It' . . . Images that Laura had long ago suppressed and pushed to the bottom of her soul came rushing back to her. The memories and emotions brought an array of strong colours to her mind – blues and purples: oh, the joy!

Time seemed to stand still. Every time she looked at the clock, the hands didn't seem to have moved. Laura wished the day away. At twenty past four I'll see her. My baby, my Jody. She felt sick with anticipation as she gazed out of the kitchen window at the sky, smiling to herself.

'What are you doing?' Mandy asked.

Laura jumped. 'You gave me a fright. I'm just enjoying the view.' She went over to her daughter and hugged her.

Mandy squealed and pushed her away. 'Get off me, Mum! What are you doing?'

'I'm hugging you because I love you.'

'Have you been eating magic mushrooms for breakfast?'

Laura threw back her head and laughed. 'No, I'm just in a really good mood.'

'Well, keep your hands to yourself. Go and hug a tree or something.' Mandy went to put on some toast.

'Let me do that. You sit down and I'll make it for you.'

'No, Mum, it's fine.'

'Please let me. I want to.'

Mandy shrugged. 'OK.' She sat down at the small round table in the corner of the kitchen and eyed her mother suspiciously.

'Mornin' all.' Lexie shuffled through the door in lace-trimmed cream satin shorts and a camisole to match.

'Coffee?' Laura asked.

'I'd love one.'

'Fantastic!' Laura enthused, filling the kettle and humming while she scooped the coffee into the mugs.

'You seem very chipper this morning, Laura,' Lexie noted.

'She's being really weird,' Mandy said, chewing at one of her already bitten nails. 'Be careful – she might try to hug you too.'

'What – a mother actually trying to hug her own child? I'll have to call Social Services.' Lexie giggled.

Mandy rolled her eyes. 'I don't like hugs.'

Lexie raised her arms over her head and stretched like a cat. 'I'd have loved a few cuddles when I was your age. For my sixteenth birthday, which she forgot, my mum gave me two packets of duty-free cigarettes.'

'Oh, Lexie!' Laura sympathized, as she buttered the toast.

'I'd love it if Mum gave me cigarettes,' Mandy said. 'How cool is that?'

'Smoking is not cool, darlin'. It gives you wrinkles round your mouth. Don't bother with it. I smoked for years, mostly to stop me shoving cream cakes down my gob, but Dougie hated it. He said it was like sleeping with an ashtray, so I gave up.'

'Was it hard?' Mandy wanted to know.

Lexie snorted. 'Does Jordan sleep on her back? Too right it was. I put on a stone in two months. Dougie said he'd have to book two seats for me on the plane if I kept eating chocolate éclairs every time I went out.'

'What did you do?' Mandy asked.

'Dougie stuck pictures of supermodels all over the kitchen, so every time I went to get a snack, some gorgeous girl was staring at me.'

Mandy frowned. 'What a dickhead. Did it work?'

'Yeah, it did. I lost the weight, but it didn't stop him cheating on me. I should have just kept eating.'

'He sounds like an arsehole,' Mandy said.

'He is. You should write one of your angry songs about him. Call it "Dougie's A Dickhead".' Lexie cackled.

'There you go, two *cafés au lait*.' Laura put down the cups.

Lexie looked up at her. 'You're cheery this morning. What's goin' on? Hot date planned?'

Laura laughed. She felt like a teenager today. 'You could say that.'

Mandy banged her mug down, spilling some coffee. 'What? Seriously? A date?'

'Don't look so surprised, Mandy. Your mum's a looker. She reminds me of that Scarlett Johansson.'

'Her mother maybe.' Laura winked at Lexie. She had an urge to climb on to the table and scream, 'SHE'S ALIVE!' Instead she sat beside them and tried to behave normally.

'Don't put yourself down. There's plenty out there that'll do that for you. You do look like Scarlett, bit older maybe, but still hot.'

'Who are you meeting?' Mandy was put out.

'I'm just joking. It's not a date, just a very important appointment,' Laura reassured her daughter. 'I'll be gone for a couple of hours this afternoon. Lexie, can you keep an eye on Mandy?'

'For God's sake, Mum, I'm sixteen not six.'

'I know, but I just –'

'Don't worry, darlin', I'll be here. We might pop into the village for our tea. Do you fancy it, Mandy?'

'What if someone sees you?' Mandy asked.

'Sod it, I need to get out. Besides, I don't reckon too many paparazzi hang out in this neck of the woods. More likely to bump into a ghost than a photographer.'

'A ghost,' Laura muttered to herself. 'That's exactly who you might be about to meet.'

Laura changed six times. She wanted to look appropriate. But she didn't know what that meant. She was a thirty-seven-year-old mother who was about to meet her long-lost child. What did you wear for something like that? A suit? A formal black dress? Jeans and a nice top? Laura tried several different outfits but in the end she opted for a blue dress, her happy colour. It was a simple cotton maxi and she wore a short-sleeved cardigan over it and flat silver sandals.

She took out the photos she had of Jody in her bedside locker and placed them carefully in her bag. She glanced at the clock. It was only twelve thirty. This day would never end.

Her phone rang. It was Frank. 'Are you sitting there watching the clock?' he enquired.

'Yes.'

'Jesus, me too. I can't sit still. I've been up all night. I met this cracking Swedish model at a book launch last night. I brought her back to the house and she's ripping the clothes off me but all I can think about is Jody. Eventually she left in a huff. She said it was obvious I was thinking about another woman!'

'Technically you were.' Laura laughed.

'I'm sitting in the office but I can't concentrate. Why don't you come up to Dublin early and we'll go for coffee somewhere near the airport and kill an hour?'

'I'd love that.'

'Have you changed your mind about the airport?'

'No. I still want to go on my own. I'll call you when I've had time to talk to her. I don't want to crowd her with people. It's just going to be me and her.'

'I'm worried you might faint with the shock of it or something might go wrong.'

Laura tucked the phone under her ear and began to tidy her discarded clothes. 'I know, and thanks, Frank. But this is something I have to do by myself.'

'I found some pictures of Jody for you. I'll give them to you when I see you.'

'Thank you.' Laura felt a lump forming in her throat.

Frank paused. Then, with a quiver in his voice, he said, 'It's just . . .'

'I know.'

'To think . . .'

'I know.'

'After all these years . . .'

'I know.'

'Alive!'

Laura closed her eyes. 'She's come back to us, Frank. Jody's coming home.'

*

Laura arrived at the airport at three o'clock. She wanted to be there, near the planes, when Jody's flight left Heathrow. She wanted to be in the airport for the whole time Jody was in the air. She wanted to be the first person Jody saw when she walked out of the arrivals gate.

While she was waiting she took out the photos Frank had given her. She hadn't seen them in years. Frank throwing Jody up in the air; Frank holding Jody on his shoulders, her face beaming with delight; Jody asleep on Frank's chest as he lay on the couch watching TV; Frank giving Jody a bottle; Frank reading Jody a story; Frank, Jody and Joan on her christening day . . .

Laura hadn't said anything to Joan. She couldn't. Not until she knew for certain. Not until she had held Jody in her arms. Not until she knew Jody was OK. Then, if everything went well, she'd tell her mother. She was genuinely worried that Joan's heart would stop with the shock of it.

How do you tell a woman who has spent years mourning the loss of her little granddaughter that she was alive all the time? That for all those years she had grieved, Jody was living and growing up with someone else. Some psycho bitch who had stolen her. Laura felt her blood pressure rising. This woman, whoever she was, would pay for kidnapping her child. Laura would make her suffer the way she had suffered. What type of a sick, evil person would abduct someone else's child? Yellow. All she could see was yellow, as rage overtook her.

She closed her eyes. She needed to stop. She didn't want to be angry when Jody arrived. She wanted to be happy, joyful, loving. She blocked the woman out of her mind and went back to the photos. Her heart-rate slowed and she allowed blue to take over from yellow.

Laura was shaking as she stared at the arrivals gate. Every time the door slid open, she thought she'd have a heart attack. Everything was a blur, except that door. She stared and watched and waited . . . and waited . . .

Finally, she walked out. Laura clutched her chest.

Jody looked around. She was fidgeting with her bag and seemed very nervous. Laura tried to lift her hand to wave but it wouldn't move. She tried to call out to her daughter but her voice was silent. She tried to walk over to her, but her feet were stuck to the ground.

Jody looked to the left, to the right and finally straight ahead, where Laura was standing. She stopped dead. Their eyes locked. Neither of them moved. While all around them people hugged, kissed, cried, cheered, laughed, pulled and pushed bags and trolleys and buggies, they stood still and stared. Drinking each other in. Too much to say, too much to process, too much emotion, too much love, too much pain, too much sorrow, too much joy, too much . . .

Jody was breathtaking. She looked the same as her beautiful baby-self, just older. The same gorgeous blonde curly hair, rosebud mouth, blue eyes, button nose . . . Oh, God! Laura's legs buckled.

A woman behind her jostled her to get by. Laura snapped out of her trance and back to reality. She moved forward, as if in a dream, arms open, but when she reached Jody, the girl took a step back.

Laura put her arms down. She had to take it slowly. She must be gentle with this fragile child. She longed to put her arms around Jody, hold her and kiss her and love her . . . her baby . . . her Jody. She had waited so long for this moment, but she could see that Jody was terrified. She forced herself to hold back, to suppress the yearning to be physically close to her long-lost angel.

She held out her hand. 'I'm Laura.'

Jody shook it politely. 'I'm Sophie.'

Laura flinched. She wanted to shout, 'No, you're not. You're Jody. I gave birth to you, I christened you. You're not Sophie, you're Jody, my Jody.' But she didn't. Instead she said, 'It's very nice to meet you.'

'You too. You look so . . . we look so . . .' Sophie's eyes began to water.

'Alike? Yes, we do.'

'I'm very . . . um . . . well . . . confused.' Sophie was crying now.

Laura put an arm gently around her. 'It's OK. This is all very overwhelming. I feel exactly the same.'

'I'm sorry. I just can't get my head around it. It's so . . . well . . . kind of insane, really.'

'I know it is. Look, let's get out of here and go somewhere quiet where we can talk. There's a hotel nearby where we can sit down and be alone.'

'That sounds like a good idea.' Sophie walked ahead, moving away from Laura's arm.

Laura watched her, tall, elegant, beautiful. She seemed very together. She didn't look damaged, not on the outside anyway.

Sophie turned around. 'Which way?'

'My car's over here.' Laura caught up with her and led her to it.

Neither of them spoke on the journey to the hotel. It was so strange. There was so much Laura wanted to say but she didn't know where to begin. How do you fill in seventeen years of a life? How do you explain what it's like to see a ghost? How do you explain what a miracle feels like?

Laura could feel Sophie's tension. They walked into the hotel and Laura led Sophie to a couch in the corner of the lobby. It was the same one she had sat on with Frank only a few hours earlier. Sophie sat at the far end, fidgeting nervously. They ordered coffee, then looked at each other. Sophie lowered her eyes.

Laura broke the silence. 'I've been waiting for this moment for seventeen years. And now that you're here I'm tongue-tied. I want to know every single detail of your life. I want to know where you've been all this time and if you're OK. What your life has been like. School, friends, what food you eat, what books you read . . . everything. But first I have to know, have you been harmed or hurt in any way?'

214

'No, not at all. I've had a very nice life. My mother –'

Laura recoiled. She felt as if she'd been shot.

Sophie bit her lip. 'I'm sorry but . . . well . . . she is my mother, as in, I thought she was my mother but now I'm not sure.'

Laura willed herself to be calm. 'It's OK.' She tried to work out how to make Sophie understand that there was no doubt. She was Jody. The minute Laura had seen her in the airport she had known. All doubt had died when she'd set eyes on her. Visual proof, she thought, that's what I need. She pulled out the photos from her bag. 'I want to show you these. I think they'll prove to you that you're *my* daughter.'

Sophie looked at the photos, slowly, carefully, examining each one. Laura watched her. Blonde curls framed her face as she went through the pictures. Her eyebrows knitted together as she tried to understand how and why. Laura longed to hold her, but resisted the urge. She didn't want to frighten her away.

'It's me. The photos are all of me, but how did I end up in London, living another life?'

Laura chose her words carefully. 'We were on a boat and I took my eyes off you, which was wrong of me. I remember a woman hovering around and I've always believed it was she who took you. Stole you.'

'What did she look like?'

'I can't remember,' Laura admitted. 'It all happened very quickly.'

'What happened when you realized I was gone?'

'I searched for you everywhere. Everyone was looking for you and the police were called. Then someone saw your sandals floating in the sea and everyone presumed you'd drowned. But I knew you hadn't. I felt it in here.' Laura tapped her heart. 'I knew you were alive. It's been hell not knowing where you were or who you were with. A living hell.'

'But that means my mother –'

'Abducted you. Yes, it does,' Laura said, through gritted teeth.

Sophie twisted the napkin in her hands. 'Laura, my mother's

not like that. She's a really honest person. She'd never just take a child. She'd never do something so awful.'

'Jody –'

Sophie looked taken aback.

Laura hated calling her 'Sophie' but she knew she had to. 'I'm sorry, Sophie, but this woman did steal you. She ruined my life and my family's lives. She is not a good person. She is a very bad person. An evil person.'

Sophie's phone rang. She looked down. The screen said 'Mum'. Laura sat on her hands to prevent herself picking up the phone and smashing it into tiny pieces.

Sophie switched it off. 'I can't speak to *her* tonight.'

Laura's heart soared.

22.

Sophie

Dublin, July 2011

She couldn't have abducted me! Sophie's mind was racing. Her head ached. She'd almost fainted when she'd seen Laura in the airport. She looked so like her. It was all so surreal. She felt as if she was having an out-of-body experience.

And now here she was staring at baby pictures of herself and talking to her mother, her real mother, her birth mother. But it was insane. Was Anna a kidnapper? She couldn't be. She would never do something so heinous. She was a good, honest person. She was the most upstanding citizen Sophie had ever met. But how else could this be explained? Laura seemed so normal and lovely. If she said Anna had stolen her then that must have been what happened. And it did explain a lot. But Sophie still couldn't believe it of her.

'What that woman did was wicked and immoral, not to mention illegal.' Laura banged the coffee-table with her hand. She was getting emotional. 'She stole you from me. You can't imagine the pain of it. It nearly killed me, my mother and Frank. We all adored you. You were our Jody, our baby girl.'

'But how could she just walk off with me? Didn't you scream?' Sophie didn't understand how it could have happened. Especially on a boat where there was nowhere to run.

Laura closed her eyes and took a deep breath. 'I was young, very young, only twenty. I got distracted briefly and when I turned around you were gone. At first I just thought you'd wandered off or were hiding under a table or something. It was only after a while that I started panicking . . . and by then it was too late.'

It sounded awful, but Sophie needed to explain to Laura that her mum wasn't a kidnapper. She couldn't have taken her. There had to be a mistake. 'I'm sorry but my mother, I mean Anna, just wouldn't do that. She's the most honest person I know. She's completely law-abiding and never even drives over the speed limit. There *has* to be a mistake.'

Laura sighed. 'There is no mistake. Look at us. We're cut from the same cloth. We are mirror images of each other. You are my flesh and blood and I did not give you up. I did not hand you over or tell someone they could take you. That woman stole you. I don't know why she did it, but no reason is good enough. You do not take someone else's child. It's wrong. It's the worst crime you can commit. I've been in Hell. Hell. I didn't know if you were alive or dead, safe or in danger, with a normal person or a psychopath. I've been so heartbroken, so worried and sick with grief. I was terrified that I'd never see you again. Everyone thought I was delusional for imagining you were still alive. But I knew it. Deep in my heart I knew it. And here you are!'

Sophie could see how much Laura was hurting. It was all so upsetting. How could this have happened? She believed Laura, but that meant her mother had done something unspeakably wicked. She just couldn't accept that Anna was such an evil person. 'But she's my mum. I mean, she's not really, not biologically, but she is. She's a nice person. I can't believe she would do something so horrible and cruel. Oh, God, this is so awful. I feel so bad for you and your family to have suffered so much.'

It was too much. Sophie began to sob uncontrollably. Last week she had been looking forward to a fun summer before art college and now she was sitting with her real mother in Dublin, discovering that the woman she had thought was her mother was actually a fake and a kidnapper.

Sophie covered her eyes. 'I'm sorry. All I can see is green.'

Laura caught her breath. 'Is that your colour for pain?'

Sophie nodded.

'Mine's orange.'

'Are you seeing it now?'

'No.' Laura smiled. 'I'm seeing mostly blue, which is my happy colour, and a little bit of beige, which is my sad colour, because you're so upset.'

Sophie stopped crying. She held up a corner of her dress. 'I wore this because pink is my happy colour.'

'It's beautiful, as are you,' Laura said softly.

Sophie blushed. Laura was looking at her so deeply and lovingly, it made her a little uncomfortable. She decided to stick to the subject of colours. It was safer, less emotive. 'It's amazing to meet someone who has synaesthesia. When did you realize you had it?'

Laura's eyes lost their intensity. She sat back on the couch and absentmindedly fiddled with her necklace. 'My first real memory of it is coming home from school when I was about six and announcing that my name was purple. My dad was thrilled. He couldn't believe I saw the world the same way he did. Our colours were different. The only one we matched on was orange for pain.'

'What's Jody?' Sophie asked.

'Blue,' Laura smiled, 'which was why I chose it.'

'My mum –' Sophie saw Laura's face fall. 'Sorry. Anna didn't understand what was going on when I started saying I saw things as colours. She thought I was autistic. She took me to lots of different doctors until one eventually recognized the symptoms. It was a relief to find out that there wasn't something wrong with me.'

Laura sat forward again, frowning. 'Did the other kids in school notice or make fun of you?'

Sophie needed to reassure her: she looked so concerned. 'No, my mu– Anna was the headmistress so no one dared be mean to me.'

Laura seemed surprised. 'Headmistress! Was that hard for you?'

Sophie thought for a moment. 'There were times when I wished she wasn't because she knew everything that went on at school. Every move I made. But she was very protective of me, too much so at times, so it probably made it easier. Otherwise she would have been quizzing me after school every day to find out exactly what was going on.'

Laura's face clouded and she gripped the table. 'Of course she was over-protective, having done what she did. What did she say to you about your past? Did she ever admit you weren't hers?'

Sophie shook her head. 'No, never. I had no idea I wasn't her daughter.'

'Do you have any sisters or brothers? Did this Anna nick any other kids?'

Sophie winced at the bitter tone of Laura's voice. 'No. Just me.'

'Was she a good . . . ' Laura searched for the word '. . . parent?'

Sophie couldn't lie. She knew Laura wanted her to say Anna was an ogre, but she couldn't. 'Yes. She devoted herself to me. My friends' mothers used to comment on how committed she was. To be honest, it was a bit stifling at times.'

Laura looked stony-faced. 'Where is she from? London?'

Sophie looked surprised. 'No, she's Irish.'

'WHAT?' Laura almost fell off the couch.

'She's from here, from Dublin. But she never came back. She refused to bring me here.'

'I'm hardly surprised. Dublin's a village, really, so someone would probably have recognized you. I can't believe she's Irish. How could she do that? What kind of a human being is she?'

Sophie twisted her ring around her finger. 'I realize this will sound strange, but she's very normal.'

Laura slammed her coffee cup down on the table. 'No, Sophie, she's not. No normal person does that.'

Sophie winced. 'You're right. I'm sorry.'

Laura closed her eyes. 'Yellow now, for anger.' She opened them and looked at Sophie. 'This is really hard for me. To know that for all these years someone else has been bringing you up just kills me. But I'm glad she was nice to you and I'm happy that you had a decent life. It just hurts so much to know I missed all those years. Those precious years that she stole from me.'

Sophie sipped some water. Seeing the pain in Laura's eyes was making her feel weepy again. 'It must have been awful. I can't even begin to imagine. To lose a child like that . . . Did you not want any more children after it happened?'

Laura stared at her. 'I'm sorry, I should have told you. I have another daughter, Mandy. She's less than three years younger than you. I got pregnant shortly after you were taken. Having Mandy saved my life. I don't think I'd be here if it wasn't for her.'

Sophie was taken aback. When she had read on Laura's website that she had a daughter, she had presumed she was referring to Jody, the daughter who had disappeared. 'Wow, I had no idea. So she's kind of, like . . .' She hesitated.

'Your sister.' Laura smiled. 'Yes, she is. She's going to be so happy when she finds out you're alive. Mandy always wanted a sister she could talk to and play with.'

'Do we have the same dad?'

Laura blushed. 'No.'

'Who is my dad?'

Laura blew out her cheeks. 'I'm sorry, but I don't know where he is. He was an American musician I met one night and . . . well . . . he left town the next day. Two months later I realized I was pregnant.'

Sophie stared at her, open-mouthed. 'That's almost the same story Anna told me about my father.'

Laura looked shocked. 'What?'

Sophie's eyes flashed. 'She said my dad was an American architect she spent one night with and then he left and she never saw him again. Is this some story you mothers make up?'

Laura leaned over and gazed into Sophie's eyes. 'No, it is not. I'm ashamed of what I did. I was young and very stupid and very immature. But you were a blessing so I can't regret it happening. As for Anna, she obviously had to make up a story that put your father out of the picture.'

'So my real dad was a musician?'

'He said he was a drummer. I believed him. He was very good-looking and charming. I wish I knew him and could introduce you to him. If it's any consolation you have a wonderful uncle, granny, and sister.'

'I always wanted a sister.' Sophie smiled. 'A little sister is pretty cool. And a granny and an uncle.'

Laura beamed at her. 'I can't wait for you to meet everyone. They'll be over the moon.'

It was so nice to see Laura smiling and not looking tortured. 'I'm looking forward to it,' Sophie enthused.

'Mandy's lovely but she's quite shy and she can take a while to get to know, so don't be put off if she's wary at first.'

'I won't. I totally understand.'

Laura started twisting her necklace around her fingers. Suddenly she seemed cross again. 'Does Anna know you're meeting me today?'

Sophie didn't want to talk about Anna. She'd much rather talk about her new sister and synaesthesia. She sighed. 'At first I didn't tell her but I know she suspected something was up because I'd been asking lots of questions about my past and then I sent her a text saying I was with you. I'd say she's going crazy. I've never spent a night away from her. She never allowed me to go on sleepovers or on school trips unless she was on them too.'

Laura reached for her hand. Sophie felt awkward but didn't want to hurt Laura's feelings, so she put it out. Laura held it tightly. 'Can I hug you? Would that be OK?' she asked.

Sophie could see in her eyes how much Laura needed to hold her. She was afraid of it, afraid of the emotions that would surface when her real mother held her. She reached over gingerly and hugged Laura, who held her so tightly that she took her breath away. Sophie could feel Laura's body heaving with tears of joy, relief, sadness for the lost years, happiness at the miraculous reunion and exhaustion from the emotions that were drowning both of them.

She let herself sink into the hug and allowed herself to feel everything Laura was experiencing. They wept in each other's arms, mourning their lost past, celebrating their new future.

When Sophie pulled away, they looked at each other's tear-stained faces and began to laugh. There was a hysterical edge to it. Sophie felt all of the emotions coiled up inside her being released. It felt fantastic.

Laura handed her a tissue and they wiped their eyes. Then she stood up and pulled out her car keys. 'Come on, let's go. I live a forty-minute drive away. Will you come and stay? Will you come home with me?'

Sophie didn't hesitate. She wanted to be with her mother. She wanted to spend more time with her, get to know her and meet the rest of the family. 'I'd love to. But I just need to ring my friend Holly. Is that OK?'

'Of course. I'm going to call Frank and ask him to take Mandy for the night. I need to break this incredible news to her gently and give her a little time to process it before I introduce you. We can sort it all out tomorrow. For now I think you need some sleep – you look exhausted.'

Sophie was relieved. She felt drained. She'd had enough emotion for one day. She didn't have the energy to meet any more people tonight. She longed for sleep. 'That would be perfect, thanks.'

While Laura rang Frank to sort out Mandy's sleeping arrangements, Sophie called Holly to see what was going on at home and to fill her in.

'OMG, I've called you, like, ten zillion times!' Holly screeched.

Sophie grinned. It was so good to hear her friend's voice. It was like putting on your favourite fleece, warm and comforting. Holly knew her: she didn't have to worry about what she said or how she felt or how Holly was going to react. She could be completely herself and totally honest. 'Sorry, I turned my phone off to avoid Mum.'

'Are you all right?' Holly sounded very serious.

'I'm fine.'

'Are you sure? Can you speak freely or is someone beside you? Say "Jeepers" if someone's beside you.'

Sophie sighed. This was typical Holly, talking in riddles. 'What are you on about? I'm totally alone. Laura's gone to call her brother.'

'So you've met?'

'Yes.'

'Is she drunk?'

'No!'

'Has she been mean to you or abusive?'

'No. Stop asking silly questions.'

'They're not silly,' Holly protested. 'I'm trying to make sure you're all right and that you're not in danger.'

It was sweet that Holly was worried about her and Sophie appreciated it. 'I'm fine, Holly. Honestly.'

'Thank God for that. So, what's she like?'

Sophie glanced at Laura, who was talking animatedly into her phone, laughing and crying at the same time. 'She's great. She's really pretty and young. She had me when she was nineteen. She's super nice but she's really angry about what happened, Holly. It's terrible – she's been so hurt.'

'So is she definitely your mum?'

'Yes. No question.'

'Is she messed up psychologically from the kidnapping? Like Mrs Havisham, all eaten up by grief?'

Sophie laughed. Typical Holly. 'It's *Miss* Havisham.'

'What?'

'The whole point of her character in *Great Expectations* is that she was jilted, never got married and remained a bitter old miss for the rest of her life.'

'Oh, my God, you've just met your long-lost mother and you're giving me English lessons! Can you please focus on what's important here? Isn't Laura a little bit weird?'

Sophie sighed. 'No, Holly, she isn't. She's just a normal person. She's lovely, actually.'

'OK, good. I'm glad your real mother is normal because your

other mother is in a terrible state. Sophie, I've got something to tell you. Please don't hate me.'

'What is it?'

'It's about telling your mum – I should probably call her Anna. We can't call her your mum any more, can we?'

'I haven't thought about that yet. Go on.'

'I know I wasn't supposed to tell her anything about where you were and what you were doing. Initially I did really well. I kept my mouth closed. But then she got really scary. She's such a good interrogator – it must be from all the years she's spent in school quizzing girls on misdemeanours – and then she went from scary to completely devastated. I mean, I've never seen anyone so upset. It was terrible, Sophie. I just caved in and told her everything.'

Sophie shuddered. She hated to think of Anna so upset, but then again, look at the misery she had caused. She hardened her heart against her mother. 'It's OK. I knew you would.'

'What do you mean?'

'Holly, you were never going to survive my mum – Anna's questioning.'

'Well, I'll have you know I did very well. I lasted about ten minutes before I broke. I know that may not be James Bond or Red Beret standards but –'

'It's Green Beret.'

'Excuse me?'

'The special forces you're talking about are Green Berets, not red.'

'Whatever, Sophie. The point I'm trying to make is that Anna came storming into the pizzeria and started hissing at me in front of the barman, then dragged me outside and was shouting at me. And I still didn't tell her anything. I only gave in when she started crying. She was hysterical.'

'Wow! Mum never cries.' Despite trying not to care, Sophie was feeling queasy at the thought of her mother being so upset.

'I know! And remember, she's not just your mum to me, she's

my headmistress too. I didn't know what to do, so I panicked and told her everything.'

'She had to find out sooner or later anyway.'

'Well, Sophie, she's doing her nut. I've never seen her like that. But when I got home from work her car was still there and the light was on in her bedroom, so she must be getting an early flight over tomorrow. I bet she called Joe. Did you ring Mark?'

'I didn't want to talk to him because I knew he'd try to persuade me to call Mum, so I just rang his voicemail when I landed and said I was in Dublin for a few days and it was a long story and I might need a place to crash.'

'Anna kept saying it was all a mix-up and that she saved you and that Laura was a terrible person and that she's a drunk.'

'Well, she's lying. We've been here for ages and Laura's only had coffee.'

'Maybe she's one of those people who keeps the bottle in her handbag and pours it into her coffee when you're not looking.'

'Holly, she didn't pour anything into her coffee.'

'Does she have the shakes or bloodshot eyes or slurry speech or anything?'

Sophie knew Laura wasn't a drunk. It was just Anna trying to sabotage everything. 'No. She's not drunk.'

'Be careful, Sophie. Some alcoholics never seem drunk and then all of a sudden, bam, they keel over. I think they're called functioning drunks. My uncle –'

Sophie decided to interrupt her friend before she launched into a long story about her uncle. 'Holly!'

'I've got it! Why don't you do that test on her? You know, the one we did in school where you ask the questions – does drinking affect your finances, does it alter your mood, have you ever got into a fight because of alcohol –'

'I am not going to start quizzing my mother about alcohol dependency.'

'Ooooh, Sophie, you called her your mother!'

Sophie's hand flew up to her mouth. 'Gosh, I did, didn't I?'

'You must like her. Is she as good-looking in the flesh as she is on her website?'

Sophie looked at Laura's animated face. She was beaming as she talked into her phone. 'Prettier.'

'Wow, lucky you! You're going to look like that when you're older. I'm going to look like my mum, which is scary.'

'Your mum's great. Oh, I forgot to tell you, guess what? You're not going to believe this.'

'I knew it, you lucky cow! Bono's your dad!'

'No! I have a sister.'

'No way!'

'I swear. My mum, I mean Laura, just told me. My sister's name is Mandy and she's a bit younger than me.'

'Wow, I hope she's nice and not a total pain, like Jessie.'

'Me too. She sounds nice, although Laura did say she was hard to get to know.'

Holly snorted. 'My mum says that about Jessie. It's mum-speak, which translates as "My daughter is a living nightmare."'

'She can't be. I'm sure she's lovely.'

'I bet she isn't, and I guarantee when she sees you walking in, all gorgeous and normal and clever and arty, she'll hate you.'

'Holly, that's really mean.'

'I just gave you loads of compliments.'

'I want Mandy to like me.'

'I'm just being honest. If you were my ghost sister I'd hate you.'

'Thanks a lot. Look, I have to go. We're driving to Laura's house now.'

'Try and smell her breath before you get into the car. I'm not dealing with Anna if you die in a car crash with drunk Laura.'

'Stop it. She's not drunk.'

'Hey, Sophie.'

'Yes?'

'Don't forget to keep notes. We'll need them for the screen-play.'

23.

Anna

Dublin, July 2011

As the night dragged on Anna continued pacing the floor, worrying herself sick. Was Sophie in danger? What if Holly had told Nancy – or one of the other girls and they'd told their parents? Her secret would be out. She'd probably be arrested. Oh, God . . . the pain! She bent over clutching her stomach. Her ulcer was blazing. She swallowed two tablets.

She didn't know what to pack. How long would she be staying? A day, two, three? Would Sophie come home with her straight away? She'd sounded very angry in her text, but Anna knew that once Sophie had met Laura she'd soon realize how lucky she was to have been saved.

She was so worried about Sophie. What if Laura was drunk and abusive to her, verbally and, oh, God, maybe even physically? Anna would kill that witch if she hurt her daughter. She looked at Laura's website for the millionth time. According to that and the other articles she had Googled about Laura Fletcher, she was a successful artist. But lots of successful artists were drunks and drug addicts. A talent for painting didn't necessarily make you a decent human being. Just because you sold a few pictures it didn't mean you were fit to be a mother. It didn't mean you weren't a wretched person who neglected your child.

Anna looked at the clock. God, it was only three. This night would never end. She sat down on her bed and tried to breathe deeply and calm down. But it was hopeless. How could she be calm when Sophie might be mixing with drug addicts and alcoholics? Laura's friends were bound to be similar to her – 'artists' who probably spent all day drinking and getting stoned. Anna had seen her drinking on the boat that day: she was a bad mother.

Anna felt sick. Sophie wouldn't be able to handle it. She was mature in some ways but very naïve in others. She had led a very cosseted life. She'd never travelled alone before. She'd never even spent a night away from home. What if Laura collected her and was drunk and crashed the car, killing them both? What if one of Laura's friends spiked Sophie's drink and molested her? What if Sophie had a fight with Laura and ran out with no clue where she was or who to run to? Anna prayed she would go to Mark or Joe. Surely she would have the sense to call them if she was in trouble. Dublin could be a dangerous place. Anna knew the bad areas all too well from her teaching days there. She raised her eyes to the ceiling. Please, God, keep her safe until I get there . . .

Not having Sophie near her was like having a limb wrenched off. Anna knew this was going to be the longest night of her life.

She arrived at Heathrow at four thirty a.m. She was desperate to get to Dublin – to be near Sophie, to explain to her, to save her once again from that terrible woman. When she eventually landed in Dublin airport, she hurried through the arrivals door and found Joe waiting for her.

He looked older, more craggy-faced, but handsome. He still had the greenest eyes, and although his hair was white now, there was lots of it. She rushed over to him and he wrapped his arms around her. She sank into them, grateful for their comfort.

'Oh, Joe, thank God you're here. I'm so worried.'

He pushed her hair back from her face and kissed her gently on the lips. 'Poor Anna, you look exhausted. Don't worry, we'll sort this out. Have you heard from Sophie since last night?'

'No. I was hoping she'd have at least sent me a text this morning so I'd know if she was alive or dead.' She began to cry.

Joe rubbed her back. 'Mark heard from her late last night. He'd had a message from her and tried to call her but she didn't answer.

Then at about eleven she sent him a text, saying she was with her biological mother and she was fine.'

'That bitch Laura! How dare she take Sophie away from me? We have to go straight to her house, Joe. We have to go now. Come on.'

'Hold on.' Joe stopped Anna. He took her bag and her hand and led her to a bench in a corner of the airport.

'What are you doing? I don't have time for this.' Anna was up to ninety – she couldn't sit still. Not now, not when her daughter was in danger. What was Joe thinking?

Joe tugged her hand and got her to sit down beside him. In his warm, measured voice, he said, 'You need to calm down and decide how you're going to approach this. You can't go barging in there, like a crazy woman. You'll just make Sophie even angrier. She's obviously furious that you never told her she was adopted. You don't want to make things worse. You have to tread softly here, Anna. There are a lot of heightened emotions involved.'

Anna crossed her arms defensively. 'What am I supposed to do? Sit around waiting for her to be corrupted by this Laura? This excuse for a mother who was too drunk to look after her own child? A woman who passed out and left her baby girl abandoned for anyone to take?'

'What do you mean "take"?'

Too late, Anna realized her mistake. Joe had always suspected something was wrong about the adoption and now she'd given him a clue. Damn. 'Nothing.'

'Anna?'

'Nothing.'

Joe turned her to face him. His green eyes bored into her brown ones. 'Anna, I want the truth, the whole truth this time. Did you adopt Sophie via the proper channels or did you ignore some of the red tape? This is really serious. You've been vague about her adoption all along. What exactly did you do?'

Anna looked at her friend, the only connection she had to her former life. Joe loved her. He would help her. He was such a good person, not one to judge. A man who had been broken-hearted when his marriage failed. A man who had fought for joint custody of his son. A man who never ducked responsibility, who had the biggest heart she knew of. A man she was lucky to have in her life. A man who thought she was perfect. A man who was about to have all of his beliefs shattered . . .

Anna looked into the distance, took a deep breath, and said, 'I didn't adopt her. I took her.'

Joe frowned. 'Took her from where?'

'From a boat.'

'A boat?'

Anna turned and held his gaze. Her voice was steady, as she said, 'The boat I took to London when I emigrated after Hope died.'

'How could you take a child from a boat?' Joe was puzzled.

'Easily. Her mother had passed out drunk at the bar. Sophie was abandoned, alone, upset, hungry, thirsty and seasick. Completely neglected.'

Joe's eyes widened as he began to understand. 'So you just took her?'

Anna's jaw set in a tight line. 'Yes.'

'You *stole* someone else's child?' Joe's mouth hung open.

'Yes.'

'But . . . how . . . what . . . Are you insane?'

'No, Joe, it was the sanest decision I ever made. If it hadn't been for me, Sophie would have drowned or maybe been taken by a paedophile or ended up living on the streets because her mother was an alcoholic. It wasn't even lunchtime and her mother was so drunk she'd passed out.'

'But how did you get away with it?' Joe said, rubbing his forehead. He looked shocked. 'Surely she woke up and realized her child was gone.'

'By the time she came out of her drunken coma, I was halfway to London.'

'There must have been an investigation,' Joe spluttered.

Anna remained composed as she related the story. 'Not really, because they found the child's sandals overboard and presumed she'd drowned.'

'How did her sandals end up in the sea?'

'I threw them over the side.'

Joe stared at her as if he was seeing her for the first time. 'Jesus Christ, Anna, how could you? How could you take someone else's child and pretend they were dead. It's un–'

'Unthinkable? Reprehensible? Shameful? Despicable?'

'Yes!'

Anna sat back and crossed her arms. 'Is it really, Joe? Is it really such a terrible crime to save a child's life? To allow a little girl to grow up in a safe, loving, nurturing environment? To make her happiness your priority? To give her a chance to become the best person she can be? Should I have left her with that pathetic excuse of a mother so she could end up like all those beautiful children I taught in school? Most of whom ended up as either drunks, drug addicts or dealers, in prison or pregnant at fifteen living on welfare. Is that better? Is that what we need to do – turn our heads and pretend we don't see it? Shrug our shoulders and say it's not our problem? Wash our hands of these innocent children's fate?'

Joe took her by the shoulders and shook her. 'It's not for us to decide. Who made you God?'

'Neglect is a form of abuse,' Anna shouted.

People were staring at them. Joe stopped shaking her. 'You can't take someone else's child. It's wrong. It's immoral.'

'No, Joe. It's immoral to leave a child in danger. Sophie was in real danger. She was crying, thirsty and sick.'

'Anna!' he snapped. 'It was not up to you to decide that the child was better off with you. She had a mother already. Maybe not a perfect one, but for all you know she could have been a good mother most of the time and you just saw her on a bad day.'

'Don't insult my intelligence! I know these women,' Anna spat. 'I watched them all those years I taught in that inner-city school. They don't change. They get worse, more abusive, more neglectful. All they think about is their next drink. I'd seen enough – I'd stood by helplessly for years while those innocent children suffered. I had to do something, Joe. I had to help her – she was so forlorn.'

'ANNA! You can't do that. If everyone went around taking children from parents they didn't think were suitable the world would be a mess. Not all children of alcoholics turn out badly. You had no right. That poor woman has spent years thinking her child drowned because she was drunk. Do you have any idea what she must have felt?'

Anna laughed bitterly. 'I'm sure she just cracked open another bottle of vodka and blacked it out.'

Joe stood up and turned away, running his hands through his hair. 'I cannot believe you would do something so fundamentally wrong.'

Anna jumped up and pulled him back. 'I saved her life, Joe. Nothing you can say will make me feel bad about that. And I've been the best mother I could be and look how well she's turned out. She's an incredible girl. She's happy, smart, full of joy and warmth and affection. I couldn't be more proud of her.'

'Well, she's not full of joy at the moment, Anna. She's full of rage because you've been lying to her all her life.' He shook his head. 'I mean, how did you even get the right papers for her? You've taken her on holidays – how the hell did you get a passport?'

Anna shrugged. 'I had Hope's birth certificate,' she said, biting her lip. 'I just used it as Sophie's and no one was any the wiser.'

Joe stared at her for a few seconds. 'Hope?' he said. He continued to look at her, and his gaze softened. 'Oh, Anna,' he whispered.

She turned away from him, hiding the doubts and fears that had been creeping into her mind all night. Doubts and fears that she had never allowed to enter her mind before. Thoughts that she had buried deep down in the bottom of her conscience. 'It'll pass.

When she sees what a terrible life she would have had with that woman, she'll understand I was right. She'll thank me.'

Joe shook his head. 'My God, Anna, can't you admit what you did was wrong?'

Anna's jaw set. 'Never, because I believe with every fibre of my being that it was right.'

'I'd never have thought you capable of something so shocking.'

'It wasn't shocking. It was instinctive and necessary.'

Joe was clearly shattered by the revelation. 'It was wrong, Anna, you have to see that.'

Anna's eyes welled up and she reached for his hand. 'Joe, you're my best friend in the world. I need you now. Whatever you think of what I did, I promise you I did it for the right reasons. Please don't judge me. Please help me get my Sophie back.'

Joe hugged her as he would a stranger in distress, and Anna knew that something had broken between them.

They drove in silence to Killduf. Anna tried calling Sophie over and over again, but she only got her voicemail. She looked out of the window at the scenery she knew so well. Ireland, her birth-place, her home. Not any more. London was her home now. Sophie was her home. This place, this country, had let her down. She had left it a broken woman with a broken marriage and a broken heart. A mother who had buried her child. A wife who had buried her marriage. A daughter who had buried her parents. An orphan, lonely and crushed.

And now here she was, seventeen years and one snap decision later, the mistress of her own destiny, the navigator of her own fate, strong, happy, fulfilled, loved. And best of all a mother, who understood what unconditional love felt like. To love another more than yourself, to value their happiness far above your own, to sacrifice for them, to work hard to give them a perfect life . . . It was all she had wished for and so much more.

'This is the village of Killduf.' Joe broke the silence. 'Do you know where the house is?'

'No.' Anna spotted a man locking the post-office door. 'Pull over and I'll ask him for directions.'

Joe did so and Anna jumped out. She ran to the man. 'Hello, sorry to disturb you, I'm looking for Laura Fletcher's house.'

'Oh, are you now?' the man said, smirking.

'Yes.'

'And what would you be wanting there?'

Anna was taken aback by the question. 'Well, it's, um . . . a private matter.'

'Oh, is it now? You wouldn't happen to be looking for a certain missing person, would you?'

Anna froze. 'What do you mean?'

'You know exactly what I mean. You're scum.'

'Excuse me?'

He warmed to his theme. 'Scum, I said. Going around preying on innocent people. Ruining their lives.'

Anna glared at him. 'How dare –'

He put his face close to hers. 'Don't try and justify yourself to me. I know your type. You're like a leech, feeding off other people's misery. That poor girl doesn't know if she's coming or going.'

'But how –'

He leaned on the handlebars of his bicycle. 'How did I know? I know everything that goes on around here. It's my business to keep an eye out for unsavoury types like you, coming here trying to force that poor young woman out of hiding. Ruining her life. Why can't you just let her be? She's happy up there with Laura Fletcher.'

'But I'm her –'

'Stalker. Oh, yes, I know all about you. I had a long chat with her. She told me how you follow her everywhere she goes. She knows that without her you'd be destroyed, you'd be nothing.'

Anna was beginning to panic – how the hell did this man know so much? When had Sophie spoken to him? Why had she told him all this? The whole village would know their secret by lunchtime. 'I need to speak to Laura Fletcher. It's urgent.'

'I'm under strict instructions to say nothing. But I will say this. Laura's house-guest is a lovely girl. Beautiful, kind, funny, warm and generous, with a body that would make a grown man weep.'

'Excuse me!' Anna interrupted.

'Don't get all feminist on me now. She's not a bit shy about showing off her assets. She's very funny about them – she calls the left one Ernie and the right one Bert.'

'What?'

'English girls are less inhibited about their bodies than Irish girls. Much less uptight, fair play to them.'

Was this man really telling her that Sophie had been talking to him about her breasts? Anna was horrified. Laura must have got her drunk or spiked her drink. Sophie would never talk about her breasts to a strange man, or to anyone else for that matter. She was very reserved.

'She isn't usually that forthcoming, I can assure you.'

'Not to you, obviously. Who'd want to tell you anything? You'd just throw it back in her face.'

'No, I wouldn't.'

'Yes, you would. It's always the same. You draw her out and then you use the information against her.'

'Look, I don't know what she told you but I've never done anything to hurt her.'

'Oh, I see. You're one of the "good" ones, are you? One of the nice ones. Someone she should trust?'

'Yes, of course.'

'I don't believe you, and neither does she any more. She's been hurt too much. Laura told her not to talk to anyone, but she said she was lonely and needed to talk to someone about it all. She said her head is melted and I'm a good listener, so she told me everything. All the sordid details. I have to say I was shocked. I never would have thought anyone capable of such a terrible act.'

Anna's heart was pounding. 'What did she tell you?'

'Playing dumb now, are you? Trying to get me to slip up? I

won't, though. I won't give the game away. She asked me not to. She's writing a book about it all.'

'A book!' Anna croaked.

The postman grinned. 'Yes, a tell-all book, leaving no details out. She said it's going to be sensational.'

Anna thought she might be sick. She ran back to the car where Joe was waiting.

'What took you so long?' Joe asked. Then, looking at her, he said, 'My God, you're green.'

'Joe, she's taken drugs or got really drunk or something. That man said Sophie was writing a book about everything that's happened and that she was talking to him about her breasts and naming them Ernie and Bert and just being really odd. We have to get her out of there before she's completely corrupted. Quick, hurry.'

'Which way?'

'I don't know,' Anna wailed.

'Stay here. I'll ask in the local shop.'

Joe went into the small grocery store and came back a minute later. 'Got it. Up here, left, second right, and it's down the end of a long lane.'

'Thanks, Joe.' Anna went to squeeze his hand, but he placed it on the steering wheel.

Five minutes later they were staring at the house and studio. They had parked a good bit back and walked closer so no one could see them. The house was lovely. It was whitewashed, with blue shutters, and set back from a cliff overlooking the sea. Anna was surprised to see it was so well kept. She had assumed it would be more run-down and tatty-looking.

She and Joe hid behind a large oak tree watching Sophie, Laura and a small blonde woman with big breasts having breakfast outside in the sun.

Sophie looked exhausted. She had black circles under her eyes. Anna longed to rush up and hug her, but Joe held her back. Laura looked completely different from how Anna remembered her. She was young and very beautiful. She was Sophie. It hurt to see how similar they were. Anna's ulcer flared.

'They could be twins.' Joe was amazed at the similarity between birth mother and daughter.

Anna couldn't hear what they were saying but she watched Sophie talking to Laura and saw the look on Laura's face. It was the look only a mother can give her own child. She was looking at Sophie as Anna did. She could see the love in Laura's eyes. The adoration . . . Anna felt as if her heart was being ripped out. She clutched the tree to stop herself falling. The emotion was too much, too painful.

'She doesn't look like a down-and-out alcoholic,' Joe noted.

'How can you tell? It's only ten o'clock in the morning, for goodness' sake.'

'Anna, she looks well, healthy, no shakes, no trembling in the hands. She seems perfectly normal –'

'Stop!' Anna sobbed. 'I can't take it. Sophie's mine. She's my baby, not hers. I don't care how normal she looks. She's a bad person. I'm Sophie's mother, not her.'

Joe caught her as she fell. He held her upright as she cried her heart out into his shoulder. 'Come on, let it out. You need to let go, Anna. How did you keep this to yourself for all these years? The stress of such a secret must have been killing you.'

Anna wiped her eyes and nose. 'I just blocked it. From the moment I walked off that boat, Sophie was mine. Nobody else's. I knew I'd done the right thing. I've never been so sure of anything in my life. I know you may think I was mad, Joe, but I did save her – her life was in danger – and I don't regret it.'

Joe wiped a tear from her cheek. 'Your ulcer was your body's way of channelling all the stress, Anna. I wondered why it never cleared up. I understand completely now. Keeping a secret like this is mind-blowing.'

'I was happy, Joe. Really, truly happy. Sophie did that, she made me happy.'

'I know.' Joe nodded. 'I know she did.'

Anna looked over at the group eating breakfast. Sophie was picking at her food. She could see Laura encouraging her to eat. 'I have to go to her. I have to explain.'

Joe held her back. 'Not now. It's too much for her. If you go in there now, guns blazing, she'll push you away. Give her a bit more time with Laura. She needs it. Why don't you leave her a message and tell her you're in Dublin with me and that you want to meet her to explain everything? Don't be angry with her. Try to sound calm and reassuring – it'll make her want to call you back.'

Anna ached to be with Sophie, but she knew Joe was right. If she barged in now, when Sophie was still so angry and raw, she'd make things worse. Besides, she could see now that Sophie was all right. And that was what mattered most.

Anna knew there was nothing she could do – Sophie would freak if she walked in on her now. She had to give her a little more time and keep the lines of communication open. She rang Sophie's mobile and watched as Sophie picked it up, looked to see who was calling and flung it back into her bag. Anna saw Laura turn away and smile – the bitch.

She composed herself and left a message for her daughter, trying not to sound desperate: 'Sophie, it's Mum. I'm in Dublin. I had to be near you. I'm staying with Joe. Please call me so we can meet up and I can explain this to you. There are two sides to every story and I think you need to hear mine. I miss you. I love you. I'm waiting for you.'

'Perfect,' Joe said. 'No one could resist that. Now, come on, let's get out of here before someone finds us lurking in the bushes.'

As they turned to go, a man strode across the lawn. He stopped dead in front of Sophie. 'Jody!' he shouted, and threw his arms around her.

24.

Laura

Killduf, July 2011

Frank's shoulders heaved with emotion. Sophie stood awkwardly beside him while he clung to her hand, tears streaming down his face.

Lexie came over, gently pulled him away and led him towards a chair. 'Come on, Frank, sit yourself down here and catch your breath.'

Frank did so shakily. 'I'm sorry, it's just so incredible . . . Jody . . . to see you . . . alive . . . so beautiful . . . so like Laura . . . I just didn't expect . . . It's such a shock . . . to see you . . . here . . .'

'It's all right, darlin' – it's normal you reactin' like this. I've only known you lot for a few weeks and I'm gobsmacked.' Lexie patted Frank's back.

Laura went over to her brother. He sniffled. 'Who would have thought, Laura? It's a miracle.'

'I know.' She smiled, getting emotional herself. 'It's hard to believe. But it's true, she's back.'

'Our little Jody.' Frank gave Sophie a watery smile.

'Now, Frank,' Lexie said, 'this girl has been brought up as Sophie all her life and I think we should respect that. So why don't we call her Sophie and make things easier for her? The poor thing's had a right shock, haven't you, love?'

Sophie nodded and rubbed her eyes wearily.

Frank coughed and pulled himself together. 'I apologize, Sophie. I'm not usually an emotional man. It's just that we all thought you were dead. Well, all of us except Laura. She never gave up hope. She always knew you were alive. And now to have you back, sitting here with us . . . well, it's just hard to believe and very, very special.'

'He's a good egg, is Frank.' Lexie winked at Sophie. 'He's been really nice to me. As has Laura. They're a lovely family. You'll fit right in.'

'Here you go, Frank.' Laura handed her brother a cup of coffee. 'I put three sugars in for shock.'

'I wish you drank. I could murder a drop of whiskey in this.'

Laura laughed. 'I'd nearly have one myself!'

'Do you not drink?' Sophie asked.

'I used to, but I gave up after you disappeared.' Laura kept as close to the truth as she could, but she wasn't about to admit to her daughter that she had been a drunk and done drugs.

'I love a drink, me,' Lexie said. 'Nothin' better than a nice glass of Cristal after a hard day.'

Frank laughed. 'Cristal! Lexie, you're a true WAG.'

Lexie grinned. 'Flippin' right I am. I know how to spend Dougie's cash, make no mistake. We used to get through cases of the stuff. Oh, we had some wild parties. Do you drink, Sophie?'

Sophie hesitated. 'Well, not really. I don't like the taste of wine, but I have had vodka and Coke, which is all right.'

'You're better off staying away from it,' Laura assured her. 'It can cause terrible problems.'

'That's what Mum, I mean Anna, always says.' Sophie caught herself. 'She says people behave really badly when they drink too much.'

Laura didn't want to hear anything that Anna had had to say. Every time she heard her name she wanted to scream. She decided to change the subject and get on to safer ground, away from alcohol. 'Guess what, Frank? Sophie's applied to go to art college next year. She's just finished her A levels.'

'Like mother, like daughter.' Frank smiled. 'That's fantastic, good for you, Jody – sorry, Sophie. Have you always been interested in art?'

'Ever since I can remember. I think it's because I see things as colours.'

'Of course, you have synaesthesia too.' Frank remembered her email. 'How incredible.'

'I suppose that was where it all started, and then I found that I really enjoyed the subject. Painting is the one time when I completely switch off from the world.'

'Just like me.' Laura's eyes shone.

'If you've got your mum's talent you'll be amazin',' Lexie enthused.

'Mum doesn't paint at all. Oh!' Sophie went red. 'Sorry, I . . .'

'It's OK.' Laura patted her hand. It wasn't Sophie's fault. She hoped that in time Sophie would only have one mum in her life – herself. 'I'm thrilled that you get so much joy from painting. I can honestly say it saved my life. On very bad days, when I missed you so much I could barely function, I'd put on some soothing music and lose myself in my work.'

Sophie smiled. 'I'm glad you had something to help you. It must have been very hard.'

'There are no words adequate to describe it,' Laura said, voice shaking.

'This woman here is the most incredible human being,' Frank said to Sophie, clasping Laura's shoulder. 'She never gave up hope. She never stopped believing you'd come back one day. Never.'

'And here you are.' Laura beamed at Sophie, whose cheeks were flushed. She could tell that all the attention was taking its toll. Sophie was shrinking back into her chair. She needed a break. 'How's Mandy?' she asked Frank, switching topics.

'She's fine. I dropped her off at Joan's on my way here this morning. She knows something's up but she has no idea what it is.'

'She'll get plenty of lyrics out of this story,' Lexie put in. 'She'll be writing songs for weeks.'

'Is she a musician?' Sophie asked.

Lexie and Frank roared laughing. 'She takes it very seriously and she tries hard, but she hasn't a note in her head,' Frank said.

'That's a bit harsh,' Laura defended her younger daughter. 'She's talented. She just needs more time to find her sound.'

'And a singer.' Frank grinned.

'She needs to tone down them lyrics an' all. They're very angry and depressin',' Lexie added. 'Then again, I like Kylie and Girls Aloud. Dougie says my taste in music is crap. He likes 50 Cent and all them rappers. I can't be dealin' with all that stuff – it's too aggressive for me.'

'What kind of music does Mandy play?' Sophie wondered.

'She says she's a cross between Alanis Morissette, Björk and Nirvana,' Laura explained.

'Oh.' Sophie was lost for words.

'"Oh" is right,' Frank agreed. 'She writes very angry songs about being trapped and feeling suffocated. There's a lot of shouting and banging on the guitar. It's not really my kind of thing. I'm more of a Michael Bublé man myself.'

'I like Lana Del Rey and Adele,' Laura said.

'Oh, me too,' Sophie said. 'They're amazing.'

'Dougie said he thought Rihanna looked like me, only she was black.'

Frank threw his head back and laughed. 'Good old Dougie. His lines are going to make your book a bestseller.'

'This book is going to get me into a lot of trouble,' Lexie observed. 'I'm not holdin' back, I'm tellin' it like it was. I reckon I'll have to go into that witness protection programme when it hits the bookshops.'

'You'll be the toast of London,' Frank assured her. 'I guarantee you the *Sun* will offer us a fortune for the serial rights. It's all looking good, Lexie, so just keep talking into the tape recorder.'

'Keep your hair on. I'm workin' hard, ain't I, Laura?'

'Yes, you are. And remember, Lexie, you can always come back and hide here if it gets too much,' Laura said. 'You're welcome anytime.'

'Thanks, darlin'. I'd love to.' Lexie turned to Sophie. 'This is a great place to chill out and get your head together. You'll love it here. It's so peaceful and the view of the ocean would lift the heaviest heart.'

'That's why I bought the house,' Laura mused.

Sophie smiled weakly. Lexie could see she was struggling. 'You look worn out, darlin'. It's been hell for you. All this findin' out you're not who you thought you was. Do you fancy a little lie-down? Come on, I'll make you a nice fresh cup of tea and you can have a nap.'

'You do look tired,' Laura agreed. 'Would you like a rest?'

Sophie nodded, looking relieved. 'Actually, that would be lovely, if you don't mind?'

'Of course not, it's been a crazy few days.' Laura stood up. 'I'll walk you in.'

'No, darlin', you sit down there and have a natter with Frank. You two have a lot to talk about. I'll go in with Sophie. I need to work on my book anyways. See, Frank? I'm not slackin'.'

Laura watched Lexie tottering across the garden on her six-inch wedges, followed by Sophie in flat pumps, head hanging low, deep in thought. 'Frank, can you believe it?' Laura said softly.

Frank didn't reply.

'Frank!'

'Sorry – what?'

'Are you looking at Lexie's bum?' Laura slapped his arm.

'Sorry, but it's a very pert one,' he said sheepishly.

'I'm trying to talk to you about my daughter and how wonderful she is.'

'She's incredible. I swear when I first saw her it was like seeing you.'

'I can't stop staring at her,' Laura confessed. 'The poor thing must be completely overcome.'

'The amazing thing is that she seems so normal. I know you told me last night that she was very together but I still can't get over it. Our little Jody has turned into a lovely young woman.'

'Frank, you have to call her Sophie. She cringes when we say "Jody",' Laura warned him. 'I hate calling her that but it's the only name she knows. We have to take this slowly and be very gentle with her.'

Frank rolled up the sleeves of his shirt. The morning sun was getting warmer. 'Sophie it is. But I find it incredible that she doesn't seem scarred or odd or in any way peculiar. The woman who took her can't have been a nutter. Sophie seems to have been treated well.'

'She may not have any obvious scars but that doesn't mean she's not messed up.' Laura didn't want anything good said about Anna: she was a stealing psychopath.

'Did she say what her childhood was like? She's got a very posh English accent – she obviously went to a good school.'

'Anna was the headmistress of the private Catholic girls' school she went to, and get this – she's Irish.'

'What?'

'Yes, Jody's – Sophie's – abductor is Irish. Can you believe it?'

'Well, I suppose the chances were high. You were on a boat from Dublin to Holyhead.'

Laura put her cup down. 'I know, but somehow I never imagined an Irish person taking her – certainly not a headmistress from Dublin!'

'Did she say if this Anna was a bit strange? Weird? Deranged? Mentally unstable?'

Laura sighed. 'No, she said she was a great mother. She was devoted to her. She seems to have done everything to make Sophie happy. It makes me sick even to say those words. But I'm glad that Sophie didn't suffer. I have to be happy about that.'

Frank thumped the patio table. 'She may have been devoted but it doesn't take away from the fact that she kidnapped your child. No one in their right mind would do that. She must have a screw loose. Underneath her headmistress guise there is an unstable individual.'

Laura looked out at the sea. The water was like glass. It was a

245

still summer morning, not a puff of wind. 'I'd only ever admit this to you, but if I'm being totally honest, I was a complete drunken mess on that boat. I have to take responsibility for that. I'm sure I didn't exactly come across as mother of the year.'

Frank's face was flushed. 'I don't care how drunk you were, she *did not* have the right to steal your child. It's called abduction and it's illegal. She put us all through hell and she should go to prison and rot there.'

'Ssssh! Don't let Sophie hear you. I don't want her to be frightened. She could bolt anytime. The poor thing is confused enough and she has a lot of loyalty to Anna. She has a big heart and a really pure soul – I can see it in her. Isn't she beautiful, Frank? Isn't she just magnificent?'

Frank put his arm around his sister and kissed her cheek. 'Yes, she is. Just like her mother.'

'At her age I was a mess. She's a much better person than I ever was.'

'You turned your life around, Laura. When are you ever going to give yourself credit for that? You were very young when you got pregnant with Jody. Dad had died, we were all grieving differently, it was a hard time, and you handled it by partying too much. You have to forgive yourself, you were just a kid. Look how well you've done, look at all you've achieved. Look at Mandy – she's great. Granted, she's a bit bolshie at times, but all teenagers are like that. She's a good kid. You did well, sis.'

Laura twirled her bangles around her wrist and tried not to cry. What Frank had said meant so much to her. It was wonderful to get feedback, especially from a man. She knew Frank was biased but it was still good to hear it.

Because she had devoted herself to raising Mandy and never allowed herself to have a relationship, she had been alone a lot, doubting her parenting skills all the time, spending nights reading or watching TV alone. All of her decisions had been made alone. Her parenting skills – the successful ones and the failures – were tested alone. Her hopes and fears for Mandy:

she had struggled with them alone. At the end of every day, even the really bad ones when they had fought and Mandy had said she hated her, Laura had gone to bed alone. No one to talk to, no one to bounce ideas off, no one to tell her if she had made the right decision, dished out the correct punishment, given the right amount of praise, loved enough, scolded enough, protected enough, cherished enough . . . Sometimes the loneliness had been unbearable.

'What are we going to do about Mum and Mandy?' Frank interrupted her thoughts.

'I'll have to tell them today,' Laura said.

Frank sucked in his cheeks. 'Jesus, Laura, I'm not sure Mum can take this. On the one hand I can't wait for you to tell her, but on the other I think she may have a coronary.'

'I know – but, oh, Frank, to see the look on her face when she meets Sophie, it'll be so brilliant. I'll finally be able to stop feeling guilty.'

'It wasn't really your fault, Laura,' Frank said, for the zillionth time.

But Laura knew it had been her fault. If only she hadn't been so drunk. But now she could give Jody back to Joan. She could watch Joan hold her precious granddaughter again. Joan would forgive her and they could rebuild their shattered relationship. Laura would be able to breathe easily in front of her mother again instead of worrying about saying the wrong thing. She was now going to be able to give Joan the one thing she yearned for – and she couldn't wait.

'I'm definitely going to tell her today,' Laura said. 'I'm not waiting any longer. Mum deserves to know as soon as possible. I'll tell Mandy first, and when she's calmed down, which could take a while, I'll tell Mum.'

Frank grinned. 'Good luck telling Mandy. She's going to be stunned.'

'I'm worried about her, Frank. It's a lot to take in, your dead sister reappearing from the grave. She's only sixteen, and it's a

247

difficult age. I don't want her going off the rails . . . like I did after Dad.'

Frank picked up a biscuit and took a bite. 'Slight difference, we put Dad into a grave and Jody's come back from one. Mandy'll be fine – she's a tough cookie. Besides, she always wanted a sister her own age. And she knows how much Jody's disappearance crushed you. She'll be happy for you. Don't worry. It'll all be fine.' He stood up and grabbed his car keys. 'Come on, I'll drive you to Mum's house. I'll distract her while you tell Mandy. Then I'll help you break the news to Mum. You might need a hand if she faints or gets hysterical.'

Laura asked Lexie to keep an eye on Sophie for a few hours while she went to Dublin to tell Joan and Mandy the news.

When they got to the house, Mandy opened the door wearing her usual uniform of black jeans, a black T-shirt, black boots and a lot of black eye-liner. She led them down the steps into the kitchen and stood facing them, leaning against the counter top, hands on hips. 'OK, what's going on? I know something's up. Don't lie to me or treat me like a child.'

'Where's your grandmother?' Frank asked.

'She had to go to the hospital – her friend Lilly had a stroke and it's not looking good. She said she could be a while. I wouldn't be surprised if she went to put a pillow over Lilly's head. All she ever does is give out about her. Apparently she's the tightest person in the world. Gran says when they meet for coffee Lilly asks for hot water and brings her own teabag and she always puts all the packs of sugar and ketchup and mayonnaise into her bag. But the worst is, Lilly nicks the flowers from cemeteries to bring to people's houses as gifts!'

Frank and Mandy snorted with laughter.

Laura put the kettle on. 'How long ago did Joan leave?' She couldn't help it. Her instinct was always to protect Mandy.

'Chill, Mum. About twenty minutes ago. Stop trying to distract me – I know something's going on and I want answers now.'

Frank held his hands up. 'I'm going to leave you guys to it. I'll be in the lounge if you need me.' He walked out, softly closing the door behind him.

Laura stood face to face with her daughter. She marvelled at how different the two sisters were – Jody was so blonde and blue-eyed and Mandy so dark. So different, yet born of the same womb.

Mandy was eyeing Laura suspiciously. Laura reached out to her, but Mandy took a step back. 'Oh, my God! You're getting married, aren't you?' she gasped.

'What?' Laura was completely blindsided.

'All this running around and going on a hot date yesterday and changing your clothes ten times and being all hyper and sparkly and joyful, it's a man, isn't it? You're in love with some guy.'

Laura started to laugh. 'Oh, Mandy, where would I meet a man? I'm either in my studio or with you.'

Mandy shrugged. 'I dunno – at one of your art-gallery things? Lexie keeps going on about how good-looking you are and how loads of men must fancy you. I never thought about you like that – I mean, you're my mother. But then when she kept saying it, I kind of saw what she meant. You're not bad-looking for your age and thirty-seven isn't that old. Lots of people get married when they're older now so . . .' Mandy fiddled with her leather cuff. 'That's it, isn't it? Please tell me he's not a toy boy.'

Laura went over and put her arms around her daughter. Mandy didn't push her away. 'Oh, Mandy, darling Mandy, wonderful Mandy. I'm not in love. Well, I am but not with a man.'

Mandy jumped back like a scalded cat. 'Are you a LESBIAN? I seriously cannot take it. Oh, my God – are you and Lexie getting it on? That's it, isn't it? That's why Lexie's in our house and why she keeps going on about how she can't believe you never had a boyfriend because you're so beautiful and talented and creative and – I cannot believe this is happening to me. My mother's a lesbian.'

'Mandy!' Laura said. 'I'm not gay. I'm not about to come out of any closet. But I do have a skeleton to unearth and it's a big

249

one. I need you to sit down because this news is kind of mind-blowing.'

Mandy lowered herself into a kitchen chair. Laura sat opposite her and spread her hands out. 'Something kind of unbelievable has happened.'

'Jesus, you're freaking me out. What? Is Frank really your dad?'

Laura frowned. 'Don't be ridiculous. You're watching far too much reality TV.'

'Are you transgender? Oh, my God, were you born a man and then had a sex change? Is your name really John?'

'No!'

'An alien?'

'Mandy, listen – '

'I'm adopted? That's it, isn't it? I'm adopted! I bet my real parents were musicians.'

'Mandy, you are not adopted.'

'Egg donor?'

'No.'

'Sperm donor?'

'MANDY! Jody's back.' Laura hadn't meant to blurt it out like that, but she needed to stop Mandy's guesses.

Mandy looked at her blankly. 'What did you say?'

Laura slowed her breathing down and explained. 'You know that I always believed Jody was alive? I never believed she drowned that day on the boat. Well, I was right. Jody's alive and well. She was taken by a woman who raised her in London as her own daughter.'

'WHAT?' Mandy stood up and waved her arms about. 'Alive?'

'Poor Jody has been living a lie for seventeen years. She saw me being interviewed on the BBC and then she recognized herself in a photo on my website. Anyway, she contacted me and arrived over from London yesterday. She was my "hot date". And now she's here, with us.'

'In Dublin?'

'In our house.'

Mandy sat down opposite her mother. 'Mum,' she said, choosing her words carefully, 'are you sure this isn't a set-up? How do you know it's really Jody?'

Laura put her hand on her heart. 'I know in here. It's her. A mother knows.'

'Are you sure? Are you absolutely certain? One hundred per cent?'

'Yes. Frank met her this morning. It's her.'

Mandy's hands began to shake. 'Jesus Christ, this is like . . . oh, my God . . . how . . . Where was she? Who took her? What does she look like?'

'Me.'

'Is she normal? Was she part of a cult? Was she brainwashed? Is she a Scientologist? Or one of those Jehovah's Witnesses? Maybe this girl just looks like you and they sent her to try and get money out of you because they heard you sold that painting to Hank Gold for two hundred grand. Seriously, Mum, I still think this is a hoax.'

'I promise you, Mandy, it isn't. And Jody – well, her name is Sophie now – is perfectly sane.'

Mandy shook her fringe out of her eyes. 'Mum, you don't get out much. You're not very street smart.'

Laura drummed her fingers on the table. How could she convince Mandy? The photos! They were still in her bag. She fished them out. 'Look, these are the pictures of Jody taken in the month or two before the boat. And these are Sophie's pictures of when she was a toddler. She says there are no pictures of her at all before these ones – no baby pictures – and Anna, the woman who abducted her, was always very secretive about her past.'

Mandy examined the photos closely, frowning with concentration. 'They look like the same baby but they could be Photoshopped. You can do anything, these days.'

'Mandy, all I can tell you is that I know this is Jody. It's her. She's back and she's dying to meet you. She says she always wanted a sister.'

Mandy's head snapped up. 'Well, I don't want to meet her. She's an impostor, and I can see you're all hyper and thrilled and I don't want you to be crushed again when you find out she's not Jody. You have to do a DNA test, Mum. You have to be sure it's her before inviting her into our house. She could be nicking all our stuff right now.'

Laura stood up and walked to the door. 'Frank!' she shouted. 'Can you come in here for a minute, please?'

Frank rushed in, looking concerned. 'Is everything all right?'

'Everything's fine, but Mandy thinks Jody is a fake.'

Frank went over and stood in front of his niece. He put his hands on her shoulders. 'Mandy, I can assure you that she is no fake. As sure as I am standing here, that girl is Jody.'

'Am I the only sane person in this family?' Mandy exclaimed. 'You believe it's her because you want to believe it. But I don't. Don't you think it's a little coincidental that, just after Mum gets lots of publicity for selling a painting for loads of cash, this girl suddenly turns up claiming to be Jody returned from the dead? Come on, guys, wake up! You're being taken for a ride. Thank God I'm here to make you see sense.'

'But –'

Frank cut across his sister: 'The only way Mandy is going to understand is by seeing her,' he said. 'Come on, let's go. I'm taking you to meet your older sister.'

Mandy folded her arms and scowled. 'Well, don't expect a happy family reunion because I'm going to kick this lookalike out of our house as soon as I see her.'

25.
Sophie
Killduf, July 2011

Sophie lay on the bed and listened to the messages on her phone. There was one from Mark: 'Dude, call me. Everyone is going mental looking for you. What's going on? Your mum and my dad are phoning every ten seconds asking if I've heard from you. What are you doing? I didn't know you were adopted although it kind of makes sense because you look nothing like Anna. Call me. We can go for a drink and talk about it. I can't believe you – Sophie the square – ran away from home. I'd no idea you had it in you. Respect!'

Sophie smiled. Mark always teased her about being straight because she never got into any trouble unlike him: he had been caught drinking and smoking hash and had almost been expelled from school several times. He knew Anna and Sophie well. He'd be a good person to talk to right now; he wouldn't be dramatic like Holly. She'd call him back and arrange to meet up. He didn't take life seriously at all – he never got flustered about anything. He'd probably think it was cool to have been abducted.

The next message was from Holly, reminding her to keep detailed notes on everything that was happening and asking her to fill her in on all the gory details. She said she'd Googled Max Clifford and he definitely seemed like the best publicist to represent her and her story. Holly had taken down his office number and was choosing outfits for them to wear to their meeting with him: 'I'm thinking smart-casual. We might have to splash out on two super-chic tailored dresses and maybe even Christian Louboutin shoes. I know they're really expensive but you're going to be a millionaire. I've been looking into it and, as your personal assistant, manager and stylist, I think twenty-five per cent is fair. Let me know what you think – and don't worry, I told my mother that you and Anna decided to go on holiday early. She doesn't suspect anything. Jessie's been snooping around, though, so I'm going to have to keep my phone with me at all times.'

There were six messages from Anna. She asked Sophie to call and talk to her. She promised to explain everything. In the second message she was crying so much Sophie couldn't understand what she was saying. She had never seen Anna lose control. It made her feel sick to hear her mother so desperate. In the past whenever Anna had had a bad day, which she did occasionally, she'd just say she had a headache and lie down in her room for a while with the curtains drawn. She never made a fuss and she'd always get up for dinner, even though sometimes she looked really awful and couldn't eat. She'd make an effort to chat to Sophie and keep her company. She had always put Sophie first.

In her last message Anna sounded calmer, more like herself, less hysterical. She said she was in Dublin, staying with Joe. She reminded Sophie that there were always two sides to every story and she asked her to call her when she was ready.

Sophie longed to talk to her. She needed her mum right now. She wanted to tell her about all her problems. She missed the person she relied on, the best shoulder to cry on, the person who knew how to comfort her, soothe her, reassure her . . . but that person was the very cause of all her confusion and turmoil. Her mother was now . . . what? Her enemy? Her kidnapper? Her abductor?

How could Anna have snatched her like that? How could she? Sophie's head began to throb again. She sat up and looked around. She was in Mandy's bedroom. It was a strange mixture of girlish and rock-chick. Although the walls were painted a lovely shade of pale blue, Mandy had covered them with lyrics and quotes. There were several written diagonally across the wall behind her bed in thick black ink:

I crawl towards the cracks of light
It's not fair to deny me of the cross I bear that you gave to me
It's my duty as a human being to be pissed off
Angst is not the human condition, it's the purgatory between what we have
and what we want but can't get

Her bookshelf was weighed down with school books and biographies of troubled musicians, like Kurt Cobain and Jim Morrison, and of female activists and singers, like Joan Baez and Janis Joplin. On the bottom shelf she had all the *Harry Potter* books and the full *Twilight* series too. Mandy had several black candles in her room, and two guitars leaned against the wall in the corner. One was electric. Her dressing-table was covered with cosmetics and jewellery. Lots of dark nail varnishes – black, grey, ink blue. She had three different black liquid eyeliners, four different mascaras, a big box of eye-shadows, four leather cuffs, six pairs of hoop and chain earrings and a long thick silver chain with a silver ball at the end. There was a little catch on the side of the ball. Sophie clicked it open and the ball unfurled to reveal four tiny hidden photos. She held them up to the sunlight: one was of Laura and another of an older woman – Sophie presumed it was Joan. There was one of Mandy with her guitar and one of – Sophie's hand shook – Sophie as a baby. The one Laura had on her website, the photo of her holding the pink blanket.

The door flew open. Sophie dropped the necklace. It landed with a thud.

'What the hell are you doing?' Mandy ran over, scooped up the necklace and snapped the ball shut. 'Who the hell do you think you are snooping around in –' She looked up at Sophie's face and gasped. 'Jesus Christ!'

'I told you.' Frank walked in behind her, followed by a worried-looking Laura. 'I said you'd understand when you saw her.'

'Sorry to barge in on you like this, Sophie,' Laura apologized. 'We've just got back and Mandy was eager to meet you.'

Mandy gaped at Sophie.

'I'm sorry about your necklace,' Sophie muttered. 'I shouldn't have opened it.'

'No, you shouldn't.' Mandy had found her voice. 'It's private. Everything in here is private. This is *my* bedroom.'

Sophie glanced up at her sister. She was so different from herself, so dark and sallow. Mandy's brown eyes bored into her, taking in every detail of her own appearance. She felt as if she was under a microscope. The adults had been more subtle about staring, but Mandy just stood there and ogled.

'Are you feeling better?' Laura asked.

'Yes, thanks,' Sophie said.

'So?' Frank watched Mandy's face. 'Do you believe us now?'

Mandy was noncommittal: 'Maybe.'

Frank nudged Laura. 'We'll leave them for a bit. Let them get to know each other.' Before Laura could object, he ushered her out. 'Girls, we'll be downstairs if you need us,' he said, and closed the door behind him.

Mandy continued to glare at Sophie, who was beginning to perspire. The room was hot from the midday sun and she was weary and drained. She sat down on the edge of Mandy's bed. The duvet cover was bright red with a black print of Che Guevara's face across the middle. Sophie longed for her own bedroom with the calming dusty pink walls, her crisp white bed linen and her favourite painting hanging on the wall opposite her bed – Turner's tranquil *Colour Beginning*.

Mandy passed the silver ball necklace from one hand to the other. 'So, you're Jody, then, are you?'

'Well, yes, I guess I am.'

'What makes you so sure? Just because you look like my mum and have her freaky colour thing doesn't make you her kid.'

Sophie began to see yellow, her colour for anger. Mandy was being very confrontational. She eyeballed her. 'That's not all. The photos of me as a small child are identical to the ones Laura has. And my mother – or, at least, the woman who brought me up, Anna – was always very vague about my birth and she has no photos of me until I was a toddler. Also, she's Irish but she never wanted to bring me to Ireland and she always seemed uncomfortable when I asked questions about my past. And then I saw Laura on the TV and something clicked. I just felt so connected to her. I knew.'

Mandy scoffed. 'Was that before or after they mentioned her big sale?'

'I beg your pardon?' Sophie had no idea what she was talking about.

'Don't play all innocent with me. You're after the money, aren't you?'

'What money? What are you talking about?' Sophie frowned. The yellow was getting brighter.

'The money Mum got from selling her painting to Hank Gold. This is a set-up, isn't it? You do look the image of my mum, but lots of people look like other people. Look at me. I'm nothing like her but I *am* her daughter. You're just one of those looky-likeys trying to get money from her. Well, you may have fooled them but not me. You're not pulling the wool over my eyes.'

Anger boiled over inside Sophie. 'Money? I don't know what on earth you're talking about. I don't want anything from you or your mother. All I want is the truth. Do you understand? The truth! And the last time I checked that was free. Do you think I want to be here? Do you think this is fun for me? Finding out I'm not who I thought I was? Discovering I'm someone else when I was perfectly happy being who I was? I hate this whole awful mess. It's making me ill. I wish I could turn the clock back. I wish I'd never seen that stupid programme, but I did, and the minute I saw Laura something inside me shifted. All the little things that had been niggling deep down suddenly came bursting out.'

Mandy pulled a cigarette packet out of her backpack and went to stand beside the open window. She lit one, inhaled deeply and blew the smoke out into the fresh air. 'OK. I had to question you to make sure you are who you say you are. My mum's been crying about you for seventeen years. I couldn't let an impostor mess with her head. I knew when I saw you that you were Jody – you're so like

Mum it's actually freaky. But I had to be extra sure. Mum couldn't handle it if you turned out to be a phoney. Neither could I. It would completely crush her and she's damaged enough already. I don't want her to be hurt any more. She's had enough shit to deal with. She wouldn't survive another blow. I've never seen her like this.'

'Like what?'

'Happy.'

'Really?'

Mandy made smoke rings. 'She pretended to be happy. She tried to be happy for my sake, but she wasn't really. Not deep down. How could she be happy when all the time she blamed herself for you disappearing? Part of her died after that. I thought she was mad thinking you were still alive, thinking someone stole you – so did Frank and Gran – but I guess Mum was right all along.'

Sophie went to join her at the window. 'I don't smoke, but I think I need a cigarette. Can I have one?'

'Sure – here.' Mandy lit it for her. Sophie took a drag and coughed. Mandy grinned at her. 'Slowly, just take little puffs.'

Sophie took a tiny pull and a small cloud of smoke drifted out of her mouth.

'Now you've got it.' Mandy reached over and pinched Sophie's arm.

'Ouch!'

'Just checking you're not a ghost. It's pretty mind-blowing that you came back from the dead. I keep thinking I'm going to wake up and it'll all have been a dream.'

'Me too.' Sophie leaned on the windowsill and sighed. 'In a way I kind of wish it was. I liked my life.'

'Really? I was bored. This drama is way more fun.' Mandy grinned. 'Wait till Gran sees you – she's going to literally die!'

'I hope not. I'd feel guilty for the rest of my life.' Sophie giggled. The cigarette was making her light-headed.

'Gran's great. She can be a cow sometimes, and she's really mean to Mum, but when you get past all the prickly grumpy-old-lady stuff, she has a heart of gold. She gives me money and lets me smoke in her house when Mum's not there, but she'd kill me if she caught me drinking. She's got a real thing about booze. So's Mum. It's a total drag. All of my friends raid their parents' booze cabinet before a night out so all they have to buy is Coke or Sprite. Then they go into the loo and mix in the vodka or gin or Bacardi or whatever they managed to steal. But the only thing to drink in this house is soy milk!'

Sophie rolled the cigarette between her fingers. 'My mum feels like that about drinking too. She's very strict.'

'What's she like, your mum? Anna?'

Sophie looked out at the cloudless sky. 'She's just a normal person and, I have to be honest, she's been a really good mother.'

'Come on, Jody –'

Sophie cut across her: 'It's Sophie. Please call me Sophie.'

'Well, your mother – as in your real mother, Laura – christened you Jody so I think it's pretty disrespectful of you to demand we all call you Sophie.'

'Look, I've got enough on my plate at the moment with everything I've just discovered. I can't take on a new name too. Not now anyway, perhaps later.'

'OK, chill, I'll call you Sophie. So, you're telling me that this Anna person is normal? Come on, seriously, how could she be? She nicked you from a boat. She stole someone else's kid. Only people who should be in mental institutions do that.'

'I know what she did was insane but she isn't crazy. Honestly, she's really . . . well . . . just . . . nice.'

Mandy stubbed her cigarette out on the windowsill and went into the little shower-room off her bedroom to flush the butt down the toilet. 'Maybe she brainwashed you so you'd think she was nice, like they do in those religious cults? So that you end up thinking normal things are weird and weird things are normal. Maybe she hypnotized you or played CDs while you were asleep. You were only tiny when she abducted you so you wouldn't even remember the brainwashing.'

259

Sophie handed Mandy her unfinished cigarette. Mandy took two long drags and flushed that away too.

'Anna's not in any cult. She's Catholic.'

'Ha! Well, some people would think that's a cult of its own,' Mandy noted.

'She's a very kind, caring, loving person, which is why I find it so difficult to believe she would do something so awful.'

'Did she ever hit you or put cigarettes out on your arms?'

'*No!*' Sophie was shocked.

'Well, I don't know why you look so surprised! That's the sort of thing weirdos do to kids. I know you keep saying she's normal but she has to have a screw loose.'

'Maybe she found me alone and I was crying and she thought I'd been abandoned or something. Laura did admit that she took her eye off me, so maybe Anna thought she was actually saving me.'

'You were on a boat and my mum was there. Anna can't have tried very hard to find who you belonged to before she bundled you under her arm and did a runner.'

Sophie ran her hands through her hair. 'I know it all seems so odd. I wish you could meet Anna and then you'd understand my dilemma.'

Mandy put her hands up. 'No, thanks. I do not want to meet that fruit-cake. I don't want to be hypnotized or dragged into her cult or whatever it is she does.'

Sophie shook her head. 'The really strange thing is I know you'd all like her.'

Mandy snorted. 'I doubt that. I'd say Mum and Gran would kill her with their bare hands if she ever came near them. She ruined their lives.'

'Anna would never do anything to hurt anyone. She's just not like that – it's all so confusing.' Sophie's eyes welled.

Mandy shifted uncomfortably. 'Let's talk about something else. Mum said you're going to art college. She's over the moon about that, especially as I can't draw.'

Sophie's eyes glistened. 'I love art. When I'm looking at a

beautiful painting or working on a piece myself, the world could be falling down around me and I wouldn't notice. It's like floating or something – it's hard to explain.'

'I kind of feel like that when I'm writing lyrics. Do you have a boyfriend?'

'No. I've been out with a few people but no one special. I'm hoping to get more experience at art college when I meet boys with similar interests and passions.'

Mandy's eyes widened. 'Are you a virgin?'

Sophie blushed. 'That's none of your business.'

'Oh, my God, you are! I thought all you English girls went to mixed schools and lost your virginity behind the bicycle shed at fourteen.'

'I was at an all-girls' Catholic school. My mother was the head-mistress and the only male teacher we had was Mr Kelly, who was about ninety. So there was no one to have sex with behind the bicycle shed, even if we'd wanted to.' Sophie shook her hair back and looked at Mandy. 'Do you have a boyfriend?'

Mandy blew her fringe out of her eyes. 'No. I'm kind of into this guy Johnny in my guitar class but he's so not my type. He's really friendly and at first I thought he fancied me but he's the same to everyone. He's just one of those sunny, happy people who is nice to everyone. I usually like bad boys – you know the dark, depressed ones who do drugs, skip school and rarely speak.'

'Have you had sex?' Sophie would never normally have asked someone such a personal question but as Mandy had asked her she thought it was all right to ask her back.

Mandy lit another cigarette. 'Five times. Once with Killian, who was just crap, but at least I got the whole losing-my-virginity thing out of the way. And then four times with Leo, who I was completely in love with, but then I found out he was shagging Sarah Ford behind my back so I told him to fuck off and wrote a song about him. Writing music is my therapy. The song's called "Two-timing Twit With The Two-millimetre Dick".'

Sophie giggled. 'Did he hear it?'

Mandy exhaled her cigarette smoke. 'I posted it on my Facebook page.'

'Wow! Good for you.'

'Revenge isn't all it's cracked up to be. I'm still kind of into Leo, to be honest, even though he's an arsehole. His willy isn't small at all.'

'Did you use condoms?'

'Duh! Of course. I don't want to end up like my mother, with a kid at nineteen. No way! It would totally interfere with my plans to conquer the world with my music.'

'I couldn't imagine having a baby so young. Poor Laura. It must have been so hard for her to deal with all that. Until a few days ago my biggest dilemma was trying to persuade my mother to let me go to a nightclub.'

'I couldn't handle it either. Mum was lucky, though. My dad was really supportive. He still is, when he's not being bitch-slapped about by his wife, Tanya.'

Sophie's eyes watered.

'What's wrong? What did I say?' Mandy looked worried.

'I'll never know my dad. Laura said she had a one-night stand with an American musician.'

'Gran told me about it. She was furious with Mum for being such a slut. She keeps reminding me of how Mum got pregnant twice by mistake – she uses it as a warning to me not to have sex. Like, hello! There is such a thing as contraception. It's a bummer that you'll never meet your dad, but on the up-side, at least you don't have to deal with a bitchy stepmother like I do.'

'The really weird thing is that it's almost exactly the same story Anna told me about my pretend dad. The only difference is that Anna said the man she slept with was an American architect.'

Mandy whistled. 'Now that *is* freaky.'

Sophie was seeing green again. 'I'm so sick of all her lies. I've had enough. I want some answers.'

She went over to the bed and picked up her phone. She had to find out the truth and only one person could reveal that.

26.

Anna

Dublin, July 2011

Anna ran into the lounge and threw her arms around Joe. 'She called!' She beamed up at him. 'She wants to meet me this afternoon at five o'clock in Killduf village square. I'll need to borrow your car. Oh, Joe, everything's going to be all right. When I explain the story to her she'll forgive me. I know she will.'

Joe pulled Anna's arms gently from his neck. He walked over to the window of his top-floor apartment and looked at the sprawling view of Dublin city. 'She may not,' he said quietly.

Anna's happiness dissipated. 'What do you mean?'

He turned back to her. 'Oh, Anna, come on.'

'Come on what?'

He took off his reading glasses and placed them on the towering bookshelf beside him. 'Put yourself in Sophie's shoes. She's just found out she's not who she thought she was. She's discovered that her mother abducted her . . . that you are not, in fact, her real mother. You need to prepare yourself for a lot of anger. I doubt very much that it's going to be a happy reunion.'

Anna sat down on the couch and fiddled with her ring – her mother's engagement ring. She had given her own engagement ring back to Barry when they had split up, telling him to give it to the daughter he was sure to have one day. He hadn't wanted to take it but she'd made him. It had been just another reminder of her failed marriage. But she always wore her mother's ring. When her mother had become very sick, she had given it to Anna and asked her to wear it for good luck. She said she knew it would bring Anna a daughter, the daughter she deserved to have. It was a beautiful ring, an emerald surrounded by diamonds. Anna cherished it and had hoped to pass it on to Sophie one day.

She looked at her oldest, dearest friend. Joe had been so supportive, listening to her crying and ranting and panicking. But she knew that deep down he was disappointed in her. He didn't agree with what she had done – he had told her so. But she knew he only felt like that because he hadn't been there. If he had been on that boat and seen the state Laura was in, he would have done the same thing. A neglected child needs to be protected.

Anna stood up and went over to him. She slipped her hand into his. 'Joe, I'm still me. Anna. Your childhood neighbour, your best friend. We've known each other since we were kids. That's over fifty years of friendship and love. Don't shut me out, Joe. I need you.'

Joe kissed her lightly on the forehead. 'I'll always be here for you. I'm just having a little trouble taking in all this information. Give me time. I need to let it sink in and mull it over. I'm a doctor, a scientist, and we live by rules and regulations. I've seen many sad cases over the years of children not being properly cared for but I didn't judge. I encouraged, I scolded, I advised, I helped, I followed up . . . but I never played God.'

Anna laid her head on his shoulder. 'She was one too many, Joe. She was the straw that broke the camel's back. I'd seen too much neglect, too much pain, too much suffering. I had to do something. I reacted instinctively. I have no regrets.'

Joe took her chin in his hand and lifted her face to his. 'That still doesn't make it right.'

Anna pulled away and went to the other side of the room. 'I was a good mother, Joe. I loved her like no other.'

'I know. I saw how devoted you were. But you're not her mother. She wasn't yours to raise. Your baby died.'

Anna swivelled around, her voice quivering with emotion as she said, 'I deserved to be a mother. I knew I'd be good at it.

Sophie has been my proudest achievement. When Hope died, I died too. I never thought I'd get over her death. I thought my life was over. My heart broke, Joe. It broke into a thousand pieces when I buried my baby.' Anna gulped back the sobs. 'No parent should have to bury a child. It's too much pain. I lost everything when Hope died, everything. My marriage, my home, my life. I ran away to London because I knew if I stayed here I'd kill myself. I didn't get on that boat meaning to take a child. I was a shadow, a dead woman walking. I was nothing, invisible, an empty shell. I never thought I'd feel anything again. I was numb. But when I saw that little girl being treated like dirt by her drunk of a mother, being shouted at and told to go away, I felt emotion for the first time in months. I felt anger, rage and fury. "No more," I said. No more broken children. No more shattered little lives, no more crushed hopes, no more missed birthdays and Christmases, no more violence and abuse. No more. It's not right, Joe. Children deserve to have a chance in life. They deserve to be loved. They deserve to have opportunities and kindness and food on the table and shoes on their feet and clean clothes and lice-free hair and baths and hope . . . They deserve hope. I do, too, and so did Sophie, and that was why I took her. If it happened again I'd do the same thing. I couldn't leave her with a mother who was passed out drunk at the bar. I just couldn't.' Anna sank to the floor and wept.

Joe rushed over to her. He picked her up and led her over to the couch. He handed her a tissue and went to pour her a large brandy. He poured himself one too. He sat down beside her and handed her the drink. He rubbed her back while she sobbed and sipped, sobbed and sipped.

'I understand why you wanted to do it, Anna, I really do,' he said. 'I saw the light go out inside you when Hope died. I know how much you wanted to be a mother. And you're right: no parent should have to suffer such an unbearable loss. Life is complicated and some people get dealt much darker cards than others, children included. And as much as we want to change things, as much as we desire to improve their lives, to "save" them, it's not up to us. If we all acted on our instincts and impulses, society would be lawless. But the important person here is Sophie. What matters most is her opinion. She's the one you have to convince. She's the one who needs the explanations. She's the one who's hurting the most.'

Anna blew her nose. 'I know. I just hope she understands. She has to. If she turns her back on me, my life is over. I can't lose two daughters, I just can't.'

A couple of hours later, Anna was sitting on a bench, watching two little boys playing. There was a small green in Killduf village square with two benches on opposite sides. In the middle were two swings and a small slide with a sandpit to the right of it. The green was surrounded by shops and businesses: a butcher, a Spar, an Italian restaurant, a shop selling everything from fishing tackle to Barbie dolls, a Supermac burger joint and two pubs. It was an attractive place but the shop fronts looked a little tired. They were in need of a fresh coat of paint. An old man shuffled by, hauling his shopping bags up the road, and a young mother pushed a buggy across the green, talking animatedly into her mobile phone.

Despite the warm day, Anna was shivering. She pulled her cardigan around her shoulders. She was sick with nerves and welcomed the distraction of watching the small boys chasing each other. One came over and hid behind her. The other followed quickly in his wake.

'Hello, are you having fun?' Anna asked them.

The two boys stopped playing and eyed her.

'My name's Anna and I'm waiting for my little girl – well, she's a big girl now – to come and meet me.'

The boys said nothing.

'What are your names?'

The younger boy in a red T-shirt, who looked about four, shook his head, but the older one, in a yellow T-shirt, piped up,

'Our mummy says we can't talk to strangers. Even people who look normal. She says the baddest people sometimes look like mums and dads.'

'Yeah,' said the smaller boy, 'and she said there are lots of bad guys in the world that want to take childrens away. They give you sweets to get you into their car and then they drive away super-fast, like a Batmobile. *Whisssssh.*'

'And – and even if they give you a Curly Wurly, which is like my most favouritist thing ever, you can't take it. Cos if you do, the bad guys will grab your hand and pull you into their van and your mummy and daddy will never see you again. Ever. You'll be in like a prison kind of thing or maybe living in a forest with wolves.' The boy in the yellow T-shirt made a wolf face to emphasize his point.

'I hate wolves. They're mean and scary.' The younger brother's eyes were wide with fear.

'Your mummy is right. You do have to be careful of strangers,' Anna agreed.

'And even old persons like you can be bad guys. Because – because bad guys can put on disguises and masks,' the older brother informed her.

'Like in *Scooby Doo*,' the little brother exclaimed.

'*Scooby Doo*'s for babies,' his brother scoffed. Then to Anna he said, 'It's actually like in *Ben 10* when he can transform himself into other people that have super-powers and stuff. So, even though you look like a regular granny you could actually be an evil person in disguise.'

'Well, that's true, but I'm not. Look at my face.' She pulled her cheek. 'See? It really is my face, not a mask.'

'Do you have any sweets?' the little boy asked.

'No, I'm afraid not, and even if I did, I wouldn't give them to you because I'd have to ask your mummy's permission first.'

'She's over there, in the shop.' The older child pointed to the grocery. 'She told us to be good and not talk to anyone we didn't know. She said if anyone tried to talk to us or show us their willy or asked us to touch their willy or to show them our willies or asked us if they could touch our willies we haded to shout loud.'

'That's very good advice,' Anna concurred. 'Your mummy sounds like a very clever person.'

'Your eyes are all red. Are you sad?' the older boy asked.

'Yes, I am a bit.'

'Why? Did you hurt yourself?' the little brother wondered.

'No. I had a fight with my daughter and she's very cross with me.'

'Why is she cross?' the little boy asked.

'Because I lied.'

'Ooooh.' They were appalled. 'Our mummy says lying is the worstest thing you can do.'

'She's right, but sometimes you do it to protect someone.'

'What does "potect" mean?' the smaller boy asked.

'It means that sometimes you lie to make the other person happy.'

'Like when Mummy asks Daddy if she has a fat tummy and he says no even when her tummy *is* really fat?' The older boy was pleased with himself.

'Exactly.' Anna smiled.

'Mummy says "fat" is a bad word, but it's not, is it? It's just a word. But she says it makes girls sad if you say it to them.' The younger brother frowned. He seemed confused by this. 'But she said "thin" is a good word and it makes girls happy when you say it.'

'Girls are weird,' the older boy huffed.

'Are you going to say sorry for lying?' the little boy enquired.

'Yes, I am,' Anna admitted, 'and I'm going to explain why I lied. I'm going to tell her I was protecting her.'

'Tell her she's thin. That'll make her happy, like my mummy,' the older boy advised.

'I lied once when Mummy asked me if I put her phone down the toilet and I said no.' The little boy's face went as red as his T-shirt as he recalled the incident.

'Did she find out you were lying?' Anna asked.

He nodded. 'Yes, and she was so cross her head nearly spinned off. She said Santa mightn't come, but he did.'

'Oh, I'm glad. I'm sure you're a good boy.'

'I am most of the time and I'll never lie again. No way.'

'Are *you* going to lie again?' The older boy was curious.

'No.'

A shadow fell over them. 'Looking to kidnap some more children, are you?'

They all looked up. Sophie was standing in front of them, arms folded, lips pursed.

Anna jumped up.

'Did she say "kidnap"?' the little boy squealed.

'Yes, I did,' Sophie said. 'You boys better run back to your mummy before this lady takes you away. She steals little children from their mummies.'

The boys scurried over to the shop and their mother.

'That was unnecessary,' Anna said.

'Really? I think not, under the circumstances. Who knows what you're capable of?'

Anna could see the black shadows under Sophie's eyes. Her daughter looked completely worn out. Anger and rage emanated from her every pore. She'd never seen Sophie like this. She was usually so even-tempered and positive. Anna knew she needed to tread very carefully or Sophie would bolt. She had to get her to sit down and listen. She dug deep and tried to remember all the tricks she'd learned in her years as a teacher and headmistress. She needed Sophie to stay and hear her side of the story.

'Sophie, please sit down. I understand you're confused but I can explain everything.'

Sophie sat on the other end of the bench, as far away from Anna as was physically possible. Anna took a deep breath and willed herself to stay in control of her emotions. 'What has Laura told you?'

Sophie's eyes flashed. 'Let's see. She told me that she was on a boat with her little daughter when someone abducted the child and she didn't see her again for seventeen years. Everyone thought the little girl was dead. Her life was completely destroyed.'

Anna maintained eye contact with Sophie, which she knew was important. She kept her tone neutral. 'Did she say anything else about the boat? About not looking after you?'

Sophie threw her hands into the air. 'Oh, I get it. You're going to blame Laura now. Well, unlike you, she was honest with me. She admitted that she got distracted for a minute, took her eye off me, and when she turned back I was gone.'

The lying wench! Anna needed to keep gently probing. 'I see. Did she mention anything else?'

Sophie glared at her. 'That her heart was broken and her life was ruined.' Anna watched as her daughter's shoulders began to shake. Sophie looked at her through tears. 'How could you, Mum? How could you do this? I don't understand. It's such a horrible thing to do. It's just awful! It's – it's psychotic. Why? Why would you do it?'

Anna rushed over to put her arms around Sophie and comfort her, but Sophie pushed her away with force. 'Don't touch me!'

Anna sat back down and looked into the distance. In as calm a voice as she could muster, she asked, 'Did Laura mention that she had been drinking?'

Sophie's head snapped up. 'She's a teetotaller!'

'Really?' Anna could feel the anger rising in her throat. Teetotaller! This woman was a compulsive liar. How dare she make herself out to be a pillar of society? How dare she pretend she didn't drink? She was a manipulative cow. 'A teetotaller? Well, she certainly didn't look like one when I saw her that day in the bar, drinking double vodkas and flirting with the barman while you sat alone, crying because you were hungry and thirsty.'

'What?'

Anna had her attention now. She was going to let her know the truth. 'Oh, yes, Sophie. Laura the teetotaller proceeded to get so drunk that she passed out at the bar.'

Sophie crossed her arms defensively. 'I don't believe you.'

But Anna could see the seed of doubt in her daughter's eyes. 'Don't you think it's a bit strange that a caring, sober mother would lose her child on a boat? You might lose sight of your child for a minute but you'd always find them again. If you were passed out drunk, you might not.'

'But –'

Anna interrupted her – she was going to give her every detail of that boat trip, even the awful things Laura had said, so she'd understand. She wanted Sophie to know she was telling the truth and that Laura was the psychotic one. 'You were sitting in that bar, curled up in a corner by yourself, crying your eyes out. You kept asking Laura for a bottle, you called it a "baba", but she started shouting at you and cursing at you. She told you to go away and leave her alone. You were sobbing your little heart out and Laura told the barman – I'll never forget it – how her life would be so great if it wasn't for you. When you came over again, looking for your bottle, she threatened to take your blanket away. You were terrified. I didn't plan on going over, I was just minding my own business reading my book, but you looked so forlorn and she was so wretched to you that I couldn't help myself. I went over and said I was going to get a sandwich in the coffee shop and I'd bring you to get some milk, if that was OK. She said, and I quote, "Fine, take her with you. You're welcome to her."'

Sophie's eyes filled with tears. 'I don't believe you.'

Anna knew she was causing her precious daughter pain, but she was damned if she was going to let that drunk rewrite history. 'It's true, every single word of it. I took you to get some milk. You were so thirsty you drank it too quickly and then you were sick everywhere. We went back to the bar to find Laura and she was furious. I offered to take you to the bathroom to clean you up and change you. She threw your knapsack at me while she continued to drink. I cleaned you up, and when we got back to the bar, Laura was disgustingly drunk so I kept you outside. You could see her but you weren't near her so she couldn't verbally abuse you any more. I sang songs to you and played games with you, and when I looked up, Laura had lost consciousness. She was so drunk that she had keeled over with her head on the bar counter. That's when I knew I had to save you. I knew if you stayed with her you'd be destroyed. She was an aggressive drunk. She was unfit to be anyone's mother.'

Sophie had stopped crying and was watching Anna intently. 'So you just took me?'

'Yes. I had to. I had no choice.'

'You kidnapped me! You can't do that. You can't just take other people's children. You're the one who always told me *never to steal.*' Sophie's face was bright red with rage. 'She was my mother.'

'She was out-of-her-mind drunk,' Anna shouted back, not caring about the strange looks passers-by were giving them. She'd had enough. She was sick of Laura being made out to be the victim when in fact she was the guilty party. It was Laura's shocking behaviour that had caused this whole sequence of events. 'She couldn't even look after herself, not to mind a child. I'd seen mothers like her before in the school I taught in. Drunk and drugged-out mothers neglecting their children and ruining their lives. I just couldn't let it happen again. I saved you, Sophie! Do you understand? I saved your life. If I hadn't taken you, some paedophile could have or you could have drowned. Your so-called mother was in an alcohol-induced coma. You might as well have been alone on that boat because you had no one to look after you.'

'Maybe Laura was drunk that day but it must have been just a bad day because she's a great person and a really good mother. She has another daughter, Mandy, and she's been a brilliant mother to her. You were wrong! You judged her on one moment.'

'She was shouting and cursing at you. You were starving and thirsty. She said she didn't want you. She handed you over to me, a stranger. She pushed you into my arms. She didn't want to have anything to do with you. You're lucky it was me there that day and not some creep.'

Sophie slapped her forehead with her hand in sheer frustration. 'What you did was not *normal*. You abducted someone else's child. How can you not see that it was *wrong*? You of all people. Ms Law-abiding Citizen, Ms Headmistress, telling everyone else how to behave properly when you did the worst thing of all.'

Anna clenched her fists and forced herself to cool down. She pushed Sophie's accusations from her mind. She had been right to take her. It had been illegal and impulsive but she had had no choice: she had had to save Sophie's life. In a quiet, calm tone, she said, 'I honestly don't think you'd be alive now if I hadn't been there that day. I have devoted my life to your happiness. Whatever accusations you want to sling at me, you know that you have been loved unconditionally. You have been adored, cherished, treasured and protected by me, every day of your life. Nothing else matters to me but you. You are everything to me, you know that, Sophie. You're my world.' Tears streamed down Anna's cheeks.

Sophie buried her face in her hands and began to howl.

Anna's ulcer seared in her abdomen and she clutched the back of the bench. The pain was horrendous. She was devastated to see Sophie so upset. Her baby girl was suffering so much, it was killing her. She reached over and gently stroked her back. Sophie didn't turn away. Anna put her arms tentatively around her daughter's shoulders and leaned in to hug her. Sophie allowed her to comfort her. Anna was so relieved. She held her tightly, wishing all her pain away.

'It's OK, Mum's here now.'

She felt Sophie's body go rigid. Sophie jerked away. 'No! You can't do this. You can't come back and make believe it's OK. It's not OK, Mum – Anna – whoever you are. You've been lying to me my whole life. Why should I believe you now? Everything I thought was real is just a lie! I'm not who I thought I was, and you aren't my mother. You're a kidnapper. Our whole life is based on falsehoods. You can't just tell me you love me and think that it's all going to be OK. It's not. I hate you for what you did. Laura is a lovely person. She's really spiritual and creative and kind and caring. She would have been a great mother. She's my real mother, you're just a – just a freak.'

Anna felt as if her stomach was being ripped out. 'Sophie, sweetheart, come on.'

Sophie stood up, pulled her bag to her chest and glared at Anna. Her eyes were red-rimmed and full of rage. 'No more. I won't listen to your lies any longer. I'm going home to be with my real family.' She stormed away.

Anna stood up to follow her but the pain in her stomach forced her down. 'They're not lies,' she shouted after Sophie. 'Ask Laura. Ask her what really happened on that boat. You'll see I'm not the one who's lying.'

As Sophie disappeared around a corner, Anna doubled over in pain. She threw up beside the bench. The ground was red with blood.

27.

Laura

Killduf, July 2011

Laura had been hovering in the garden since Sophie had left. She was like a cat on a hot tin roof. What was Anna going to say? Would she persuade Sophie to go back to London? Would she take her away again? Would she tell Sophie how drunk Laura had been on the boat and how she'd neglected her? Oh, God, she felt sick at the thought. She didn't want Sophie to think badly of her. She'd only just got her back. She couldn't bear her daughter to know what a terrible mother she had been. She wanted Sophie to see the new Laura, the reformed Laura, the Laura who had spent seventeen years working so hard to make amends for all her mistakes. The Laura who had grown to love her from afar, the Laura who had beaten herself up every day for having been so immature and selfish. The Laura who had tried to be the best mother in the world to Mandy to make up for the error of her ways. The Laura who yearned to make up to Sophie for letting her go. She looked at her watch: one minute since she'd last checked – damn.

Lexie tottered out with a tray. She refused to wear flat shoes even though Laura had told her she could break her leg on the uneven grass. Even at breakfast Lexie always had her high-heeled slippers on.

'I'm four foot eleven, darlin'. I never go anywhere without my heels. I look like a flippin' midget without them,' Lexie had told her. 'Dougie said I looked like one of them Oompa Loompas from *Charlie and the Chocolate Factory*. Cheeky bugger!'

Lexie had kept to her room for most of the day, discreetly

tucking herself away to work on her book, while Mandy, Laura and Frank were coming to terms with Sophie's arrival.

She walked across the grass, set the tray on the table, gently guided Laura to a chair and told her to sit down. 'Now, I want you to drink this. It's one of them calming herbal teas I found in the kitchen. Personally I think they taste like muddy water, but I know you like 'em. I'm a builder's-tea girl myself.' She handed Laura a mug. 'Get that down your neck. You're all of a doo-da and you need to chill.'

Laura smiled up at her new friend. 'Thanks. Sophie went to meet Anna and I'm terrified of losing her again.'

Lexie sat down beside her, facing the magnificent view. She poured herself some tea. 'She had to meet her at some point. She needs to have it out with her, find out what's what. It's only normal. She'll be back.'

Laura sipped her tea in silence while Lexie tapped on her iPhone. 'Between Frank and Dougie, I can't get a moment's peace. Frank's stalking me for them new tapes, but I'm a bit behind, what with all the drama here. He says I have to get me finger out, he's payin' the ghost writer a ton of cash and he's sittin' on his arse cos I ain't sent the new tapes up to him yet. I'm a bit stuck, to be honest. I got to the part where I find out about Dougie stickin' his dick where it don't belong an' it's hard to talk about the emotions. Made me feel, well, sad and pathetic, really.'

Laura smiled at her. 'I'm sure it's awful to have to dredge up all those feelings again. Ignore Frank, take your time.'

'The thing is, since I got away and come here, I see things differently. Over in London I was wrapped up in bein' a WAG and all that. You know, I was lovin' the money and the lifestyle, especially since I come from nothin'. But being here with you lot and seein' how you live, without all the bling and the parties an' all, well, it's made me think. What's important in life? I see you livin' here beside the sea, wakin' up to the most beautiful sight every morning and goin' into your studio and workin' at something you feel passionate about and I think, What the hell am I doin' with my life? I spend my days shoppin' and going to the gym and gettin' me hair done. It's an empty life, innit?'

Laura leaned forward. 'No, it isn't. You're twenty-six, you had a really difficult childhood, you deserve to have fun and enjoy yourself.'

Lexie sighed. 'But I've been doin' it for years now and I'm bored with it all. I want something else. I want to be my own person, not just Dougie's wife, although I do still love the bugger. I actually got a text from him – do you want to read it? It'll give you a laugh.'

'Of course.'

'Brace yourself, darlin'.'

Lexie I hear u is writn a bk. If u tel em I cryd wen we woz wachin X-factr I wil tel em that u waid 9 stone 11 wen u gav up smokin. I hope u is alrit. Wher r u Lex? I is sory abt ur sister. It was off side but I woz out of me hed on vodka. I mis u Lex. We woz gd togeda. D Gaffer sez I m playin like a fukin criple. Cant score a goal to sav me life. I need u Lex. I m on d bench nxt wk. I m etin tak outs & dem Doritos al d time. D Gaffer sez I need 2 looz a stone & get me hed sortd. I m ded lonly Lex. I hate livin by meslf. I no I woz a prik & I shagd ur sistr but wil u tink bout comin bak. I wil try me best not 2 get drunk & go of wid uder birds. I luv u. Dougie

'Wow, that is some text.'

Lexie giggled. 'He really poured his heart out. Poor Dougie, he started bunkin' off school at thirteen so readin' and writin' aren't his strong points. I always read, not big posh books or anything, but me mum's Mills & Boons and me nan's Danielle Steels. The only thing Dougie reads is the scoreboard.'

They both cracked up laughing. Lexie put her phone on the table and picked up her tea. Laura watched her. Behind the laughter she could see sadness. 'Are you OK? It must be hard hearing how much he misses you and how things are going badly for him in his career since you left.'

Lexie's eyes were hidden behind her sunglasses. 'He deserves it, Laura. That prick put me through the wringer. He made a fool of me, and then when I lost it with him about goin' with them slappers, he went and had sex with my sister. What kind of person does that?'

Laura nodded. 'Fair enough. He was horrible to you.'

Lexie's right leg jiggled. 'The really annoyin' thing is, I do feel for him, the stupid bugger. Football is his life. I know how much bein' on the bench will hurt him. I know what he's like when he's unhappy – he just eats. I'd say he's a tub of lard now. Maybe I should go back and stick some photos of David Beckham and Ronaldo up on the fridge door. Give him a taste of his own medicine.' She giggled.

'Well, it would certainly teach him a lesson.' Laura grinned.

Lexie broke a tiny corner off a chocolate biscuit and popped it into her mouth. 'The stupid thing is that I love him. I know it's mad and he'll never be faithful but I love him. Dougie knows me – he gets where I come from, how much I needed to get away from my past. He's the same. He grew up in an estate like mine, full of junkies and losers. I'm totally myself with Dougie. No pretendin' I watch the news or read the papers. No pretendin' I give a shit about politics or understand the first thing about taxes and stocks and shares. I can take me makeup off and go barefoot with Dougie. He knows I'm a short-arse.' Lexie looked at her six-inch wedges. 'I don't have to pretend my family's normal or that me dad's got a decent job and isn't locked up. And best of all,' Lexie's lip began to quiver, 'he doesn't mind that I can't have children. He's fine about me not being able to give him little Dougies. Most men would struggle with that. So . . .'

Laura took Lexie's manicured hand in hers. 'Oh, Lexie, I can see that this is really hard for you. But my advice to you is, follow your heart. If there's one thing I've learned over my messed-up, grief-filled life, it's that you have to grab happiness while you can. If you think being with Dougie will make you happy, then maybe you should talk to him. I know what it's like to live half a life, to spend every day wondering what if, if only . . . Don't do it to yourself. If you think Dougie's the man for you, then talk to him and see if you can sort it out.'

Lexie pulled her sunglasses up, her eyes red. 'What about the cheatin'?'

'Obviously you'll have to set rules. If he's unfaithful again, you walk and never come back. He loses you for good. Remind him that losing you also means that his career will suffer and he'll end up with nothing.'

Lexie thought about this. 'He shagged my sister.'

'I know that's a hard one to get past.'

'Even though she's only a half-sister, she's still family.'

'Look, I'm not for a second condoning his –'

'Condo-what?'

Laura smiled. 'Sorry. I mean I'm not forgiving or excusing his actions.'

'Good, because that mortified me that did. I looked a right fool with my husband havin' sex with me sister. Like a flippin' *Jerry Springer Show* we was.'

Laura wanted to reassure Lexie. 'What he did was shocking and appalling. All I'm saying is that, if you really love him and think you'd like to give it another go, don't let pride get in your way. Obviously it's a risk. He could cheat again, but I suppose that at least if it doesn't work out this time, you'll walk away with no regrets and no what-ifs.'

'ARE YOU INSANE?'

They spun around to see Mandy standing behind them, holding her guitar.

'You nearly gave me a bleedin' heart attack,' Lexie puffed.

Mandy's face was like thunder. 'Mum! How can you tell Lexie to go back to that love-rat Dougie? I can't believe you'd encourage her to walk back into that shitty relationship. Don't do it, Lexie. Have some pride.'

'Keep your hair on, darlin',' Lexie told her. 'We're just havin' a discussion.'

Laura looked up at her younger daughter. 'I'm not telling

Lexie to go back to him, but I am suggesting that she looks at all her options.'

Mandy was having none of it. 'But he treated her really badly and she deserves to be treated like the incredible person she is.'

Lexie patted Mandy on the back. 'Stop! You'll have me bawlin' in a minute.'

'I agree.' Laura didn't want Mandy getting the impression that she thought cheating was all right. 'Lexie deserves the very best, but she loves Dougie and he's asked her to come back. I just thought it might be a good idea for her to meet him and have a chat.'

Lexie smiled at Mandy. 'Don't worry, darlin', I'll be all right. Lexie's a tough old bird. Now, that's enough about me. What do you reckon about your new sister? Never a dull moment around here, eh?'

Mandy plonked herself opposite them with her back to the view. 'It's pretty mind-blowing.' She put her guitar down beside her.

'Writing a song about her, are you?' Lexie grinned. 'I'd guess you've got enough material for an album after what you found out today.'

'It's actually pretty cool. I've got all these ideas and I'm trying to get them down on paper before I forget them.'

Mandy had been great about Sophie, Laura thought. She'd expected her to be much more difficult, but the two girls had been up in her room together for ages, and when they'd come down they'd seemed to have bonded. Laura was thrilled to see them getting along. She was so proud of the way Mandy had handled it that she decided to ignore the smell of smoke and leave Mandy alone for today.

'So, how do you feel about havin' an older sister?' Lexie asked.

'It's pretty freaky when you consider she was supposed to be dead and then she just turned up, seventeen years later, alive and, like, normal. I thought she'd be really messed up and weird but she's actually kind of a square.'

280

'She's wonderful,' Laura said. 'So thoughtful and polite and clever and –'

'She's not that clever,' Mandy interrupted. 'It took her seventeen years to figure out her mother was a stranger who abducted her.'

'She was only nineteen months old when she was taken. She knew no other life.' Laura felt defensive for Sophie. She didn't want anyone, not even Mandy, criticizing her. As far as she was concerned, Sophie was perfect.

'I can't believe she's not more messed up in the head. She seems very together and mature for her age. And her accent is dead posh. She didn't go to school round my way, I can tell you.' Lexie cackled.

'Her accent is gorgeous,' Laura gushed.

Mandy frowned. 'It sounds a bit put-on.'

'That's just cos you're used to listenin' to me. I'm as common as muck. Sophie sounds like royalty and I sound like Barbara Windsor.' Lexie roared laughing.

Laura leaned back in her chair, smiling. 'I just can't believe how together she is – she's so poised. She told me she always got top marks in her exams.'

Mandy picked at the blue-black nail varnish on her index finger. 'I told you she was a square. She might study ten hours a day but she has no clue about life, real life. She's very innocent in lots of ways.'

Lexie took another tiny bite of her biscuit. 'I wish I'd been more innocent when I was younger. Too much too young is no good, mark my words.'

Laura turned to her. 'Lexie, at twenty-six, you *are* young.'

Lexie brushed some crumbs off her skinny jeans. 'I feel old, darlin'. I've been pregnant, had a botched abortion that left me barren, been kicked out of home, had a boob job, Botox, filler and veneers . . . got married and now I'm about to get divorced.'

Laura stroked Lexie's hand. 'Hopefully the next decade will be less dramatic for you.'

'No!' Mandy sat forward. 'That's the whole point. You've lived. You've experienced life and you're interesting because of it. You haven't sat at home studying, wrapped in cotton wool, having your dinner cooked every night, like I have.'

Mandy was so impatient to get away from home and spread her wings. Laura constantly had to rein her in. From the day she was born she had tried to assert her independence, always pushing boundaries and demanding more freedom. But Laura had made such a mess of her own life that she couldn't let go. She knew it was hard for Mandy that she was over-protective, but how could she not be? The last thing she wanted was for Mandy to get drunk, do drugs and end up pregnant in her teens, as she had. Life was complicated and at times very cruel. She didn't want Mandy to experience that side of it until she was older. She wanted her to enjoy her youth and not be jaded, worn out and shattered in her early twenties, as she had been.

'There's plenty of time to experience life,' Lexie echoed Laura's sentiments. 'Stick at your books for the moment. Go to college and get a degree so you can support yourself and not rely on some dodgy footballer or your boobs for money.'

Laura glanced at her watch again. Sophie had been gone for more than an hour. 'Do you know where they were meeting?' she asked Mandy.

Mandy shook her head. 'No. But I wouldn't worry about it, Mum. She's really pissed off with Anna. I'd say she's giving her a complete bollocking right now.'

'So she should,' Lexie said. 'Bleedin' kidnapper! What the hell was she thinkin'?'

'I'm just worried she'll persuade her to go back to London with her. I couldn't stand it if she leaves. I've only just got her back.' Laura began to get upset.

'Relax, Mum, she's not going anywhere. She likes it here.'

'Can you believe she has synaesthesia as well and wants to go to art college? Isn't that amazing?' Laura was like a young girl in love.

'Unlike me who can barely hold a paintbrush,' Mandy grumbled.

'You're talented in other ways,' Laura reassured her. 'It's just so wonderful to know that the synaesthesia gene is still in the family.'

'Joan and Frank don't have it and they're great,' Mandy snapped.

'Of course they are. I'm just saying it's nice for me to have someone who understands how I see the world. It's very special.'

'Weird, if you ask me,' Mandy muttered. She picked up her guitar and started to pluck the strings. She began to sing in a low voice:

> 'One sister has colours on her mind,
> The other is colour blind,
> But I think you'll find,
> She's defined by other things . . .
> Ohohohohohoh.
> The ghost returns,
> Life upturned,
> Will she get burned by the mirage
> Ohohohohoh . . .
> Mother in love with this new dove,
> Fits like a glove,
> I'm feeling the shove coming,
> Ohohohoh . . .'

Mandy's voice fizzled out.

Lexie patted her knee. 'Lovely, darlin'. Is that a new one?'

'Yeah, I've only just come up with it.'

'Excellent,' Laura said, staring at the gate, completely oblivious to what Mandy was singing. Her whole focus was on Sophie coming back. She stood up abruptly. 'I can't sit here for a second longer. I'm going to find her.'

'*No!*' Lexie and Mandy both jumped up, but it was too late: Laura had sprinted off.

*

After she'd gone about five hundred yards she saw Sophie in the distance. She was walking slowly down the lane towards the house. Her shoulders were shaking. As Laura got closer she saw that her long-lost daughter was sobbing. She rushed towards her, arms outstretched, eager to comfort her. She was delighted that Sophie's reunion with Anna had clearly gone badly.

'Sophie!' she called, and ran towards her. Sophie stopped dead. Laura ran to her but Sophie ducked away.

'Are you all right?' Laura asked. Sophie's eyes were red and puffy from crying.

Sophie took a deep breath. 'I need to ask you something. If you lie to me, I will never speak to you again. I'm sick of all the deceit. I can't take any more.'

Laura swallowed hard. 'All right.'

'Were you drunk on the boat that day?'

Laura fleetingly considered lying, but she knew she couldn't. She had to be honest. She had to explain. 'Yes, I was. I –'

'WHAT? How could you get drunk with a baby to look after?' Tears streamed down Sophie's face.

Laura spoke slowly and deliberately. 'I was twenty. I was immature and stupid and overwhelmed with being a mother. I had a few drinks, which was a really stupid thing to do but, believe me, I've paid for that mistake.'

'Define a few drinks. Were you tipsy or passed out drunk at the bar like my mother just told me?'

Laura felt her heart constrict. She willed herself not to get upset. 'At the end of the boat journey, I did fall asleep briefly.'

Sophie's mouth hung open. 'How could you do that? How could you be so neglectful? I was a baby. I needed a mother to look after me. How could you get so drunk that you blacked out? How could you not care about me? How could you just leave me on my own to fend for myself? What kind of person does that? I would never leave a small child on their own while I got drunk.'

Laura began to see yellow. She was getting angry now. Clearly Anna had slated her to Sophie in an attempt to justify her evil

284

deed. 'Hold on a minute. I admit I was drunk, I admit I made a huge mistake, but I did not neglect you. I loved you. I was just too young and immature to be a responsible mother.'

'You *did* neglect me. You were in a coma!'

'It was only that one time and I haven't touched a drink in seventeen years.'

'Did you really shout at me and push me away and tell Anna she could take me?'

'*No!*' Laura shouted. But she was shaken. Had she said that? Had she pushed her baby girl away? She had been so drunk she couldn't remember. She had gone over that day in her mind a million times and she had a horrible feeling deep inside her that she had pushed Jody away. Damn that bitch Anna. Damn her.

Sophie was becoming hysterical. 'Anna said that you told her to take me, that you said your life would be better without me.'

'I DID NOT!' Now Laura was seeing all yellow. 'How dare that woman tell you that? I may not have been the best mother but I *didn't* give you away. I died that day.' Laura thumped her chest. 'My heart stopped beating when you were taken. I did not give you up. She TOOK you, she STOLE you.'

Sophie wiped her eyes with her sleeve. She was having trouble breathing. 'How can you take something if it's being looked after? How can you abduct a child if its mother is holding its hand?'

'I may have let go of your hand but that was not an invitation for someone to snatch you. I've paid dearly for my behaviour that day.'

'What about me? I've paid too.'

Laura squeezed her hands together. 'Sophie, believe me when I tell you my life was ruined that day. I died inside. The only reason I didn't kill myself was because I got pregnant again with Mandy. I haven't touched a drink since. I've spent my life making up for that awful day. I've been the best mother I can be to Mandy, and I will be to you too, if you let me.'

'But Anna said you didn't want me.' Sophie broke down.

Laura wanted to scream, jump up and down and thump the nearest tree. She wanted to find Anna and wring her neck. How dare that bitch tell her beautiful child that she hadn't wanted her? Laura knew she had to calm down, for Sophie's sake. She went over to her and placed a hand gently on her sobbing daughter's shoulder. 'Of course she said that. She's trying to justify her evil actions. Don't you see? She's trying to make out that I was a worthless mother so her kidnapping you doesn't seem so vile. But it is vile. It's the worst thing you can do to someone. It's unforgivable.'

Sophie began to calm down. Laura's soothing tones were working on her. 'I'm so confused,' she said. 'Everything is red and green. I feel as if I've lived ten years in the last week. So much has happened and I don't know who I am or what I am or who anyone really is. My life has been completely upended.'

'Of course you're confused, you poor dote,' Laura sympathized. 'Sit down here and we'll do some yoga breathing.' She pointed to a tree stump. Sophie sat down and they began to breathe deeply, in and out.

Just as Sophie was calming down they heard a rustle. They looked up to see Joan storming down the path, followed by Frank and Mandy.

Joan was furious. 'What the hell is going on? Frank told me –'

Laura turned to face her mother. As she did so, Sophie came into view. Joan stared at her and fainted.

28.
Sophie
Killduf, July 2011

'You killed my granny, you ghost freak!' Mandy shouted, as she crouched down to see if Joan was still breathing.

'I'm sorry, I –' Sophie was terrified.

'Don't be silly! She's just fainted.' Laura glared at Mandy.

Frank slapped his mother's cheek gently to bring her round. Joan's eyes fluttered open. She saw Sophie and fainted again.

'See? She's killing her!' Mandy cried. 'Her heart can't take it.'

'Be quiet,' Laura barked. 'She'll be fine. It's just the shock.'

Frank put his arms under his mother, picked her up and carried her to the house. He laid her on the couch in the lounge and put a cushion under her head.

'What did you tell her?' Laura asked him.

Frank sighed. 'I thought she knew – you said you were going to tell her today so when I called in I said, "What about Jody coming back? Isn't it a miracle?" and she went mad. I had to drive her straight down. She thought the whole thing was some hoax.'

'Ooooh,' Joan moaned, coming round again.

Lexie was clopping down the stairs in her heels. She came into the room, got her very strong scent out of her handbag, sprayed some on a tissue and waved it under Joan's nose. 'Oooooh.' Joan opened her eyes. 'Get that dreadful smell away from me.' She pushed the tissue aside and sat up.

'That's Beyoncé's perfume that is.' Lexie looked surprised. 'It's supposed to drive men wild.' Ignoring her, Joan stood up and looked at Laura, Frank, Mandy and then Sophie. Her lined face scrunched into a deep frown. She peered closer and closer until she was almost nose to nose with Sophie. Then she reached out to touch her. Sophie was completely freaked out. She hated Joan's cold hands groping her face. It was so awkward and embarrassing. She tried not to pull away as Joan stroked her hair and muttered, 'Jody . . . Jody . . . my Jody.'

Sophie hated the name 'Jody'. It made her feel queasy. It was a green name, a bad name.

'Is it really you, Jody? Have you come back to us? Am I dreaming? Is this real?' Joan's voice shook. 'Is it true, Frankie? Is it her?'

Frank nodded. 'Yes, it's really her. I told you, Mum, she's come back to us.'

Joan touched Sophie's hands and arms. 'Jody, my Jody.' She began to cry.

Frank put his arm around her. 'It's all right, Mum. It's been a shock to us all.'

Joan turned to Laura, who was crying. 'She came back, Laura. She didn't die?'

'No, Mum, she didn't.'

Joan stared at her daughter. 'You were right, she didn't drown. I never believed you, but you were right. Our Jody's back, our little angel.'

Laura went to her mother and tried to hug her, but Joan stepped away. She stood on Sophie's toe in her eagerness to avoid Laura's affection. Sophie didn't squeal: she bit her lip and gingerly moved her toe.

Joan gripped her hand. 'Where have you been, Jody? Where did you go?'

Sophie really wanted to pull her hand out of Joan's vice-like grip. 'I've been living in London,' she answered. She hated all these questions. She'd answered them already. She'd been over it ten times. She wanted to lie down on Mandy's bed and sleep. She was drained. She couldn't take any more emotion or scrutiny today.

'But how?' Joan asked. 'How did you end up there?'

Sophie remained quiet, trying to muster up the energy to

answer yet more questions. Mandy was studying her closely. She stepped in: 'Gran, she was abducted by a nutter who took her to London and she grew up there. She went to an all-girls Catholic school, you'll be delighted to hear! And she's actually very normal, considering.'

'Abducted? Oh, my God.'

Abducted, nutter . . . That was her mother they were talking about. Anna, who had been a good mother, not insane, not a psychopath . . . but she had kidnapped her. Oh, God, it was all too much. Green, green, green.

Joan let go of Sophie's hand and sank down into the couch.

'I think Joan needs a drink, real alcohol,' Lexie said. 'I've got a stash in my room.' She rushed upstairs to get some vodka.

Joan peered at Sophie. 'Who was the monster who took you? What kind of human being would do that?'

Sophie squirmed. More horrible name-calling. 'She's not a monster,' she said. 'She's actually a nice person.'

Joan wagged a finger in her face. 'She is a monster. We thought you were dead. I nearly died myself of a broken heart. You were my baby, my angel, the love of my life. That day finished me. I'm a broken woman. That person needs to go to jail and rot there for the rest of her days.'

Sophie knew Anna had done a terrible thing, but prison? Lock her up in a cell with some murderer? No.

Laura was watching her. She said to Joan, 'It's OK. Sophie's home now.'

'Sophie?' Joan spat.

'That's her name. She's asked us to call her that. We need to ease her back in, Mum,' Laura said firmly.

'Here you go, Joan, get that down you. It'll put hairs on your chest.' Lexie handed Joan a large vodka, which she knocked back.

Joan's eyes narrowed. 'My granddaughter's name is Jody and I will not be calling her anything else. That monster stole seventeen years of her life. She's not taking her name too.'

Laura sighed. She whispered, 'I know, Mum, but this isn't

about Anna – the woman who took her. It's about Sophie being confused and frightened. It's not her fault so please just work with me.'

'Jody,' Joan said, completely ignoring Laura's plea. 'You were christened Jody, and for nineteen wonderful months I fed you and dressed you and rocked you to sleep and sang you lullabies and took you to the park and taught you how to walk and loved you with all my heart. I will not be calling you by any other name.'

'I understand,' Sophie said, not wanting to have an argument with the woman. Joan frightened her: she was so full of anger and bitterness. She hated being called Jody, but she'd let it go with Joan.

'Where is this woman who stole you from us? I want her arrested immediately.'

'Mum!' Laura warned. 'Stop.'

Joan lashed out at her: 'Don't you dare tell me what to do. If it wasn't for you being a drunken mess on that boat we wouldn't have lost Jody.'

'MUM!'

'Drunk?' Mandy frowned. 'Mum's a Pioneer.'

Joan laughed bitterly. 'She was out of her mind with drink that day. We all thought Jody had drowned because she was neglected, but now we know that a complete stranger walked off with her in broad daylight because her mother was too drunk to notice.'

'Steady on, Joan,' Lexie defended Laura.

'Be quiet, Mum. Laura's suffered enough,' Frank snapped.

'Laura's suffered enough, has she?' Joan hissed. 'It was me who raised that child. It was me who rocked her back to sleep when she cried. Laura was never there. She was too busy partying and cavorting to look after her own baby. I'm the one who sat up with her at night giving her bottles. I'm the one who changed her nappies. I'm the one who was teaching her how to talk. *Me*.' Joan beat her chest. 'Not you, Laura, or you, Frank. Me! Do you even know what her favourite food was? Stewed pear. Do you know what her first word was? "Gany" – for Granny! I did everything. She was my baby, my Jody. I died with her that day on the boat. I *died*.'

Sophie was shocked. Laura had never said Joan had done all the parenting. She hadn't said she'd been partying while Joan looked after her. Laura had hidden all this from her. Sophie was beginning to wonder if she was as great as she seemed.

'That's not fair,' Lexie said. 'Laura's a great mum. I've seen her here with Mandy and she's totally devoted.'

'I can't believe Mum was partying and drinking.' Mandy was astonished.

'Your mother was wild and completely irresponsible, and it wasn't just drink either,' Joan continued.

'MUM!' Laura yelled.

'Drugs?' Mandy gasped.

'Stop it!' Frank said. 'That's enough, Mum. Laura's spent seventeen years eaten alive with guilt. She doesn't need any more.'

'It's the truth,' Joan snapped.

'Were you really drunk when Sophie was snatched on the boat?' Mandy pulled Laura's arm so she was facing her.

Sophie could see that Laura wanted to run away, just like she did. She looked devastated. Joan was making everything worse with her accusations and revelations. Sophie wished she would go away again. Everything had been better before she'd arrived. Granted, all of their lives had been turned upside down, and things had been extremely emotional and confusing, but the atmosphere had been mostly joyful, not bitter and twisted as it was now. Joan seemed so angry with Laura.

Laura looked at her younger daughter. She took a deep breath. 'Yes, Mandy, I was. I drank too much that day and I have lived with the regret and guilt every moment of the last seventeen years.'

Mandy was incredulous. 'You were so drunk that you let someone nick your own kid?'

Laura clenched her teeth. 'Yes.'

'And you lecture me on my behaviour?'

'I don't want you to make the mistakes I did or have to experience the pain I have.'

'Were you so drunk you blacked out? How could you get that drunk with a baby to look after?' Mandy wouldn't let it go.

Sophie felt physically sick. She couldn't listen to much more of this. It was as if all the air had been sucked out of the room.

'Hang on a minute,' Frank interrupted. 'Your mum wasn't much more than a child herself when she had Sophie. It's a huge responsibility for a teenager. And she made a few bad decisions, but who hasn't? Unfortunately for Laura, hers led to a horrendous outcome. But she has learned from her mistakes and has been a brilliant mother to you.'

'It's OK, Frank. Mandy should know the truth.' Laura sank down on to the edge of the couch. 'Yes, Mandy, I was so drunk I passed out. My disgusting behaviour did give this Anna woman the opportunity to kidnap Sophie. But what I did does not give anyone the right to abduct a child. It's still wrong, immoral, illegal and completely unforgivable.'

Joan waved a long finger in Laura's face. 'If you hadn't been drunk none of this would have happened and all of our lives wouldn't have been ruined.'

'STOP!' Sophie screamed, holding her hands over her ears. 'STOP IT, ALL OF YOU.'

She ran out of the lounge and up to Mandy's bedroom, where she locked herself in.

She threw open the window and gulped fresh air into her lungs. She could hear raised voices downstairs, then a knock on the door. 'Please go away. I need to be alone for a bit.'

'That's all very well but you're in my bedroom and I'd like a bit of time out myself,' Mandy said, through the keyhole.

Sophie reluctantly unlocked the door. Mandy stalked past her and flopped down on her bed. Sophie locked the door again. She wasn't letting anyone else in. She'd had enough.

'Jesus, what a day this has been. You couldn't make this shit up.' Mandy chewed a fingernail.

Sophie leaned out of the window and looked at the sky.

'Are you OK? Too much drama?'

Sophie turned to her sister. 'I'm used to a very quiet life and this has been . . . well . . . just . . .'

'A kick in the teeth.'

'No, more of a –'

'Smack in the face? Punch in the nose?'

'I feel as though I've been run over by a freight train. I was finding it difficult to breathe down there.'

Mandy kicked off her boots and lay back on the bed. 'Me too. I cannot believe my mum was a lush. She's so square now.'

Sophie longed to be alone. She didn't want to talk about the day any more.

Mandy rolled on to her side and rested her head on her hand. 'What do you think of Joan? In fairness, you didn't see her at her best. She was being a bit of a bitch down there.'

'She seems awfully bitter,' Sophie ventured.

Mandy blew her fringe out of her eyes. 'So would you be if you'd just found out your beloved granddaughter, who was like your own daughter to you, wasn't dead.'

'I suppose so. She's a bit mean to Laura, though.'

Mandy pulled some cigarettes out of her bedside locker and lit one. 'Well she deserves it – getting so pissed that she passed out and let someone take you. That is seriously messed up.'

Sophie bit her bottom lip. 'Don't you think she's paid for her mistake?'

Mandy blew smoke rings. 'Yes, I guess she has. God, my head's melted. I'm going to take my guitar down to the beach and write some tunes. Do you want to come?'

Sophie yearned to be alone. 'No, thanks. Do you mind if I stay here and just rest for a bit?'

Mandy shrugged. 'Sure.' She stubbed out her cigarette and picked up her guitar.

As Mandy walked out, Laura walked in. Mandy brushed past her. Laura looked worn out. 'Are you all right, sweetheart?' she asked Sophie.

'I'm fine, but I really need to be alone for a bit.' Sophie had to be firm: she couldn't face any more emotional conversations.

'I'm sorry about that. Joan is just coming to terms with it all. Can I make you some dinner?'

'No, thank you. I just need some quiet time.'

Laura looked crestfallen. 'All right. If you need anything just ask.'

Sophie locked the door after Laura had left and lay down on the Che Guevara duvet. Her head was pounding. She closed her eyes. Green, red and yellow swirled around.

She opened them and tried to do the yoga breathing Laura had shown her. In and out, in and out. Her phone vibrated. It was Holly. Yes! Holly: her familiar old pal to whom she could say anything.

'Hi.'

'God, you sound awful,' Holly said.

'I am awful.'

'Go on, spill the beans.'

'I'm too tired to go into details.'

'No way! You have to tell me everything.'

Sophie closed her eyes. 'I met Mum.'

'Which one?'

'Anna. She confessed to kidnapping me.'

'No!'

'Yes. She said Laura was passed out drunk, and had told her to take me.'

'No!'

'Yes. She said Laura was horrible to me so she took me to save me.'

'Wow, Anna the superhero.'

Sophie smiled. 'I'm not sure superheroes abduct children.'

'Go on.'

'I confronted Laura. She admitted to being drunk, but she hasn't had a drink since.'

'A lot of people do that – you know, become all holy when something bad happens. Like Paris Hilton found Jesus when she was in prison for drunk-driving and said she wanted to build a Paris Hilton playhouse for sick kids.'

'Well, Laura does seem to have changed her life. She's a really good mum to Mandy.'

'What's *she* like?'

'She's nice . . . at least, I think I like her. I'm still getting to know her. She's very different from me. She's really into music and plays the guitar and writes her own songs and stuff.'

'What kind of music?'

Sophie sat up and peered at the bookshelf. 'I haven't heard her sing so I'm not sure, but I think it's quite dark. She has lots of books about old singers I've hardly heard of, like Joan Baez.'

'Dad loves her but she's, like, a hundred years old. Your sister sounds a bit weird.'

Sophie thought about Mandy. Was she weird? 'No, she isn't. In some ways she's a lot more worldly than I am, even though she grew up in this little village and I grew up in London. She's had sex and –'

'Sophie, nearly all of our friends have had sex. You're one of the very few who haven't.'

'I know.'

'Seriously, what are you waiting for? Just get it over with. Do what I did. Choose a guy you know likes you, drink at least four vodka and Cokes, lie back and close your eyes.'

'Why close your eyes?'

'Because then you won't see his face getting all red and boggle-eyed. Honestly, boys look like frogs when they're having sex. With your colour thing, you'd be seeing lots of greens and that could really ruin it for you. But then it's done and all the wondering and waiting is over and you can move on to someone you actually fancy and maybe enjoy it.'

Sophie shuddered. 'You're not making it sound very appealing.'

'I probably chose badly. Luke had a really spotty back – I could feel the lumps with my hands.'

'Gross!' Sophie giggled. She was delighted with this distraction from her current situation.

'And he grunted like a rhinoceros and shouted dirty things at me.'

'You never told me that.'

'I was too embarrassed.'

'What kind of things?'

'Things like "You know you want it, you whore" and "How's that, you filthy bitch?"'

'But he's such a quiet, reserved guy!' Whenever you spoke to Luke he went purple with embarrassment and looked at the ground. He was painfully shy. He had a huge crush on Holly, who thought he was a complete nerd and had never given him the time of day until six months ago, when she'd decided to lose her virginity and wanted to do it with someone who worshipped her and wouldn't tell tales after the event.

'I know! That's why I chose him to be my first. He was a quiet geek who thought I was a goddess.' Holly laughed.

'It's true what they say, "It's always the quiet ones!"' Sophie chortled.

'When he got to the end of his performance he made this insane noise – *gaaaah guh-guh-guh*.'

They shrieked with laughter.

'It was like the Incredible Hulk or something,' Holly continued, 'but then he turned back into normal Luke. He got dressed without looking at me, shook my hand and said, "Thank you so much for a wonderful evening."' Holly couldn't go on, she was laughing so much.

'Shook your hand?' Sophie was practically choking.

'I know! After calling me all those rude names, he shook my hand as if we'd just had a business meeting.'

'Oh, Holly, that's so funny.'

'Perhaps you should find a nice Irish boy and get it over with there. Maybe one of Mandy's friends.'

'She's nearly three years younger than me.'

'I'm sure they'll have older brothers.'

'Holly, I can barely think straight with everything that's going on. I really don't think losing my virginity in the middle of all this chaos would help.'

'It would be a good distraction,' Holly suggested. 'Imagine if you met Colin Farrell's younger brother or something. That would be amazing.'

'I'm in a remote village outside Dublin surrounded by crying women all accusing each other of awful things. It's unlikely I'll have the opportunity to meet anyone. I'll be lucky if I get home with my sanity intact.'

'Did your mum mention me?'

'No, she was too busy trying to excuse her psychotic behaviour.'

'Were you glad to see her?'

Sophie looked out at the sea. 'Yes, I was. But I have no idea what's going to happen next. It's all such a mess. I've just met Laura's mother and she fainted when she saw me – Mandy thought she was dead.'

Holly whooped. 'It's crazier than *The Osbournes*! I hope you're writing it all down. Honestly, Sophie, there's so much potential in this story.'

'Yes, but it's my life. This craziness is my new reality.'

'Shit! Jessie's coming, gotta fly. Love you, Sophie, stay strong.'

The phone went dead. Sophie looked around the room and saw a stack of white paper in Mandy's printer. She went over to the desk and pulled a few sheets out. She picked up one of Mandy's pencils, sat down at her desk and began to draw. She welcomed the warm blanket of oblivion that encompassed her as she lost herself in her art.

29.

Anna

Killduf, July 2011

Anna cried the whole way back to Dublin. It had been so wonderful to see Sophie but heartbreaking too. Sophie was so angry with her, and when she had said that Laura was her real mother, it had been like being stabbed with a hot poker.

Anna had never seen Sophie like that. She hated herself for what she was putting her daughter through. She had hoped this would never happen. Sophie finding out the truth had never been part of her plan. After seventeen years she had almost begun to relax. Sophie was going to art college. Anna had done what she had promised to do. She had raised a wonderful, balanced, caring, clever human being, who was about to go out into the world and enrich it.

Now everything was broken, destroyed. She couldn't let it end like this. Laura had been a terrible mother, a wretched mother. How dare she pretend to Sophie that she hadn't been drunk? How dare she pretend she had been a good parent? It was nauseating to think of her spinning her story and pulling Sophie into her web of lies and deceit. It made Anna sick to know that Sophie was staying with this person, listening to her falsehoods and, even worse, believing them.

There was no way Anna would let this go: she was going to fight for Sophie. She was going to do everything she could to get her daughter back. Laura had no right to steal her away. She wasn't her mother: she had given up that right when she had neglected her and pushed her away on the boat.

Sophie was Anna's daughter, no one else's. Biology had nothing to do with it. Loving, nurturing, caring, minding, encouraging, nursing, teaching, nourishing, protecting: they were the things that made you a mother. Anna had devoted her life to bringing up Sophie. She had spent seventeen years putting Sophie's happiness before her own. She had invested everything she had, financially, emotionally and intellectually, in making her daughter's life perfect. There was no way in hell Laura was going to walk into her life now and take her away. Sophie was Anna's life. She was damned if she'd give her up without a fight.

When Anna arrived back to Joe's apartment he was waiting for her. She collapsed into his arms and told him everything . . . except that she had vomited blood.

Joe sat her on the couch, placed her feet on a footstool and handed her a gin and tonic. But when she took a sip, it burned her stomach so badly that she winced. Joe noticed straight away. 'Damn, it's flared up, hasn't it?'

'It's fine.'

'Anna, I saw your face. It must be bad if one sip is causing you so much pain. God, I hope it hasn't ruptured. Have you coughed up any blood?'

'No.' Anna didn't want Joe fussing. She needed to focus on getting Sophie back.

Joe went into the kitchen and came back with a glass of milk. 'Drink this, and take two Lansoprazole. That should help.'

Anna gladly took the tablets and drank the cold milk, which was soothing. She rested her head on a cushion and let the tablets work their magic.

Joe sat down beside her. He took her hand. 'I want you to get some tests done. I'll arrange for them tomorrow morning. I have a horrible feeling all this stress may cause the ulcer to rupture.'

'I can't tomorrow. I have to go and talk to Laura.'

Joe took his glasses off and placed them on the coffee-table. 'You're no good to anyone if you're sick. A ruptured ulcer is very serious. I'm booking the tests for first thing in the morning. You can see Laura after that.'

Anna finished her milk and put the glass down. 'I'll get the tests done in the afternoon. I'm going to Killduf at the crack of dawn tomorrow to talk to Laura. I'm sorry, Joe, but getting Sophie back is my priority. Nothing else matters.' Anna kissed his cheek. 'I know you've got my best interests at heart, but Sophie comes first.'

'She always does.' Joe smiled sadly. 'Sometimes too much so. She's eighteen and you have to let her go.'

Anna gritted her teeth. 'Not now, not yet and definitely not like this. I'm going to make sure Sophie knows the truth and that that witch admits the terrible things she did and said. There is no way I'm backing down.'

Joe rubbed his eyes. 'When you're like this there's no point trying to change your mind. I'll book the tests for after lunch.'

Anna reached for his hand. 'Thanks, Joe. I'm sorry about all this. I'm sorry I lied to you and hid the truth. But I had to – you can see that now, can't you?' Anna was desperate for his approval, for him to say he understood and agreed with her actions. 'You understand now that I did the right thing, don't you? I know it seems extreme, but it was that or she would have died.'

'She might have been fine.'

'She wouldn't.'

'Anna!'

'It was the right thing. My instinct told me so.'

'You had lost Hope. You were still grieving.'

'No! I took her because she was in danger.'

'She was the same age as Hope.'

'I know, but – but that wasn't it. I saved her, Joe. I saved her.'

Joe looked at her, his eyes full of sorrow. 'You also saved yourself.'

'But that's not why ... No, Joe ... I was only thinking about Sophie and her safety.'

Joe remained silent.

'Joe?'

Joe looked at his hands. 'I can't, Anna. I can't tell you I approve. I understand why you did it but that doesn't make it right. A child belongs with its mother.'

'Not when she's a danger to her.'

'You don't know she was for sure. You made a snap decision that changed those people's lives.'

Anna stood up and glared at him. 'I made the right decision, I know I did.'

'And just how do you think Laura's going to react when you march into her house uninvited?' Joe's voice was tight.

'I'm going to give her a piece of my mind for all the lies she told Sophie. I'm going to make her tell Sophie the truth about that day.' Anna's mouth set in a hard line. 'I'm not leaving until she does. She'll have to throw me out.'

'I really think that's a bad idea. She's only just got Sophie back. Let her have a few days with her.'

Anna stood up. 'I will not let her poison Sophie with her lies and her truth-bending. No bloody way. I'm going to show her she can't just take my child away.'

'Like you did to her,' Joe quietly reminded her.

Anna tossed and turned all night. She slept in the spare room. Joe wasn't ready to let her into his bed. It hurt her that he didn't agree with her actions, but she tried to block it out and focus on what she was going to say to Laura. She knew she had to keep calm and take the upper hand. She slept fitfully. At four o'clock she woke up with a searing pain in her stomach. What if Laura called the police and reported her crime? What if she ended up in prison? No! Anna decided she would simply tell the judge that Sophie had been in mortal danger. No judge would rule against her: they'd see that she'd done what she'd had to do, and Sophie would testify that she had been a great mother. But didn't most courts rule with the mother, the biological mother? Yes, but only if she was fit to look after the child, which Laura was clearly not . . . Anna gave up on sleep and sat up. She turned on the light and tried to distract herself by reading, but the fears and doubts continued to eat away at her. As the sun rose, she was vomiting blood in the bathroom.

On the drive down, Anna practised her speech. She went over all the things she wanted to say, all the things she wanted to remind Laura of – how she had shouted at Sophie and said how much better her life would be without a child and how she had asked Anna to take her away.

At exactly half past seven, Anna parked the car at the end of the lane and walked up to the house. She was wearing light grey trousers and a pink blouse. She had put on some makeup so she would look less old and tired. She had seen how young Laura was and felt very old compared to her. And she knew she looked even older than her fifty-seven years due to the recent trauma and lack of sleep.

When she got to the house, it was quiet. She tiptoed to the kitchen window and peered in. No one was up. She was about to go around to the front of the house when she noticed someone in the studio. She walked slowly to the large glass window and looked in. Laura was sitting cross-legged in the middle of the floor, eyes closed, meditating. She was wearing loose linen trousers and a blue cotton T-shirt. Her blonde curly hair was held up with a clip.

She looked so like Sophie that Anna stopped in her tracks and stared. They could have been sisters. Laura looked so different from the drunken girl on the boat. She was a woman now, a beautiful woman.

Her beauty belies her bad heart, Anna thought grimly. She steeled herself, opened the door and stood in front of Laura, blocking the sunlight and the view. Laura opened her eyes. They were the same deep blue as Sophie's. Anna glared at her. 'I don't think I need to introduce myself.' She folded her arms across her chest.

Laura blinked a few times, taking the situation in. She slowly uncrossed her legs and stood up. She was taller than Anna, younger and fitter. It struck Anna that if they got into a fight, she'd lose. Laura would easily knock her down.

Laura was staring at Anna, open-mouthed. She was taking in every detail of her face as if she was memorizing it. Anna decided to take control of the situation. 'Where's Sophie?'

'I don't remember you at all.' Laura frowned. 'I thought I would. I thought when I saw you I'd recognize you from the boat. But you're a total stranger to me. Nothing about you is familiar.'

'Where is she?' Anna persisted. 'I'm here to take my daughter home.'

Laura flinched. 'Excuse me?'

'You heard me.'

'I think you mean *my* daughter,' Laura reminded her. 'And she *is* home.'

Anna laughed bitterly and waved a hand around. 'You think this is her home? You must be joking. Her home is in London, with me. It's the only home she knows.'

Laura's eyes flashed. 'How dare you come in here and demand to take my daughter away again? Have you no remorse? Have you no shame? Are you insane? You abducted her! There is no way that's ever going to happen again.'

'Have you conveniently forgotten that you were passed out drunk that day? Have you forgotten that you said you wished you'd never had her, wished she would go away, handed her to me . . . asked me to take her. I didn't steal her. You *gave her away*.'

Laura's face was bright red. 'You're a psychopath. Yes, I was drunk, but that did not give you the right to kidnap my child. Mothers drink sometimes, they make mistakes, but that does not give strangers the right to take their kids away. I loved her. She was my baby, my Jody. Your actions put me in Hell! Do you understand – HELL!'

Anna clenched her fists and willed herself to be calm. She felt as if the ulcer was burning a hole in her chest. 'Sophie was in Hell. She was crying with hunger and thirst, and you were shouting at her and telling anyone who would listen how much you wished she wasn't around. Is that what you call being a mother? Is that your twisted view of love?'

Laura blanched. 'I was twenty. I was naïve and immature. I didn't mean anything I said. I loved her. I loved my little girl.'

'Well, it didn't look like it to me. You were horrible to her.'

Laura jabbed a finger at Anna. 'Who the hell do you think you are, coming into my house and accusing me of being a bad mother? You abducted someone else's child. What does that make you? Mother bloody Teresa?'

Anna pushed a stray hair off her face and put her hands on her hips. 'No, it doesn't. It makes me a human being who saw a child being wilfully neglected and, instead of turning away and allowing her life to be ruined, took action.'

'Oh, you took action, all right! You *stole* her. You made her live a lie for seventeen years. You ripped my family apart. My mother adored Jody, and so did my brother, Frank. She was loved and cherished in our home. You stupid cow, you took her away from a loving family.'

Anna was caught off guard: she hadn't thought about an extended family. She hadn't known there had been a loving grandmother and an uncle. Still, how caring could they have been, allowing Laura to take a baby on holidays when she clearly had a drink problem and was a danger to herself and Sophie? She walked over to the window and looked out at the sea. 'I know what I saw and you were toxic. You would have ruined her life. How can you justify shouting at a baby because she was hungry? You treated her like dirt. All you were interested in was your next vodka. If I hadn't taken her, the police would have.'

Laura spun Anna round to face her. 'Are you insane? You saw one moment in our lives, one incident, and you decided to play God. She wasn't yours to save. She wasn't yours to take. She was *my* baby. Mine! She belonged to *me*!' Laura was thumping her chest with her fist.

Anna moved away from her. 'Calm down.'

Laura lost it. 'CALM DOWN? YOU STOLE MY CHILD. YOU RUINED MY LIFE.'

Anna looked into Laura's rage-filled eyes, and said evenly, 'I saved her.'

'She wasn't yours to save!' Laura shrieked.

Anna's eyes narrowed. 'I gave her a great life. I loved her more than you ever could. I brought her up to be the incredible human being she is.'

'*Lies!*' Laura shouted. 'Her whole life is based on lies. You have lied to her every day. You're not her mother, you're a monster.'

Anna's plan to remain composed, at all costs, went out of the window. She glared at Laura. 'Don't you dare call me a monster. You're the monster. Sophie is a stable, happy girl because I took her and nurtured her and gave her the life she deserved, the life every child deserves, in a stable and loving environment.'

Laura stared at her, incredulous. 'A child belongs with its mother, not a stranger. You are *not* her mother. You did not give birth to her. You did not have the right to make any decisions regarding her life. What you did was illegal and immoral!'

'It's immoral to mistreat a child.'

'It was one bad day. Jody was adored at home. She was doted on by my mother, who has barely spoken to me for seventeen years because she thought I'd killed my baby girl. Do you have any idea what that's like?' Laura burst into tears. 'You destroyed my life. My mother called me a murderer. Are you proud of yourself now? I've spent seventeen agonizing years not knowing what happened to my baby. I almost went insane wondering if she was dead or alive. Believing she was out there somewhere, but where? With whom? Safe? In pain? Suffering? Being raped? Being abused? I had no idea. You put me through hell. How can you live with yourself? What kind of person does that? Only an evil one.'

Anna was close to tears herself. She had thought Sophie was

alone in the world, but for her mother. She felt sick thinking about the grandmother's suffering – but how could she have known? Where was the grandmother that day? Why did she leave Laura to look after Sophie when clearly she was a drunk? 'I'm not evil. I've been a wonderful mother to her. Sophie has been happy every day of her life with me. I never once shouted at her or made her cry or feel unwanted, or let her go hungry or thirsty. You were unfit. Maybe it was because you were young, but I know I made the right decision that day. Look at her – look at how wonderful she is.'

Laura was gulping back sobs. 'She would have been wonderful anyway. I'm her *mother*. I loved her.'

'You didn't love her. No one treats a child they love like scum.'

Laura screeched, ran over and pushed Anna towards the door. 'You stupid bitch! Don't tell me I didn't love my own child! I want you out – get out! You're the one who's toxic. Go back to the hole you crawled out of.'

Anna was surprised by the force with which Laura was pushing her out of the door. She began to push back, but Laura was stronger. So Anna dug her nails into Laura's arm. Laura yanked it away and Anna ducked under the other. Laura grabbed her again. Anna pinched her. Laura squealed and let go, but then she grabbed Anna's wrist and squeezed it tightly. Anna reached out with her free arm and pushed Laura's chin up, wrenching her neck. Laura scrambled and grabbed Anna's hair. They ended up pulling, pushing, pinching, thumping, slapping and wrestling on the studio floor.

Laura rolled over and jumped up. Before Anna could catch her breath, Laura grabbed her right arm and dragged her out of the door on to the lawn. Anna scrambled to get up, but Laura was too strong. She was pulling her with force and determination. Anna roared, 'Let go of me!'

Laura ignored her. She was dragging her towards her car. Anna had to get free. She dug her nails into Laura's hand. 'OW!' Laura loosened her grip.

Anna scrambled to her feet, but Laura dived on top of her, crushing her to the ground. Anna gasped for breath.

'*Stop it!*'

Sophie was running towards them. She grabbed Laura's arm and pulled her off Anna.

'Kick her arse, Mum,' Mandy bellowed, following hot on Sophie's heels.

Anna rolled on to her stomach and gulped air. The two girls were in their pyjamas.

'What are you doing?' Sophie demanded.

'Beating the shit out of each other.' Mandy grinned.

Anna smoothed down her shirt. The sleeve was ripped, her hair was a mess and she had scratches on her cheek. Laura's top was torn, her hair clip lay broken on the ground and she had red fingernail marks down her left arm.

'Way to go, ladies. That was a serious catfight. You were killing her, Mum. Respect.' Mandy held her hand up to high-five Laura, but her mother wasn't paying her any attention. Laura and Anna were both staring at Sophie.

Anna rushed over to her. 'I'm sorry you saw that, sweetheart. Laura attacked me. She didn't like being faced with the truth.'

Sophie shrugged her away. Laura laid a hand on Sophie's shoulder. 'Sorry, pet. Anna stormed into my studio and tried to justify kidnapping you.'

Sophie moved away from her too. 'Stop, both of you, please, just stop.'

Mandy stood in front of Anna with her hands on her hips. 'So you're the nutter. You're the psycho-freak who stole my sister. How do you sleep at night? Don't you have nightmares about what you did? Or are you one of those people who have no conscience, like serial killers and Hitler and stuff?'

Anna peeled her eyes away from Sophie to look at Mandy. She was so different from Sophie: they didn't look like sisters or relations of any sort.

'What have you got to say for yourself?' Mandy demanded. 'Nothing? Don't you care about ruining people's lives?'

Anna had seen hundreds of Mandys in her years as headmistress – she was an angry teenager, all swagger and attitude, yet underneath, completely insecure. In a very firm voice she answered, 'I'll let your mother explain the circumstances under which I took Sophie from you. Although she'll probably be too ashamed to admit them.'

Mandy narrowed her eyes. 'I know all about her being drunk. But that's not who she is now. She's all into clean living and yoga and organic food. The strongest thing she drinks is herbal tea.'

'Maybe that's the case now, but back then it was bottles of vodka.'

'Who are you?' a voice behind them said. They all turned. Joan was standing at the kitchen door. She was wearing a pair of Laura's pyjamas and her hair was askew. She walked towards them. 'I thought I'd dreamed it all about Jody coming back. But I didn't, she's really here.' Joan's eyes welled.

Laura put her arm around her mother's shoulders. 'Mum, this is the woman who took our Jody. She's had the cheek to come down here and try to take her back to London.'

Joan came over and put her face right up to Anna's. Her skin was etched with deep wrinkles and her eyes were full of rage. She breathed deeply as she examined Anna. Anna wanted to move away but stood her ground.

Joan raised her right hand and slapped Anna's cheek hard. The sound resonated above everyone's gasps.

Mandy whooped. 'Good on you, Gran.'

Anna held her hand up to her stinging cheek. She looked at Sophie, who was crying.

Joan poked Anna in the chest. 'You stole seventeen years of my life. I was forty-three when Jody died – at least, we thought she'd drowned. I'm sixty now but I look eighty. That's what grief does to your face. Do you have any idea of the agony you put this family through? You might as well have shot us all dead with a gun. It would have been less painful. I loved that child more than anything. She was the joy in my life. When I woke up every day the only thing I wanted was to see her smiling face. You took that away. You left us with nothing. *Nothing*.'

Anna shifted uncomfortably. Joan's unhappiness was hard to take. She had simply never even imagined Sophie had a loving grandmother waiting for her at home. Her face was ravaged by years of pain. Joan was only three years older than Anna but she looked twenty years her senior.

Anna's stomach was lurching. She couldn't throw up in front of everyone. She took a deep breath. 'How could you let Laura take Sophie on that boat? She was incapable of looking after her. If I hadn't saved her she probably would have drowned.'

Joan's eyes widened. 'I didn't know! I was in Galway – my sister Angela broke her leg and needed my help. I had no idea Laura was going to England for some party. I'd *never* have let her take Jody on a boat. Never in a million years. I knew what she was like, immature and irresponsible.'

'And unfit to be a mother.' Anna drove the knife in.

'No, she isn't. She's a great mum,' Mandy piped up. She continued, 'She's a bit of a stalker and a control-freak at times, but I get it. She lost one kid and didn't want to lose two.'

Laura gave her a watery smile.

Anna ignored Mandy and focused on Joan. 'Laura was out of her mind drunk. What would you have done if you'd seen it? What would you have done if you'd heard your precious grandchild pleading for food and milk and being shouted and cursed at?'

Joan eyeballed Anna. 'I'd have asked questions. I'd have looked into the situation. I would have asked the girl if she had a friend waiting for her, a mother or a brother or someone I could call. What I would *not* have done is take a child from its mother. What I would *not* have done is play God with other people's lives.'

Anna sighed. 'She thrust Sophie into my arms. She told me to take her. She wanted her out of her sight, out of her life – she said so! I've loved Sophie unconditionally for seventeen years. She's grown up to be an incredible person. I'm proud of what I've achieved and I still believe I did the right thing. Just because she had a normal grandmother doesn't mean that her drunken mother wouldn't have put her in other dangerous situations or damaged her for life. Laura was a mess.'

Joan looked at Laura, who was listening closely. 'She stopped drinking and sorted herself out.'

Anna threw her hands up in exasperation. 'She only gave up *after* I took Sophie, after she got a wake-up call, after she realized what a terrible mother she was. If I hadn't intervened she'd probably still be drinking and Sophie would be at the bottom of the sea.'

Laura rushed over, waving her finger in Anna's face. 'You robbed me of my right to see my child grow up,' she roared. 'I never got to take her to school on her first day, to dress her up on Hallowe'en, to see her in the nativity play, to teach her how to swim and play tennis and paint, cook her favourite meals, build sandcastles with her and read books to her. You stole those memories.'

Joan put her hand on Laura's arm. 'You were a mess at the time,' she reminded her. 'You were heading down a dark path, Laura. The boat wasn't the first time you put Jody's life in danger, with your drugs and your drinking. Anna here has a point. You only stopped drinking when you got pregnant with Mandy.'

Laura yanked her arm away. 'I was in Hell after Jody disappeared. I thought I'd caused my baby girl's death. You called me a murderer, Mum. You made me feel like a piece of shit. I would have killed myself if I hadn't found out I was pregnant again. Mandy was what saved me, not having my child abducted.'

Mandy bowed. 'You're welcome.'

'Sophie saved me,' Anna said quietly.

'Your actions almost killed us all,' Joan told her.

'Please stop. I can't take any more.' Sophie was holding her head. 'Green . . . it's all green. My head's splitting.'

Anna and Laura both rushed over to comfort her.

'Easy, ladies, no more physical violence, please.' Mandy stood between them.

'Open your eyes, pet. Look at me and take deep breaths,' Anna said, holding Sophie's face.

'Look at this. Focus on this.' Laura held a pink scarf in front of Sophie. 'Focus on your happy colour.'

Sophie looked from one to the other.

'Come on, sweetheart, I'll take you home. You can be back in your own bed in a few hours. Come with me,' Anna begged.

Sophie looked at her and slowly, sadly, shook her head. 'No. I'm staying here with my family.'

'Good old Sophie. Laura one, Anna nil,' Mandy cheered. '*Bon voyage*, Anna, you nut-job. Try not to abduct anyone on the flight home.'

Anna gulped back the wail rising in her throat. She felt her stomach contract. She knew she was about to throw up blood. She didn't want Sophie to see it – she didn't want her to worry. She forced a smile, straightened her shoulders, looked at her precious daughter, the love of her life. 'I'll be in Joe's if you need me. I love you.'

She walked back down the lane, head held high as her heart shattered.

30.

Laura

Killduf, July 2011

Sophie pulled the curtain back and stepped out of the dressing room.

'Oh, you do look classy in that,' Lexie enthused. She was wearing a black wig and huge sunglasses so no one would recognize her.

'Stunning,' Laura agreed.

Sophie was in a pale lilac chiffon blouse, embroidered with tiny cream spots, and a pair of ankle-grazer white jeans. She looked young and fresh and beautiful. Laura wanted to hold her, inhale her loveliness and never let go. She couldn't believe she was taking her little Jody shopping. Miracles do happen, she thought.

'Do I really?' Sophie asked. She looked at herself in the mirror.

'Yes!' Lexie and Laura answered.

'Can we go now?' Mandy looked up from her iPhone.

Laura frowned at her.

Mandy sighed. 'Fine. I'll shut up and let you all worship at her feet,' she grumbled, under her breath.

Sophie turned. 'What was that?'

'Nothing.' Laura glared at Mandy.

Lexie walked over to fix the bow on the back of Sophie's blouse. 'You'll have 'em queuing round the block, darlin'. You're a natural stunner. Not like me, who has to get up before the bleedin' birds and put on my foundation with a shovel, then my false eyelashes, eyeliner and blusher, clip in my hair extensions and stick on my nails. It's exhausting sometimes.'

'I think you look lovely with no makeup on,' Sophie responded.

Lexie kissed her cheek. 'Bless you and your perfect manners. I look like crap without my slap on, but I do appreciate your sayin' that.'

'She's right, Lexie,' Laura said. 'You don't need any of it. You're gorgeous without it. Honestly.'

Lexie examined herself in the mirror, smoothing down her skin-tight strapless black sundress. 'Thanks, ladies, but I need my war paint. It's like a kind of armour for me. When I'm all done up I feel I can cope with the world. With my face on, I feel stronger and braver.' She shrugged. 'I dunno, I suppose it's like my costume or something.'

'I get that.' Mandy looked up from her phone. 'I'd die without my fringe. I can hide behind it if I need to. I'd feel really exposed without it.'

'Exactly.' Lexie smiled at her.

'My paintbrush is my armour,' Laura confided. 'I can escape from anything when I'm working.'

'Me too,' Sophie agreed.

'I still can't get over how incredible those sketches you did are,' Laura said.

Sophie's face flushed with pleasure. 'They're very raw, but thanks. If I have any talent it's because of you.'

Laura beamed at her. She felt ten feet tall whenever Sophie said she liked the same thing she did, or felt the same way or thought the same thought or saw the same colour. It was like being in love. Her heart fluttered every time she looked at her precious daughter.

Mandy made vomiting noises in the corner, which Laura ignored. Over the last week, as Sophie had settled into the house, they had got to know her better and grown to love her more, but Mandy had become less accepting of her. She was being difficult and bolshie. Laura was relieved that she was spending the weekend at her dad's. It would give her some real quality time with Sophie. Lexie would make herself scarce, as she always did when Laura and Sophie were alone. She knew how much Laura needed to be with her daughter.

Sophie came out of the dressing room in her old jeans and a black T-shirt Mandy had lent her. It had a picture of Joan Baez on it and a quote: *I've never had a humble opinion. If you've got an opinion, why be humble about it?*

'Now try these on.' Laura handed Sophie a beautiful pair of beige Miu Miu sandals with a high wedge heel.

'Oh, they're amazing.' Sophie tried the right shoe on and admired it. But as she was about to try on the left, she saw the price tag. 'Oh, gosh, I couldn't allow you to buy me these. They're much too expensive. You've let me choose so much already. I really don't need them.'

Laura fell a little bit more in love with her elder daughter. 'Sophie, I've been waiting seventeen years to do this. Please let me spoil you.'

Sophie glanced at Mandy, who was studiously ignoring them.

'Go on, darlin', let your mum splash out on you. If my mum had offered me Miu Miu shoes I'd have bitten 'er hand off. I do love designer shoes. Louboutins are my favourite. Dougie liked me in them an' all. Actually, he used to like me with nothin' but me Louboutins on.'

They all roared laughing.

Laura picked up her handbag. 'Come on, let's get these wrapped up and go for a nice lunch.'

The shop assistant wrapped Sophie's purchases – two sundresses, three T-shirts, two blouses, one pair of blue jeans, one pair of white jeans, two skirts, one pair of sandals, one pair of Miu Miu wedges, two cardigans, a denim jacket, two pairs of pyjamas and some underwear.

Lexie cleverly steered Sophie away while the final amount was being calculated. The bill came to fourteen hundred euros. Laura gleefully handed over her card. She didn't care about the money. All she cared about was the complete and utter joy of being able to treat her precious girl. The very action of buying her daughter clothes made her feel like her mother. It was what mothers did. They went shopping with their daughters. They bought them things to wear. Laura had never had that with Sophie. She'd never been able to do nice things with or for her. It felt wonderful. She felt young and carefree, reckless and ecstatic.

Mandy sidled up beside her. 'I'm fine, thanks, Mum. Don't worry about me. I don't need anything. Thanks for asking, though. In case you don't remember who I am, I'm Mandy, your daughter, the one who's been living with you for the past sixteen years and three months.'

Laura looked at her younger daughter's grouchy face. She kissed her forehead. Mandy recoiled. 'What are you doing? Jesus, Mum, you've gone all mushy since Sophie turned up. Go and slobber over her.'

'I love you, Mandy. I love every hair on your grumpy head.'

'Whatever. Go and stalk Sophie. I've had sixteen years of you. It's her turn to take the pain.'

Laura chuckled and walked ahead to link arms with Sophie. It was a blue day . . . magnificent aqua blue.

They found a nice restaurant with a terrace. It was a treat to sit outside and have lunch: summers in Ireland were erratic so you had to make the most of the sunny days. Recently the weather had been fantastic. Since the day Sophie had walked into their lives the sun had shone. Laura knew it was the universe smiling down at them.

They sat at a round table and ordered their food. Lexie's phone beeped. She read the message and laughed: 'It's Dougie. He's not happy with me.'

'Why?' Mandy asked.

'Because my reply to his last message wasn't very positive.'

'What did you say?' Sophie wondered.

Lexie leaned over. 'To fill you in on the back-story, Dougie cheated on me when we was married – a lot. So I left him. Now he's all lonely and fat and playin' crap football so he wants me back. But I told him I needed some time to myself. I said I ain't comin' runnin' every time he clicks his fingers. So he sent me a

315

text sayin' if I won't come home for him, will I at least think of Pelé and Maradona?'

'Pelé and Maradona?' Laura grinned.

'Our Chihuahuas.' Lexie giggled. 'Dougie named 'em. I wanted to call 'em Dolce and Gabbana but he was havin' none of it.'

'Do you miss them?' Mandy wanted to know. 'I wish we had a dog. I'd love a black Lab but Mum's allergic.'

'To be honest, I can't stand 'em. All they do is pee everywhere and chew my shoes. Dougie bought 'em for me as a present but I never liked dogs, really. They're not even proper dogs, more like big rats. I took 'em for a walk round the garden on the first day and they was so knackered they slept for two days. Who wants dogs you have to carry around all the time?'

'Do you miss your husband?' Sophie asked.

Lexie took a sip of her sparkling water. 'Yeah, I do. But he was a right dickhead, shaggin' all sorts. To be honest, if I hadn't met Frank and come over here, I'd probably be back with him already. I figured I was worth nothing on my own. But coming here, away from it all and staying with you lot, has made me think about my life and what I'm doin' with it. You made me feel brilliant about myself. I don't want to be with someone who cheats on me now. I want a decent bloke who treats me right. I look at all you've been through and I can see that you can survive anything. I was too scared to leave Dougie before, but now I can see that what you wear or the size of your diamonds isn't who you are. Besides, I don't want to be a WAG any more. I want people to know me and respect me because of what I do. Look at Posh Spice – people respect her now she's got her own career as a designer. So I've decided I'm goin' to take the money from the sale of my book and start my life over.'

'Good for you,' Laura enthused.

'What are you going to do?' Mandy asked.

'Glamour photography! There are way too many men photographers and some of them are up to no good, tryin' it on with the young girls. So I've decided I'm goin' to do a course, set up my own studio and take the pictures of the page-three girls and the glamour models. I think they'd be more comfortable with a woman staring at their bits. I know I would've preferred it. I learned a lot about lightin' an' all when I was modellin' so I reckon I'll be all right.'

'That's a great idea,' Laura said. 'How totally inspired of you to think of that.'

'It's thanks to you lot, really,' Lexie said, sounding emotional. 'Honestly, comin' here's changed the way I see myself.'

'What about Dougie? Are you going to go through with the divorce?' Mandy asked.

'I'm goin' home to London and I'll see him. Listen to what he has to say and then decide. But I know Dougie. He won't be able to be faithful – he's too soft. So I reckon it's over. Sad, but life goes on. Look at you lot, what you've gone through, you're happy now. I will be too, on my own terms.'

'That deserves a toast.' Laura raised her glass. 'To Lexie's new career and life.'

'Cheers, darlin', and here's to you guys – livin' proof that you should never give up hope.'

Later that day, when they were lounging around in the garden, enjoying the sun, they heard a car pull up. Lexie was sunbathing, lying on her stomach. Laura was flicking through baby photos of Sophie. Mandy was sitting in the shade, strumming her guitar and writing down lyrics. Sophie was in the kitchen, getting everyone a drink.

'That'll be your dad,' Laura said to Mandy.

'He's dying to meet Sophie,' Mandy said. 'He thought I was winding him up when I told him yesterday.'

'I know. I had him on the phone for an hour last night,' Laura said. At first David had been brilliant about it, thrilled for her, Joan and Frank. He had said all the right things about Laura deserving this miracle and how she was a great person and a great mum . . . It had been so nice to hear those things from him. It had meant a lot, especially with Joan knocking her all the time. But then he had started pushing her to press charges against Anna. He wanted to get the police involved and lawyers. He said they must get her locked up for what she had done, it was a heinous crime and on and on, but Laura wasn't ready for that. She didn't want to get into it yet. And she knew that Sophie would be upset if she thought they were plotting to lock Anna up. She had asked David to give her a few more days to think about it, but he had been reluctant to agree. He wanted to act now, while they knew Anna was still in Dublin, before she had the chance to bolt.

They heard the car door close, hurried footsteps and then a loud cough.

Laura looked up and saw David standing at the edge of the grass, staring openly at Lexie's naked bum.

Tanya came around the corner, hot on his heels. 'What on earth?'

'Sophie?' David asked.

Laura and Mandy roared laughing.

'Don't be ridiculous, David,' Tanya hissed. 'She's the footballer woman I told you about.' Addressing Lexie, she said, 'Can you please put some clothes on?'

Lexie looked up lazily from her magazine. 'Sorry, darlin', but I always sunbathe in a thong. I like a nice brown bum, don't you?'

Laura cheered silently: good old Lexie, she took no crap from anyone.

'Close your mouth, Dad, you're drooling.' Mandy grinned.

'It's indecent,' Tanya barked.

Lexie pulled her enormous Gucci sunglasses up on to her head. 'If it was hanging around my ankles I'd agree with you, darlin'. But it ain't. I do my lunges every day to keep it nice and perky. Dougie always said my bum was better than Kylie's.'

'I'm David, Mandy's father.' Laura tried not to laugh as David reached down to shake Lexie's hand. Tanya's face was like curdled milk.

'Nice to meet you. I'm Lexie Granger. I've heard good things about you, David. Laura tells me you're a stand-up bloke. I admire that.'

David blushed. 'Well, thank you.'

'And you've done a good job with Mandy here.' Lexie winked at her. 'She's a bit lippy, but she has a good heart.'

'My sentiments exactly.' David chuckled.

'Sorry I took so long.' Sophie walked towards them. She was wearing her new powder blue sundress and her feet were bare. The sun was shining behind her, giving her an almost other-worldly glow.

David spun around and gaped at her. Sophie froze. 'Jesus Christ,' he whispered. 'She's you, Laura – it's uncanny.'

Laura went over to him and took his hand. 'I know.'

'She's just like you were when I first met you.' His voice shook slightly.

'She came back to me, David.' Laura coughed back tears.

David looked from Sophie to Laura and back again. 'It's . . . well . . . it's miraculous.'

'Yeah, yeah, twins, looky-likeys, we all know. She got Mum's blue-eyed, golden-haired genes and I got your dark-haired, brown-eyed crappy ones.'

'So you're not a figment of Mandy's vivid imagination.' Tanya's eyebrows tried to rise but her Botoxed forehead didn't allow it. 'I was sure this was one of her little dramas to get David's attention.'

Mandy rolled her eyes. 'You were wrong, as always. As you can see, my ghost sister is back from the dead. She's actually been alive all the time, living in London with the unhinged oddball who abducted her.'

David continued to stare at Sophie. Laura could see she was feeling awkward. She stepped towards her. 'This is David, Mandy's dad, and his wife Tanya.' She introduced them. 'And this is my beautiful daughter, Sophie.'

'I thought her name was Jody,' Tanya said.

'It was, but she's been Sophie for the past seventeen years and is more comfortable with that name.' Laura was firm.

Sophie held out her hand. 'It's very nice to meet you both,' she said, shaking theirs.

David cradled her hand in his. 'It's incredible to meet you. I can't believe it, I just can't believe it. What a wonderful and amazing thing to happen. How are you? Are you OK?'

'I'm fine, thank you.' Sophie gently pulled her hand away.

David was concerned. 'So you weren't harmed or –'

'No, I was very well looked after,' Sophie interrupted, wanting the conversation to end.

'I told you, Dad, her kidnapper was a headmistress and apparently was nice to her.' Mandy summed up Sophie's life.

David turned to Laura. 'Did you call the police like I told you?'

She shook her head.

'But you must!' he exclaimed. 'The woman has to be locked up. She kidnapped a child. Imagine what else she could be capable of. She's a pariah – you can't allow her to roam the streets freely. She could abduct another child. I'll find you the best criminal lawyer in town. They'll throw the book at her. She'll never see the light of day.'

'No, please!' Sophie implored him. 'She's not a bad person, she's really not.'

'You've been brainwashed to think that,' David said. 'These people are very manipulative. They're masters of deceit and mind games.'

Sophie's face crumpled. 'She's not like that. She's a good person. She was good to me, really good to me. I had a great life.'

Tanya ran her ruby red nails through her hair. 'Let's not be hasty, David,' she said. 'The girl seems perfectly normal, considering her ordeal, and once you get the police involved, the media will get wind of it and it'll become a three-ring circus. We don't want to be embroiled in some freak show of child-kidnappers. Think of the headlines – think of your career.'

David was adamant. 'Justice must be done. Laura thought her

child was dead. She suffered horrendously. This person must pay a price for what she did.'

Sophie sank down into the nearest chair. 'Please don't tell the police. I'm begging you. I'm not messed up and I'm not brainwashed. I'm just a normal girl who thought her mother was her mother. And Anna is a really nice person. I know what she did was awful but she's been a brilliant mum to me and I can't let her go to jail. I can't.' Sophie began to hyperventilate. Laura ran over to comfort her. Lexie handed her a glass of water.

David crouched in front of her. 'I'm sorry, I didn't mean to upset you, but you must see that she has to pay for her crime. If she did this once, she could do it again. Surely you wouldn't want another family to suffer like Laura's has.'

'There, there, darlin', catch your breath,' Lexie said protectively.

Sophie dried her eyes. 'My mother, I mean Anna, would never hurt anyone. She's not like that. All the other mothers were in awe of how devoted she was to me and how much time and energy she spent teaching me new things, broadening my mind, helping me develop as a person. She took me everywhere – ballet, opera, cinema, theatre, art. She was a really wonderful mother and she couldn't hurt a fly. She's not a threat to anyone. And she is suffering, she's suffering terribly. We've never been apart before. I got a fright when I saw her a few days ago because she looks so broken. I understand what she did was wrong and illegal and all of that, but you mustn't send her to jail. She doesn't deserve it. She's in her own private Hell now, I know she is. I know how much she's hurting.' Sophie sobbed into her hands.

Laura decided to step in. As much as she wanted Anna to burn in Hell, she didn't want Sophie to be upset. Sophie loved Anna and there was nothing Laura or anyone else could do to change that. Even with all the information, even knowing that Anna had kidnapped her, Sophie was still defending her. Laura also didn't want to scare Sophie away. If they pushed her too much she might run back to London. Laura couldn't bear that. She needed to be near Sophie.

And if they did tell the police, if they did take Anna to court, what would they get out of it? A long drawn-out battle, money spent on lawyers' fees. Sophie would have to testify and probably Mandy, too. Laura had had enough drama in her life and, besides, she knew as a mother that the worst pain she could inflict on Anna was to keep Sophie away from her, down here in Killduf. That was a personal prison, an emotional prison, a fate far worse than being locked up.

'David!' Tanya barked. 'Drop it. The girl doesn't want a court case and neither do we. Can we please go? I have an appointment at five thirty.'

'Getting more rat poison injected into your face, are you?' Mandy drawled.

'Don't knock it, darlin', it's flippin' brilliant.' Lexie grinned.

'I have never had Botox,' Tanya exclaimed, her frozen forehead stating otherwise. 'I just have very good genes on my mother's side.'

Mandy snorted.

David stood up. Looking at Sophie, he said, 'Please think about what I said. I really feel that letting this woman walk free is the wrong thing to do. If you change your mind, call me. Laura has my number.'

Laura went with David, Mandy and Tanya to the car.

'Jesus, Laura, you can't allow that woman to walk free. What she did was abominable,' David said.

'Drop it, Dad. Sophie doesn't want to do it and Mum won't do anything Sophie doesn't want.'

'Forget about it, David. Leave them alone,' Tanya snapped.

'Thanks for the offer, and I will think about it. But for now my priority is spending time with Sophie and making sure she's happy and safe here with us.'

David opened the car door. 'I understand, but don't rule it out.'

'Get a move on,' Tanya hissed. 'I'm late.'

Laura leaned through the car window. ''Bye, love, have a nice time.'

'It'll be a break from watching you fawn all over Sophie. Try not to smother her with love, Mum. You don't want to suffocate her.'

Laura blew her a kiss. 'Goodbye, my ray of sunshine.'

'Drive,' Tanya ordered.

Laura watched them go. She hoped Mandy would enjoy being with her dad and getting some attention. She knew she'd been focusing on Sophie, but how could she not? But she had to be careful not to shut Mandy out. She had to make sure she included her and gave her some quality time too.

But for now Laura was going to enjoy every second of her time alone with Sophie, her daughter. They had a lot of catching up to do.

31.

Sophie

Killduf, July 2011

Sophie continued ignoring Anna. Her mother rang every day and left a message on her phone, telling her she loved her, she missed her, and asking her to forgive her and let her back into her life.

Sophie found the messages really upsetting. She could hear the pain in her mother's voice. She knew how much she was hurting Anna with her silence, but she couldn't face talking to her. She wasn't ready. She felt obligated to stay with Laura and spend time with her 'real' family. They had suffered so much from losing her. They deserved her time and devotion. And she wanted to get to know them too.

Sometimes, though, it all got too much. Sophie found the constant attention draining. Joan was the hardest to deal with because she was so intense and didn't try to hide it, like Laura did. Sophie could feel Laura watching her all the time, but at least she held back. Joan insisted on touching her or holding her hand or asking her incessant questions. She would often start crying when Sophie told her about the things she had done or the places she had gone. At times, it was difficult to handle.

And Mandy, with whom she had got on well initially, was suddenly cold and distant. Sophie could see that all the attention she was getting was hard for her sister. But it didn't give her the right to be rude. The worst part was that they were sharing a room and Laura had insisted that Sophie sleep in Mandy's bed while Mandy slept on a blow-up mattress on the floor.

It was great having Lexie around: she always defused the tension. Sophie adored her. She was wise and kind, and seemed to sense when Sophie was feeling overwhelmed.

Sophie was lying propped up on Mandy's bed, sketching. Laura was in her studio working on an overdue commission and Lexie was in her bedroom working on the last few chapters of her book. Sophie was feeling calm and enjoying the peace, when she heard Mandy singing in the garden.

> 'Mother stalker where have you gone,
> Your light's shining on the long-lost spawn,
> You worship at her feet every day,
> Ignoring everything I have to say.
> We were two and now we're three,
> What does this mean for meeeeee?
> I rock and you know it,
> With my clever wit.
> I write awesome lyrics,
> And play my guitar,
> But, no, I don't paint and see colours,
> Like my ghost sister does.
> So I'm dumped on the trash heap,
> Disregarded like a . . .

'Sheep, leap, keep, cheap? Oh, yeah, cheap.' Mandy sounded excited. She continued to sing:

> 'Disregarded like some cheap
> Piece of material you no longer need,
> You must be careful and pay me some heed.
> I'll run away and then you'll be sorry,
> You dissed me like – um, calamari?

'No – porry, lorry, norry, morry? Damn I need to change that line.

> *'I'll run away and you'll be so sad,*
> *I'll go and stay with my dad,*
> *Even though his wife is a nightmare,*
> *And treats me like an au-pair,*
> *I'll be happier there . . . nananananananana.'*

The bedroom door opened and Lexie popped her head in. 'What do you reckon, Sophie? Is Mandy the next Rihanna? Eminem? Lily Allen?' They giggled.

Lexie came and sat on the end of the bed. She was wearing a fuchsia velour Juicy Couture tracksuit with silver wedge-heel runners. 'How are you doin', darlin'? Is your poor head completely melted? I reckon you've had more to deal with these past few weeks than most people 'ave in a lifetime. Are you seein' them colours now? Green's your bad colour, innit?'

Sophie nodded. The last couple of weeks had been a swirl of red and pink, and when she thought of Anna all alone, she saw green for pain.

'Don't mind Mandy and her mad songs. It's just her way of expressin' herself. It's been hard on her too, I reckon. She's only sixteen, bless her. It's a terrible age. You don't know which way is up.'

Sophie laid her head back on the soft pillow. 'Lexie, my life used to be so normal and, well, boring, really. But I liked it that way. I went to school, went home, had dinner with Mum, did my homework, we'd watch TV together or my friend Holly would come round and we'd listen to music in my bedroom and that was it. A very mundane life. Holly was always talking about travelling and seeing the world but I was happy to stay in London and go to art college and live with Mum. I know it sounds a bit lame but I liked spending time with her. How many children get to spend their lives with someone who lights up every time they see them? My mum thinks I'm the best thing in the world and she told me so every day. But now everyone thinks she's a monster.'

Lexie crossed her legs, making herself comfortable on the bed. 'The way I see it, you was lucky. Laura was in a bad way that day, and you could have been nicked by a bad person, someone who could have harmed you. But instead you was stolen by someone who really wanted a kid. I know Anna keeps going on about saving you from Laura, but I think she saved you cos she wanted a kid herself. Seems to me she was born to be a mum and yet she never had no children. Why is that?'

'I don't know. She never talked about her past and just said she had me late in life and that my dad was a one-night stand but she was thrilled to be pregnant.'

Lexie stood up. 'I hope you don't mind, darlin', but I've been doin' a bit of snoopin'. Something just didn't seem right about her story. It just didn't add up – nickin' a kid because her mother was drunk. I felt there had to be more to it. I dunno, maybe it's because I know what it's like to want kids and not be able to have 'em. Anyways, when you told me your surname was Roberts, I started searching on the Internet for an Anna Roberts and the year you was taken, but nothing came up. But then I stretched it to two years before you was taken and I found a match.' Lexie pulled a piece of paper out of her pocket. 'I printed this out two days ago. I've been waiting for the right time to give it to you. I didn't want nobody else to see – it's too personal. I reckon it'll help you understand why Anna done it, though.'

Sophie unfolded the piece of paper with trembling hands. It was a death notice from the *Irish Times*, dated 24 January 1993: Hope Sophie Roberts – beloved infant daughter of Barry Roberts and Anna Roberts (née Hogan).

Sophie looked at Lexie. 'What does . . . what is . . .'

'It means that Anna had a baby girl who died, and that baby would have the been the same age you was when she saw you on that boat and stole you.'

'Who's Barry?'

'Looks like Anna was married to a bloke called Barry Roberts. I reckon after the baby died they split up. It happens to lots of couples who lose a child. She probably decided to go to London and start a new life, then saw you on that boat, bein' ignored an' all, and something inside her flipped and she took you.'

'Poor Mum.' Sophie began to weep. 'I had no idea.'

Lexie drew Sophie to her and held her as she sobbed. 'How could you know? How could anyone have guessed? It explains a lot, though, don't it? Poor old Anna.'

They sat like that for a while, Sophie crying, Lexie comforting her.

They heard voices outside. 'Yo, I'm looking for Sophie. Is this the right gaff?'

'Um, yes, but who . . .' Mandy was stuck for words.

Sophie bolted from the bed and rushed to the window. 'Mark?' she exclaimed.

He looked up. 'Hey, babe, what's up?'

Mandy was staring at him open-mouthed. Mark was wearing jeans and a navy blue T-shirt, and his hair was gelled up in a small Mohican. His skin was brown from the sun and made his green eyes – the same colour as his dad's – even more striking.

'I'm coming down,' she said.

Lexie stuck her head out of the window. 'Cor, he's a bit of all right,' she whispered. 'Is he your boyfriend?'

Sophie laughed. 'No. He's my oldest friend. He's like a brother to me.'

'Look at Mandy's face. She'll catch flies if she don't shut her mouth soon.'

Sophie ran downstairs and out into the garden. She threw herself into Mark's arms, thrilled to see a familiar face.

'Dude, you look like crap,' he said, taking in the dark shadows under her eyes and her skinny frame.

'You look great.' Sophie grinned.

'I know, the tan rocks. Seriously, I'm scoring some top-class birds at the moment.'

'Hello! Are you going to introduce me or what?' Mandy frowned.

'Sorry. Mark, this is my half-sister Mandy. And, Mandy, this is my oldest friend, Mark.'

'Nice guitar,' Mark said.

'Thanks. Do you play?'

'Yeah, I'm in a band. I play bass.'

'Cool. What kind –'

Ignoring her, Mark turned back to Sophie. 'So, your mum is totally freaking out. I've been sent down to talk sense into you.'

'You! Talk sense to me?' Sophie giggled.

'I know, it's a first, right?'

'I like your T-shirt. I'm a Grateful Dead fan too,' Mandy said.

Mark looked blankly at her. 'What?'

'The Grateful Dead.' Mandy pointed to his T-shirt.

'Is that who these dudes are? I just grabbed it from my room-mate this morning. All my gear is rancid. I haven't made it to the launderette in, like, weeks.'

'Charming!' Sophie laughed. It was so nice to see him.

'So, what's the story? Are you, like, hanging here for a while or what? Dad told me to come back with concrete information.'

'This is where she belongs. We're her family,' Mandy said.

'Wooooooooow.' Mark was staring over Mandy's shoulder. 'That is a magnificent rack.'

'Hello.' Lexie beamed at him. 'Nice to meet you – Mark, innit? Any friend of Sophie's is a friend of mine. I'm Lexie.'

'Very nice to meet you.'

'Look up, darlin'. Me face is up here.'

Mark grinned. 'Sorry, but they are impressive.'

Lexie cupped her boobs. 'Best surgeon in London. Ten grand they cost.'

'Money well spent.' Mark ogled them.

'So, what you doin'? Tryin' to get our Sophie to go back to Anna?'

Mark held up his hands. 'I come in peace. Don't shoot the messenger. I was sent down to make sure Sophie's OK and to ask her to call her mother. My dad thinks Anna's in a very bad way. He's worried about her.'

'So she should be, bloody kidnapper,' Mandy said.

Mark turned to her. 'I know it looks like she's a psycho, but she's actually a cool person. You should cut her some slack.'

Mandy went bright red. 'Um . . . well, I suppose . . .'

'The only reason Sophie here is so normal – well, square and boring and perfect – is because Anna, like, worshipped at her feet.'

'I am not!' Sophie thumped his arm playfully.

'Dude, your idea of fun is a game of Scrabble.'

'Bugger off! It is *not*!'

'OK, Trivial Pursuit.'

'What do you like?' Mandy asked Mark.

'Sex 'n' drugs 'n' rock 'n' roll.'

Mandy blushed an even deeper shade of red.

'I like a karaoke night myself,' Lexie admitted.

'I know a really good karaoke bar I'd like to show you.' Mark raised an eyebrow suggestively.

'Steady on, Romeo, I'm a married woman.'

'And your point is?' He smirked at her.

'You cheeky bugger!' Lexie cackled. 'Right, I'm going inside to finish my book tapes before Frank shoots me.'

'You're unbelievable,' Sophie scolded him.

'I'm only human – she's a hottie.'

'Is blonde your type?' Mandy asked, looking at Mark from under her fringe.

'I don't have a type. I'm open to all offers.' He winked at her.

Sophie wanted Mandy to go away so she could talk to him properly. 'Hey, why don't we go for a walk on the beach?' she suggested.

'Cool,' Mandy said.

Sophie was not letting Mandy come: she needed some space. 'Actually, Mandy, I was kind of hoping to talk to Mark alone. We haven't seen each other in ages.'

Mandy's face darkened. 'Be a bitch, why don't you.'

'I'm not. I just want to talk to my friend.'

'What about when I want to talk to my mum or my granny or

my uncle and all they're doing is staring at you and following you around? Do I make you feel like shit? Do I make you feel like a spare tool?' Mandy stormed off.

Sophie called after her, 'I'm sorry I didn't –'

Mark pulled her towards the beach. 'Forget it. She's got the hump. You don't need that negative energy around you.'

He slung his arm around her and she leaned into his shoulder. It felt so nice, cosy, familiar. They walked down the steep steps that led to the beach. It was a cloudy day but the air was warm. They took off their shoes and paddled in the cold sea water.

Mark then walked over to a sand dune and sat down. He took out some tobacco and grass and began to roll a joint.

Sophie stopped him. 'Before you smoke it, tell me about Mum. Have you seen her?'

'No, I've been away doing some gigs so I haven't called over to Dad's place.' He rolled as he talked. 'I swear, when he last called me up and told me Anna had abducted you, I thought I'd fried my brain with weed. I kept asking him to repeat it. Of all the people in the world, Anna? In a million years I'd never have imagined it.'

Sophie lay back, her head behind her hands, her toes nestling in the sand. 'Tell me about it. I still can't believe it.'

Mark lit his joint and began to smoke. He offered some to Sophie. For once she was tempted: she'd have liked to smoke it and get away from her reality. But she was afraid: what if she reacted badly or something? She couldn't very well arrive back to dinner stoned out of her head. Laura would flip. She didn't want to disappoint her.

'What shall I do, Mark? Tell me what to do.'

He exhaled a long thin line of smoke. 'Do what feels right. You're not a kid any more. You can make your own decisions. If you want to stay here and get to know your birth mum and your weird half-sister, stay. If it feels too freaky, go back to Anna for a while. Or you can crash with me if you want to get away from it all. It's a bit of a dump, but we've got a couch and it's yours if you want it.'

'Thanks. It's good to know I've got somewhere to run to. I just feel that whatever decision I make will hurt someone and I hate that.'

Mark lay down beside her. 'Sophie, stop worrying about everyone else. Stop trying to be perfect. Just do what you want to do. Think about yourself and stop people-pleasing. Seriously, dude, you need to live a little. Shake off the convent-school Catholic-guilt thing.'

'It's easier said than done. I only left school three weeks ago!' Sophie reminded him.

'Why don't you come out with me and my mates? Some chick from college grew up in a mansion in Wicklow and her folks are going away so she's throwing a massive party the week after next. It'll be a free-for-all. You can bring Morticia Addams if you want.'

'Who?'

'Your sister with the black hair and the Gothic vibe. She needs to lighten up. What is it with your family? Anna's way too uptight too. Blow off a little steam, drink some vodka, loosen up.'

Sophie laughed. 'And end up like you? Permanently stoned and at one with the universe?'

Mark grinned. 'It's pretty cool – you should try it some time. Bring your friend with the *Baywatch* tits.'

Sophie rolled on to her side to face him. 'Lexie is not going to come to some college house party.'

'Man, I'd like me a piece of that arse.'

'Forget it. She's married to Dougie Granger.'

'The Chelsea footballer?'

'Yes.'

'What the hell is she doing here? Is this some kind of commune?'

'No, she's hiding from him while she writes her autobiography. They've split up.'

Mark waved his joint in the air. 'Sophie Roberts, abducted

child, living with WAGs and Goths. A few weeks ago you were a nice quiet schoolgirl!'

'I liked it that way.'

'Fuck it, Sophie, this makes you a lot more interesting – and look at the up-side. You've got a lot of material to put into your paintings now! You can channel all that anger and confusion and heartache into awesome art.'

'Thanks, Mark, you've really cheered me up. I was feeling very low and overcome before you arrived. I really needed a friend to talk to. Someone who knows me and Anna and my former life. You know?' She turned to him – but he was sound asleep, the end of his joint burning in his hand. Sophie removed it from his fingers, put it out and leaned her head against his chest, enjoying the comfort of his presence.

A few days later, Laura was putting the dinner plates on the table. 'Ta-dah! Thai green chicken curry,' she announced.

'Very posh.' Lexie grinned.

'Laura! You've outdone yourself.' Frank winked at her.

'It's Sophie's favourite.' Laura beamed, and Sophie winced. She could see Mandy's face going bright red.

'I hate curry,' Mandy snapped.

'Thanks, Laura, it looks lovely.' Sophie picked up her fork, determined to be polite.

'It's too bloody spicy. I can't eat it.' Mandy pushed her plate away.

'I made it mild. Try it,' Laura encouraged her.

Mandy took a small bite. 'Gross.'

'You're spicy enough as it is.' Frank laughed.

'I think it tastes dead nice,' Lexie said. 'Me and Dougie used to get takeaway once a week on a Sunday night. He likes the real spicy one, the red one, innit? I used to get the yellow one. We'd watch a movie and roll up to bed.'

'Is it all right for you?' Laura asked Sophie. 'Is it too spicy? Is it not spicy enough?'

Sophie squirmed. 'It's perfect. Really delicious.' She put a large forkful into her mouth.

'I suppose I'll just have rice, then, will I?' Mandy enquired.

'I got that ice-cream you like for dessert,' Laura continued, to Sophie, completely ignoring Mandy. Sophie wished she'd stop: Mandy was difficult enough as it was and she didn't need Laura making it worse. 'You said Häagen-Dazs strawberry shortcake was your favourite, didn't you?'

Sophie nodded, still chewing. She just wanted the subject to be changed.

Mandy pushed her chair back from the table. 'My favourite is chocolate chip cookie dough, in case you're interested. I don't actually like strawberries. But don't worry, I'll be too full after my bowl of dry rice to need dessert.'

'Poor neglected Mandy. I'll bring you an extra large tub of it next time I'm visiting.' Frank nudged her, and she thumped his arm.

Sophie could feel Laura watching her. 'I was thinking we might take a trip next week, maybe go to West Cork – it's really beautiful down there,' her mother said.

'No!' Mandy banged the table. 'You may try to starve me by cooking food I don't like, but you're not dragging me to West Cork. The Keystone Jammers are playing and Dad got me tickets.'

'Do you really like them?' Sophie asked.

'Duh! They're, like, the best band ever. Have you heard "I Hate My Boyfriend, He Deserves To Die A Painful Death"?'

'Yes – I think their music is really aggressive and unsettling, actually.' Sophie was getting fed up with Mandy biting her head off.

'Unsettling? What are you? Ninety? They're amazing. They say things that everyone thinks but is too bloody scared to admit. Like "Parents Treat Us Like We're Retards But Expect Us To Get Straight As". Or "My Dad Hits Me And Then Tells Me He Loves Me, He's Going To Wake Up One Day With A Fork In His Eye". Come on, it's exactly what the bastard deserves if he hits you. I think they're amazing.'

Sophie took a sip of her water and tried to remain calm. 'I

think they're antagonistic. There were riots at their last concert. Some kids got injured.'

'Riots?' Laura was shocked. 'That's it. You're not going.'

'Oh, great. *Now* you remember I exist,' Mandy retorted. 'Thanks, Sophie, thanks for trying to ruin everything.' Turning back to Laura, she said, 'I'm going to this concert and *nothing* you say will stop me. Dad said I could.'

'Steady on.' Frank tried to calm things down. 'Your mum's just worried. Do you have seated tickets or standing ones?'

'Seated.'

'Well, then, you'll be fine.'

'Not if there's a riot she won't,' Laura said.

'A few kids threw a few punches in the mosh pit. Jesus, it wasn't a bloody war.' Mandy was exasperated.

Laura wasn't convinced. 'It sounds dangerous. I'll talk to your dad.'

Mandy swung around and glared at Sophie. 'Any other little gems of information you'd like to tell us about? Anything else you'd like to say to ruin my bloody life?'

Sophie flushed. She could feel herself getting annoyed. 'I'm not trying to ruin anything. I'm just being honest.'

'Well, maybe you should go back to your psycho mother and be honest with her.'

'MANDY!' Laura roared. 'Don't you ever say that to her again.'

'Why? She's allowed be honest, why can't I? Or are there different rules for the daughter and the ghost sister? Let me guess, she does whatever the hell she wants and I suffer the consequences. Like starving to death because you cook food I *hate*, being ignored completely and having to sleep on the bloody floor in my own bedroom!'

'Oi!' Lexie pointed a finger in Mandy's face. 'That's enough. First of all, you don't speak to your mother like that and, second, it ain't Sophie's fault she's your long-lost sister. Do you have any idea what it's like for her? Comin' into a new family and finding out her old dear's actually a stranger who nicked her off a boat. Why don't you think about how she feels and stop feelin' sorry for yourself? I know it's hard for you, with Sophie getting all the attention and all, but give her a break. Now, zip it and eat your rice.'

Mandy put her head down and ate in silence. Sophie's stomach twisted.

'So, how's the final chapter coming along?' Frank asked Lexie, trying to break the tension.

'You'll be pleased to hear it's done. I finished it this morning.'

'Fantastic.' Frank kissed her cheek. 'Well done.'

'Wow, finished already, that's amazing.' Sophie was thrilled the focus was on someone else.

'Congratulations, Lexie, it's a wonderful achievement,' Laura enthused.

'What does that mean?' Mandy looked up.

'It means it's time for me to go home and sort out my life.'

'When will you leave?' Sophie was upset. She loved Lexie. She couldn't bear the thought of her disappearing. Lexie was her rock of sense on this emotional roller-coaster.

'Tonight. I've booked my flight for first thing tomorrow.'

'What?' They were all shocked.

'Look, it's better this way, I can't do goodbyes. Too hard. And I know if I stay another day in this lovely house with you lot, I'll never leave. You feel like family to me. So, Frank, I need you to drop me to the airport hotel.'

'Of course, if that's what you want.' Frank patted her hand.

'That sucks.' Mandy was upset.

Lexie pulled Mandy's fringe back and looked into her eyes. 'Thanks, darlin', I'll miss you an' all. You've been so nice to me, lettin' me come in and live with you.'

'We'll really miss having you here,' Laura said. 'It's been lovely getting to know you.'

'And what a time to be living in this house! It's certainly been colourful,' Frank added.

'I wish you could stay longer.' Sophie's voice cracked. A huge lump was forming in her throat.

Lexie hugged her. 'I do too, darlin', but I can't hide away for ever. I have to go back and sort out my divorce and find a photography course and get on with my life. My new life.'

'Will you stay in touch?' Mandy asked.

Lexie smiled at her. 'Course I will.'

'You'll see her again soon. She'll be over to promote her book when it becomes a huge bestseller,' Frank said.

Everyone was very downcast.

'Well, thank you, Lexie, for being such a wonderful friend to all of us.' Laura was really going to miss this gorgeous, bubbly, sensitive and kind soul.

Lexie's eyes filled. 'I have to tell you lot that this has been the best few weeks of my life. Honest. I came here feelin' crap about myself. I felt worthless – a useless WAG, whose husband cheated on her. But you've made me feel so welcome and you've been so nice to me and supportive and encouragin'. I went from feelin' like nothing to feelin' ten feet tall – and for a midget like me that's really something! And just seein' the way you all look after each other and love each other and treat each other nice, it's made me want more for myself. I want this. Well, not the baby-snatchin' part,' she gave them a weak smile, 'but the rest of it. What you have here is special. Real special.'

Sophie gave up fighting her emotions and cried into her dinner.

Lexie put her arms around her. 'Don't cry – you'll set me off. Come on, darlin', you're goin' to be fine.' Lexie stood up. 'Sod this. I can't eat. Frank, get your keys, we're off. Otherwise I'll end up cryin' all night. I have to make this quick and painless.'

Frank went up to get Lexie's large pink suitcase.

Downstairs in the kitchen, Lexie hugged them one by one. To Mandy, she said, 'Goodbye, darlin', keep doin' your thing. You're a very unique girl. Don't change for no one but go easy on your mum and your sister.'

Holding Sophie close to her chest, she whispered, 'Decide what's best for you and follow your heart. It'll all work out, you'll see. Call me anytime.'

Finally she tottered over to Laura. 'My friend, my mate, thank you for openin' your home and your heart to me. I ain't never felt so welcome.' She hugged Laura tightly and quietly said, 'You deserve to have Sophie back in your life, but don't try so hard. You're smotherin' her. Let her get to know the real you, the incredible you, in her own time. You won't lose her again. You'll win her for ever.'

Laura fought back tears. 'Thank you. And you're to go back to London and shine. Let the world see what an incredible person Lexie is. Find yourself a man who deserves you and treats you well. And find a way to be a mum – you have so much to give to a child.'

Sophie knew she shouldn't have listened but she was thrilled that Lexie had advised Laura to give her some space. It was exactly what she needed.

By the time Frank had heaved the suitcase down the stairs they were all crying.

'Come on, ladies, she's not emigrating to New Zealand. London is a short flight away. You'll see her again.'

Lexie linked his arm. 'My Frank, the man who saved me. Seems to be your thing in life. You saved Laura from going down the tubes and now you've saved me. You're a regular knight in shinin' armour.'

Frank laughed and guided her out to his car. 'Come on – before I have to swim out of here with all this crying.'

They followed her to the car, where she turned to face them. ''Bye, everyone, and thanks. I mean it, thanks for lettin' me be part of your family. I love you all.'

Laura, Sophie and Mandy waved their friend off, all of them missing her already. Things had always seemed brighter when Lexie was in the room.

They walked back into the kitchen.

'I'm sorry, Laura, I'm just not hungry. May I be excused?' Sophie asked.

'Me too,' Mandy said.

'Sure, of course. I've lost my appetite too.' Laura scraped the chicken curry into the bin.

32.

Anna

Dublin, July 2011

Anna sat up in the hospital bed and stared at the door. She had been vomiting blood since her meeting with Sophie. When Joe had discovered how bad she was he had rushed her straight to hospital.

She was connected to a drip. They had run some tests. She was waiting. Joe had gone to hurry things along. He was frantic. She was calm. The worst thing that could happen to her had already happened. She'd lost two daughters: her baby Hope and now Sophie. She was completely numb.

The door swung open and Joe walked in, followed by a tall, self-assured man in a grey suit. Joe introduced them. 'This is John Garvey. He's going to be performing your gastroscopy.'

'Gastroscopy?' Anna asked.

'We need to stem the bleeding and repair the damage. You'll be given a sedative, intravenously into your arm, while we insert the gastroscope, via your mouth, into your stomach to get a good look at what's going on. I'll wash out the blood in your stomach and duodenum. When I can see the ulcer clearly, I'll inject an adrenalin and fibrin glue into it to minimize the chance of it bleeding again later. All going well, we should be able to . . .'

All Anna heard was noise. She couldn't take in the information. She felt so tired, so old and so very weary. Even her bones ached. She wanted to sink back into the fluffy pillows, close her eyes and sleep for a very long time. She wanted to block out the voices in her head, the images of Laura and Joan, Sophie and Mandy, the cruel words and the harsh realities. She didn't care about her ulcer, she didn't care about the procedure. She just wanted to sleep.

She closed her eyes.

'You're going to be fine.' Joe kissed her forehead.

'We'll keep you in for twenty-four hours. I'd like to make sure there's no further bleeding or complications,' John Garvey added.

'Thanks, John, for everything.' Joe was effusive. 'I owe you one.'

The doctor left the room and Joe stroked Anna's hand. 'He's the best in the country. I asked him to perform the gastroscopy. I didn't want some junior practising on you. You're going to be fine but, Anna, you have to stop all this craziness or the ulcer will come back more aggressively. You have to look after yourself, stop running around and getting yourself into a state. You have to let her go, let Sophie make her own choices. She knows the full story now. She knows you love her and you're here for her. She's an adult. There is nothing more you can do. You have to stop before you kill yourself.' Joe's voice broke.

Tears slipped down Anna's cheeks from under her closed lashes. Stop? How do you stop loving your child? How do you stop caring about her? How do you stop wondering if she's all right? How do you stop praying she'll forgive you? How do you stop begging her to come home? How do you stop being her mother? How do you stop?

Anna's phone beeped. She sat bolt upright and grabbed it. It was a text from Mark: *Saw S, she OK. Needs space to sort head out. Will b in touch when more info. Don't sweat it, she cool.*

Joe snatched the phone out of Anna's hand and switched it off.

'Give it back. Sophie might call,' Anna shouted.

'*Enough!*' Joe bellowed. 'You are about to have surgery for a bleeding ulcer. Enough.'

Anna turned to the wall. It would never be enough. She would never stop.

Anna insisted that Joe go home and get some sleep. The procedure had gone well; the bleeding had been stemmed. Joe's eyes were puffy from lack of sleep. He needed to get proper rest. Besides, she wanted to be alone. She needed to think, to clear her mind.

She felt calmer after the gastroscopy. Maybe it was the lingering sedative, maybe it was the drip attached to her arm filling her with antibiotics, maybe it was the fact that she had to stay still, but she was glad of it. For the first time since Sophie had left, her heart wasn't racing, her stomach wasn't burning and she wasn't in a fog of grief.

She took the time to reflect on recent events and try to decide what to do. She knew that Sophie wasn't going to come back to her any time soon. She knew that Sophie needed to get to know Laura and her new family. Although Anna hated admitting it, she knew she would be safe with them. Laura had clearly got her life together and was no longer a drunk.

Anna could see that phoning Sophie all the time wasn't helping. By trying so hard to pull her back, she was pushing her away. She had to allow Sophie the space to make her own decisions. She had to trust that she had brought her up well enough to make the right ones. She had to step back and let Sophie work out who she was and who she wanted to be.

Anna had to admit her part in this mess and take responsibility for her actions. She had stolen someone else's child. When you said it like that, it sounded wrong, awful and criminal. But it hadn't been like that. It had been instinctual and maternal and entirely for Sophie's protection. Anna had assumed that Laura would end up like the mothers she had seen at her school gate – lifetime drunks and drug-users, women who would sell the clothes from their children's backs for a fix. But Laura hadn't turned out like that: she was normal and stable. Anna wondered what would have happened if she'd left Sophie there. Would Laura have stopped drinking? Had the shock of losing Sophie woken her up to her destructive behaviour? Would Joan have protected her granddaughter until Laura had sobered up? But Joan hadn't been there that day on the boat to save her granddaughter from harm. Anna had *had* to take her. Hadn't she?

Anna lay back on her pillows and closed her eyes to block out the headache that was beginning to split her forehead in two. She had done what she thought was right. There was no point in looking back. She had to look forward. She had believed she was saving a child's life . . . but if she was being totally honest – and for the first time since that day she forced herself to be – she had to admit that taking Sophie had filled the hole in her life that Hope's death had left.

She had never meant to hurt anyone, although she knew now she had and that was hard to live with. But she had done everything possible to make Sophie happy. And now . . . Well, now she had to accept that Sophie was furious with her. She had to respect Sophie's anger and resentment and hope they would subside. She had to hope and pray that Sophie wouldn't forget the past seventeen years of unconditional love.

Anna pulled her bag up from the floor and placed it on her lap. She took out a notebook and pen and began to write a love letter . . .

My darling Sophie,

I'm writing to tell you that you are free. I'm letting you go. I'm giving you wings, which is what every mother needs to do at some stage in their child's life. I wish with all my heart that things were different. That you hadn't found out this way, that you hadn't been so hurt. But I realize that I can't change what is. I can only explain my part in it.

I took you that day because I knew I could give you a better life. I took you that day because you were being neglected. I took you that day because I fell in love with you. I took you that day because I believed that I could be a good mother.

I never told you this but I had a baby girl – Hope – who was born early and only survived a few minutes. My ten-year marriage to Barry didn't survive the grief of Hope's loss. He was a lovely man but we grieved differently, separately, and it tore us apart. We broke up and I found myself with nothing. No marriage, no home, no baby. No family. My heart was broken so I did the only thing I could. I ran away. I got on that boat with the intention of starting my life again in London. I was running away from grief, sorrow, bad memories and myself. I had to do something to change my life or I'm not sure I would have made it. I was in a very dark place.

And then I saw you and Laura on the boat. And she was awful to you. I know she has changed and sorted her life out and I'm glad, but back then she was a terrible mother. I suppose something inside me snapped and I reacted. I didn't think. I just went with my primal instinct to protect you from harm.

My actions that day led to seventeen incredible years. I have loved every minute of being your mum. I have been proud of you every day of our life together. You allowed me to love unconditionally. You gave me the gift of motherhood. You made my heart soar every time I looked at you. You saved me. You gave me back hope, and love. You unlocked my dead heart and made it sing again.

I will always be your mother, whether you want me to or not. I will always love you, adore you and cherish you. I will always be here for you.

I will wait for you every day of my life.

But for now, I'm setting you free. Be safe, be well, be wonderful, my darling girl.

Love always,
Mum xx

The next day, when Joe came to collect her from hospital, Anna posted the letter to Sophie, then asked Joe to drive her out to Hope's grave. He wanted to take her straight back to the apartment and tuck her up in bed, but Anna begged, 'Please, Joe, I need to do this. It's part of my healing. Please.'

He finally agreed and linked her arm as they walked through the graveyard, looking for Hope's headstone.

'There,' Anna croaked, pointing to the little white cross. She walked over slowly and bent down. 'Hope Roberts, 24 January 1993. *Sometimes love is for a moment. Sometimes love is for a lifetime. Sometimes a moment is a lifetime.*'

That was when the dam broke and Anna finally let go of it all: the grief, the fear, the terror, the worry, the heartache, the love, the loss, the lies, the hiding, the pretending, the guilt, the pain. It all came flooding out.

She wailed, she wept, she screamed, she beat the earth with her fists, she allowed herself to feel everything. The years of pent-up emotion and stress, the suppressed sentiments and feelings all tumbled out.

Through it all, Joe sat on the other side of the headstone and the only thing he said was 'Let it out. Let the poison out. It's eating you up inside.'

Eventually Anna's sobbing slowed. She was spent. There was nothing left inside her. She sat in the grass beside Hope's grave and wiped her face with a tissue Joe handed her.

'Feel better?' he asked.

Anna paused. The strange thing was, she did. She felt as if something buried deep inside her, like a sickness, had come out. As if the crying had expelled it from her being. All the grief for Hope, the worry about Sophie finding out the truth and the guilt about what she had done that she had buried at the bottom of her soul had been ripped up and spat out. She felt like an empty shell, suddenly and violently relieved of so much anxiety and strain. She felt as though she had purged her past and faced her demons.

She hugged her knees to her chest. 'Yes, I do, actually. I feel . . . I can't explain it . . . it sounds so odd . . . but I feel relieved.'

Joe smiled. 'Of course you do. You've been harbouring a terrible secret for years. No wonder your ulcer was so bad. The pressure of carrying that burden around was literally tearing you up inside.'

'You're right. I only realize it now that the secret is out. I suppose I was living on a tightrope, always covering my tracks, always watching what I said, hiding my past and discarding the first forty years of my life. There was no Anna before Sophie. That person didn't exist.'

Joe stood up and stretched his legs. 'But that Anna did exist. I knew her and she was wonderful. Life dealt her some very hard blows but there were good times too. You were a happy child, your parents were mad about you and so was Barry. In the beginning you and he had a great relationship, but Hope's death broke you. It's OK to look back now. You can talk about your past and show Sophie where you grew up and went to school and worked as a teacher and the church you got married in, and all the things children like to know about their parents. In a way this liberates you from the shackles you had to impose on yourself.'

Anna thought about it. He was right. She was free to tell Sophie about her marriage, show her the wedding photos, the house she'd grown up in and all her favourite places in Ireland where she had gone on holidays as a child. If Sophie forgave her, she'd take her to Kerry. She had very happy memories of summers spent in Dingle on the beautiful sandy beaches, swimming in the freezing water, collecting shells, building sandcastles and eating ice-creams in the rain. She could tell Sophie everything. She could talk to her about the years she had struggled to get pregnant and how she had so desperately wanted a child, and that when she'd been pregnant with Hope, she was sure it was going to work out. But it hadn't and it had broken her. She'd tell Sophie about meeting Barry and falling in love, their honeymoon in Capri, and how happy and carefree she had once been. Maybe she'd take Sophie there one day and stay in the same hotel. Maybe . . . if her daughter forgave her.

'Anna!' Joe shook her arm.

'Sorry, I was miles away.'

'We need to get you home. You must rest.'

Anna looked down at Hope's grave. It was surrounded by weeds and overgrown grass. 'I can't leave her like this. I have to make it nice for her. I've neglected her for seventeen years and it's time I made it up to her.' She looked up at her best friend, her Joe. 'Will you help me?'

'Of course I will.'

Anna looked into his kind green eyes. 'Thanks, Joe, I'd be lost without you. You're all I've got.'

'You've got Sophie too. She'll come back to you. Give it time.'

Anna prayed he was right.

33.

Laura

Dublin, July 2011

Laura had an urgent call from Frank, asking her to meet him in his office at eleven. He said it was important. Laura was reluctant to be apart from Sophie, but Frank had sounded very serious and said he'd explain face to face.

When Laura arrived at his building and crossed the lobby to his office, she could hear raised voices. She walked in and came face to face with David, Tanya, Joan, Mandy and Frank, sitting in a circle drinking coffee and arguing.

'What the hell is going on?'

Frank rushed over to her. 'Don't be alarmed. David called a meeting to discuss some of the legal issues arising from Sophie's return.'

Laura glared at David. 'I thought I made myself clear. I'm not ready to press charges.'

'I know. Look, we're not suggesting taking any immediate action, we're just meeting to discuss possibilities and options. Joan and Frank were keen to look at the legal implications of Jody's abduction.'

Laura looked at her mother.

'I want that woman locked up,' Joan declared.

Frank guided Laura to a chair beside David. 'It's no harm to talk it over.'

'Why is Mandy here? She's too young for this,' Laura hissed at David.

'I am bloody not,' Mandy contradicted. 'This affects me, too,

347

you know. There's no way you're making any decisions about this without me.'

'I can assure you, Laura, I'd rather be anywhere but here.' Tanya pouted. 'But I'm going to make damn sure this does not turn into a public embarrassment for my family. I don't want salacious media attention on my doorstep. If anything is going to happen, it'll have to be done quietly.'

'For once we agree on something.' Laura smiled grimly and put her handbag down beside her.

David cleared his throat. 'I called this meeting because I firmly believe that this woman – Anna Roberts – who abducted Jody needs to be brought to justice.'

'Hear hear,' Joan said.

'Lock her up.' Mandy cheered.

'She deserves to be punished,' Frank said, 'but let's not be too hasty.'

'If we press charges the media will get hold of the story,' Tanya reminded them. 'Why can't you just threaten her legally and scare her off?'

'You could hire underworld thugs to rough her up and tell her to get a one-way ticket to Australia,' Mandy suggested.

'You've been watching too much TV.' David frowned.

'Anna committed a terrible crime,' Frank said, 'and she shouldn't be allowed to walk away scot-free, but we need to think carefully before we get the police and lawyers involved.'

'I know she kidnapped her, and it was awful, but she didn't harm her.' Laura surprised herself by defending Anna. 'Sophie seems to have had a good life.'

'She does seem remarkably together,' Frank agreed. 'She's turned out to be a smashing girl.'

'That's nonsense!' Joan raged. 'She was *born* that way. Jody had the loveliest nature I ever saw in a child. That woman had nothing to do with it. Jody was always going to turn out well. She was a wonderful baby. That woman had no right to take her and she wouldn't have been able to if Laura hadn't been passed out drunk.'

'Mum!' Frank snapped.

'What?' Tanya swivelled around to face Laura. 'Were you?'

'Thank you, Mum. Yes, Tanya, I was.'

Tanya pursed her lips. 'Well, that makes it all clearer. Anna obviously thought you were unfit to look after a child.'

'Of course she did, as would I, if I'd seen a poor child neglected by her mother,' Joan added.

'Laura was twenty!' Frank exclaimed.

'Little more than a child herself,' David defended her.

'*I* wasn't drinking myself into drunken comas at that age,' Tanya observed.

'You were too busy staring at yourself in the mirror,' Mandy muttered.

'You should get a mirror and look in it from time to time,' Tanya riposted.

'Don't you dare –'

'Please, can we all just focus on the issue at hand?' David pleaded.

'Whether Laura was drunk or not doesn't change anything. It does not justify abducting a child,' Frank pointed out. 'For God's sake, if everyone took a child they saw beside a drunk mother, the country would be in chaos.'

'Passed out is different from drunk,' Tanya reminded him.

'Thank you, Tanya.' Laura was furious that David's wife was witnessing all of this. It was so humiliating. 'I know I acted appallingly and, believe me, I have paid a huge price for it. But Frank's right. Regardless of my behaviour, Anna did *not* have the right to take my child.'

'It was abduction, which was and is a criminal offence,' David reminded them all.

'So we get her locked up in jail with all the other criminals and throw away the key. She'll never see Jody again and that'll be the end of it,' Joan said.

'No, it won't.' Mandy shook her head. They all turned to look at her. 'It won't be the end of it. Look, I'm on your side. I agree that Anna should be punished, but Sophie adores her. It'd be like you all saying that Mum should be locked up and never allowed see me again – I'd never forgive you.'

'Thanks, Mandy.' Laura's throat was tight.

'Don't get all emotional on me, Mum. I'll lose my train of thought. Where was I?' Mandy frowned. 'Oh, yes. Although what Anna did to our family was shocking, she was never mean to Sophie. In fact, she was a great mother to her and Sophie loves her. Sure she's angry with her and she's confused, but she still loves her. You can't wipe out seventeen years of devotion. It would kill Sophie to see Anna in prison.'

'But she knows now she was abducted. She knows her mother is a criminal. She knows who her real family are. Surely she'll understand that justice must be done,' David said.

Laura sighed. 'Yes, but, David, don't you see? Anna is the only mother Sophie has ever known. It was just the two of them for her whole life.'

Joan slapped her hand on the desk. 'Not her whole life. She had a loving family here for nineteen months.'

'She doesn't remember any of that,' Laura reminded them.

'I don't remember anything until I was three when I fell off the slide and broke my arm and Mum was hysterical,' Mandy said. 'She kept screaming, "I'm a bad mother, I'm a bad mother," and the doctor kept saying, "But accidents happen, she'll be fine."'

Laura shuddered. Whenever anything happened to Mandy she overreacted: it was the guilt.

'You're a great mother,' David said, pressing Laura's hand.

Tanya scowled at him. 'Can we move on? I don't want to be here all day.'

'I want justice for seventeen stolen years,' Joan said. 'I haven't had a day's peace since the child disappeared. My life was ruined that day. Ruined.'

'Come on, Gran, she's back. Can you at least cut Mum some slack and crack a smile? Look, I find the whole grumpy-old-lady thing funny but it's time to lighten up.'

Laura smiled gratefully at Mandy.

Joan, though, was furious. 'Don't you speak to me like that, young lady. You have no idea what I've been through. Your mother's actions have caused me a lifetime of pain.'

'Jody's back now, Mum. Let's focus on the future,' Laura said, through gritted teeth.

'You might be able to forget, but I can't. You don't just wake up one morning and forget years of suffering and misery. Maybe you can push the past away and pretend it never happened but I can't. I can't forget. I suffered so much, I –'

Laura jumped up, her face bright red with anger. 'Jesus Christ, Mum! You weren't the only one who suffered. I did too. I've been sick with grief. Part of me died that day too. Forget? Do you honestly think an hour went by, over the last seventeen years, when I didn't think about my baby? I was in Hell. And I had the guilt to deal with as well. It's a bloody miracle I didn't go insane with it. It ate me up.'

Joan's cheeks flushed. 'You can't blame me for your guilt. It was *your* fault she went missing. You let her go.'

'I know! I beat myself up about it all the time. And if for one second I did forget about it, you were always right behind me reminding me of it. Never letting me forget what a failure I was. Never letting me forget what a disappointment I was. Even when Jody was born you made me feel worthless.'

'You were nineteen! What mother wants their teenage daughter getting drunk and having sex with a stranger? Of course I was furious with you. Of course I was disappointed. None of that was what your father and I wanted for you.'

Laura thumped her chest. 'I was heartbroken when Dad died. I loved him. He made me feel brilliant about myself, but you always made me feel like crap. I was never good enough for you. I was lost without Dad. I went off the rails because I missed him so much. I was devastated – why can't you see that? I wasn't a bad person, I was a heartbroken teenager.'

'It's always about you,' Joan sputtered. 'Poor Laura. Poor little Laura. What about me? He was my husband! I missed him too. My heart was broken too. I had to raise two kids on my own. I was so lonely I thought I'd die from it. I was grieving too, Laura.'

'But you never talked about him. You never asked me how I was feeling. I needed you, Mum. I needed to talk about Dad and how sad I was, but you never let me. Whenever I brought up his name you changed the subject.'

Joan closed her eyes. 'I had to. It was too painful. Harry was my rock. I was lost without him. I was only just keeping myself together. I was trying to stay strong for you and Frank. But you never see that. All you see is your own pain. All you ever see is Laura's side of the story.'

Laura threw her arms into the air in exasperation. 'Jesus, Mum, I was sixteen when he died. I was just a kid.'

'You were out of control. I didn't know what to do with you. And look what it led to – look at all the sadness you caused us.'

Frank stepped in. 'Come on, guys, calm down, don't say things you'll regret.'

'I've been biting my tongue for years,' Laura spat. 'I've had it. I'm sorry I've been such a let-down to you, Mum, but I'm doing the best I can. And it would be really nice if for once in your bloody life you'd give me a break. Jody's home now, back where she belongs. Can you please just let me enjoy this time with my daughter without constantly reminding me of my terrible deeds? I didn't do it on *purpose*! I was young and naïve and, yes, selfish and stupid but I wasn't an evil person. I made a mistake and I've paid for it every day for seventeen bloody years. You have to stop blaming me, Mum.' She began to sob. 'You have to stop now. Please just STOP! I can't take any more.'

There was silence in the room as Laura sat down unsteadily and tried to regain her composure. Mandy touched her mother's hand gently.

Joan sank back into her chair and took out a tissue. She wiped her eyes. 'You weren't a let-down, Laura. You were a lovely child, like Jody. But you were a nightmare of a teenager and that's just fact. I have no intention of ruining anything for anyone and I very much object to your accusation that I always made you feel bad about yourself. That's a very cruel thing to say. I embraced Jody with both arms. I loved her and minded her like my own. You seem to forget that part.'

'I haven't forgotten,' Laura said quietly. 'You were amazing with her and I'll always be grateful to you. She adored you. I know I was a mess, and I'm not proud of it.'

Tanya clapped her hands. 'I think that's enough family drama for one day. David, can you move things along? We need to collect the girls from ballet at two.'

David stood up. 'Right. We should agree on a plan of action. Do we want to explore pressing charges?'

'Definitely.' Joan was adamant.

'I'm not sure it's the right thing to do,' Frank said.

'Laura?' David asked.

Laura put down her untouched cup of coffee. 'I want to, I really want to see Anna brought to justice, but I'm worried about Sophie. We have to think about Sophie.'

'She'll get over it. Children are very resilient,' Tanya informed her. 'But, David, how are you going to keep it out of the papers? I am not having our family dragged through the tabloids like some kind of freak show. I'm telling you right now, if this comes out there'll be hell to pay.'

'He's familiar with that. He lives with you,' Mandy muttered. Frank chuckled.

'What did you say?' Tanya glared at Mandy.

'She said he knows you well.' Laura saved her daughter.

Frank sat behind his desk, fiddling with a pen. 'Laura's right. We need to be very careful around Sophie. She's had a lot to deal with lately. It might be a step too far to suddenly announce we're going after Anna.'

'She's too fragile at the moment,' Laura told them. 'We need to give her time. And I think we should take a step back too. It's a really emotional time for all of us. It's not the right time to be making big decisions. My priority now is Sophie's happiness. The last thing I want to do is hurt her.'

'But surely Jody will want justice too,' Joan added. 'Now that she knows the truth, she'll want that woman to pay for her sins.'

Laura shook her head. In a very firm tone, she told them, 'We are not going to send Anna to prison because, if we do, the very person we've waited for will leave again. Look, I want justice too, but Sophie loves Anna. By hurting Anna, we hurt Sophie. All we should be focusing on is making sure Sophie feels safe with us and happy. Let's not do anything to upset her or make her run away.'

'She is a lovely girl,' Joan conceded.

'So are we saying that we do nothing? Let Anna walk free?' David asked.

Mandy shook her fringe out of her eyes. 'Look, guys, I've spent a lot of time with Sophie over the last week – seeing as we're sharing my bedroom – and she's incredibly normal and together. She's not damaged at all. There was no weirdness in her life. Anna treated her like a bloody princess, from what I can see. Sophie has turned out to be, like, the perfect daughter – intelligent, studies hard, really polite, never rude, kind of a nerd, really, but a nice one.'

'She does have beautiful manners,' Joan agreed.

Mandy continued, 'So we have to admit, much as we hate to, that Anna did a good job. In fact, Sophie is the most normal of all of us. The crazy part of this whole drama is that Sophie is the one who had the normal life. While we were all living with ghosts of the past, secrets and lies, she was just being a normal kid, with an adoring mother, growing up in London.'

'Even if Anna was a good mother she still committed a terrible crime,' David reminded his daughter.

'I want to see her suffer for her sins.' Joan was not backing down yet.

Mandy patted Joan's arm. 'I know you do, Gran, and I get it. But you're not thinking about Sophie. You're only thinking about yourself. If you really care about Sophie and you want her to be happy, then you'll back off. Because I'm telling you now, if you go after Anna, you'll lose Sophie. If that's a risk you're willing to take, go ahead, but don't say I didn't warn you. Mum's right.

Sophie loves Anna and she would never forgive us for putting her in prison. Never. So stop thinking about your hurt and your revenge and think about Sophie, her feelings and her future. Locking up the person she loves most in the world, the only family she has ever known, is the worst thing you can do.'

Laura smiled at Mandy, her eyes welling. 'You're right, you clever girl. You're absolutely right.'

'I think she might, in time, come around and see our point of view,' David argued.

'Dad,' Mandy said, 'she freaked when you mentioned going to the police yesterday. She was hyperventilating at the idea of it.'

'But that woman did wrong,' Joan insisted. 'I can see she did our Jody no harm, and that she brought her up well, but she wasn't hers to raise. She stole her, Mandy. She left a gaping hole in our family and a lot of bitterness.'

'Yes, Gran, I know, but if you love Sophie, then you won't do something that you know will hurt her. You'll put her feelings before your own. Because that's what you do when you love someone. You suck it up.'

There was silence in the room – except for Tanya's impatient sighing – as Mandy's words sank in.

Frank spoke first: 'Mandy's right. Let's drop it and focus on Sophie.'

David beamed at Mandy. 'My daughter has just shown that she would make a very good lawyer. I'm impressed with your persuasive arguments. I take on board what you said and I think we should wait and perhaps reconsider. Well done.'

Mandy flushed with pleasure.

'Joan?' David asked. 'Where do you stand?'

Joan patted Mandy's cheek. 'When things settle down I want to have another meeting, but for now I'll "suck it up".'

'Good. This meeting is adjourned,' David announced. 'Thanks for coming, everyone. Mandy, let's grab a burger and talk about your future as a lawyer.'

Mandy grinned and walked out arm in arm with her dad,

Tanya clipping behind them in her heels. 'But, David, we have to collect the girls from ballet.'

David walked on. 'Go ahead. Mandy and I will get the bus home.'

'But, David . . .' Tanya tottered after her husband.

The front door shut behind them. 'Are you OK?' Frank asked.

Laura nodded. 'Fine, thanks. I'm glad we've decided to leave it. I feel relieved, actually.'

Joan came over with her bag and coat.

'Do you ladies want to grab lunch?' Frank asked his sister and mother. 'I've got an hour before my date.'

Joan rolled her eyes. 'Will you ever settle down, Frankie? I'd love to see you with a nice wife and children of your own.'

'Don't hold your breath.' Frank grinned. 'But sure you've got two beautiful granddaughters now to keep you busy.'

'How old is this date?' Laura asked.

'Twenty-eight, and she looks like a young Cindy Crawford.'

Laura laughed and Joan groaned.

'So, do you want to grab a bite to eat?' he asked again.

Laura shook her head. 'Thanks, but I'm keen to get back to Sophie. I know it's ridiculous, but I can't bear being away from her for even five minutes.'

'It's not ridiculous. It's perfectly normal after all you've been through,' Joan said.

Laura was shocked. Was her mother actually being nice to her? She didn't know what to say, so she distracted herself by fumbling in her bag for her car keys.

'Can I come back with you?' Joan asked. 'To see Jody?'

'Of course, sure.'

'I'll just pop to the cloakroom first.'

While Joan went to powder her nose, Frank and Laura stared at each other.

'Was she nice to me?' Laura whispered.

'I think she was. It's a miracle. Joan's thawing.'

'Two miracles in one week! I can't take any more.' Laura laughed. It was a good day, blue blue blue.

34.

Sophie

Killduf, July 2011

Sophie sat on her bed – the bed in Lexie's old room. It had been made up with crisp white cotton sheets, which reminded her of her own room back in London. It seemed a lifetime ago that she had been there, living her old life. A lifetime since she had seen Laura on the TV that night. That fateful night . . .

The cream wallpaper was covered with little pink flowers. Sophie liked it – it was cheerful. This bedroom didn't make her feel anxious like Mandy's did. It was a haven for her. She was able to escape up here without feeling like an intruder and without Mandy barging in all the time.

The room was very simply furnished, just a double bed and a small wooden desk and chair under a big window that looked out over the sea. There were two paintings on the wall. Sophie could tell they were Laura's. She recognized her style. One was of a stormy sea, with crashing waves, all dark blues and blacks with small white reflections of the moon. She could feel Laura's anger emanating from the canvas. It was very powerful. The other painting was of a naked woman, bent over in the foetal position, her long black hair covering her face. Although you couldn't see her face, you could tell she was crying. You could sense her pain. Sophie found it difficult to look at because it was so poignant. The woman in the painting could be either of her mothers: they had both suffered so much.

Sophie kicked off her sandals and curled her feet under her. She reread Anna's letter for the tenth time. It still made her cry.

She felt as if something between them was broken. She wondered if they'd ever be the same again, Anna and Sophie, mother and daughter.

She had thought she knew her mother so well. She had thought she knew her better than anyone but it had turned out she didn't really know her at all. She'd had no idea that Anna had been married or had had a baby who had died. It hurt her to think Anna had hidden all those secrets from her. She felt as if her mother was a stranger now.

Green and yellow – pain and anger. She'd been seeing those colours since she had first received the letter two days ago. She felt so sad for Anna: it must have been awful to bury her baby girl. Sophie couldn't imagine the pain. But it hadn't given her the right to steal someone else's child. No matter which way you looked at it, it had been wrong. But Sophie had been happy – really, truly happy – with Anna. She had been loved and cherished and cared for and given everything a child could wish for; she had always felt completely safe and secure. But now she felt the opposite. She felt lonely and raw and hurt and betrayed and wounded and, most of all, confused. It was such a mess.

Sophie really missed Lexie. She had received one text from her, telling her to keep her chin up and follow her heart. It was difficult in the house without Lexie to balance things out. Mandy was still grumpy and Joan was still difficult to deal with. She was so intense: she wanted Sophie to sit with her all the time and listen to her stories. She'd heard them at least three times, but she felt she had to be polite and humour her grandmother.

She didn't know what to do about Anna's letter. She needed to clear her head. There was only one thing that would take her mind off it. Sophie pulled out one of the sheets of paper she'd taken from Mandy's printer and began to sketch. She missed her easel, paints and brushes and longed to use colours again. She knew she could ask Laura but she was afraid Laura would crowd her if she did. She was afraid that Laura would watch her while she painted and she didn't want that. She needed to switch off and let herself go.

Sophie began to sketch and time stood still as she lost herself in her art and switched her mind off for a few glorious hours.

Later that day, when she checked her phone, there was a message from Joe. It was the first he had left. He sounded tired.

Sophie, I know this is a really difficult time for you, and I'm sorry you have to go through this. But you only know what you know. The last seventeen years of your life were real, it was your reality and it was a good one. You were lucky to have a mother who adored you. You were loved more than most kids out there. Don't shut her out for too long. Don't forget all the good times, there were lots of them. Your mother is devastated. She misses you terribly. Call me anytime if you want to chat or cry or rant or rage. I'm here for you. Mind yourself. 'Bye for now.

Sophie closed her eyes and made herself remember the good times. She thought about all the fun she'd had and how much time and effort Anna had put into making her life perfect. She remembered all the themed birthday parties and the magical Christmas mornings, the Easter-egg hunts, baking cakes and cuddling up to watch Disney movies together . . . She missed Anna. She missed her mother.

Sophie decided it was time she called Anna. She hated to think of her being so upset, and she wanted to make contact, but she wasn't ready to talk to her yet. She had to take it one step at a time. She rang into her voicemail. It was strange – she felt so awkward and uncomfortable. Her fingers shook as she dialled the number. 'Hi, it's me, um . . . well, it's Sophie. Your letter arrived. Thanks, I appreciate it. I'm so sorry about your little baby Hope. I would like to meet up soon to talk. I'm just not quite ready yet. I'll call you in a few days to arrange it. OK, 'bye. Take care.'

Sophie hung up and called Holly immediately. She needed to hear a familiar voice.

'Hi, Holly.'

'Oh, my God, it's been, like, ages! I've been going out of my mind with worry. I thought they might have taken you away to some remote part of Ireland to, like, a safe-house or something where no one would ever find you.'

Sophie laughed. 'Holly, what on earth are you talking about?'

'Well, I just thought that maybe Laura had decided to make you cut all ties with your old life and taken you somewhere with no mobile coverage or Wi-Fi. I've been really worried, particularly as I just spent four hundred pounds on a dress for our meeting with Max Clifford.'

'Holly! I told you that's not going to happen.'

'You might change your mind and I want to be prepared. Mind you, I'll have to stop eating pizza or I won't fit into the dress, and it's gorgeous – midnight blue satin with one shoulder. I look really hot in it, if I say so myself. But working in a pizza restaurant is a bad idea. I've put on six pounds. If I don't stop eating large slices of pepperoni deluxe, I'll end up looking like Jessie. Urgh!'

'How is Jessie?'

'Still a complete nightmare. She keeps coming to the restaurant and asking me if I have any leftover pizza. As if she's not fat enough. And I found her going through my phone messages when I came out of the shower yesterday.'

'Oh, God! Did she see any of mine?' Sophie panicked. She didn't want anyone to know where she was or what was going on in her life. If Jessie found out, the whole world would know her secret and she'd die if that happened.

'Give me some credit, I'm not a complete moron and I've lived with the little snoop for fifteen years. I know what she's like. I delete all of your messages as soon as I read them. So she didn't find anything. Besides, she's not remotely suspicious, just thinks you're on holiday with your mum. Your secret is safe with me.'

'Thanks. I don't want anyone to find out about this.'

'I know. Don't worry.' Holly stifled a yawn.

'Tired?'

'I've been doing double shifts all week so I could spend more time with the cute new waiter I told you about – William.'

'And?' Sophie asked. She was loving this girly chat. She missed being a regular teenager. She missed gossiping with Holly and talking about boys for hours.

'And . . . nothing.' Holly sighed. 'I've given him all my best lines, batted my eyelashes at him and worn the best push-up bra on the market, but he just acts as if I don't exist.'

'Well, if he doesn't see how fabulous you are, forget about him.'

'Oh, Sophie, I do miss you. You always say the right thing. Which, by the way, is why you'd be fabulous on TV. I'd be a disaster, putting my foot in it constantly, but you'd be amazing, so composed and articulate. Honestly, Max Clifford is going to love you.'

'Holly –'

'Yeah, yeah, I know, you probably won't ever want to go public with your story, but it's fun for me to imagine what-if! Mind you, Max is representing Lexie Granger at the moment so he'll be busy with her.'

Sophie sat bolt upright. 'Really?'

'Yes! Apparently she's written a book about her life and Max Clifford said there are loads of juicy bits about Dougie. It's all over the papers here. Lexie was on Lorraine Kelly's show this morning with Max and he was saying how all the newspapers are offering masses of money to serialize her book.'

'How did she look? What did she say?' Sophie was dying to know how Lexie was getting on.

'Well, she had these really long false eyelashes on – they looked ridiculous on morning TV – she was poured into her jeans, and she must have had another boob job because her boobs were bursting out of her top.'

'Did she seem happy?'

'Why are you so interested in Lexie Granger? You always used to say WAGs were just bimbos who had no careers of their own and lived off their husbands.'

Sophie winced. 'I was wrong – stupid and judgemental.'

'Not really. A lot of them are like that.'

'You shouldn't judge someone until you know them.'

'OK, Mother Teresa!'

'Go on, Holly, tell me more about the interview.'

'Well, I suppose she did look quite happy. She said she isn't mean about Dougie in the book but that she is honest about their marriage. She said she's sad that things didn't work out but they've talked and hope to remain friends.'

'Did she say anything about what she was going to do now career-wise?'

'No. I'm sure she's just going to live the high-life on the money she'll get from the divorce and the book sales, the lucky thing. The *Daily Mail* said they reckon she'll get ten million in the divorce.'

'Wow, good for her.' Sophie was thrilled to hear that Lexie was going to be financially secure. She'd be able to set up a fantastic studio now for her photography and not depend on a man for money.

'Enough about WAGs. How are you? What's going on? Is Mandy still being a pain? Have you seen Anna yet? Is Laura still off the vodka?'

Sophie smiled. 'Mandy *is* still being a pain. She's jealous of all the attention I'm getting from Laura. I see her point, it must be difficult, but she can be really rude sometimes.'

'You should tell her to sod off. Remind her that you're catching up on seventeen years and that she's lucky to have a fabulous sister like you in her life.'

'Thanks, but I'm not sure if that approach would work. I just try to keep out of her way as much as possible. Things with Laura are good. She's so cool, Holly. Honestly, she's so lovely and well . . . young. She's more like an older sister, really.'

'That sounds great. But what about Anna?'

Sophie sighed. 'I left a message on her voicemail. I'm just not ready to talk to her yet. I need a little more time. You won't believe this – I found out she had a baby who died. She was born the same time I was.'

'What?'

'I know, and she was married too. But the baby – Hope was her name – died and Anna's marriage broke up and she was devastated and wanted to start a new life, which was why she was on the boat to London that day.'

'This story just keeps getting more incredible by the minute. Poor Anna, how awful. My aunt Margaret had a baby who died and Mum said it took her years to get over it. Anna obviously took you because Laura was drunk but also because she was desperate to replace her little girl.'

Sophie chewed her lip. 'It looks that way. Holly, it's all so complicated. I don't know who to feel more sorry for, Anna or Laura. They've suffered so much, and they both made terrible mistakes but they're really good people. Honestly, my head's constantly pounding. I don't know what to do. Every decision I make hurts someone.'

'You have to do what feels right. Follow your gut. Are you seeing loads of green?'

'Tons – and yellow because I'm still angry with Anna for taking me and with Laura for being so drunk.'

'Look on the bright side. You'll never have to look for inspiration for your paintings – your life's so much more extraordinary than anyone else's.'

Sophie laughed. 'True.'

'I'd better go. I start my shift at seven. I'm going to give William one last chance. I've rolled up my skirt so it's really short and I've had my hair blow-dried. If he doesn't fancy me tonight then I give up. Are there any nice Irish boys over there?'

'I haven't met anyone apart from the family, but Mandy met Mark and I think she fancies him.'

'Judging by his photos it'd be difficult not to. I think I should come over and check him out. But until I can work out how to get there – without my mum being suspicious or Jessie following me – keep that grumpy sister of yours away from Mark. I need some action.'

Sophie grinned. 'OK, I will. Talk soon.'

'Very soon, please. Don't leave it for long. I miss you, Sophie. My family's driving me insane – I need you and Anna and your sanity next door.'

'OK, 'bye. Good luck with William!'

Sophie hung up and smiled to herself. She felt better, as she always did after talking to Holly. It reminded her of her old life. Her good life. Her happy life. Her stress-free life. Her life . . .

35.

Anna

Killduf, July 2011

Anna chose a table opposite the door of the café. She wanted to see Sophie the minute she walked in. Then she wouldn't miss a second of this meeting. She had been ecstatic when Sophie had finally called and asked to see her.

They had arranged to meet in the coffee shop in Killduf. Anna had arrived half an hour early and was already on her second coffee. She tried to read the newspaper the waitress had offered her, but she couldn't concentrate. Every time the door opened her heart skipped a beat.

Joe was worried about her. He said she needed more rest and recuperation after her procedure and that she was supposed to avoid stress. But he knew it was pointless to try to stop her seeing Sophie. Nothing would stop Anna being with her daughter. Besides, Anna had told him, the ulcer had settled down since the gastroscopy and the tablets were easing her discomfort. She just felt a bit tired. But not now, not today. Today, she felt hopeful, excited and nervous. She prayed they wouldn't argue. She prayed their meeting would be different from the last one when Sophie had screamed at her, called her an abductor and stormed off.

Anna needed to be calm. She needed to let Sophie talk, but she also needed to be Sophie's mother. She could sense how lost and lonely Sophie was. She knew her inside and out. She knew every bone in her body and every hair on her head. She understood Sophie better than anyone else could. She loved her more than anyone else could.

But Anna knew that she had betrayed Sophie's trust in the worst way – with lies and deceit. She knew that Sophie was reeling from the betrayal. She knew that Sophie needed to lash out at her and blame her. But she hoped against hope that Sophie would come around to seeing that she had done the right thing at the right time. That she would understand Anna had saved her on that day, in that moment, on that ship when she was being neglected by her drunken mother.

The door opened and Sophie walked in. Anna had almost forgotten how breathtaking Sophie was. She was wearing new clothes: a lilac blouse, white jeans and sandals. Laura must have taken her shopping. Anna felt her chest tighten. 'Relax!' she scolded herself. 'You must keep calm and composed.'

Sophie saw Anna and came over to her. When she reached her mother, she hesitated. Anna stood up and took control. Resisting the urge to hug her daughter and never let her go, she simply leaned over and gave Sophie a kiss on the cheek. Her daughter looked relieved and sat on the chair opposite.

'It's so good to see you,' Anna said.

'You too.' Sophie blushed.

Anna could see how uncomfortable she was. She needed to make Sophie relax. She didn't want her to run away again. She wanted her to feel safe and secure.

'Would you like a latte?'

'Yes, please.'

Anna ordered it and turned back to her daughter. 'You look lovely. How are you? How are you getting on?'

Sophie twisted her necklace. 'I'm fine. I'm just . . . um . . . just trying to work things out.'

'I know. It must be hard for you.'

Sophie looked surprised. 'Well, yes, it is.'

Anna sipped her coffee. She put her cup down and looked directly into her daughter's blue eyes. 'I'm sorry, Sophie. I'm sorry about everything that happened and the way it happened. But I'm not sorry that I got to be your mum. It's been a pleasure and a privilege and I've cherished every single moment of it.'

Sophie's eyes began to water. 'But it still wasn't right . . . You can't just steal a child because your own baby died.'

Anna caught her breath. She had to be careful. She mustn't get emotional. She needed to be the parent here. She had to explain things in a measured way. She placed her hands on the table. 'Sophie, I was devastated when Hope died, but that's not why I took you. What I saw on the boat that day was neglect, pure and simple. I saw a baby being treated appallingly and I acted on instinct. I honestly never, ever, intended to take you. I did not get on that boat with the intention of taking someone else's child. The thought never entered my mind. But when I saw Laura passed out on the bar counter, something in me clicked and I knew I had to protect you. It's very hard to explain. Maybe it's because when I taught in the school in Dublin I saw so many innocent little lives ruined by alcoholic parents. I honestly don't know, but I can't regret having been your mum. It's the best thing I've ever done.'

The waitress came over and handed Sophie her latte. Anna could see she was struggling not to cry. 'But I wasn't yours to take and Laura *is* a good mum. And Joan was helping her to bring me up.'

Anna shook her head. 'Laura was not a good mum then. She might be now, but back then she was a mess.'

Sophie stirred her coffee. 'Joan told me that Laura was a wreck. But she stopped drinking and she's great now.'

'*Now*,' Anna emphasized. 'Laura only stopped drinking because you were taken. Look, Sophie, I truly believe that if I hadn't taken you with me, you would have drowned, or something else awful would have happened. A small child cannot look after itself on a ship full of strange people in the middle of the sea.'

Sophie didn't say anything. Anna was hoping maybe she had got through to her.

Sophie rolled a sugar cube between her fingers. 'I can see why you did it, but that doesn't make it right. They suffered so much when I disappeared. While I was having a great life in London, they were all broken-hearted in Dublin. I just wish things had been different.'

Anna leaned forward. 'I know you do. But, Sophie, none of us can change the past. We can –'

'We can only live today and look to the future.' Sophie smiled. 'I haven't forgotten your favourite mantra.'

Anna was thrilled to see her daughter's smile, even if it was only a small one.

'Why didn't you tell me you were married?' Sophie asked.

Anna sat back. She decided to be honest. No more lies. 'Because I didn't want to think about the past. Because I was living my own mantra – I wanted to focus on the present and the future with you. Also, because I thought it was better not to talk about my past in case I said something that would make you suspicious.'

'What was his name?'

'Barry Roberts.'

'How long were you together?'

'Ten years.'

'Were you happy?'

'Initially, yes. When we first got married things were wonderful. We were extremely happy. But then we started trying to have children and I kept having miscarriages. The longer it went on the more of a strain it put on our relationship. When I got pregnant with Hope we really thought this was it. We thought, finally, our time had come – we were going to be parents. Everything went really well . . . until . . . until she was born prematurely and only survived a few minutes.' Anna coughed to clear the lump forming in her throat. 'After that the marriage was over. We were so unhappy. I knew he'd be better off without me. Better off with a younger woman who could give him the children he deserved. So I told him I was leaving and I could see he was relieved. It was the right thing to do.'

A tear ran down Sophie's cheek. Anna had to look away or she knew she'd cry too. 'I'm sorry, it must have been awful,' Sophie murmured.

'Yes, it was, but it all happened a long time ago and I've had so much joy in my life since then, with you, that I honestly haven't looked back.'

'Do you know what happened to Barry?'

'No. Joe is the only person I kept in touch with. I left Dublin a broken woman. I had to leave because I was falling apart. And then you came along and, literally, saved my life.'

'It's so hard because I don't know what to do and the one person I always go to when I need advice is you. But you're the cause of all this so I can't talk to you about what to do and where to go, who to be angry with and who to forgive and . . . uh . . . uh . . . oh, God, my head feels like it's spinning off. Green, everything's green.'

Anna slowly got up and went to sit beside her. She took Sophie's hand in hers. 'I want you to listen to me. I'm always here for you and you can talk to me about anything. I know this is awful for you. I know you're incredibly confused right now and angry and upset. And I know you're furious with me, but life isn't black and white, Sophie. It's mostly grey. I did what I did, and I'm sorry I put Laura and Joan through so much pain. That was never my intention. I didn't know Joan existed. But it happened, and I believe that we found each other for a reason. We saved each other. I can't regret my decision. I can only try to make you understand that I did it out of love and I never meant to hurt anyone. I thought I was saving you from a life of hell. You were so small and vulnerable and upset. I couldn't leave you there, I just couldn't.'

Sophie sobbed.

'The last few weeks have been hell for me too. Watching you go and live with Laura has been the hardest thing I've ever had to do. But I understand that I need to step back and let you get to know your other family. Although I hate not seeing you, I think it's important that you spend time with them, and I'm not going to stand in your way or make you feel guilty about it. All I want is for you to be happy.'

Sophie wiped her eyes. 'I know you took me because you thought it was the right thing to do. I just wish everything wasn't such a mess. Whatever I do now, whatever decisions I make, I hurt either you or Laura.'

Anna could see that Sophie really needed her to let go. Her daughter needed her to say she was OK with being left behind. But Anna also wanted to make sure that Sophie knew she'd be waiting for her whenever she decided to come back – whether it was in a day, a month or a year.

Anna took a deep breath and gave up her most precious gift: 'You have to follow your heart. Do what feels right. If you need to be with Laura and her family, then that's where you should be. Stay for as long as you want. Get to know them, let them see how wonderful you are. I will *always* be here for you. No matter how long we're apart, I will always be waiting for you with open arms. I love you and I want you to be happy.'

Sophie fell into Anna's arms. 'Thank you . . . oh, thank you.'

Although Anna's heart ached, she knew she'd done the right thing. She prayed that by letting Sophie go she'd win her back.

36.

Laura

Killduf, July 2011

Although she missed Lexie terribly, Laura had to admit that her departure had been well timed. Sophie had moved into Lexie's room and Mandy had her bedroom back, which made her less tetchy.

Laura tried to take Lexie's advice and forced herself not to crowd Sophie or follow her around or stare at her all the time. It was hard, really hard, and she hated Sophie being out of her sight for more than a minute, but she knew Lexie was right. She had to give Sophie breathing space and allow her to get to know her slowly.

In an attempt to stop focusing on her so much, Laura began to paint again. Just an hour or two a day, but it was familiar, soothing, and she could switch her mind off, a relief after the roller-coaster of emotions she had been on lately.

The tactic seemed to work, because one afternoon, for the first time, Sophie sought her out. She came into her studio and asked if she could borrow an easel and some paint.

'Of course.' Laura was thrilled. 'I'd love to see you paint.'

'Well, I'm nothing compared to you. I mean, your work is so incredible. It's so . . . um . . . passionate and emotional, and when you look at the different pieces, it feels as if they're speaking to you.'

Laura beamed. 'Thank you. That's such a lovely compliment. I'm thrilled you like them. But I have to be honest: for every good canvas you see, there are hundreds of bad ones.'

Sophie smiled. 'You're very modest.' She set up her easel at the other side of the room. Then she asked shyly, 'I was wondering, who do you admire? Who inspired you when you started painting?'

Laura walked over to the shelf behind her. It was weighed down with books on every type of painting and painter, from ancient Malaysian cave paintings to Damien Hirst. She pulled a large book out and placed it on the table beside her easel. Sophie came over to look. 'This is one of the people who most inspired me.'

Sophie stared at her, mouth open. 'I adore Georges Braque. *Houses at L'Estaque* is one of my favourite paintings.'

Laura wanted to scream with joy, but composed herself. 'Really? That's incredible – me too.'

They grinned at each other. 'Who else do you like?' Laura asked.

Sophie listed all of her favourite artists and they scoured Laura's books, finding pictures she particularly liked, discussing their merits and virtues. Then Laura showed her daughter some of the more obscure artists she had learned from and been inspired by.

Sophie was blown away. 'You know so much.'

Laura smiled. 'Yes, but I'm a lot older than you are. I've had more time to learn.'

'You're not that much older,' Sophie said. 'Honestly, none of the mums at school looked like you. You look so young and . . . well . . . amazing. Not like a mum at all, really, more like a sister.'

Laura winked at her. 'Thanks. I'll take any compliment I can get.'

They spent the afternoon painting side by side. It was utter bliss. For once there was no awkwardness. Laura wasn't fussing over her and Sophie wasn't trying to please. They were their true selves, united by a passion for art that transcended self-consciousness. They talked about art, colours, synaesthesia, the different surfaces to paint on, brushes, oils, solvents, varnishes, using gold and liquid leaf, technique, inspiration, motivation, style, ideas . . . It was a warm and relaxed atmosphere for both of them. Laura felt as though she'd died and gone to Heaven.

After a long silence, when they'd concentrated on their work, Sophie took a deep breath. 'Do you think you'll ever be able to forgive Anna for what she did?'

Laura forced herself to keep painting. 'I don't know, Sophie. If you want me to try I will, for your sake. But it's a lot to ask. I feel robbed of so much.'

'I understand completely. I just thought that maybe in time you might see that she didn't set out to hurt anyone. I know it was wrong, but she thought she was saving me.'

Laura gripped her paintbrush. 'Yes, but she wasn't saving you, she was stealing you. Look, Sophie, more than anything I want you to be happy and I can see that Anna was good to you. But she wasn't your mother, and it's a long road back from seventeen years of grief. But for you I'll try.'

'Thanks, Laura. I really appreciate it. Can I see your painting?'

She came over and marvelled at her mother's work. Laura reciprocated when she saw Sophie's. She was genuinely impressed. 'You have real talent, Sophie, and a unique style. You're going to be something special.'

Sophie beamed. 'You're not just saying that, are you?'

Laura looked into her daughter's eyes, her own blue eyes. 'No, I'm not. You really are special. And I want to help you in any way I can.'

'Can I come and paint with you every day?'

Laura forced the cry not to come out of her mouth. 'I'd love that.' When Sophie turned back to her easel, Laura punched the air.

Early one morning, Laura was in her studio painting. Joan was coming to spend the day with them, so she wanted to get a few hours' work done before her mother arrived. Laura knew Sophie found Joan hard going. Joan would sit Sophie down and tell her endless stories about when she was a baby, often crying as the memories became too much. Sophie was extremely patient, but Laura could tell she found Joan's visits draining, so Laura liked to be around to help her out.

Mandy and Sophie were still asleep when a delivery van pulled up. The man got out carrying a heavy box. Laura opened her studio door and beckoned him over. She signed for the delivery and went to find scissors to cut through all the tape with which the box was secured.

She pulled back the flaps and saw a bunch of folders – there were five. They were bulging with documents. On top lay an envelope addressed to Laura Fletcher.

What was this? She opened the envelope and read the note.

I thought you might like to see these. I'm sorry. Anna

Laura dropped the note as if it had burned her fingers. With trembling hands she pulled the heavy folders out. They were marked (a) 1994–6; (b) 1997–2001; (c) 2002–2005; (d) 2006–2009; (e) 2010–

She opened folder (a) and cried out. Photos of Jody, her little Jody, when she was the same age as Laura remembered her. They must have been taken just after the abduction. She was at a birthday party: some little girl was two and Jody was sitting beside her blowing out the candles. Laura felt physically sick. She turned the pages. Hundreds of photos interspersed with medical records, dental records, paintings Sophie had done, a big Santa with his beard made of cotton wool, school reports, a curl of her beautiful blonde hair, her favourite book – *The Very Hungry Caterpillar* – photos of her in Hallowe'en costumes, dressed as a witch, a fairy, a lion ... Laura turned the pages, lost in time, in stolen memories, drinking in the past, soaking up every detail. She cried through the first folder, her baby, her missing child. There she was, beaming out from the pages as she grew, went to school, had birthday parties and a life Laura had played no part in.

But by the time she opened the second folder Laura's sorrow

had turned to rage. How dare this woman steal these memories from her? *She* should have taken these photos and celebrated these milestones. These were the moments she had dreamed of, begged for, missed. The loss of these memories had been tearing her up inside for all these years. Her own daughter's history had not included her for even one second. Anna had robbed her of seventeen years.

Laura was distracted from her rage in the third folder by the beginning of Sophie's talent for art shining through her classwork. She was astounded at the paintings Sophie had been doing at twelve and thirteen. She was proud of her daughter's achievements in all subjects, but it was in art that Sophie had excelled. Laura felt such a strong connection to her on a creative level. It made her feel closer to Sophie now that she had seen the beginning of her journey as an artist.

By folder four Laura was awed by the amount of detailed information Anna had collected and stored so carefully. It was a complete treasure trove of information – visual and written – about Sophie's life. Her every achievement – even the insignificant ones – had been recorded.

Laura had kept a handful of particularly nice things Mandy had brought home from school and she had filed away a few of her school reports, but nothing like this. Anna had kept a record of every single thing Sophie had ever done. There were even ticket stubs from the first concert she had gone to, her first ballet, her first opera . . . The detail was staggering.

The fifth folder was only a third full. The last page had photos of Sophie's final day at school. She was standing with her arm around another girl – Holly – who featured throughout every folder. Sophie looked so happy and carefree. Laura examined the picture more closely: the girl in it radiated happiness and contentment. Her face showed no strain, no dark shadows under her eyes, no forced smile. She was a different girl from the one Laura knew. This girl didn't have a care in the world. She looked confident, joyful, ready to embrace the next chapter in her life.

But all that had changed since she had discovered that her life – her lovely life – was a lie and her mother an impostor.

Laura sat back and looked out at the sea. She hated allowing the thought to enter her mind, but she had to admit that Sophie's life had looked idyllic. In every photo she had been happy.

Anna had been a good mother – no, a great mother. A better mother than Laura had been to Mandy. Maybe even a better mother than Laura would have been to Sophie . . .

Later that day when Joan was telling Sophie a long story about how she used to love watching a particular *Tom and Jerry* cartoon – a story Sophie had now heard at least three times – Laura interrupted them. 'Mum, could I borrow you for a second? I need to show you something.'

Reluctantly, Joan got up from the couch and Sophie scampered off to her bedroom. She followed Laura to her studio, grumbling about being disturbed mid-story. 'What is it you need me to see so urgently?' she demanded.

'This.' Laura pointed to the box and handed her mother the first folder. 'They arrived this morning. I thought you'd like to look at them. Anna sent them to me.'

'What on earth – how dare that woman –'

Laura held up her hand. 'I know, Mum, but just look through them. They're the story of Sophie's life and how she became the person she is today.'

Laura lined up the folders in sequence and sat back as Joan opened the first and gasped. 'Little Jody! There she is, just as I remember her. Oh, Laura, look at her lovely little smile.' Joan cried as she turned page after page and learned about her granddaughter's life in London.

Initially, just as Laura had, Joan raged about lost years and precious stolen memories. But as the folders went on she, too, was awed by the detail Anna had included.

She got to the final photo and sniffed. 'Well, she certainly likes keeping records. It's very thorough.'

Laura smiled. 'It certainly is. Look at that last photo.'

'Her final day in school.'

'Do you see how happy Sophie looks?'

'She looks happy now.'

'Come on, Mum, let's be honest here.'

'Well, all right, she looks a bit strained now, but that's only to be expected. She's had a shock. We all have.'

Laura picked up a paintbrush and ran her fingers through the soft sable hair. 'Sophie asked me to forgive Anna.'

Joan's head jerked up. 'I hope you told her it was out of the question.'

'No, I didn't. I said it would be very difficult but I'd try, for her sake.'

'Could you?'

Laura sighed. 'Forgive her? No. I don't think I ever will. But I can see, although it galls me to admit it, that Anna was a good mother. A really devoted mother. The folders are incredible.'

'You would have been a good mother. Once you grew up a bit and stopped drinking. You were foolish and selfish, like most young girls, but you would have been a good mother eventually, when you matured.'

'But when she saw me that day on the boat I was a bad mother. I was awful. I treated Jody so badly. Oh, God, Mum, I hate myself for it.' Laura began to cry.

Joan hesitated. Then, slowly and nervously, she placed her arm around her daughter's shoulders. It was the first time she had touched Laura in seventeen years. Laura's sobs turned into wails.

'There, there.' Joan patted her shoulder. 'You've paid for your sins, Laura – God knows, we all have. I've been angry for as long as I can remember. It's been eating me up. But I've been thinking a lot about what Mandy said, about putting Sophie's feelings before my own – even I'm calling her Sophie now! And I realize that Mandy was right. I have to leave my bitterness aside or it will ruin the precious time I have left with my family.'

Laura wiped her eyes. 'Come on, Mum, you're only sixty.'

'Yes, but I'm an old sixty. And I don't want to spend the rest of my life being angry. I don't want Sophie to know me as a bitter old woman. We've got her back and it's time to rejoice. It's time to let go of the past.'

Laura gave her mother a shaky smile. 'You're absolutely right. We do need to move forward. So what do we do about Anna?'

'Anna is in her own private hell,' Joan said. 'She has deeply hurt the person she loves most in the world and that's her punishment. We know all about hurting in this family. Now it's Anna's time to feel it and I hope she feels it acutely.'

Laura covered her face with her hands. 'I'm sorry, Mum,' she sobbed. 'I'm sorry I hurt you and Frank. God, I've hated myself for so long.'

'No, pet,' Joan said, dabbing her own eyes with a tissue. 'I'm the one who's sorry. I've been angry with you for so many years. I was so consumed by my own grief and pain that I didn't care about anyone else. I should have talked to you, I should have forgiven you, and I should have supported you more with Mandy. I'm sorry, Laura. I've been a bad mother to you.'

'No, you haven't.' Laura hiccuped. 'I understand why you blamed me because it *was* my fault. I blamed myself.'

'No more blame. You're my only daughter and I'm not going to waste any more time being angry. Let's start again. Can we do that?'

Laura was crying too much to speak. Joan put her arms around her grown-up baby girl and rocked her gently, soothing her as a good mother should.

37.

Sophie

Killduf, July 2011

Sophie found Laura at her computer in the kitchen, surrounded by paperwork. 'Hi, Laura, sorry to disturb you. I just wanted to let you know that I'm going to a party tonight with Mark.'

Laura looked alarmed. 'What party? Where?'

Sophie had anticipated this. She was used to having an over-protective mother. She was ready with details. 'It's a house party in Wicklow. The house is called Pegasus. Hannah is a friend of Mark's from college. He's going to pick me up and drop me home. I'll have my phone with me, so if there's any problem I'll call you.'

Laura shuffled her papers. She was visibly agitated. 'But I don't know Mark. I wasn't here when he called the other day. I didn't meet him. Who is he?'

Sophie remained calm but firm. She needed to get out of the house and have some fun. She felt cooped up. 'He's my oldest friend and he's like a brother to me. He's a great guy. Please don't worry. I'll be fine. I'm going to get ready now. He's picking me up at eight.'

Before Laura could ask any further questions or try to dis-suade her from going, Sophie ran upstairs. She had decided to wear the new white ankle-grazer jeans and Miu Miu wedges Laura had bought her. She was still trying to choose a top when her door flew open.

'Are you really going to a party with Mark tonight?' Mandy asked.

'Don't you ever knock?' Sophie pulled a blue T-shirt over her head. 'Yes, I am. Why?'

'Can I come?'

'No.'

'Why not?'

'Because you're sixteen and you won't know anyone and I'm not looking after you. I need to go out and have some fun on my own. I've been cooped up here for ages.'

Mandy sat on the bed. 'Please take me. It's been hard on me too, you know. And you won't have to mind me. I'm perfectly capable of making friends. I swear you won't see me from the minute we walk in. You have to take me, I'm begging you. I need to let off some steam too. Come on, Sophie, it's been a crazy few weeks. My head is wrecked from it all.'

Sophie sighed. The last thing she wanted was her little sister tagging after her. But she knew things had been difficult for Mandy and she did feel guilty about all the attention she'd had from Laura while Mandy had been more or less ignored.

'OK, but you'd better not get drunk or into any trouble. I'm not being your guardian.'

'Brilliant! I promise you won't even know I'm there.' She jumped up and headed towards her bedroom. 'By the way,' she shouted over her shoulder, 'you should wear the pink top – it's hot.'

Sophie took off the blue top and put on the pink one.

Mark turned up to collect Sophie at ten past eight. Sophie ran out to greet him.

'Are you stoned or drunk?' she asked.

He clambered out of the car. 'Dude, I've just got out of bed. I was gigging last night and then we partied till dawn. So the answer is no.'

Sophie hugged him. 'Thank goodness. Laura wants to meet you. She's worried that you're an unsuitable companion for the evening. Please be on your best behaviour and don't mention Anna.'

'My brain isn't that fried.'

'Sorry, I'm nervous. Oh, and Mandy's coming.'

'The angry Goth chick?'

Sophie nodded. Mark shrugged. 'OK, cool. My mate Ross digs Goths so she might get lucky.'

Sophie grabbed his arm. 'No! She is not to get lucky or drunk, or smoke joints or anything. Laura will kill me if anything happens to her.'

'Jeez, relax. I'll warn him off her if you like.'

'I would.'

'Are we allowed have fun? Or do we have to sit around drinking water and talking about art all night?' Mark pinched her cheek.

'Get off me.' Sophie giggled and swatted his hand away. 'Mandy's only sixteen. I just don't need any more drama in my life.'

Mark grinned. 'I get it. Don't worry, I'll make sure she doesn't end up in prison or knocked up.'

Laura came out to meet Mark. She insisted on smelling his breath to make sure he hadn't been drinking.

Mandy hid her face in her hands. 'I'm sorry about my mother – she's a freak.'

Mark smiled. 'No, it's cool. I get it. She had a bad experience with one kid going missing for years so she's entitled to be nervous.'

Laura attempted a smile. 'Thank you, Mark. Right, well, have fun and call me if you want a lift home. Do not even think about getting into a car with anyone who has been drinking. I'll be waiting up for you anyway so it's no problem to collect you.'

'We should go.' Sophie made a move towards the car.

Laura kissed her goodbye. 'Please be careful,' she whispered. 'I couldn't take it if anything happened to you. Not now, not when I've just got you back.'

'I promise I will.' Sophie put her seatbelt on.

Mandy jumped into the back. 'Drive,' she hissed at Mark. 'Please just put your foot down before she tries to come to the party with us.'

'She's pretty hot. I dig older chicks. Do you want to invite her?'

381

Mandy squealed.

They drove out, leaving Laura waving forlornly.

The house was huge. It was like one of those old country piles you see in magazines. There must have been three hundred people there. Music blared from enormous speakers in the vast hall. The bar had been set up in the kitchen. There was every type of alcohol imaginable. People were drinking beer, vodka, gin, wine, whiskey, rum . . . Some were making cocktails, others were smoking bongs, and a small group were snorting cocaine on the corner of the kitchen counter.

Sophie was shocked about the open cocaine use but was trying not to show it. Wait until Holly hears about this, she thought. Mark introduced them to lots of people but Sophie couldn't remember anyone's name. The music was so loud it was difficult to hear anything. So she just nodded and smiled and said hello.

Mandy kept trying to talk to Mark about music and bands, but he was far too busy eyeing up the talent to listen.

'Do you like the Keystone Jammers?'

'They're all right but I don't see them lasting.' He squinted over Mandy's shoulder.

'So who are you into?'

Mark shrugged. 'I like loads of different bands.'

'Like who?'

Mark faced her. 'Dude, I plan to get wasted and score with one of the many hot women here tonight. If you want to talk to me about music, you have to get me during the day. It's party time now. My priorities are drink, drugs and sex.'

'Fine. Don't let me hold you back,' Mandy snapped.

Sophie felt sorry for her sister. Mark could be unintentionally cruel at times. Thank God she'd never fancied him. He was fun as a friend but he would be the worst boyfriend in the world.

While Mandy turned to pour herself a drink, a tall, slim, blonde girl in a short, tight gold-sequined dress threw her arms around Mark and pulled him into the corner where the bong was being passed around.

Sophie felt a bit self-conscious. She didn't know anyone and she wasn't feeling very confident or sociable. She wished Holly was with her. She needed a drink to help her relax.

Mandy was at the kitchen counter, pouring herself a large vodka and Coke.

'Could you pour me one?' Sophie asked her.

'Sure, here you go.' Mandy handed her sister a drink. 'Don't worry about Mark. He's a bit of a slut.'

Mandy glared at her. 'I don't give a shit about Mark. He's a loser.'

Sophie took a big glug of her drink, then another and another. It felt like heaven. The alcohol kicked in and she could feel herself relaxing.

Mandy raised her glass and knocked the contents back in one. She poured herself more.

'Don't you think you should take it easy?' Sophie said.

'What?'

'I don't want you to get drunk. You're the youngest person here and I don't want anyone taking advantage of you.'

Mandy took a long sip of her second drink. 'I'm not the convent-school virgin here. I can look after myself. I've been doing it for sixteen years. I don't need your help.'

Sophie took another sip of her vodka. 'I don't want Laura blaming me if anything happens.'

'My mother isn't capable of blaming you for anything. In case you hadn't noticed she worships the ground you walk on. Sophie, the perfect daughter with the synaesthesia and the talent for art.'

Sophie began to see yellow. 'It's called genetics. Why don't you try to stop being so angry all the time?'

Mandy put her face close to Sophie's. 'Why don't you stop being so bloody perfect?'

'I'm not perfect.'

'You never put a foot wrong. You're so bloody polite all the time and it's irritating. Yes, Laura, no, Laura, oh, thank you, Laura.'

'I see. So should I behave like you? An immature, rude, disrespectful idiot?'

'At least I'm not an uptight bore. Why don't you just have a few drinks and lighten up?'

'Don't speak to me like that.' Sophie was seeing all yellow now.

'Why?' Mandy's eyes flashed. 'Because you're the chosen one? The prodigal daughter back from the dead and everyone has to worship at your feet? Well, I'm sick of it, and of you, and of all the fucking drama you brought with you.'

'Well, I'm sick of you and your attitude towards me. Do you think I like the fact that my life is based on lies? Do you think I wanted to find out I'd been abducted? Do you have any idea what it feels like?'

Mandy polished off her drink. 'Oh, boo-hoo, poor little Sophie. She's so confused. We must protect her and make her feel welcome. Nothing and no one but Sophie matters. Her happiness is all we care about. To Hell with everyone else.'

People were beginning to stare at them. But Sophie didn't care: her blood was boiling. 'It must be nice for you to have somewhere else to channel your anger. I understand completely why you have so much inside you. I mean, it must have been terrible for you growing up with a mother – who was actually your mother – who adores you and a father who loves you. Not to mention a grandmother and an uncle who also think the world of you. How many parent figures do you need, Mandy? Just how much love and attention can one person expect to get in life?'

'Fuck you and your little Miss Princess of England act, with your perfect looks and your talent at art. Could you be more nauseating? You come crashing into my life and wreck it. My mother doesn't even know I exist any more. Neither does my gran nor even Frank. And what the hell would you know about growing up with a stepmother who hates the sight of you? You in your little cocooned world, the headmistress's daughter who never did anything wrong, the perfect student, the perfect daughter, the perfect human being. You make me want to puke.'

Sophie finished her drink and slammed down the glass on the table. 'I'm going to leave before I say something I regret. In the meantime you might try growing up, you silly little girl. You're behaving like a petulant child. It's pathetic.' Sophie stomped away from her.

She was overcome with yellow, the most intense yellow she'd ever known. She had to calm down – it was blinding. She went to find Mark to talk to him. He was lying on a couch, surrounded by adoring girls, stoned out of his mind, laughing hysterically at his little finger.

Sophie turned and went upstairs. She reached the first landing and found six people sitting in a circle. They looked nice, normal and not completely drunk or stoned. She stood apart, watching them. A good-looking floppy-haired boy was trying to remember the last line from Yeats's 'When You Are Old' but he was stuck.

'"And hid his face amid a crowd of stars,"' Sophie quoted, emboldened by the vodka.

The boy looked at her and grinned. 'Thank you.' He beckoned her to sit down beside him. 'I'm Freddie,' he said. 'And this is Sarah, Grace, Kate, Liam and Nigel.'

Sophie raised her hand in a little wave. 'Hello, I'm Sophie.'

'I love your accent,' Kate said.

'Oh, thanks.'

'Where are you from in England?' Grace asked.

'London,' Sophie said.

'Beautiful, clever and foreign – an intoxicating combination,' Nigel said. He was wearing a red smoking jacket and a cravat, which looked a bit pretentious but he seemed friendly.

'Have a drink,' Freddie said, pouring some brown liquid into a small glass.

'What is it?'

'Jägermeister.' He handed it to her. 'Just knock it back, like a shot.' He demonstrated by drinking his.

What the hell? Sophie needed something to get her through this party. She drank it. They all cheered. The game was: you had to quote a verse of a poem but if you hesitated or got stuck, you had to drink a shot of Jägermeister.

Sophie thought it sounded easy. She had an excellent memory, but the drink had a very strong effect on her. She felt woolly-headed, light and airy, confident and funny. Everything was funny. She stumbled over her quotes, laughed hysterically and drank shot after shot after shot . . .

'Wake up, you stupid cow!' a voice shouted in Sophie's dream. 'Wake up!' it shouted again. She felt herself rocking from side to side. She must be in a boat. Maybe she was dreaming of holidays.

Ouch! Someone had hit her. She opened her eyes. Two angry black circles were staring back at her. Who was it? She recognized her. She tried to figure it out but her mind was all fuzzy.

'Sophie, can you hear me?'

Ouch! She'd hit her again. Sophie opened her eyes fully. Mandy. It was Mandy. What? Where was she? She looked around. She was lying in a bed – naked!

'Arrrrgh.' She sat up, holding the sheet to her chest. 'Where am I? Why did you take my clothes off?'

'You took them off all by yourself, or at least the guy I just threw out of here did.' Mandy pulled Sophie's pink top over her head.

Sophie's eyes widened. 'What guy?'

'The one with the floppy hair, the one you were in bed with.' Mandy handed Sophie her knickers and jeans.

But Sophie was too shocked to concentrate on getting dressed. 'What did I do?' she wailed. 'Oh, my God, Mandy, what did I do? Did I have sex with him?'

'How the hell should I know?'

Sophie pulled the sheet over her head. 'I don't remember – I don't remember anything. Oh, God!'

Mandy grabbed the sheet, heaved Sophie to her feet and quickly dressed her. 'We can talk about this on the way home. It's three a.m. and Mum's doing her nut. She's called me about fifty times. I told her we were having fun and lost track of time but we were on our way home. And then it took me bloody ages to find you. I didn't think you were such a slut.' Mandy grinned.

'What did I do? I can't remember if I had sex or not. What kind of person does that? A cheap tart.'

'Lighten up! You got drunk and horny – it happens.'

'But I don't even know if he used protection or not.'

Mandy pulled the sheet back and looked around the floor. 'I don't see any condoms.'

Sophie started crying. 'I'm going to get a sexually transmitted disease. Oh, God, maybe he had Aids. I could be pregnant with an Aids baby!'

Mandy shook her. 'Calm down. Don't start imagining the worst-case scenario. You probably didn't even have sex. Put your sandals on and I'll see if I can find him and suss out what happened.'

Mandy rushed off to find Freddie, the floppy-haired Lothario, while Sophie crawled around trying to find her shoes, which she eventually discovered under the bed.

When Mandy came back, she was sitting on the floor bawling her eyes out. 'My life is such a mess,' she howled. 'I hate this. I want my old life back. I don't know who I am any more. I never would have got drunk and slept with a stranger in London. It's not who I am.'

Mandy sat down beside her. 'OK, turn off the taps for a minute. I have good news. Old Floppy-hair said you passed out before he got any action. He was very disappointed.'

'So I didn't?'

'No, you didn't.'

Sophie threw her arms around Mandy. 'Thank God! I'm so

387

relieved. Oh, thank you, Mandy, thanks for finding out. You're the best.' She punched her fists in the air. 'Hurrah, I'm not a slut and I'm not pregnant.'

'And you don't have an STD.'

'Yes, that too!'

'Come on, we have to get home before Mum blows a fuse.'

'Let's find Mark.'

Mandy roared laughing. 'Mark is so stoned he doesn't know what day it is. I've called a taxi. It's on the way and I said we'd wait at the front gate.'

The two sisters left the party, the older one leaning unsteadily on the younger one's arm.

They sat on a bench at the grand entrance to the house. Mandy lit a cigarette and inhaled deeply.

'I'm sorry,' Sophie said quietly.

'What?'

Sophie looked at her sister. 'I'm sorry for barging into your life like this, out of the blue, and turning it upside down. I've been so wrapped up in my own pain and confusion that I haven't thought much about how difficult it must be for you.'

'I'm glad you're back. Mum's been half a person all my life. She tried her best to be a great mother, but half of her was broken-hearted. A big part of her died when you disappeared. She used to fall apart every year on your birthday in January and then again on the day you disappeared in August. I dreaded those days. They were a nightmare.' Mandy shuddered at the memory. 'But it's over now. No more of those dark days. The other good thing about you coming back is Gran. She's actually becoming human. She even smiled the other day, which, believe me, is a rare sight. I always hated the way she was so mean to Mum – they had such a messed-up relationship – but since you came back it's better. It's still far from normal, but it's definitely improving.'

Sophie smiled. 'Thanks for saying that. It must have been awful for you growing up with all that tension and grief. It can't be easy for you now either, with me getting everyone's attention.'

'To be honest, it's a relief. I've had all these adults homing in on me all my life. It's exhausting and claustrophobic. And, besides, to see Mum so happy is brilliant. She used to be so sad – even when she was happy she was still sad. But now she's like a teenager in love or something. She's all bouncy and carefree and just . . . well . . . joyful, I guess. I'm not saying all this isn't weird for me, but I'm glad she's happy. It'll just take a while to get used to it.'

Sophie pushed her hair back and sighed. 'I just don't know what to do. My mum, Anna, wrote me this amazing letter and it made me realize how much I miss her. It's always just been me and her, the two of us, no other family at all. And I know she's really hurting. Her heart is broken. Whatever I do hurts someone. If I stay here, Anna's upset. If I go home to London, Laura will be devastated.'

Mandy blew out cigarette smoke. 'The way I see it, you have to do what feels right for you. You can't spend your life trying to make other people happy. If you're not happy, they won't be either. I've seen it with Mum. She always tried to be normal on her dark days, when she really missed you, but I knew she was faking it and I hated it. I felt so bad for her but I had to play along too. I'd have much preferred it if she'd been honest and said, "I'm having a bad day so I'm going to stay in bed. I'll be OK tomorrow." The pretending was worse than the truth. My advice to you is to be honest with yourself and everyone else. If you want to go home and be with Anna for a while, do it. As long as you keep in touch with Mum, and come back to see her regularly, she'll get over it.'

'But I love being here. It's so nice having a real family and finding out who I really am and where I come from. I feel so connected to Laura, but she doesn't seem like my mum. She's like a really close aunt or an amazing older friend or something.'

Mandy flicked ash on the ground. 'Of course she does. You

met her when you were already grown-up. You never knew her as a kid. She'll probably always feel like that cool aunt or friend. I reckon Anna will always feel like your mum because she *was* your mum.'

'For a sixteen-year-old, you've got a lot of insight.'

Mandy grinned. 'I grew up in a house full of ghosts and secrets. You, on the other hand, grew up in a happy-clappy bubble. I learned to read situations and emotions very early on.'

'I always wanted a sister.'

'Me too, and my dad's two shrimps don't count – they're too young. Besides, I know Tanya will turn them into complete nightmares. So, you're all I've got.'

Sophie tucked her arm into Mandy's. 'You're great.'

'That's the drink talking.'

'No, that's Sophie/Jody Roberts/Fletcher, or whoever the hell I am, talking.'

They were still laughing when the taxi pulled up.

38.

Anna

Dublin, August 2011

Anna pulled her cardigan around her. Although it was late August, there was a strong wind that made her shiver. Where was this place? She glanced down at the directions again: a small black gate in the wall, they said. Anna walked down the lane again, carefully scanning the wall, and then she saw it. It was a very narrow black gate, almost completely covered with ivy.

She pushed it open and walked through. On the other side there was a tiny park. It had a small fountain in the middle and four benches placed in a circle around it. Joan was sitting on a bench, reading a book. Anna took a deep breath and walked towards her.

'Hello, Joan.'

Joan looked up. 'Hello. You found it, then.'

Anna smiled. 'Just about. It's very hidden.'

'That's why I like it,' Joan said, packing her book into her bag. 'Hardly anyone knows it exists. It's a little hidden treasure in the middle of a noisy city.'

'How did you come across it?'

'After Jody . . . Sophie disappeared, I used to walk for hours every day, trying to get away from my grief. And on one particularly bad day that first year she was gone, I found myself wandering down the lane and stumbled into it. It was so peaceful and quiet, a little oasis. It was the first time in a year that I'd felt some semblance of calm. It's been a haven for me all these years. I've cried here, wailed here, raged at God here and prayed here.'

Anna nodded. 'I need to find somewhere like this now. I thought when I went back to London to get the folders to send to Laura that being back in my house would be a comfort. Somewhere full of good memories, but it's too far away from Sophie now. I need to be near her, even if she won't see me.'

Joan patted the seat. 'Come on, you look exhausted.'

Anna sat down. 'I'm not sleeping very well.'

'I know how that feels,' Joan retorted.

Anna said nothing. She was nervous. She didn't want a scene. She was feeling very fragile and raw. She missed Sophie terribly. She couldn't handle Joan having a go at her.

As if sensing her concern, Joan said, 'I didn't ask you here to shout at you or throw blame in your face. I wanted to meet you to clear the air and to have an honest and frank discussion about everything that's happened. If Sophie is to be truly happy then we need to find a way to move forward. I'm doing this for her. She's suffered enough. We've all suffered enough.'

Anna was hugely relieved. 'I really appreciate that. And I'll do anything in my power to make Sophie happy.'

Joan looked directly at Anna. Her expression was intense, but not hostile. 'We've had a lot of dark years filled with bitterness, heartbreak and grief. When I looked at the folders you sent Laura, it broke my heart to see all the birthdays and Christmases and Hallowe'ens we missed. But I have to admit that Sophie looked happy, she looked loved and she looked cherished.'

'She was,' Anna whispered. 'She really was.'

Joan continued, 'I've thought a lot, over the last few weeks, about you and what you did, and although it was wrong, not to mention criminal, I understand why you took her.'

'Really?'

Joan nodded. 'I understand the instinct to protect a child from harm. You did a terrible thing for the right reasons. I've done a lot of soul-searching recently and I've decided to forgive you. I've spent seventeen years being angry. But Sophie's back now and I don't want to spend any more time being bitter. I want to make her life happy and uncomplicated. She's had enough to deal with – she doesn't need feuds. Besides, Sophie loves you, and if we don't forgive you and continue to push you away, we may lose her again. And I will never let that happen. So I'm forgiving you.'

Anna choked back tears. 'Thank you. It means a lot. I never meant to hurt anyone. I just wanted to save her. I truly believed Sophie was in terrible danger.'

Joan patted Anna's bony shoulder. 'I know what a mess my Laura was back then. I understand why you took Sophie – seeing her mother passed out drunk like that was awful. Laura was unfit to look after a child. She was dealing with her own demons and I should never have left her in charge of Sophie.'

Anna fished a tissue out of her pocket. 'I never planned to take her, I swear. It was as if something took over my body and I found myself carrying her away. I just felt instinctively, deep in my gut, that I had to save her.' Anna wiped her nose. 'Sophie was so small and upset and forlorn. Honestly, I had no idea I was going to take her until it was done.'

Joan sighed. 'Well, we can't rewrite history. And, if I'm being honest, you did a wonderful job raising her. She's the loveliest girl I ever met. And those folders are a remarkable record of her life.'

Anna struggled to keep her emotions in check. 'Thank you again. Every moment with her has been a gift.'

'She was born a little dote.' Joan sniffed. 'I think I loved that child more than my own two. And then one day she was gone and I was devastated.' Joan's voice shook as she struggled to maintain her composure.

Anna looked at the older woman's face, etched with pain as she recalled her loss. Anna knew she couldn't change what she had done, but she could see how much she had hurt the woman and she felt physically ill. She reached out and laid her hand on Joan's arm. 'I'm sorry.'

Joan nodded sadly. 'I know you are, but it's time for all of us to move on. I'm determined not to waste the precious years I have left full of rage. Not now, when I have my beautiful granddaughter back. Our little angel is home. I have to let go of the past so I can enjoy the future with her.'

'I think that's a very good plan.' Anna smiled. 'Thank you for being so generous. I can see how much heartache my actions caused you. But all I saw that day on the boat was an unfit mother and a neglected child. If I had known that Sophie had a doting grandmother at home, waiting for her ... well, things might have been different.'

'It is what it is,' Joan said. 'And the important thing is that Sophie's all right. She's more than all right. She's magnificent.'

'How is she?' Anna asked. She hadn't seen Sophie in weeks and it was killing her. After that meeting in the coffee shop, she had stepped back as she had promised. She hadn't even called, although Sophie had sent her texts every couple of days to say she was OK. It had been torture – she'd missed her daughter so much.

'She's doing really well. That awful strained look has gone from her face and she's stronger, more sure of herself and, I suppose, of us. She's got to know us now and she's carved out her own place in the family. She's painting a lot with Laura, which she loves.'

The idea of Laura and Sophie painting side by side, together, bonding, connecting over their love of art made Anna's stomach churn. She felt as if she was losing her daughter to this family. It was agony to let go.

'But,' Joan continued, 'she misses you, and she'll never be truly happy until she knows that she's not hurting anyone.'

Anna threw her hands into the air. 'But that's just it. Whatever she does, whatever decision she makes, will hurt someone.'

Joan stiffened. 'Well, Anna, you had her for seventeen years, so it's our turn to spend time with her now. You surely can't deny that.'

Anna sighed. 'Of course not, but it's very difficult to let go of the person you love most in the world. I'm trying, Joan, I'm really trying. I've stepped back, I've let you have her, but I'm not going to pretend it's easy. It's killing me not to see her.'

'I know all too well how that feels.'

Anna shook her head. 'I'm sorry. I just love her so much.' She wiped away a tear.

'We all do,' Joan reminded her. 'Actually, I have good news for you. Sophie wants you to come to the house on Saturday.'

Anna's head snapped up. 'Really?'

'Yes. Here, she told me to give you this.' Joan fished an envelope out of her pocket and handed it to Anna.

Anna opened it. 'Please come to the house on Saturday. I need to talk to you. Sophie.' Anna looked up at Joan. 'Surely Laura won't want me at her home.'

'It's what Sophie wants that matters, remember?'

'Yes, but –'

'No buts. I'm not going to pretend Laura's delighted about it – she's still struggling to forgive you. I think it will take her a long time to get there and I'm not sure she ever will, but Sophie has asked her to try so she's doing her best. You have to admire her for that.'

'I do. I'm grateful,' Anna said quietly. She was thrilled she was going to see Sophie, but she would have preferred to see her on her own, somewhere neutral, away from everyone's watching, judging eyes.

'Laura's a really good person. She's suffered so much, but now that Sophie is back, the change in her is incredible. She's found her light again. She's found her smile, her laugh, her joy. I'd forgotten what she was like. I didn't just lose my granddaughter that day on the boat, I lost my daughter too.'

'I'm glad Laura's happy, honestly, and I hope she can find it in her heart to forgive me.'

'I do too. So will I tell Sophie you'll come?'

Anna hesitated. What could Sophie have to say to her in front of Laura and her family? Her heart was racing. Was Sophie going to tell her that she had chosen them? Was her precious daughter going to tell Anna to go away for ever? Oh, God! Please don't let it be that. But, whatever it was, Anna had to go. She ached to see Sophie. There was no option but to say yes, whatever the outcome.

39.

Sophie

Killduf, August 2011

Sophie surveyed her clothes. She wanted to wear something from her old life and something from her new life. After all, that was what today was about – old and new coming together. The mother who had raised her and the mother who had given birth to her. The family she knew and the family she had discovered. The old, cosseted, naïve Sophie and the new, independent, worldly-wise, wounded Sophie.

She peered at herself in the mirror. Outwardly she looked the same; inwardly she was a completely different person. The last two months had turned her world upside down, shattered every belief she had ever had, crushed her spirit and dragged her kicking and screaming into a reality she could never have imagined possible.

She smiled ruefully. Were any other eighteen-year-old girls about to sit down and talk to their biological mother and their kidnapper mother? What would her convent-school friends say if they could see her now?

School friend: 'Hi, Sophie, how was your summer?'

Sophie: 'Interesting. I found out that my mother abducted me and my real mother was a drunk.'

That was the problem. There was no one to talk to who could understand what she was going through. No one could say, 'When it happened to me, I did this . . .' There were no books on how to cope when you'd found out your mother was a child-snatcher. She, and only she, had to work through her pain, her grief, her anger and her loneliness. Only she could make the decisions that would help her move forward with her life, her new truth, her new reality.

And Sophie knew that she had to face it and deal with it before it destroyed her and everyone she loved. While she had lost the mother she knew and cherished, she had gained the family she had always craved. In the beginning she had thought she had to choose, that to embrace one meant turning her back on the other . . . but now she knew that wasn't the case. Yes, she was going to hurt people, but she had to put everyone's feelings and emotions to one side and decide what *she* wanted, what *she* needed, to be able to move forward with her life. She had to protect herself and work out a way to live in this dysfunctional family unit without losing her sanity. She had to take control of her own destiny.

Anna clung to Joe's arm for support. She felt sick with nerves. As they came around the corner into the garden, she stopped. A huge banner hung between the house and the studio. It said *Happy 2, 3, 4, 5, 6, 7, 8, 9, 10, 11, 12, 13, 14, 15, 16, 17, 18th birthday, Sophie!* Enormous multicoloured bouquets of half-deflated balloons swayed in the breeze.

Anna's hand flew to her mouth.

'Easy,' Joe said, squeezing her arm. 'Come on now, they're entitled to throw a party for her.'

'I'm losing her, Joe.' Anna stifled a sob. 'I'm losing her to them. I can't bear it.'

'Hey, we've discussed this. You had to let her go and you did. It was the right thing to do. She needs to get to know her other family. Don't forget all their years of loneliness and suffering. You have to be fair, Anna, you have to let them have her for a while. She'll come back to you because you're her mother. Now, come on, deep breath and smile.'

As they approached they could see everyone spread out across the garden.

Laura was pouring tea. She was wearing a beautiful turquoise dress that matched her eyes. She looked so young and happy. She was laughing at something Joan was saying.

Anna recognized Frank as Laura's brother – there was a strong family resemblance. He was talking to a small woman with very blonde hair.

'Go on, Lexie, what did you say?' He grinned.

'I told him to get off his fat arse and go joggin'. I said, "Look, Dougie, I ain't coming back, so you need to stop stuffin' cheesy Doritos down your gob and get fit. Otherwise you'll lose your career as well as your wife."'

Frank roared laughing. 'Have you spoken since?'

'No. I changed my phone number three days ago so he couldn't call no more. He was calling me ten times a day and it was wreckin' my head. Funny thing is, I thought I'd be the one who wasn't able to move on, but I'm fine. I do miss the bugger sometimes, but I know I made the right decision. I'm quite enjoyin' my freedom and I'm gettin' chatted up everywhere I go. It's incredible how many men fancy me since the papers said I'd get ten million in the divorce.'

'You deserve every penny,' Frank said. 'And the auction for your book is going very well. HarperCollins came in with a big bid this afternoon. I'll go back to Random House in the morning and see if they'll go higher.'

Lexie kissed him. 'You're brilliant you are.'

Mark was sitting on the grass between Mandy and Holly. Mandy was strumming her guitar and rolling her eyes at Holly, who was giggling at everything Mark said.

'You are *sooooo* funny. I never knew Irish guys were so witty,' Holly said.

'I never knew English girls were so hot.' Mark winked at her.

'I never knew two people could be so lame.' Mandy groaned.

'So,' Holly twirled her hair around her index finger, 'you must have lots of groupies hanging around at your concerts.'

Mark chortled. 'A few.'

'I'm sure you'd fit right in,' Mandy drawled.

Holly glared at her. 'Do you have to be so hostile? Don't you have a song to write about hate and rage and, I don't know, anachronisms or something?'

'Duh, I think you mean anarchy,' Mandy grunted.

'Whatever.' Holly flicked her hair and turned back to Mark. 'So, can I come to your next concert and hang out backstage?'

'Backstage!' Mandy laughed. 'They're not the Kings of Leon! They play small pub venues.'

'Dude, I'll have you know we played to sixty people last week,' Mark said.

'Wow, sixty's a lot.' Holly batted her eyelashes at him.

'We're actually playing next weekend. It'll be fun. Maybe you could come and help me warm up before I go on.' Mark arched an eyebrow as Holly swooned. Mandy made gagging noises behind them.

Sophie was keeping watch out of the bedroom window when she saw Anna and Joe arrive. She noticed that Anna was clinging to Joe. She'd never seen her look so vulnerable. Anna had always been in charge and in control, but now she looked thin and frail. Sophie's heart melted. This was, after all, the woman who had devoted her life to raising her and making her happy. But she was also the woman who had stolen her. Sophie sighed. Thank God Anna had Joe. Wonderful Joe, who was always there to support her through thick and thin.

Sophie saw Laura stiffen when Anna and Joe stepped out of the shadows into the light. Her mouth set in a tight, tense line. She didn't move towards them but stayed back, standing still, glaring at Anna. Her hostility was almost palpable.

Sophie left her room and ran downstairs to greet Anna and Joe and try to smooth things over. Their arrival was going to ruffle more than a few feathers.

Anna's face lit up when Sophie ran towards her. She looked radiant. She was wearing a lilac top that Anna had bought her and cut-off jeans. The dark shadows under her eyes had gone, as had the strained look from her face. She looked like herself again, beautiful and joyful. Anna could have stared at her for ever.

'I'm so glad you came,' Sophie said, kissing her lightly on the cheek. 'It's really good to see you.' Her lips quivered.

Anna tried desperately not to cry. She hadn't seen Sophie for so long, and now she was in Laura's home, on Laura's territory, surrounded by Laura's family. Anna was the outsider and she felt it acutely.

'You too, sweetheart.' Anna wanted desperately to hug her tight and never let go. She longed to smell Sophie's hair and touch her skin. But she knew not to. 'Baby steps,' Joe had warned her, in the car on the drive down. 'You've been doing really well allowing her the space to get to know Laura. Don't crowd her now. She'll come back to you when she's ready.'

Anna had listened to his advice. But it was so hard when she yearned to be physically close to her daughter.

Joe pecked Sophie on the cheek. 'It's great to see you. We've missed you.'

'Me too.' To Anna, she said, 'You look lovely.'

Anna had worn Sophie's favourite colour – pink. It was a very plain shift dress, but it went some way to hiding her huge weight loss. 'So do you.'

Frank came over, breaking the tension. 'Hello, Anna, and you must be Joe.' He shook Joe's hand. 'Sophie's told us a lot about you.'

'All good, I hope.' Joe winked at Sophie.

'There is only good.' Sophie smiled.

Joan, Holly, Mark and Lexie came over to say hello. It was awkward but everyone was trying really hard to be 'normal'.

Laura hung back, with Mandy standing close by her side, like a bodyguard. Mandy was wearing a black T-shirt that said *Ghost sisters rock*. Laura was stone-faced.

When Sophie had told Laura that she wanted Anna to come and visit, Laura had been upset and angry. Things had been going so well. The last few weeks had been bliss. She had spent hours with Sophie, painting, talking, getting to know her and becoming close to her. Laura had adored every second of it. She had been able to forget about Anna and the past and just focus on her beautiful baby girl. And then Mandy had suggested the birthday party – seventeen years of birthday parties in one big night. They had all been so excited about preparing for it, and Frank had arranged for Lexie and Holly to fly in from London, and it had been so special, just the family and some very close friends celebrating the return of their lost girl. Laura couldn't remember feeling happier than when they had all sung 'Happy Birthday' while she watched Sophie blow out her candles surrounded by her real family. Her flesh and blood.

Mandy looked at her mother. 'You OK?'

Laura squeezed her daughter's hand. 'Yes, thanks. I just need a moment.'

'Don't sweat it, Mum. The kidnapper won't win. Sophie loves you. She's not going to leave you.'

'I'm so scared, Mandy. I can't do it again. I can't let her go. It's too painful.'

'Listen to me. I will not let anyone ever take Sophie away. She's your daughter and my sister. She belongs here, with us, and nothing and no one is going to change that.'

'Have I told you lately how wonderful you are and how much I love you and how you coming into the world saved my life?'

'Don't start getting all mushy on me.'

Laura put her arm around her daughter and gave her a tear-stained kiss. 'You are my rock. I'd be lost without you.'

Mandy wriggled away. 'Gross, Mum! You're making my face all wet. Go and slobber over Sophie.'

Laura smiled. 'Thank you.'

Mandy shrugged. 'You're welcome, I guess. Now, come on, let's get over there and fight our corner.'

'I see you had a party,' Joe said to Sophie, as a stray balloon flew by.

Sophie blushed. 'It was Mandy's idea.'

Anna tried to force a smile. 'Looks like fun.'

Laura strode over. 'Yes, it was. It was a big day for this family. After all, we'd missed seventeen of her birthdays.'

Anna flinched.

Mandy piped up, 'Lexie organized the balloons and I did the banner and Mum made an incredible cake.'

'That sounds great, doesn't it, Anna?' Joe prompted.

Anna nodded, not trusting herself to speak.

'It was super-fun and Sophie looked divine in this *amazing* dress Laura bought her, all sparkly and fabulous,' Holly enthused. 'And look at her present – it's, like, OMG stunning.' Holly pointed to Sophie's wrist.

It was a diamond and white-gold bangle.

'It's beautiful.' Joe again broke the silence.

'We wanted to spoil her,' Joan said.

'It's flippin' gorgeous,' Lexie added.

'It's a lot more than I've ever got,' Mandy noted.

'It's a very special occasion,' Laura reminded her.

'You look a bit peaky, darlin'. I think you'd best sit down,' Lexie said to Anna, who felt as if she was going to faint. It was all too painful.

'She had surgery not long ago,' Joe announced.

'What?' Sophie looked upset.

Laura froze.

'It was nothing.' Anna scowled at him.

'It was not nothing and you were supposed to rest.'

'Are you OK? Was it your ulcer?'

'I'm fine, pet. It was a little procedure and it's over now.'

'You look very thin and pale,' Sophie said.

'That's just stress.' Anna stared into Sophie's eyes.

Sophie looked away. 'Don't do that. Don't make me responsible for your life. I won't do it.'

Anna gasped.

'Sophie!' Holly exclaimed.

'Go easy on her, darlin',' Lexie said.

Mandy looked at Laura and raised an eyebrow. Laura nodded imperceptibly.

'Sorry,' Sophie muttered.

Joan stepped in. 'Now, everyone, this is an emotional time for all of us. Let's not say anything we'll regret. Anna, come over here and sit down.' She took Anna by the arm and escorted her to the garden table and chairs.

Sophie turned to Laura. 'Will you come over too? I need to talk to you both.'

Joan waited until Laura was sitting down, then whispered in her ear, 'I know this is hard but you have to put Sophie first. And don't worry, she loves you.'

Anna sat bolt upright in her chair, while Laura sat beside her, wrapping her arms around herself defensively.

'Tea?' Sophie asked.

Both women shook their heads. They sensed something was coming and they were nervous.

Sophie sat down opposite them, placed her hands on her knees and leaned forward. 'I've asked Anna to come here today because I wanted to speak to you both together. I know it's not easy for either of you, but I need you to hear me out.'

'Of course,' Anna said.

'Go ahead,' Laura added, crossing her legs to stop them shaking.

'I've been doing a lot of thinking and soul-searching this summer, and while I've been shattered, shocked and very angry, I realized that that was getting me nowhere. At one point I felt as if I was going mad. I couldn't sleep, I had no appetite. I think I was on the verge of a breakdown. This whole revelation has been really difficult. I'm not who I thought I was. Everything I believed to be true was a lie and I had to find a way to deal with it and to understand why everyone had behaved as they did.'

Sophie paused and took a sip of water. Her fingers trembled. 'I'm not saying I have all the answers or that I've sorted everything out in my head and made peace with it, but I've come up with a plan that will, I believe, be fair to everyone and allow me to stop feeling guilty all the time. Which is ironic because I'm the innocent party in this mess, yet I've been riddled with guilt for the last eight weeks.'

'You have nothing to feel guilty about,' Laura said. 'You were abducted. How can that be your fault?'

'It's not your fault your mother was a drunk who neglected you,' Anna put in.

Sophie jumped out of her seat. 'STOP! Both of you, just stop it!' she shouted. 'Do you want the world to know the truth about what you did? Do you want people to know that you were neglectful and you are a kidnapper?' She shook a finger from one mother to the other. 'Do you want this to get out so people can call us freaks?'

The two women sank back into their chairs, shocked at Sophie's outburst.

'I'm sick of the fighting and blaming,' Sophie continued, in a calmer tone. 'It's getting us nowhere. I need you to stop hating each other. You have to find a way to forgive and move on. You can't chop me in two and have half each. I'm a person, and I want both of you in my life. You are both my mothers – so get used to it. I've had to.'

Anna looked at this angry person and saw that Sophie had changed irrevocably. She was no longer her little girl. Her innocent, sweet, gentle child was a wounded, hurt and furious woman. And she had every right to be. She had been let down by everyone in her life. Anna needed to help her daughter. She needed to make this easier for Sophie. After all, wasn't true love all about compromise and sacrifice?

Anna cleared her throat and turned to Laura. 'I'm sorry for what I did. But at the time I honestly thought it was the right thing. I thought she was in real danger. But I can see the heartache and pain I caused and I'm sorry for that.'

Laura's head was bent. She twisted her bracelets around her wrist. 'I've tried to forgive you, for Sophie's sake, but I'm not there yet. I don't think I will be for a very long time. You stole my baby and for seventeen years I had no idea whether she was dead or alive. I admit that I was partly to blame. I was a mess at the time and I have to take responsibility for my own actions. But whichever way I look at it, you taking my daughter, kidnapping my baby, was wrong.'

'I –' Anna went to speak but Laura raised her hand to stop her.

She looked up at Sophie, her beautiful Sophie. Clenching her fists she said, 'I've not finished. Although I haven't forgiven you, I will say this. You did a great job bringing her up. She is an incredible girl. I'm going to take some genetic credit for that, but I can see that you were a very good mother. She seems to have had a very happy life in London and I'm glad. I'm glad she was treasured and loved the way she deserved to be.' Laura's voice began to quiver. 'Those files you sent me were . . . well . . . incredible. I know that if I want to keep Sophie in my life I have to accept you too. You come as part of the package.'

Anna bit her lip. 'I really appreciate you saying that.'

Sophie's eyes glistened with unshed tears. 'You see? That wasn't so hard.'

Anna and Laura avoided eye contact. This conversation was one of the most difficult things they had ever endured.

Sophie shuffled about in her seat. 'So, I've made a few decisions regarding next year.'

'Are you going to take up your place in art college?' Anna prayed Sophie would say yes.

'No. I called them and deferred it for a year.'

'But – but you wanted to go so badly.' Anna was devastated. Sophie had been ecstatic when she had been offered her place.

'That was before all this happened,' Sophie pointed out. 'This is not a decision I've made lightly but it's a decision that I'm happy with. I've decided to spend the year commuting between London and Killduf. I want to spend time with my new family and also with you. I want the time and space to sort out my head. I need to process everything that's happened and, hopefully, next year I'll be ready to start my course and the next chapter of my life.'

'I thought you'd stay here for a year and paint full time with me.' Laura looked crushed.

Sophie took her hand. 'I'll be here tons and there'll be plenty of time to paint together – I know you can teach me so much. I can't wait to learn more from you.'

'Do you think she's talented as an artist?' Anna asked.

Laura nodded. 'I think she's quite brilliant. She has a real gift.'

Sophie flushed with pleasure.

Anna smiled. 'I thought so, but I wasn't sure. Art isn't my forte.'

Sophie was so talented, beautiful, young and fragile. Laura knew she had to stop fighting Anna or she'd lose Sophie. She had to accept that Anna was part of Sophie's life and, although she hated it, if she kept pushing Anna away, she'd only end up hurting the one person she wanted to protect. For Sophie's sake, she had to find a way to tolerate this woman. She looked up at Anna. 'Well, you encouraged Sophie, which is the most important thing for a young artist.'

Anna looked out over the glittering sea. Let go, she urged herself, let go for Sophie's sake. You owe it to her. Do it for her. 'You know, Laura, I spent my life dreading Sophie finding out she wasn't mine, and these last few weeks have been horrendous, but I believe now that it's a good thing she found you. Sophie needs to know who she is. You can teach her so much about art and talk to her about synaesthesia – and now she has the sister she always wanted too. I miss her terribly but I know she's happy here, safe and loved. It makes it a little easier to let go.'

'I want to be generous. I want to tell you I forgive your actions, but I can't. There was too much pain. But I can see that you loved her and cared for her and she's turned out to be a wonderful person.'

'Thank you,' Sophie said, kissing them both on the cheek. 'Thanks for trying. That's all I ask.'

She called the others over, and they gathered around the garden table, fidgeting uncomfortably. You could have cut the atmosphere with a knife.

Sophie took a deep breath. 'I've done a lot of thinking and

planning and plotting over the last few weeks and I've come to a few decisions. One is to divide this next year between London and Killduf.'

There were murmurs of approval all round.

'The other is how to explain this mess to the rest of the world.'

'Oh, my God, have you decided to tell?' squealed Holly. 'Can I call Max Clifford? This is going to be huge!'

'No, Holly! Not now or ever. I've come up with a story that will protect my two mothers. It will keep Anna out of prison and Laura's neglect a secret. I need to thank Frank, Joan and Laura for helping me with the details but especially Frank, because he's the one who has the most to lose in this.'

'What's going on?' Anna froze.

'It's all right,' Joan assured her.

Frank smiled at Sophie. 'From this day forth, I will be Sophie's biological father. We'll be telling everyone that I had a brief fling and Sophie is the result. I had no idea she existed until she turned up on my doorstep a few weeks ago. The fact that she looks the image of my sister Laura and has her talent as an artist, along with synaesthesia, can be explained away by genetics. Sophie said that Anna told her friends in London that Sophie was the result of a fling, so it all ties up relatively neatly. The real story can *never* get out. Only the people here know the truth and it has to stay that way to protect Laura, Anna and Sophie.'

'It's flippin' genius, that is,' Lexie said. 'Cos if the media got hold of the real story, you'd all be dragged to Hell and back. I've had a taste of it with my divorce and, let me tell you, those tabloid hacks are a vicious lot.'

Anna blinked and tried to process the information. Sophie came over to her. 'Do you see? It's the only way we can explain my turning up like this without everyone knowing you stole me or that Laura abandoned me. I hate having to lie, but it's the only way I can protect you both.'

Anna saw that Sophie wanted to shield her from harm. She had spent her life protecting Sophie and now the daughter was defending the mother. The child had become the adult. 'Thank you,' she muttered.

'Are you absolutely sure?' Holly asked Sophie. 'We could have had such fun making a movie.'

Sophie smiled. 'Yes, Holly, we are sure, and you are sworn to secrecy for ever.'

Holly crossed her heart. 'I'll never breathe a word of it. Not even if I'm tortured on one of those waterboard things.'

'Well, Frankie, it's official, darlin', you're a knight in shinin' armour . . . and a daddy!' Lexie giggled.

'He was always selfless,' Joan said.

Laura hugged her brother. 'He's the best.'

'Oh, God!' Mandy groaned. 'This is so hard! The amount of material I have for incredible lyrics is unreal but now I can't use any of it.'

'Thank Christ for that.' Frank grinned.

'There's one last thing.' Sophie hopped nervously from one foot to the other.

'More? You're turning into quite the drama queen.' Mark chuckled.

Anna wasn't sure she could take any more. She felt weak and her head was spinning. She leaned against Joe, whose strong arms held her upright.

Laura closed her eyes. Everything was green, dark green, as fear gripped her. What now? What was Sophie going to say next?

Joan took her hand. 'It'll be all right. Sophie needs to take control of her life. Let her do this.'

Sophie was beginning to see red. She needed to get on before she lost her nerve. This last thing would give her control of her life. She had to make them see who she was. She had to show them she was her own person, a unique combination of her old and new lives. A product of her once uneventful existence and her new earth-shattering reality.

'I have decided to change my name legally to Sophie Fletcher. One half of me belongs to Anna, the other to Laura. But the name is mine. I'm happy with my decision and I will not be changing my mind.' Turning to Laura, Joan, Frank and Mandy, Sophie added, 'No more Jody. I'm sorry, but she's gone. She died that day on the boat and a new person was born. Please understand that I can't be that ghost. I'm real, I'm here and I'm me.'

Frank had his arms around his mother and sister. Mandy was standing beside Laura, linking her arm. They all had tears in their eyes.

Sophie gulped back the sob in her throat. 'And, Anna, I'm not Roberts, I never was. My family name is Fletcher. It's who I am and I'm proud of it. I can't be the old Sophie any more. I'm me.' Sophie broke down.

Everyone rushed to her side.

'I think it's a wonderful name. It's a new beginning,' Joe said, hugging her.

'It's a perfect compromise.' Frank patted her back.

'We may have lost Jody that day, but this summer we gained you, and you're a precious gift,' Joan said, tears streaming down her face.

Sophie turned to Anna, who was trembling. 'I see you, my sweet Sophie, I see you.' Anna wiped a tear from her daughter's face.

Sophie then looked at Laura, who was sobbing, 'Welcome to our family, Sophie Fletcher. I've been waiting for you for a very long time but you were worth every second.'

'Crikey, I should have worn me waterproof mascara.' Lexie dabbed her eyes.

Sophie reached out to hold both her mothers' hands. 'I always used to wish for a dad,' she smiled ruefully, 'but now I have two mums and I'm OK with that. I know the road ahead will not be smooth. I understand that you'll never be friends. But I'm your daughter, both of you, and nothing and no one can change that. So let's try and move forward as a very abnormal, peculiar and weird but amazing family. Can we, Anna? Laura?'

Laura and Anna locked eyes and slowly nodded. They would try anything for the love of Sophie.

Acknowledgements

My deep and heartfelt thanks go to:

Rachel Pierce, my editor – I am so grateful for her invaluable advice and encouragement; and Patricia Deevy, for championing me from the beginning; Michael McLoughlin, Cliona Lewis, Patricia McVeigh, Brian Walker and all the team at Penguin Ireland for making the publishing process so enjoyable. To all in the Penguin UK office, especially Tom Weldon, Joanna Prior and the fantastic sales, marketing and creative teams. To my agent Marianne Gunn O'Connor for her passion and commitment. To Hazel Orme, for her meticulous copy-editing. She is a true gem.

To Anwen Hooson and Maura Brickell, for their hard work on the publicity front. To Cliodhna Hand, for her honest and humorous insight into the life of a teacher. Thanks to my friends for their love, loyalty and laughter.

To Mum, Dad, Sue, Mike and my extended family for their unwavering support and cheerleading.

To Hugo, Geordy and Amy – you make my heart sing.

And to Troy my best friend and soul-mate.